Miss You Forever

ALSO BY

JOSEPHINE COX

QUEENIE'S STORY

Her Father's Sins
Let Loose the Tigers

THE EMMA GRADY TRILOGY

Outcast
Alley Urchin
Vagabonds

Angels Cry Sometimes
Take This Woman
Whistledown Woman
Don't Cry Alone
Jessica's Girl
Nobody's Darling
Born to Serve
More than Riches
A Little Badness
Living a Lie
The Devil You Know
A Time for Us
Cradle of Thorns

JOSEPHINE COX

Miss You Forever

HEADLINE

First published in 1997 by
HEADLINE BOOK PUBLISHING

1 3 5 7 9 8 6 4 2

British Library Cataloguing in Publication Data

Cox, Josephine
Miss you forever
I. Title
823.9'14 [F]

ISBN 0 7472 1380 1

Typeset by Palimpsest Book Production Limited,
Polmont, Stirlingshire
Printed and bound in Great Britain by
Mackays of Chatham PLC, Chatham, Kent

HEADLINE BOOK PUBLISHING
A division of Hodder Headline PLC
338 Euston Road
London NW1 3BH

THANK YOU, HILARY.

Some time ago, my friend Hilary Joel told me about an old woman who was found wandering the streets. She died in hospital alone, a pauper. Sadly, the authorities were unable to trace any friends or relatives.

Try as I might, I could not get the old woman out of my mind. Imagine being all alone in the world, with no one to care whether you lived or died.

In my imagination, I began to weave a story around her.

The woman is Kathleen.

This is her story.

CONTENTS

PART ONE

1912
THE OLD
WOMAN'S TALE

Chapter One

———◦———

'GO ON, YOU old hag. Get back to the slums where you
belong!'

The taunts rang in Kathleen's ears. Tripping and stumbling over the cobbles, she hurried away, wincing beneath the
onslaught of abuse and objects that followed her.

'You'd better run, old woman.' The jeers were merciless. 'If
you're not out of sight in two minutes, we'll set the dogs on
you.' As if to endorse the threat, the two bull mastiffs growled
threateningly, straining at their leashes, mouths dripping saliva
at the thought of sinking their fangs into her soft, ancient flesh.

'What you got in that bag, then, eh?'

'Huh! Crown jewels I shouldn't wonder, by the way she's
clutching it.'

The dogs went crazy to be loosed. 'They fancy that scraggy
mongrel of hers for dinner,' someone yelled, and they fell about
laughing.

As she fled, Kathleen prayed the thugs would not carry out
their threat. She knew the danger, for they were no different
from many others who had made fun of her along the way.

The old woman had lost count of the times when she'd
been jeered at, spat at, laughed at, or chased away at the sharp
end of a pitchfork. People were wary of newcomers, especially
'newcomers' with no fixed abode or means of earning a living.
Generally, they tended to pour scorn and contempt on such
as Kathleen. Being made unwelcome was something she had

3

learned to live with. There were times when she met with kindness and compassion, but these occasions were few and far between.

Too old and too tired to run any more, she yearned to put down roots, but with each passing year the prospect grew more unlikely.

In her lonely treks Kathleen Peterson had travelled the length and breadth of Britain. She had tramped across the green fields of the Emerald Isle and climbed the hills of Scotland. She had stayed in the Welsh valleys, travelled every nook and cranny of England, but her heart always brought her back to her native Blackburn.

Yet Kathleen had neither home nor family, no one who would miss her if she never returned. Her life was in the diaries she so jealously guarded, and in the mangy old dog she had found snuggling up to her when she awoke in an alley one cold February morning.

He was a dolly mixture of black and brown, with a long, meandering splash of white down his nose, and a speckle of grey round his whiskers. He had one black ear that had been broken in a fight and hung sadly over his head like an eye-patch, while the other ear remained upright and finely tuned to every sound. He reminded Kathleen of an old man she had known as a child; he, too, had had a black eye-patch and grey speckled whiskers that twitched when he talked. His name was Mr Potts. 'What else can I call you?' she had asked the dog, and so he was given the old man's name.

The two of them became fast friends. They made a comical sight as they walked the streets, Kathleen in her dark shawl and boots, with a threadbare tapestry bag over her arm and her long grey hair in thick plaits that reached down to her waist, and the odd Mr Potts, head cocked to one side as he peered from under one ear, his body so close to her heels as they went that he might have been attached.

Having been on the road since first light, Kathleen had arrived in Liverpool. She had fourpence in her purse, earned from sweeping an undertaker's yard in Sheffield. She was hungry and cold, and, having consulted with the wise old Mr Potts, had decided that Liverpool was as good a place as any to stay awhile. 'The market should be opening soon,' she explained. 'With a bit of luck we might go away with a bag of sweet potatoes.' She hadn't tasted a sweet potato in ages and her mouth watered at the prospect.

'Are you still 'ere, old woman? I thought we told you to piss off!' The four thugs who had taunted her earlier had followed her to the docks. 'What'ya got in yer bag, eh?'

Kathleen didn't have to look round. She recognised the voice. 'Come on, Mr Potts,' she urged. 'Let's be off, before they come after us.'

In spite of her scruffy, neglected appearance, the old woman spoke in a soft, genteel tone that might have shocked the rough crowd who saw her only as an object of derision. Like many others who had never taken the trouble to know her, they would have been astonished to learn that Kathleen Peterson, the unkempt and aged vagabond who tramped the roads and carried all her worldly possessions in a grubby tapestry bag, was once a fine, respected lady.

Gasping and exhausted, she came to a busier part of the docklands. Here, men hurried at their labours, talking, shouting and whistling, great ships waited to be loaded and offloaded, trolleys were pushed back and forth and there was an air of hustle and bustle. One of the men, catching sight of her, touched his cap and bade her a cheery 'Morning, luv.'

Kathleen turned nervously, wondering if her pursuers were following. They were, and her heart sank. If only she was younger, stronger, she might give them a run for their money.

The man paused in his work. He had seen the fear in her eyes and noticed how the thugs hovered a short distance away. He bristled. 'Bothering you, are they, luv?' When she nodded, he walked away, spoke to a mate, and together they approached the four thugs. On seeing the burly dockers, Kathleen's pursuers made off like the curs they were.

'They'll not bother you any more,' the man promised. 'Where are you headed, luv?'

'Nowhere in particular.'

He regarded her with concern. There was an air of dignity about the old woman that startled him. Her smile was bewitching, and her dark brown eyes were arresting, deep and troubled yet filled with the brightness of a summer's day. He bent to stroke the dog, who backed away. 'Not very friendly, is he?'

'He's hungry, that's all.' Kathleen fussed Mr Potts, and he sidled up to the docker, his tail wagging.

The docker laughed, ruffling the dog's ears. 'Pity he's not fierce though,' he commented, 'or them devils might not have been so keen to tail you, eh?' Mr Potts rubbed so hard against him he nearly lost his balance. 'By! He's a funny-looking dog an' no mistake.'

Kathleen laughed. 'That's because he's not a dog,' she joked. 'He's an old man in disguise.'

'You ought to be more careful, lady,' the docker warned. 'This area is known for thuggery and such. Anyway, what brings you out on a cold January morning? I should have thought you'd be tucked up in yer bed.' The old woman was cold, he could see. With only a thin skirt and a ragged old jumper covered by a shawl, she was trembling. She and the cur were both pitifully thin, he noticed.

Kathleen's answer shamed him. In a soft, genteel tone that shocked him, she explained, 'Some of us don't have a bed to tuck up in.'

'I'm sorry,' he murmured, digging in his pocket and taking out a coin. 'It's all I've got on me,' he apologised, 'but yer welcome to it.'

Putting up her hand she smiled. 'I don't want your hard-earned money. You've been kind enough. I'm very grateful, but now we'd best be on our way.' She turned, heading away from the docks.

'Wait a minute!' With her soft smile and independent manner, she reminded him of his old mother, though the old dear had been rough and ready to look at, with a cavernous mouth and kind, wrinkled eyes, while this old lady had clear, striking eyes and a set of teeth that would put a younger woman to shame. 'Where will you go?' he asked.

'Here and there.' Experience had taught her to be careful with strangers. Even with the kind ones.

Heading towards the old cobbled square where she knew the market was held every Saturday, Kathleen took a detour which brought them into a back alley. 'Might as well find a warm place to have our breakfast,' she said, peering into the back yards as she passed the tiny terraced houses. 'Folks are still abed,' she noticed, looking up at the bedroom windows and seeing how the curtains were still tightly drawn. 'It's Saturday,' she muttered with a little smile. 'Hard-working folk deserve a lie-in, and who can blame them?' Still wary of the thugs who had threatened her, she glanced nervously behind. 'Looks like we've lost the devils,' she smiled. 'We'll be safe enough now.'

One of the yards was open. Its tall, wooden gate was split from top to bottom and hung from its hinges as though it might have been ripped off by some marauding drunk. From the house could be heard raised and angry voices.

'As long as they don't come out for a bucket of coal, we should be safe enough,' Kathleen decided, with a wry little smile. 'Be quiet and no one will be any the wiser,' she said, wagging a finger at the mongrel. She noticed the coal-hole door was ajar. Cautiously, she went inside; it was dark and cold, but not as cold as the street outside. 'Seems cosy enough,' she remarked. 'I'm sure no one would mind if we made ourselves comfortable for a while. And we can finish off the last of that pie, before it goes sour on us.'

Finding an old sack lying on the ground, she took it out and shook it, sending the black dust flying through the air. Then she laid it in a clean corner of the coal cellar and sat herself down, with the dog at her feet as always. As the cold struck through her thin skirt, she shivered. 'It's a hard life, Mr Potts,' she sighed.

Waiting for any little titbit she might have for him, Mr Potts sat on his bony haunches, eyes bright and ear cocked, intently listening to every word the old woman uttered.

'It's not like it used to be, is it?' the old woman pondered softly. 'There was a time when you could walk the streets and be safe, when you could pass the time of day and not be afraid somebody might snatch your bag or run you through when your back was turned.' She chuckled. 'It doesn't matter to you though. All you're concerned about is having a full belly and a warm place to lay your head, and nobody can blame you for that, can they, eh?'

Her kind brown eyes misted over, her voice falling to a whisper. 'As for me, what does it matter? Who is there left to care about a silly old fool like me?' She gave a sad little grunt. 'Nobody, that's who. Never mind,' she remarked wisely; she was not one to dwell on the downside of life. 'When the time comes, we can say that we were here, and we made a difference. In the end, that's all that counts.'

Smiling into the dog's eyes, she cradled his hairy face between her two hands. 'You might be a funny-looking thing, and you might have very little to say for yourself, but you've been a friend to me, and I'm grateful for that.'

Impatient now, the mongrel began to whimper, scratching at her with his paw.

She rummaged in her bag. 'Let's see what old Kathleen's got for you.' Laughing, she confessed shamefully, 'I weren't the only one watching the butcher throw his leftovers away. I'll have you know I fought off a hungry cat for this particular juicy bit, though in the end I couldn't see the cat starve and gave him a piece. So, you see, your dinner isn't as big as it might have been. Mind you eat it slowly,' she cautioned, taking out a muslin cloth and opening it to reveal a half-eaten meat pie. 'It might be all we get between now and tomorrow morning.'

The dog enjoyed his titbit. Kathleen was delighted to find another treat skulking in the bottom of her bag; the fat muffin had been given to her by a grateful woman whose purse she had retrieved from the pavement only yesterday. 'I'd forgotten all about that,' she said with a laugh. 'I must be going senile.'

She shared the muffin, and afterwards took a drink from a small stone jar. 'There's nothing better than a drop of cider to finish off a meal,' she declared, licking her lips in appreciation.

From somewhere in the distance, a clock chimed the sixth hour. 'Too early for the market yet. We'll be all right here for another hour. By then the traders will be set up and the ground rolling with fruit and veg that's fallen from the barrows.' It might be bruised and battered, but it was good enough for the two of them, she thought.

The light from the house shone into the coal hole. 'I think I'll write for a while,' she murmured. 'Lord knows it's been a curious day.' From her bag she took out a pen and a small exercise book. In the half-light she could see well enough, though not without squinting.

Using her bag as a desk, she opened the book and began to write in fine, meticulous lettering.

KATHLEEN PETERSON
SATURDAY THE 12TH JANUARY,
IN THE YEAR OF OUR LORD, 1912.

Another year, another journey. Another day, another trial.

I've travelled a long way since Christmas, and now find myself here, in Liverpool. This time, God willing, I plan to stay.

Maybe here I will find a measure of peace, a way to forget. A way to leave it all behind and never think of it again.

Oh, if only I could, if only it were possible . . .

Overwhelmed by a surge of emotion, she could not go on. Instead she sat a while, head back and eyes closed, while the past came again to haunt her.

Kathleen could not say when it all began to go wrong. There had been times when life was good, and times when she despaired. She had known love and laughter, and sadness of a kind that would stay with her until her dying day. Once, a lifetime ago, she had a promising future, a family, and reason to hope.

Now, it was all gone, and she was reduced to foraging for a living. Yet she still had her pride. She mended her clothes and washed them in the brook. She bathed in the stream, combed her hair into tidy plaits and retained a semblance of dignity. When there was work she took it, and when there was not, she lived off the land. She never begged and took no favours, and always believed that something better would come along; that somehow, life would get easier.

But it never did, and with each passing day she grew older and more weary. Her bones ached in the winter, and her skin burned in the summer. At the end of a particularly bad day, her feet might be blistered and her spirit close to being crushed, but Kathleen didn't complain. What was the use of that?

She gave a long, withering sigh, opened her eyes and stared at the page before her. 'So much to tell,' she murmured, 'and no one to listen.' Memories swamped her. So many. Too many.

She placed the pen between the pages, then closed the book, and carefully returned it to her bag. 'My old eyes aren't what they used to be,' she whispered, 'I'll wait till the light's better.'

In the house the row continued. 'Somebody's certainly got a temper,' she commented. 'Hope they leave us be.' Undaunted by the raging voices, she slid down and crossed her arms over her precious tapestry bag. 'I'll just close my eyes for a minute.'

This was always a sign she was settling to sleep. The dog knew it, and normally when she closed her eyes he would curl down beside her. But not this time. This time he remained wary, one ear cocked and a low, hostile growl issuing from his throat.

The old woman didn't hear it, for she was already asleep, warmed by the cider, and dreaming dreams of long ago.

While she slept, the four thugs crept up on her.

'The old hag's asleep,' the ringleader hissed.

'With no interfering docker to save her this time,' chuckled another. 'Let's get a look inside that precious bag of 'ers.'

———◆◦◄———

INSIDE THE HOUSE, Rosie was being subjected to the same old threats and bickering that had peppered her marriage from day one. 'You're always the bloody same! What does a man have to do to get his rights? It's been three days since you let me get anywhere near you. What's the sodding excuse now, eh? Have I to knock you down and help meself?' The man paused, his grip tightening on her arms and making her squirm. 'If it's roughing up you want, why don't you bloody well say so?'

'If you forced yourself on me, you might live to regret it.' She realised the burst of defiance might cost her dearly.

She wasn't wrong.

Without warning, he raised his fist and knocked her to the ground. 'Sod you!' He stood over her, eyes blazing. 'Now are you satisfied? Can you see what you're doing to me?'

Rosie Maitland was a small, pretty woman, with a soft heart and caring ways, while her husband Jake was a big brawny fellow. In his own selfish way he loved her, but he was possessed of a terrible jealousy and a hard, spiteful nature. When roused to anger, like now, he made a formidable sight.

He stared down on her, his face twitching with emotion. 'I provide for you, don't I?' he demanded. 'I pay the bills and keep everything straight. I never refuse if you want something for the house, and I work bloody hard, don't I?'

When she didn't answer immediately he gave her a nudge with his boot and raised his voice. 'I said, I take care of everything, don't I? I never deny you anything reasonable. ISN'T THAT SO, WOMAN?'

In that moment, Rosie hated him. 'No, you never deny me anything.' He never denied her anything, as long as it met with his approval, she thought bitterly. But he denied her the things she craved, like the smallest measure of independence, pretty clothes and the friendship of other women. Oh, she had friends at the charity hospital where she worked but she was not allowed to have anyone back to this house – the house she worked to furnish and maintain; and if she didn't immediately tip her wage packet up the minute she came through the door on a Friday night, there was hell to pay.

A terrible look of suspicion came into his eyes. 'You're not cheating on me, are you?' he hissed. 'Because if you are, I swear to God I'll swing for the pair of you.'

Her soft, honest voice made him feel ashamed. 'You can trust me, Jake. You know I would never cheat on you.' The defiance had gone and in its place was a degree of resignation. But the hatred remained. The hatred always remained.

Astonishingly, his manner changed. Reaching down, he took her in his arms and held her close. 'I don't mean to be hurtful,' he apologised, nuzzling her neck. 'But you shouldn't deny me my rights. It drives me crazy.'

She tried not to cringe from his touch. 'Tonight,' she promised. 'I'll be feeling better by then.' Anything to appease him.

'Why not now?' He licked her mouth with the tip of his tongue.

'No, Jake. Tonight.' She looked at the mantelpiece clock. 'You'd better go or you'll be late for work.' A tough, unforgiving foreman, Jake was one of the most despised men on the docks.

Squeezing her face between his rough hands, he whispered into her mouth, 'God! I wish I didn't love you so much!' Then he kissed her abruptly, grabbed his coat and strode out into the yard, and straight into the ruffians. 'Hey! What the hell's going on out here?'

The thugs might have stayed and fought, but one look at this big, powerful man with a face as dark as thunder and fists the size of hammers and they were off in a rush, over the wall and down the alley.

'You thievin' buggers!' Jake yelled after them. 'I know yer faces. I'll be looking out for yer!'

Rosie ran to the door. 'What is it? What's going on?'

He returned to give her a parting kiss, so hard and demanding it bruised her lips.

'Nothing for you to worry about,' he told her. 'A few louts prowling about, but they'll not be back, I can promise you that.'

'What did they want?'

'Whatever they could lay their hands on, I expect.'

'But there's nothing in the yard worth stealing.'

'There you are then. Like I said, nothing for you to worry about.' He held her for a moment. 'Don't forget what you promised,' he whispered fondly. 'I'll be looking forward to it.'

'You'd best hurry,' she said, drawing away. 'You know how you like to start the shift before anybody else.' He insisted on being there first, to see the men arrive, to glare at them and make certain they would be penalised if they were even half a minute late. He liked it when they were late. It justified his existence.

'Till tonight then, me little beauty.' A quick, spiteful tweak of her breast, and he went off to his work, whistling merrily.

Inside the coal hole the old woman lay unconscious, her faithful friend lying beside her, his head bleeding. Only the occasional flickering of one eye gave a small sign that there might still be life.

As the old woman regained her senses, she called out for him. There was no reply; no familiar whimpering or nuzzling of a wet nose against her. Only a terrible stillness, a silence that was frightening.

As Rosie turned to go back into the kitchen, she thought she heard a noise. Swinging round, she called nervously, 'Who's there?' Indignant now, she warned, 'You'd better clear off! The police are on their way.' Rosie waited and listened. There were no more sounds. 'I must be hearing things,' she snorted.

She was just about to close the door when she heard it again, a soft, agonised moan. Aware that one of the ruffians might still be lurking, she took up a heavy shovel and went cautiously towards the coal hole. She found the old woman crouched over the dog.

'Mr Potts it's all right, I'm here . . .' The old woman's voice trembled with fear. A sob catching her words, she turned her eyes to Rosie. 'They've hurt him,' she croaked. 'They've hurt my dog.'

Horrified, Rosie dropped the shovel and ran to her. 'Dear God!' Gently, she helped the old woman into a sitting position, shocked when her hands were warmed with blood. 'Oh! You're hurt too.'

In the half-light the old woman stared up at her with surprised brown eyes. 'Help him,' she whispered.

Rosie followed the old woman's troubled gaze. She feared the mongrel was past all help. 'I'll see to him,' she promised, 'but you mustn't try to move any more. I need to go for help, but I won't be long, trust me.'

<hr />

THOUGH RETIRED FROM work these many years, Bill Soames was strong as an ox and had a heart of gold. He and his good wife Amy were the best of neighbours. 'Course I'll help,' he said, on answering the door to a frantic Rosie. 'You're the nurse. Just tell me what to do.'

It took only a minute for Rosie to explain what had to be done, and while she ran back to the old woman, he brought his old flat-cart round to the alley. 'She's badly hurt,' Rosie warned. 'You take her weight while I keep her still. Gently now.'

Together they carried the old woman outside where they wrapped her in one of Rosie's blankets and made sure she was safe for travelling. 'I'll stay with her,' Rosie said. 'You'll have to take it slow, Bill. Go by way of the canal, that way we'll avoid the cobbled roads.'

Bill's wife stayed behind to close up the house and keep an eye on the sorry Mr Potts. 'Poor little devil,' she murmured, stroking his soft fur. 'What kind of monsters did this? Attacking an old woman and killing her dog? They should be hanged.'

When Mr Potts seemed to sigh, she drew back, astonished.

'Lord above! I thought you were done for. You must be tougher than you look. Like the old woman, eh?' Delighted that he still drew breath, Amy took it upon herself to tend Kathleen's brave little friend.

◆◆◆

T HE RUFFIANS WERE never found, and after eight long days it was still touch and go whether the old woman would survive the vicious attack. She had lost consciousness on the way to hospital and remained in a coma.

Rosie worked long hours to watch over her. She sat by her bedside and talked to her as though Kathleen could hear. She described the weather, and she read from the pages of the newspapers; she sang softly, and picked out the humorous incidents at the hospital in an effort to amuse Kathleen. But it was all to no avail. Kathleen slept on. And with every day that passed, it seemed the old woman's life was disappearing with it.

The ward was quiet now. Beyond the curtain the sky was darkening into evening. Above the door, the big round clock rhythmically ticked away the seventh hour.

Rosie arrived to take over the shift. This was her favourite time. Behind her she left a husband whose appetite to satisfy himself on her was insatiable and obnoxious, while here in this place there were people who valued her, people who trusted her. It was a good feeling.

Taking off her coat, she made her way along the ward, checking that everything was as it should be. That done, she hurried towards the far end of the ward where the doctor and the other ward nurse were in discussion by the old woman's bed.

'In a way it might be a blessing if she goes,' Dr Naylor remarked as she approached. A kind old gent, disillusioned with the way things were, he had developed his own philosophy. 'She doesn't appear to have any family, and she's old and apparently homeless.' He sighed from his boots.

Leaning forward he gently prised open her eyelids. 'She won't last long in my opinion. It's a pity, I know, but there's nothing more we can do.' He looked at the old woman's face. 'Amazing what a bit of soap and water will do, don't you think?' he asked softly. 'When she was brought in she looked like any other old vagabond, but now . . . Well, I mean, she has a certain, oh, I don't know . . . a kind of gracious beauty – the look of a lady.' He laughed at his own ramblings. 'Who knows, she might be worth a fortune, and here she is, ending her days in a charity ward.'

'She does have a fine face, doesn't she?' Rosie agreed. It was a good face, with strong features, high cheekbones and a full, plump mouth. The eyes were closed, but the long dark lashes and gently arched brows gave the impression of vitality beneath.

When she was brought in her hair had been covered in coal dust and her hands were blue with cold, but now, with the long grey hair combed into deep, shining waves about her shoulders, and her slim hands stretched out on the blanket, Kathleen had the look of a woman who had been a real beauty in her time. 'How old do you think she is?' Rosie asked, intrigued.

Dr Naylor shrugged. 'It's hard to say. She may have been living rough for some time, and such a life will age a person. But her skin is surprisingly good, and her hair has a remarkable sheen.' He picked up one of her hands. 'See here, how firm and clean her nails are? Whoever she is, and however she came to be a vagabond, this lady took great care of herself. Normally we find months of dirt ingrained in the nails, and the same beneath the breasts; the feet, too, are usually diseased, but not this woman's.' He laughed softly. 'She has healthier feet than I have, and God knows how many miles she may have trudged along the roads.'

'How old though?' Something about the old woman had stirred Rosie's heart.

He shook his head. 'She could be in her late fifties, early sixties. Like I say, it's difficult to be precise.'

'I wonder if she has a family somewhere.'

'Who knows? We're not paid to do detective work, my dear. We're here to mend bodies if they can be mended. She received a vicious battering. I believe she may go in her sleep, and that would be a merciful thing. I suspect it won't be too long before we have the use of her bed.' With those words, he moved on to the next patient.

As Rosie considered his harsh comments, her colleague stepped forward. 'Ain't no good dwelling on it.' A scrawny creature with a dark scraping of hair beneath her white cap, Nell Salter had a thin, whining voice that made cats want to mate.

Rosie didn't answer.

'That old woman's been here over a week,' Nell persisted. 'The doctor's right. There's nothing else we can do for her, and you can't deny we do need the bed.'

Drawing her aside, Rosie was sharp. 'That "old woman" is a charity case, and this a charity hospital. It's gentry with consciences who keep this place open,' she reminded Nell. 'Spoiled gentry with fat wallets and purses, who make themselves feel good by helping the less fortunate. Not one of them has ever shown their face through these doors. They have no idea of the terrible things we see here, and by and large they don't want to know. But I'll tell you this, Nell Salter, for all their privilege and arrogance, I don't believe there's a single one of them who would want to see this old woman thrown out to die on the streets.'

Feeling aggrieved and inadequate, Rosie was hitting out at everything and everybody. She was incensed by Nell's casual attitude. Here was a woman who had taken on the responsibilities of nursing yet was incapable of administering a few kind words to those in her care. Most of all, Rosie was hitting out at the way things were between her and Jake. Life was a bag of tricks, and whatever trials it set her, she was never ready. Maybe it's me, she thought bitterly. Maybe I'm the one at fault and everyone else is right. It wasn't the first time she'd questioned her place in the order of things. No doubt it would not be the last either.

'I know the old dear is gravely ill,' she said to Nell, 'and I know we've done all we can, but she's strong and might just surprise us all – if you and the good doctor aren't too hasty in writing her off!'

'Whoa! Don't go mad at me.' Nell was taken aback by the

outburst. Usually Rosie was quiet enough. It was true she cared more than most, even at times being reduced to tears, especially if the patient was an infant. But to see her fly off the handle like this was something altogether new. 'Don't take it so personal. You're not blaming yourself because she was attacked in your yard, are you? We take patients like her all the time. Drunks, paupers, orphans – destitutes who don't have a soul in the world to care what happens to them.' She cast a glance at Kathleen. 'Like her,' she added thoughtlessly. 'Tramps and suchlike.'

Rosie rounded on her. 'People! Not once have you called them people, but that's what they are, just like you and me.'

Nell shook her head. 'Oh, no,' she snapped. 'Not like you and me, Rosie. We work bloody hard for a living, and if you ask me, so could most of the rabble who are brought in here. Like you, I do my job. I nurse their wounds and I fetch their bedpans, and I loathe every minute of it. I do it because at the end of the week I get paid, and that's all.' Red-faced with anger, she cursed herself for revealing the truth.

Rosie had always suspected as much but she was still shaken by the admission. 'If that's how you really feel,' she accused angrily, 'you shouldn't be here.'

'And neither should *she*!' Nell waved a hand at Kathleen. 'That old nobody is taking up valuable space. The sooner she goes the better, and it can be out the back door in a box or out the front door on her own two legs. Either way will do, as long as it's soon!'

Conscious that the old woman might be able to hear what was being said, Rosie moved to the desk in the centre of the ward and Nell followed. 'Is there anything new that I should know about?' she asked.

Nell handed her the clipboard. 'Nothing,' she replied curtly. 'Except Mrs Tyler seems to have developed a raging thirst. You'll need to watch her or she'll have you running yourself ragged.'

Rosie glanced through the clipboard. 'Thanks,' she said, and before she could go on, Mrs Tyler began calling for a drink. 'I'll see to her.' Rosie's shift didn't start for another ten minutes but she was never a clock-watcher. In fact, if truth be told, she would rather be here than at home with Jake.

It took only a few minutes to help Mrs Tyler to a drink of water, but during that time Nell Salter took the opportunity to rifle Kathleen's bedside cabinet. Something the doctor had said earlier had made her curious – 'Who knows, she might be worth a fortune,' that was what he had said, and it made her wonder what the old woman carried in that tapestry bag she had been clutching when she was admitted.

When Rosie returned to the desk she noticed the screen drawn round Kathleen's bed. Quickly, she went up the ward and there, on the other side of the screen, was Nell furtively going through the old woman's tapestry bag. 'For God's sake, Nell! What do you think you're doing?'

Red-faced and excited, Nell continued to turn things out of the bag, on to the bed. 'D'you remember how she clung to this bag when she was brought in?' she whispered excitedly. 'Like it had valuables inside.'

Rosie couldn't believe her eyes. 'Have you gone out of your mind?'

'You heard what the doctor said,' Nell hissed. 'What if she really is worth a fortune? The old hag's on her way out so she'll not need it any more. We could help ourselves and no one would be any the wiser. It's only what we deserve, Rosie.'

Stepping forward, Rosie challenged her. 'Put it all back,' she ordered in a harsh whisper, 'and we'll say no more about it.'

'Don't be daft!' Defiantly Nell turned the bag upside down, spilling its remaining contents on the bed: a torn notebook with a pen tucked inside; food crumbs; a twig shaped like a hook with a bit of twine on the end for fishing; a bone comb; and various other bits and pieces.

'You disgust me!' Gathering up the old woman's belongings, Rosie made a grab for the bag. In the tussle, a small bundle fell to the floor with a gentle thud.

'Christ, Rosie!' With trembling fingers, Nell bent to pick up the package. 'I bet this is stuffed with money.' In a frenzy of greed she pulled at the ribbon that held it secure.

Over the years the ribbon had frayed and as Nell tugged at it, the whole thing came apart in her hands. 'Christ Almighty!' Angrily, she flicked through the books, throwing them to the ground with anger. 'Notebooks!' she cried hoarsely. 'Nothing but notebooks and pages of scribble!'

While Rosie bent to her knees to retrieve the books, Nell picked up the bone comb; a handsome thing, it had marbled teeth and a slim, gleaming backbone inlaid with mother of pearl. 'Looks like it might be worth a bob or two,' she said, eyes glittering. 'It won't be a fortune but it's better than nothing.'

'Steal it and it will cost you your job,' Rosie promised.

'I don't think so,' Nell sneered. 'One word about this and I'll make out it's *you* who's the thief.' She smiled. 'I'm a very convincing liar. You'd best think on it, Rosie Maitland. I've got two brothers who would turn the world upside down for me. They wouldn't take kindly to you spreading lies about their little sister.' Her face darkened. 'Keep it shut or you'll pay dearly.' As quickly as her face had darkened, it brightened again with a smile. 'I'm feeling a bit peckish. I'll get off home now and see what me mam's got for supper.'

Shaken by the events, Rosie gathered up the exercise books. 'Brothers or not, I won't keep quiet about what she's done,' she muttered. 'Stealing from patients who can't defend themselves!'

A small voice made her sit up. 'Rosie?'

Grabbing the books and scrambling up, Rosie was astonished to see the old woman looking straight at her; astonished, too, at the timeless beauty of her dark brown eyes. 'How long have you been awake?' It shamed her to think the old woman had heard every word.

Kathleen smiled. 'Rosie . . . lovely name.'

'Did you hear . . . everything?'

Kathleen's next words confirmed it. 'Is it true? Am I really on my way out?'

'Don't let her upset you.'

'Please, is it true?'

Rosie couldn't find the words to answer but her silence spoke for her.

'Mr Potts?'

'He's recovering. Don't worry, he'll be well looked after, I promise.'

Her smile became a sigh. 'I'll miss the silly old scruff.' Suddenly, two plump tears sprang from her eyes and trickled to the pillow. 'So much to tell,' she whispered. 'So much.'

'Sleep now.' Rosie held her hand for a moment, and when she believed the old woman was asleep, she began piling the books up, her intention to tie them with the frayed ribbon as best she could before returning them to the bag, and the bag to the cupboard.

'The comb was given to me by a boy I used to know.' Kathleen's memories grew stronger. Oh, what a glorious summer's day it had been, and how much in love they were. In her mind, it was only yesterday.

'I'll get the comb back for you if I can,' Rosie promised. It was obvious the comb meant a lot to the old woman.

With a surge of strength, Kathleen raised herself on to one elbow. Looking into Rosie's surprised eyes, she told her, 'I want you to know . . . about me.' Falling back on to the pillow, she reached out and placed her long fingers over Rosie's small, workworn hand. 'In the books.' She paused, her old heart glowing. 'It's all there,' she whispered. '*Everything.*'

'Have you no family?' Rosie was deeply moved.

'Only you,' came the sad reply. 'The books are all I have to give,' she murmured. 'They're yours now.'

Still Rosie made to return them to the cupboard but Kathleen saw. 'Cherish them,' she pleaded, her eyes brimming with tears. 'For me.'

Worn by the effort, Kathleen drifted into a fretful sleep. With the books on the bed before her, Rosie sat by her bedside, her gaze sweeping the old woman's face. 'You must have been very beautiful when you were young,' she mused. 'Who are you? How did you come here?'

From somewhere down the ward a voice called out. Rosie went to investigate. It was Mrs Tyler, wanting another drink. 'I'll 'ave a gin, if yer please,' she grinned with her toothless mouth.

Rosie had to smile. 'It was too much gin that brought you here in the first place,' she chided. 'You can have a cup of water and then you can go to sleep, before you wake the whole ward.'

'I want a piss!'

'You want a lot, don't you?' For all her irritating traits, Mrs Tyler always made Rosie smile.

'It's all that bloody water.'

'So you don't want it then?'

'I want a drop o' gin.'

'Sorry.'

'Bugger off then. I can't get any sleep wi' you standing there.'

Rosie 'buggered off', back to Kathleen who appeared to be peacefully sleeping. 'Sleep well,' Rosie whispered, and was about to return the belongings to the cupboard when she paused. 'So much to tell,' the old woman had said. 'Yes, I can imagine,' Rosie murmured. Fingering the notebooks, she thought for a moment, and then nodded. 'All right, I'll read them, but I can't promise when I'll have the time.'

It was quiet on the ward that night and Rosie laid the books out on her desk. They were tattered old things of a kind used by schoolchildren or clerks, or the foremen at the docks – she had seen the very same type curled into Jake's overall pockets. The books were numbered from one to twenty, with the name Kathleen Peterson written on each one. 'Nell was wrong,' Rosie murmured. 'There was a fortune in the bag after all. Not a fortune in money or jewels, but a hoard of memories, the precious memories of one woman's life.' And now they were entrusted to her. The responsibility suddenly seemed overwhelming.

She took up the first book and opened it.

There, in that quiet place, in the soft glow from the lamp, Rosie settled into her chair, turned the page, and began to read.

PART TWO

1855
THE GIRL

Chapter Two

TREMBLING WITH FEAR, Kathleen hugged her rag doll close to her heart. 'Adam's been naughty,' she whispered. 'Father's whipping him again.' Placing a finger over the doll's lips, she urged, 'Ssh! He mustn't hear us.'

Crouched inside the closet, the five-year-old child quivered at the sound of her father ranting and raving, the crack of the whip as it rose and fell, and her brother Adam's cries. 'Adam's hurting,' she told the doll, a tumble of tears creating a smudged trail down her white face. 'It's all my fault,' she quietly sobbed. 'Adam's being whipped and it's all my fault.'

Upstairs in her room, Kathleen's mother heard it too. Arms folded and face pinched with fear, she paced the floor. 'I should go down,' she muttered, 'but God forgive me, I'm too afraid.' She continued to pace, back and forth, to the window, then to the door, agonising over whether she should intervene, fearing that if she did it might be her on the receiving end of that whip.

Years before, when she first met the man who was now her husband, she had been courageous and bold. Over the years he had eroded her self-confidence until now she was little more than a coward.

In the town of Blackburn, Elizabeth Peterson was a fine example of what a squire's wife should be. When the sun came up, she spent the long lonely days doing what was expected of her. She performed her duties with grace and accomplishment; she displayed active interest in her husband's work; ran a big house with no apparent effort; marshalled and supervised the servants and made certain her children had the best nanny and governess money could buy.

When the sun went down, she lay in her bed while her husband took his satisfaction. At times, and because it seemed to pleasure him, she even feigned a measure of satisfaction herself. But the truth was she hated every minute of her existence, seeking her happiness wherever she could find it, at whatever cost.

Her husband had a foul and vicious temper which he often vented on his only son. Robert Peterson had longed for a son who might take after himself; a son who would grow tall and strong, with a fierce and ruthless nature to match his own. When he first cast eyes on his newborn son, the disappointment showed in his eyes. 'No matter that he's weak and puny,' he vowed, 'if I have to punish him every inch of the way, I'll make him the man I want him to be.'

The baby slept and his father woke him. The infant loved to walk and his father made him run. The boy loved to paint; his father made him climb trees. When his son was four years old, Robert Peterson rallied the servants to show them how fearless his son was. Demanding their attention, he hoisted the small boy on to the back of a stallion, parading him round the grounds. Then he sent the animal into a frenzy by slapping it hard with a crop. It shot forward at a gallop, with the boy clinging on for dear life, obviously terrified and begging his father to get him down.

Laughing, the man took the boy down, carried him indoors and then viciously beat him. 'Don't ever again humiliate me in front of the servants!' he thundered. 'Like it or not, you are my son – though I wish to God you weren't. Puny coward that you are, you carry my name. Robert Adam Peterson is a proud name, with centuries of tradition behind it. Don't ever forget that!'

The boy was afraid of water, so when he was eight, his father threw him into the sea and watched him almost drown before he sent a servant in to rescue him. 'Another disappointment!' he declared, striding away in disgust. 'Another humiliation!' It was an incident the boy was never allowed to forget.

The latest 'humiliation' had taken place this afternoon, when young Adam, now ten years old, was in the garden with his sister Kathleen, whom he adored. They had been swinging from the lower boughs of an apple tree when Kathleen dropped her doll, which fell on to an area of rockery some ten feet below.

Horrified, Kathleen would have gone after it, but her brother made her wait while he went down to retrieve the doll. The doll was broken, and he was cut and bruised. Kathleen was distraught. The whole episode was witnessed by the governess, who rushed out and took them both inside. Inevitably, the tale was related to the master and, in spite of all protests that Adam had been brave in clambering down to recover his sister's doll, the boy was blamed and viciously punished.

Now, trembling as though she herself was receiving the terrible blows, Elizabeth Peterson remained in her room, knowing that she was a greater coward than her son would ever be.

Her son's cries ceased and a terrible silence permeated the house. 'Oh, dear God, let him be all right.' She went to the door and gingerly opened it. Burying her head in her hands, she began to sob. 'I daren't go to him, I'm afraid. God help me, what kind of woman am I?'

Suddenly a piercing scream rent the air. Quickly Elizabeth slammed shut the door and leaned against it, her arms spread out as though to fend off an intruder. 'Don't kill him,' she kept saying. 'Please, don't kill him.' Yet she made no move to stop it.

Pressed deep in the closet, Kathleen felt the silence, and she too was startled by the sudden, high-pitched scream.

Suddenly she could bear it no longer. With immense courage, she flung open the door of the closet, ran to the drawing room where she burst in, her eyes filling with horror at the scene before her.

Adam was small for his age, with a shock of fair hair and dark, blue eyes. Now, though, his eyes were closed in pain; he stood against the wall, his arms reaching up and out against the wood panelling. From the waist down he was naked, his blood-stained legs and buttocks criss-crossed with a weird pattern made by the lash.

When the beatings stopped, he made no move. It was as though he was welded to the wall, his small body only barely managing to keep upright, his heart infused with a strength that only made his father more determined to break him. He wanted Adam to beg for mercy. Exasperated that not once had his son shown any sign of doing so, he had paused to rest his arm and then wielded the whip one last time with all the power he could muster. It was this that had made Adam scream in agony.

Robert Peterson didn't even look to see who had burst into the room. He kept his eyes on the boy and yelled, 'Get out, damn you! *Get out!*'

Kathleen stayed by the door, tears rolling down her face at the plight of her brother, who was her only friend. So shocked was she that her tongue wouldn't say the words that rushed to her mind. She remained quite still, clutching her broken doll, her gaze focused on Adam and only the soft sound of her crying permeating the awful silence.

Robert swung round, his features crumpling with shame when he saw who stood there. 'Oh, Kathleen!' He rushed across the room. 'No, sweetheart, you mustn't see this.' He reached out to her, his face suffused with love. 'Come on, let Daddy take you out of here.'

Holding the doll close, Kathleen backed away. 'Go away. I don't like you.' For the first time in her young life she knew hatred. It was a bitter thing, but not as bitter as seeing her brother cut and bleeding. 'You're hurting Adam!'

'Don't be silly, darling.' He loved her so very much. In many ways she had been some measure of compensation for the son he craved but could never have. 'Adam has been bad and he has to be punished.' When she didn't move, he picked her up and strode out of the room with her.

She fought him with such ferocity, he was taken aback. Hitting out with fists and feet, she could only think of her brother. 'Leave him alone! I hate you! I hate you!'

He put her down, and when he looked into her tear-filled brown eyes, a great tenderness overcame him. 'You don't understand,' he said. 'This is men's business, and you're not supposed to see.' While she quietly sobbed, he went on, 'Don't ever say you hate me, Kathleen. I couldn't bear that.'

Kathleen wasn't listening. With a determined twist of her arm she broke free and before he could stop her she had run back to the room and her beloved Adam. She found him slumped on the floor, face down. 'It's all right, Adam,' she sobbed, falling to her knees and stroking his hair. 'I won't let him hurt you. I won't let him.'

In two strides her father was across the room. Taking her by the arm, he propelled her into the hallway and on up the stairs, yelling as he went, 'Elizabeth! Elizabeth, where the hell are you?'

Like a frightened mouse she came scurrying out of her room. 'I'm here, Robert,' she said in a remarkably calm manner. 'Whatever is it?' She had grown adept at feigning ignorance when the occasion warranted. The less she pretended to know about what went on, the easier it was to strike it from her conscience.

His eyes swept her pretty face. 'I thought I told you to keep Kathleen away from the drawing room.' As he spoke he came closer, making her tremble.

'But I thought the governess had her safe.'

'You're bloody useless! You've allowed Kathleen to see a punishment. Damn it, Elizabeth! You know how I feel about that.'

'I'm sorry. It won't happen again.'

For a moment he was silent, his gaze intent on her face. Kathleen was like her mother, he thought; the same chestnut-brown eyes and long dark hair. He loved them both. Hated them too, for the power they had over him. The girl was still innocent, but the mother was knowing; too knowing. There were times when he could have willingly killed her, and times when he loved her until she cried out for mercy. 'The governess,' he demanded drily. 'Where is she?'

'I thought she was in the garden with the children.'

'When I'm finished with the boy, find her. Send her to me in the study.'

'Let me take Kathleen.' She reached out but did not make a move towards him.

He kept hold of Kathleen. Suppressing the rage inside him, he bent to address her in soft, loving tones. 'You never have to be afraid,' he promised. 'I would never punish you.' When she cowered away from him, he persisted, 'I love you, more than anyone else in the world. You know that, don't you, sweetheart?'

She raised her small face to his dark, passionate eyes. 'You hurt Adam,' she accused brokenly. 'I don't love you any more. I only love *him*.'

'Don't talk like that. Come on now, give your daddy a kiss.'

'No!' Kicking out, she caught him on the ankle with her boot. Insane jealousy took hold of him.

'Adam is a coward,' he hissed, shaking her. 'I don't want you to love him, do you hear?' Damn and blast that boy, he soured everything. 'He broke your doll, didn't he? He had to be taught a lesson.' He made himself smile. 'If you forget what you saw downstairs just now, Daddy will take you shopping in London. We can go on the train, or we can go in the carriage. You can choose. Just you and me, sweetheart, and I promise you, we'll find the best, most expensive, most beautiful doll in the world.' Foolishly he took hold of her broken doll. 'You don't want this old thing any more, do you? Adam's spoilt it – like he spoils everything!'

Nothing could console her. Snatching back her doll, Kathleen tore away from him and ran to her mother who, startled and afraid, tolerated the child clinging to her skirt. 'What am I to do?' she asked nervously, keeping her hands clasped. 'I honestly thought the governess had her safe.'

He glared at his wife. 'The governess,' he reminded her. 'In my study in ten minutes. See to it!' Inwardly fuming, he turned and went down the stairs.

He didn't return to the drawing room. Instead he stormed into the kitchen. 'It seems I pay people for doing nothing,' he snapped at the three servants he found there. 'Where is the housekeeper?'

Being the boldest and least expendable, Cook spoke up. 'I believe the housekeeper went up to inspect the bedrooms, sir.'

He looked around the room. As usual it was spotless, with food on the table and sideboard in various stages of preparation; and a particular favourite of his cooking in the oven. The aroma of steak and onion pie filled his nostrils and made his stomach rumble. 'Get her,' he ordered. 'I'll be in the study.' With that he strode out, leaving them gasping with relief that they still had their jobs.

'It ain't often he shows his face in 'ere,' Cook remarked, brushing a whisper of baking powder from her eyebrow.

'What d'yer reckon he wants with Mrs Glover?' With her thin face, thick lips, and wispy hair escaping from beneath her cap, Nancy Tomlin made a comical sight. She wasn't too bright but she was a wonderful worker with a heart of gold, and Cook had a special place in her heart for her.

'It isn't for us to question the master,' she said curtly. 'Run upstairs now and tell Mrs Glover the master's been here looking for her, and that she's to make her way to the study.'

While Nancy ran to find Mrs Glover, the butler stepped forward, his face dark with anger. 'You know why he wants her,' he said quietly. 'You heard the lad's cries as well as any of us. He's taken a terrible thrashing and now Mrs Glover will be made to shut him in his room until the master is ready to let him out again.'

Cook was a round, homely woman with kind eyes and a kinder nature behind her sharp tongue; she had seen things in this house that touched her deeply. 'It should be the governess who deals with that, not Mrs Glover,' she snorted with disgust. 'The governess!' she declared haughtily. 'Jumped-up nothing, if you ask me, not fit to take charge of a dog. What's more, I shouldn't be at all surprised if she gets paid more than all of us put together.'

'I didn't know you were so set against her, Mabel. You've never said before.'

'That's because I know when to keep my mouth shut.' She glanced about, ever nervous they might be overheard. 'It's true though,' she went on in a quieter voice. 'That young madam is paid good money to mind the children. Oh, I'm not denying they've learned their tables and the pair of them can read and write as good as any I've seen afore. But she doesn't care for them like she should. Since the master got rid of the nanny and gave the task to this one, she's neglected the children shamelessly. They're put at all manner of risk. Time and again they go off on their own, across the fields and down to that fast-flowing brook. My God, anything could happen, and her nowhere in sight.'

'Aye, well, happen that's not such a bad thing, the young 'uns going off on their own, I mean. Being left to their own devices has taught 'em to look after theirselves. I bet you could set 'em down in the middle of a jungle and they'd find a way of surviving. Still, you're right, the brook's a dangerous place for the children to be. I've said as much to the master and was swiftly told to leave such matters to them as know.'

'The master's a fool!'

'If I were you, I shouldn't worry too much. And anyway, the boy swims like he were born to it. As for the lass, well, she's not afraid of anything.'

'Aye, John, I'll not deny they're a capable pair, God love 'em. But they're too young to be wandering off on their own. That fancy madam should be doing the job she's paid to do.' Sighing, Mabel wiped her nose with the back of her hand. 'She's worse than useless. Never anywhere to be found when she's wanted, except when the delivery men call. Oh aye, she's to be found then, right enough. Making cow eyes and showing off her ankles to all and sundry.'

John gave a grin. 'Well, you must admit she has got a well-turned ankle.'

Being round and lumpy, and never having had her ankles complimented, Mabel snorted disapprovingly. 'If it was up to me, I'd have her out the door before she knew what day it was!'

'Yer not jealous, are you?' John teased. 'Because you needn't be. Haven't I told you before, Mabel Down, you're the finest woman that ever walked on two legs – pretty or not.'

He had thought to please her. Instead he got a sharp tap on his knuckles with the rolling pin. 'My legs are as good as anybody's,' Mabel retorted, adding with a chuckle, 'for getting me about, that is.'

The butler's mind was already on other things. 'Mind you, we all know why he keeps her on, don't we, eh? She's his fancy bit, that's why. Time and again young Nancy's heard him creeping up the back stairs to her room, and many's the time he's not come out till morning.'

'Be careful what you say,' Mabel warned. 'Walls have ears.'

John shook his head in anger. 'The way he thrashes that lad, we should shout it from the rooftops!'

'What good would that do? I know he's a bad-tempered, merciless devil, and I know he takes it out on that poor boy, but when all's said and done, he is the boy's father.'

'More's the pity. Adam is a good lad. He'd die before he'd let any harm come to that little lass, and the master knows it.'

Mabel nodded. 'There's a lot of jealousy there, I reckon,' she murmured. 'The master dotes on the girl, and he can't stand anybody else near her, especially the boy, who he seems to hate like poison. And for no good reason that I can see, other than he's never going to make a master huntsman because he doesn't like riding the horses. The lad hates the idea of killing things. I mean, look how the master went berserk when the boy refused to lay traps for the rabbits. And there was nearly murder when he caught the boy down by the brook with an easel and paintbrush.' She shrugged her ample shoulders. 'It's true the lad's not the same strong build as his father, and he prefers painting to killing. But there's nowt wrong with that.'

'If he only opened his eyes he'd see how Adam is a son any man could be proud of. He isn't built big, I'll give you that, and he doesn't have the same killer instinct his father has, but he's no coward. He has the heart of a lion and he knows the difference between right and wrong. In my book, he's a better man than his father will ever be.' John nodded his head, as though agreeing with himself. 'The master knows it too, and that's why he whips the lad until he draws blood.'

'I'm well aware o' that. We *all* are.' Her heart went out to both the children. 'But we're only paid servants in this house, John.' She squared her shoulders. 'Don't forget what happened to old Mr Potts. That man tended the gardens for nigh on twelve years but he were sacked in a minute when he made a comment to the master about the boy being too small to take a man's punishment.'

'Aye, but he had the guts to speak up.'

'It didn't help though, did it? What can any of us do, eh? Who could we tell that might believe us? And how long do you think we'd be in a job? Once we opened our mouths we'd be out of here quicker than you can draw breath, and there wouldn't be a lady nor gent in the country who would ever give us work again. Troublemakers, that's what they'd call us, and likely we'd starve to death in a gutter somewhere.'

'Hey, now, that's a bit strong.'

'It's the truth. What's more, even if we did stand up and tell the world, the gentry would stick together like they always do. The master would still flog the boy, and the law would still be on his side.' Mabel rolled up her sleeves, plunged her arms into the baking bowl and sent a fine spray of flour into the air. She sneezed. 'Tell me I'm wrong. Go on. Tell me I'm wrong.'

Frustrated and angry, John slammed his fist on the table. 'If you ask me, it's not the boy who should be flogged, it's that bastard.' He blushed. 'If you'll pardon the strong language, Mabel.'

Shaken by the ferocity of his outburst she turned to regard him. He was a small man, white-haired and ferret-like. But there was something about him that made him tall among other men; a strong, good-looking face and elegance that made him attractive to her. 'It's all right, John,' she said kindly. 'I know how you feel.'

'All the same, I shouldn't let my tongue run away with me, not in front of you, I shouldn't.'

When he smiled, she was afraid her deeper feelings might show. So, setting her features into grim disapproval, she sharply rebuked him. 'You're right! In future mind your language. I'm partic'lar who comes in my kitchen!'

Bowing his head, John muttered something incoherent. He had a secret fancy for this big, bustling woman. She was kind and generous, and knew how to laugh. What's more, she made the best meat pie and veg he'd ever tasted. It made him determined that one fine day he would take Mabel for his wife. It was something to look forward to and it kept him going. It kept him here, in this house, waiting on a man he detested, when he would rather be a million miles away. He would have been gladdened by the cheeky twinkle in Mabel's eye, as she looked away. Since John's fleeting kiss under the mistletoe, many a foolish dream was raised in her old heart.

<hr />

Mrs Glover made her way towards the master's study at a smart pace. A tall, trim lady, with strong, proud features and her white cap fluttering as she went, she might have been a galleon in full sail.

'Come!' As always after administering a beating, Robert Peterson was in a state of great excitement.

Mrs Glover knew of the beating. Like everyone in the house, she had suffered the boy's punishment as if she herself was on the receiving end. 'You want me to take the boy to his room,' she said without preamble. She had done it so many times before.

'You know the procedure,' Robert snapped. 'See to it.'

Only when Mrs Glover had departed the room did he relax. 'Damn her!' he snarled, downing a glass of whisky. 'Damn them all!'

It was only a matter of minutes before there came another, softer knock on the door. 'Go away, bugger you!' He was in no mood for visitors.

The voice was so low and vibrant it seemed to be in the room with him. 'I was told you wanted me.'

At the sound of the voice, Robert laughed out loud. 'Come in, you slut,' he replied jovially. Stretching out his legs, he raised his feet to the desk, awaiting her entry with the air of a gentleman at ease.

The door opened. He kept his gaze down, staring into the bottom of his glass.

The door closed. He smiled, but still did not look up. 'You have a lot to answer for,' he murmured.

She made no move, but answered softly, 'Don't be angry with me.'

'Lock it.'

'What?'

'The door. Lock it.'

'You won't beat me, will you?'

'Lock it, damn you!'

The click of the lock made him glance up. He liked what he saw. Connie Blakeman was neither short nor tall; she was fair-haired and pleasantly feminine, with soft features and pale eyes that were sometimes blue and sometimes green. She was both cunning and naive, and had a way of winding men round her little finger. She took one cautious step into the room.

'The boy has had a thrashing.' His smile was evil.

'I know.'

'Your fault.'

'I know.'

'Come here.'

Just a little afraid, but knowing she only had to smile and he would be at her mercy, she went to him. 'I wasn't far away,' she said. 'I wandered into the spinney. I really thought the children were right behind me.'

Swinging his legs down, he let her fondle him. 'I should

have known you were too young to look after them.' Opening her blouse, he kissed her bare breasts. 'Only eighteen.' He grinned at her. 'Elizabeth was right. You're too young for such a responsibility.'

She was kissing him, sending him wild. 'You've never complained before.'

'That's because I don't give a sod what anyone else thinks.' Clutching the neck of her blouse, he tore it from her shoulders. For a long, awful moment he stared at her breasts, small ripe fruits, pointed to a dark, erect nipple. Stirred deep inside, he caressed them like a man starved. 'You're always warm,' he murmured, rolling his face over the pink, supple skin. 'Warm and soft.'

She laughed softly. 'You've ruined my blouse.'

He didn't smile. 'You'll have to go,' he said, peering at her from beneath heavy eyelids. 'You know that, don't you?'

Uncertain whether it was the drink talking or the man, but either way feeling confident that he would never send her away, she teased, 'Do you want me to go this very minute?'

'Not yet,' and now he did smile. 'We haven't finished our business.' His mouth covered her nipple and his hands moved up her skirt. Suddenly he was pushing her to the floor, his weight bearing down on top of her. 'What will I do without you?' he moaned, pushing up her skirt and feasting his eyes on her bare flesh.

While he watched, she drew down her underwear, sending him wild when she exposed the darker, more secret area. 'Do you want me?' she invited, spreading her legs. 'Go on then, take me.' Bold and unashamed, she arched her back and waited, eyes and fists closed, limbs trembling, anticipating the unbearable rush of pleasure.

She wasn't disappointed. 'You little witch!' With a swift, brutal movement, he tore away his own garments and was into her with one long, direct thrust. In their wild and frenzied passion, they were oblivious of the fact that their cries could be heard outside the room.

'Cor!' It wasn't the first time Nancy had burst into the kitchen with eyes sticking out like hat pegs and hair flying. 'You should hear the noises coming from the master's study,' she exclaimed. 'It's like there's murder going on!'

Mabel grabbed her by the arm and propelled her to the range. 'There *will* be murder going on,' she promised, 'if you leave this kitchen again without my say-so. Now stir that pot until it bubbles. If just one piece of meat sticks to the pan, my girl, I shall want to know the reason why.'

With that she returned to her baking, one eye on Nancy, the other on the door. 'They're like a pair o' dogs on heat!' she muttered, dropping generous dollops of plum jam into the pastries.

At that moment John returned from his tour of the house. He, too, was well aware of what was going on in the master's study, and he arrived in a fluster. The sounds rose to a climax. Mabel reddened; John coughed and rolled his eyes with embarrassment, then with the calm dignity that set him apart, he closed the door and asked, 'Is there a cup of tea going?'

'There might be,' Mabel told him, 'but you'll need to make it yourself. Us women are too busy.'

But she wasn't too busy to sit and enjoy a cup with him afterwards, and even Nancy was allowed to join them.

'It's frightening, ain't it?' Nancy said, looking from one to the other with her big round eyes.

'What is?' John asked curiously.

'Never you mind!' Mabel intervened, reddening again. 'There's been enough said on that partic'lar matter. Now eat your cake or I'll throw it out for the birds.'

Threatened with having her cake taken away, Nancy tucked in, trying to forget all about the 'frightening' noises coming from the master's study. They sounded like the noises her mam and dad made and soon after there was always a baby. But the master wasn't like that, she thought. He and the mistress were gentry, and everybody knew that gentry were different. And anyway, the mistress was upstairs with the girl. She knew that because just now she'd been summoned to take up a tray of tea and dainties.

———◆———

UPSTAIRS, ELIZABETH SAT by the window, her sorry gaze fixed on the far-off hills. On the settee behind her Kathleen slept fitfully.

'You don't know how lucky you are,' Elizabeth murmured, shifting her gaze to the child. 'You're unhappy now because your brother has been hurt, but you don't know anything yet.' She sighed, letting her gaze linger a moment. 'Poor little Kathleen.' She smiled sadly. 'All too soon you'll be a woman, and then your heartaches will really begin.'

She turned away, quiet for a moment, then spoke aloud, letting her feelings flow from within. 'I should never have got married,' she whispered. 'That was a bad thing.'

Having few people to talk with, Elizabeth often conversed with the birds roosting in a wide-spreading apple tree outside her window; at this glorious time of year it was in full bloom, the sweet scent of its blossom wafting in through the open window. 'I might have loved him once, but not any more.' She shuddered. 'I can't bear him to touch me.'

After a moment, she rose from the chair and crossed to the settee where Kathleen was sleeping. 'I know I'm not a good mother,' she murmured, gazing down at the girl's innocent face. 'But I have tried. You can't know how hard I've tried all these years, until now there's nothing left. I never wanted children, but he insisted. I want to leave him, but I can't. He's the one with all the money, you see. I want to leave you and your brother too, but I don't know how.'

She felt ashamed. 'None of it is your fault. You're such a lovely, generous little thing, but I can never love you as you should be loved. Maybe it's because he smothers you and I can't bring myself to go where he's been, or love what he loves.' A sob caught her voice. 'Or maybe it's because I'm afraid to love you in case he finds out. Adam loves you, and he gets beaten for it.'

She wrung her hands, alone and desperate in that great, cold house. 'I'm so afraid,' she muttered, 'so afraid of what he might do. And, oh! If he should ever find out the truth! I daren't even think about it.'

She wasn't talking about her love for Kathleen now, but about her love for another man; a man who gave her comfort and listened to her as though she mattered.

She sat down on the settee and began stroking Kathleen's long, dark hair. 'You're so pretty,' she whispered. 'One day you'll fall in love with a good man, and it won't matter that your mother couldn't love you. You'll forget about me, and the beast who thinks he fathered you.'

She clamped her hand to her lips and lowered her voice. 'Must be careful what I say, Kathleen. Let him believe he's your father, and you must believe it too, because that's the way it should be. But the truth is you were conceived in love,' she whispered, 'not out of fear, like your brother.' Now that she had spoken the secret out loud, she felt strangely free of her husband. 'No one knows, except me,' she murmured. 'And no one ever will.'

She sat awhile, dreaming and wishing, and knowing there would come a day when she might be brought to answer for her sins. But for now she had little thought for herself. 'When you leave this place, as you surely will one day,' she whispered to the child, 'I pray you will put him out of your life. And you must forget me because I've let you down badly.' A tender smile crossed her sad features. 'Not Adam though. You must never forget what Adam means to you. Unlike you, he does have his father's blood running through him, but thank God he's not tainted by it. Nor is he tainted by my weakness. Adam has taken my own father's nature, he's kind and strong. Be thankful, Kathleen, thankful that he's your brother and your friend. Adam knows you better than anyone, and he knows how lonely you are.' Taking Kathleen's fingers in her own, she put them to her lips and softly kissed them.

'Adam will always look after you,' she promised. 'No matter what happens, you must always remember that.'

Suddenly she heard angry, raised voices. Going to the door, she edged it open, silently listening but not surprised. She had seen this particular confrontation coming for some time; ever since he had brought the girl into the house. She knew it would be only a matter of time before he threw her out, like so many before her.

'You bastard!' It was Connie Blakeman's voice. 'You mean you really are throwing me out?' Trembling with rage, her voice dropped to a low, threatening tone. 'What if I open my mouth about you and me, eh? What if I tell all and sundry how you've been taking advantage of a decent, hard-working girl who wanted no part of you.'

'Huh!' His laughter echoed through the house. 'You? Connie Blakeman? Whose father's a useless nobody and whose mother sells her favours on the market corner for a bob a time? Who do you think would listen to a no-good whore like you?'

'You're the one who's no good!' she yelled. 'For all your money and fancy things, you're less of a gent than my dad is. He ain't a drunken old bastard like you. He don't beat his kids raw neither, and he don't rape his wife!'

Incensed, he took her by the hair. 'One day that big mouth of yours will get you hanged,' he hissed, and while she continued to struggle and scream, he marched her to the front door where he wedged the toe of his boot up her backside and kicked her down the steps. She landed in a painful heap at the bottom. 'Now be off with you,' he said, staring down at her. 'And I warn you, don't try slurring my good name or you'll be very, very sorry.'

As he slammed the door on her, she continued to shout threats and obscenities. 'You'll be the sorry one, Mr high and bloody mighty! 'Cause when my brothers hear what you've done, they'll be round here, I can promise you that!'

Bruised and hurt, she hobbled away, spitting blood. Occasionally she glanced back, her face wreathed with loathing.

Like him, she was a vindictive creature. And she never forgot an insult.

———◆◆◆———

LATER THAT NIGHT, when the house was quiet, only the children were awake; Adam because he was in too much pain to sleep, and little Kathleen because the image of her brother bleeding against the wall would not let her sleep.

Softly she clambered out of bed and put on her robe. Barefooted, she made her way out of the room and down the long draughty corridor. She had to see him. She had to know he was all right.

Adam had been sitting by the window, tears streaming down his face at the memory of his humiliation. 'I hate him!' he muttered, wiping away his tears. 'I hate him!'

When the door handle softly turned, his heart turned over with it. For one awful minute he believed it was his father come to hand out more of the same punishment. Defiantly, he stood with his back to the window and his eyes on the door. 'I won't show him I'm afraid,' he muttered. 'I won't!'

When he saw Kathleen's worried face peer into the room, he sagged with relief. 'It's you!' he gasped, going across the room to draw her inside. 'What are you doing? You should be in bed asleep.'

'I couldn't sleep, Adam.' To see him out of bed and walking towards her, was too much of a relief. She began to cry; big rolling tears and racking sobs. 'He whipped you. Daddy whipped you and I don't like him any more.'

'Aw, come here.' With his arm round her shoulder, he took her to the chair and sat her down. 'You don't have to cry,' he chided. 'I'm all right, aren't I?' His back felt as tight as a drum and if he breathed too deeply the wounds seemed to pop open and it was agony. 'I want you to go back to your own room, and go to sleep. Will you do that?'

She regarded him in the moonlight that gentled in through

the window. He seemed all right, but she wasn't certain. In fact there were suspicious smudges on his face. 'He's made you cry, hasn't he?' She had never seen Adam cry and the realisation was a shock. She couldn't know that he had cried many times before; he never let her see, he had too much pride for that.

'Maybe a little,' he grudgingly admitted. He had never lied to Kathleen, and he never would.

'I don't like him any more.' As she spoke, the tears trembled over long lashes. 'Can I stay with you, Adam?'

He shook his head. 'It's best if you go back to your own room.'

'Please.' She couldn't rid herself of the awful things she had witnessed. 'If he comes to get you, I'll make him go away.'

He smiled at her then. 'Oh, Kathleen, you're a silly billy, and I do love you.'

'Can I stay then?'

'Course you can.'

After tucking her up in bed, he watched while she fell asleep. 'Does your back hurt?' she asked dreamily.

'Not too much,' he said. 'Go to sleep.'

'Cuddle me.' She held up her arms and he cradled her close, until at last she drifted into a contented slumber.

Still in a considerable amount of pain, he sat in the chair, watching her sleep and thinking he would kill his father if he ever laid a hand on little Kathleen. 'I'll never let him hurt you,' he whispered. Then he lay forward on the bed and fell asleep.

It wasn't a contented sleep. His back was on fire, and he burned with anger.

One day he would be a man. When that day came, the tables would be turned and his father would never again dare to take a whip to him.

Chapter Three

THE BLAKEMANS WERE renowned for their arrogance and aggression. Their reputation spread far and wide, from the narrow streets beneath the shadow of Blackburn's cotton mills to the fresh green lands of the Ribble Valley. On Saturday nights they scrapped outside the pubs, and in the confines of their own home they fought among themselves.

There were fourteen Blakemans. Aggie, aged forty-eight though she looked much older, was a small, wiry woman with iron-grey hair and a tired stoop to her thin shoulders. Her husband Bob, ten years older, was big and burly, a quiet, amiable fellow, content to spend his days at the mill and his nights with his feet up by the fire.

When the rowing started, as it usually did when their bellies were filled with their mam's stew, or the landlord's booze, he would close his eyes and feign sleep until it was all over. 'Let them get on with it,' he used to tell his wife when the boys were younger. 'They'll soon wear themselves out.' Now, with each one still at home and no sign yet of marrying, he wished to God he'd slung them out on their ear when they were small enough not to challenge him.

It was too late now. They'd got their feet well and truly under the table and were waited on hand and foot by their tired old mam. Even if he did ever pluck up courage to show them the door, he'd likely be the one to end up face down on the pavement.

So, much to the aggravation of his long-suffering wife, he let it all ride over him. Having fathered eleven strapping boys and one good-looking, wily girl, he felt he had contributed his lot to society.

The sons ranged in age from nineteen to thirty-two, and were as different from one another as washing on a line.

Nathan was the eldest; the biggest in size, the biggest coward, and the most cunning of all his siblings.

Then came Jack the liar, who idolised and imitated him.

Robby was named after his father but was more violent. Bold and fearless, he was also without mercy or compassion.

Steve was the handsome one. He was also a troublemaker and loved to drop poisonous suggestions into an otherwise innocent discussion until there was murder in the air.

Luke was the sensible one. Much like his father in height and build, he had the bluest eyes, the quietest nature, and was the only reasoning voice in any heated moment.

The remaining six looked to these five for guidance but invariably erred on the harder, more violent side.

Only two of the sons had regular jobs. Luke ran cargo up and down the canals. Jack worked for a local club-owner and was the dandy of the family. Both men valued their small measure of independence but neither had yet shown any inclination to move away from home and family.

Home was a converted warehouse on Penny Street. It had three floors, a cellar, and endless dilapidated rooms, many with rotting floorboards. Ten sons shared five rooms, and the eldest, Nathan, had a room of his own. The parents slept downstairs in the back room, and Connie had a small box room, kept for the few occasions when she deigned to visit, which was as little as possible because she hated the warehouse and everything in it, including her family.

They ate in the kitchen; a surprisingly sunny room, where Aggie had surrounded herself with the best she could steal, buy or borrow. There was a fine old dresser arrayed with cooking implements, peg rugs and pretty curtains, and a table made out of old doors and cupboards, smoothed down and nailed together, so it was big enough to seat the whole family at once.

At mealtimes, when everyone was seated, they made a formidable sight. While they ate, there was not a word spoken, but when the last mouthful was swallowed and the meal over, the talking would start, with everyone impatient to get a word in. Inevitably, the rows would soon follow, and one by one the family left the room, the quiet ones first, the aggressive ones last, until only Aggie was left in the kitchen, to clear away and reflect on this huge, disappointing family she had raised.

Usually Bob would sit back, enjoy his pipe and let them all get on with it. Tonight, though, he and the others had a certain matter on their minds. The matter was Connie who had arrived home unexpectedly three days ago and was saying very little.

From under heavy brows, Bob discreetly regarded her. She looked as pretty as ever, he thought, but she wasn't happy. No, not happy at all. 'You still haven't told us what brought you home, luv,' he said, sucking at his pipe. 'Is there summat you want to tell us?'

Peeved and humiliated, she gave him a scathing glance. 'I can deal with it!'

Feeling rejected, he shrugged his shoulders. 'All right, please yerself.' He got up and left the room.

'Will yer be going back to the Peterson place?' Aggie asked. She hoped so, because Connie was the hardest of her children to deal with. Whenever the two of them were in the same room together, there was an uncomfortable, brooding atmosphere. It hadn't always been that way. Right up until Connie was fifteen, they had shared most secrets. Now they didn't know how to converse without rowing. Maybe it was because Connie was no longer a girl but a woman, eighteen years old with ambitions that frightened Aggie, who was a contented, simple soul.

Connie didn't answer. Instead she kept her gaze down and her features impassive. She didn't know whether to tell the truth dressed up with lies, or to say nothing until she had devised a plan to get back at that swine, Peterson.

Aggie turned away with a sweeping glance at the rest of her children, secretly wishing she'd never given birth to any of them – except maybe Luke, who was the best of a bad bunch.

'We're all behind you, Connie,' Steve declared, bristling. 'We're your brothers, after all, so if there's a problem, we should know about it.' He was always ready for an argument with somebody.

Robby, too, was itching to punch someone. 'That's right,' he snarled. 'If the bastard's been trying it on, we'll have to teach him a lesson, won't we?' He glanced about, looking for reassurance.

Connie wasn't sure if that was the right way to go about it. Oh yes, she wanted Peterson beaten to a pulp, and she knew Steve and Robby would do it for the pleasure, but there was always a chance that she might get back in Peterson's good books. If she was wrong, then her brothers could do their worst, but she had to try. Returning here had been a trial. After three days, she couldn't wait to get out again. Another chance, that was all she wanted. She still had plans for herself and Peterson and couldn't, wouldn't, believe it was all over.

Steve was insistent. 'If he has been trying it on, you'd better tell us. We've a right to know.'

'Mind your own bloody business!' she snapped. 'If I want your help, I'll ask for it.'

'Leave her be,' Luke ordered. 'Connie's right. She'll let us know when she's ready.' He read Connie better than most and thought she might have Peterson well in hand.

A short time later, they all went their different ways. Aggie looked around at the dirty plates and the piles of washing-up still to be done. 'Sometimes I wonder why I bother,' she groaned, collecting up the dishes and going back and forth until everything was piled into the big pot sink. 'Lazy buggers, that's what my lot are, every bloody one!'

She had rolled up her sleeves and made a start when Connie returned. 'I'm sorry I snapped at everybody, Mam,' she said. 'Only I don't want them knowing what happened.' She didn't really want her mam to know either but she needed to talk to somebody. With no friends to confide in, that left only her mother.

Aggie paused to look at her, at the small slim figure and the bold brassy face that made men go weak at the knees. God forgive her but she didn't like her own daughter. 'He hit yer, didn't he?' she remarked, returning to the washing-up. 'I saw the bruises when you were coming out of the washroom the other day. Like you say though, it's none of our business.' She had enough on her own shoulders without taking on the weight of Connie's troubles.

Dejected, Connie threw herself into the nearest chair. 'You don't give a bugger, do you?'

'Course I do. Same as you gave a bugger for me when you took yerself off to greener pastures.'

'I'm not like you, Mam. I've got ambitions.'

'Oh yes, and don't we know it.'

'I mean to be a lady. I mean to have fine clothes and a carriage to run me about. The only way I can manage that is to marry a man who's loaded.'

'Well now,' Aggie remarked acidly, 'Peterson is loaded, that's for sure. He's also married.'

'Being married don't matter.' Growing excited, Connie gave away more than she intended. 'Robert Peterson owns eight cottages and endless acres of farmland. He's got interests all over the city, and more money than he knows what to do with. He fancies me rotten. There's nothing between him and that stupid wife of his. She won't give him what he wants but I will, and one day I'll get my reward, you see if I don't.'

Aggie turned to stare at Connie with disgust. 'I married yer father for better or worse, and I bore him an army o' sons that took me figure and took me strength. There were times when I could have gone off and left him to it, times when I never knew where the next penny were coming from, and all of you small and hungry, wanting clothes, wanting things I couldn't give yer. Me and yer dad had a hard life, and things ain't so much better now, even with more money coming in.

More money in, more money out, and never enough, that's the story of my life.'

'It's not much of a life to be proud of, is it?' Connie remarked spitefully.

'Mebbe not, but you've nothing to be proud of either, young lady. The minute you turned of age, you walked out that door when you could have been helping me and fetching another wage into this house. But oh no. You chose to go swanning off to yer fancy man and yer precious ambitions.' There was a sob in her throat as she went on, 'I'll tell yer this an' all, you think yer pretty, don't yer? But I were prettier than you. I could have had any man I wanted – even the ones with money. I could have left yer dad and made my life easier, but I never did, and shall I tell yer why? Because I had respect for meself, that's why.'

With immense cruelty, Connie told her, 'Peterson says you sold yourself on street corners.'

For a moment it seemed as if her mother had not heard, but then she lowered her gaze, took a deep breath and said very softly, 'Sometimes, when the money's short and you've nothing in the cupboard to feed the young 'uns, a woman might be driven to . . . desperate measures. I'm not denying I did things I'm ashamed of, but that were a long time ago, and I hope I've paid me dues.'

'You bloody old hypocrite! Who the hell d'you think you are to preach at me? What I'm doing ain't no different than what you did.'

Rage coloured Aggie's face. 'That's where you're wrong, my girl! You're whoring for greed, for yerself, and what you can take a man for. I whored because my kids were hungry and there was no other way. It were a long time ago, and it stopped soon as ever your dad got better pay. Now I'd sooner starve before I'd sell my body to any man, rich or poor.'

'Any man would be better than Dad. What's he ever done that you can be proud of? What's he ever given you, eh? And when will he provide you with the things a woman should have – money put away and clothes you might be proud to walk the streets in? When did you last go on a holiday? When did he buy you a present? Huh! You'd have been better off staying with one o' the men who *paid* for your favours.'

'You ungrateful little swine!' Striding across the room, Aggie took Connie by the shoulders and shook her hard. 'You don't know what you're saying. Your father's been good to me in his own way. He's worked his fingers to the bone, and he's done all any man can do for his family. And you have the bloody nerve to compare him with the no-goods *you* ferret out! He's worth ten o' the buggers. I'll grant you he's not rich and never will be, and he's not able to give me fine things, even if I wanted them, which I don't. But he's hard-working, and he's never raised a hand to me in all the years we've been wed. So don't you ever think he's less than the cowardly creature you've been bedding.'

'Get your hands off me.'

'Think on then,' Aggie warned, releasing her daughter and feeling ashamed. It wasn't in her nature to be violent, but this arrogant little sod brought out the worst in her. 'Your father never knew what I did all those years back, so keep your mouth shut or I might have to flay you alive.'

There was a moment of quiet, during which Aggie returned to the sink and Connie reflected on her mother's anger. 'If he *had* hit you, what would you have done?'

Aggie thought a moment. 'Much as I love him, I'd have packed me bag there and then. I would never stand for any man nor woman raising their fist to me.' She looked into Connie's small, cruel eyes and thanked the Lord she was not made in the same mould. 'Like I said, I have respect for meself.'

'And you think I haven't?' Her mother's words had managed to make her feel ashamed and that made her angry. 'You think I have no respect for myself, is that what you're saying?'

'If you like.'

'Well, you're wrong! Why do you think I've come home?'

'I wish you'd tell me.'

When Connie hesitated, Aggie answered for her. 'You've come home because he's thrashed you, and then he's thrown you out. I'm right, aren't I? The grand man used you for his own ends and now he's had his fill and doesn't want you any more. Come on, now. Own up and shame the devil.'

'We had an argument, that's all.'

'Just an argument, was it?' Aggie knew Connie was fooling herself. 'And now here you are to lick yer wounds before you go, cap in hand, begging him to take yer back in. But he won't want you back now, will he? Yer soiled, aren't yer? He's dirtied his hands on yer and now he's washed 'em clean.' A wave of pity overwhelmed her. 'Oh, Connie, why don't yer come home for good? I'm sure we could try not to murder each other.'

'No!'

'Yer only fooling yerself if yer think he'll have yer back. Rich man Peterson is rid of you, and now he's off looking for the next conquest.'

Leaping to her feet, Connie raged, 'Shut up, damn you!'

'Face the truth, my girl.'

Bristling with hatred, Connie shouted, 'All right, he did thrash me. So what? Maybe I deserved it. Time and again he had his way with me, and I enjoyed it. What d'you think to that?'

'I think you're a damn fool.'

Relentless, Connie went on, 'Me and Robert Peterson have been lovers right from the first, and it's been bloody wonderful. But then we had a silly argument and, yes, he called me a whore and threw me out. I suppose you're satisfied now.'

'No, gal. I'm just sorry you can't see him for what he is.'

'You're jealous, that's all. Because your life's been one long drudge, you can't bear to see me making something of myself. Well, I don't give a monkey's what you say. I'll wait a few more days, till he comes to his senses, then I'm going back, and nothing you can say will change my mind.' With that she flounced out, straight into her brother Steve. 'And you keep your nose out,' she ordered, realising he must have heard every word. 'If I find out you've been anywhere near him, you'll be sorry.'

'Wouldn't dream of it,' he said softly. But as she went on her way, he had a cruel gleam in his eye.

'So!' Robert Peterson stood by the fireside, hands clasped behind his back and a look of disdain on his face as he addressed his gamekeeper. 'The poachers got away yet again?'

'Empty-handed though,' came the reply. 'Half a dozen rabbits and a string of fine, plump fish abandoned in the escape and now delivered to your own kitchens.'

'That's not the bloody point, man!' Robert hated the idea of his lands being plundered. 'I want these poachers caught and punished.'

'They will be. They're a cunning bunch but it's only a matter of time before I have 'em red-handed.'

'One month.'

'Beg your pardon, sir?'

'I'll have these poachers caught and punished, or I'll have your job away. Got that, have you?'

'Yes, sir.'

'Good. See to it then.' He stared at Matthewson until he had backed out of the room and closed the door. 'Useless bastard!' Robert Peterson hated everything and everyone at that moment.

Elizabeth was in the hallway when Geoff Matthewson came out of her husband's study. 'Good morning, Mr Matthewson,' she said politely.

Acutely aware that the maid was waiting by the door, he returned her greeting in the same polite manner. 'Morning, ma'am.' He nodded his head and gave a quiet, knowing smile. Then he waited for the maid to open the door, passed through it and went on his way.

Wasting no time, Elizabeth hurried up the stairs to her room where she ran to the window, her eager gaze following his progress across the fields.

The gamekeeper was a fine figure of a man, with fine brown hair and kind blue eyes. The very sight of him did her heart good. When he was gone from her view, she sat on the window seat, her eyes closed and her heart racing. Another hour, that was all. Just one more hour.

Exhilarated, she went to the wardrobe, where she rifled through every garment, until she found the one she wanted: a simple, pretty gown in fine white fabric with a low, sweetheart neckline and tiny red rosebuds trimming the hem and sleeves.

Quickly, she put it on and admired herself in the long mirror. 'Why shouldn't you have someone to love you?' she asked herself softly. She stepped out of her shoes and into her ankle boots which she laced tightly. She brushed her hair until it shone and then tied it into the nape of her neck; she touched her mouth with colour and her cheeks with rouge, and gave herself one last look in the mirror. 'I hope he likes my new dress,' she murmured. 'But then he seems to like me in anything. Not like Robert, who only sees what's underneath.' Her pretty features crumpled with sadness.

A few moments later she rang for the housekeeper. 'I have a crippling headache, Mrs Glover. A walk in the sunshine might do me good.' She had learned to lie beautifully. 'I shall be gone for about an hour, maybe a little more.'

'Quite right, ma'am. It's a glorious day.'

'With the governess dismissed and no one to take her place, I'm sorry you've been burdened with extra responsibilities.'

'I understand, ma'am.' Oh, she understood all right. The master had had his fun and now everyone else was paying. 'I'm sure it won't be for too long.'

'I'm interviewing a young woman for the post in the morning. Let's hope she will take some of the weight from your shoulders.'

Mrs Glover nodded, but she had reservations. If the new candidate was young and pretty, she wouldn't last any longer than the one before, and the one before that.

Elizabeth saw the look of disillusionment cross the older woman's face. 'I know what you're thinking,' she commented wryly, 'but rest assured, if I can arrange it, the new governess will be of a more mature and responsible nature.'

Mrs Glover smiled. 'Thank you, ma'am. Go for your walk

and don't worry. I'll keep an eagle eye on the children, see they don't come to any harm.'

'If the master wants me, please explain how I'm taking the air to rid me of this terrible headache. And that I should not be too long away.' If she only had the courage she would be gone and never return to this house, or the man, or, God help her, the children.

'Of course,' said the housekeeper and took her leave.

Downstairs in the kitchen, Mabel set the children outside with a picnic, close to the window where they could be seen. 'Mind you don't go wandering off now,' she chided, 'or you'll get a tanned arse an' no mistake.'

'You said arse!' little Kathleen giggled. 'That's a naughty word.'

Mabel was unruffled. 'Yer right,' she agreed. 'It is a naughty word, but you'll still get it tanned if yer run off.'

The children settled to their picnic and Mabel went inside chuckling. 'I've just been given a wigging by the little madam out there,' she said as Mrs Glover came into the kitchen.

'Did you deserve it?'

'Aye, I expect so. I mean, I did say a naughty word, after all.' With a few moments to spare, and it being a time when the servants gathered in the kitchen for their tea, she then put out the goodies on the kitchen table. 'Help yerself,' she told the others. 'Heaven only knows we've earned it.'

Settling down, they discussed the recent business of Connie Blakeman and the master, which consequently led on to the matter of a new governess. 'The children are a delight,' Mrs Glover said, 'but I can't do them justice with their learning.'

'Nor should you,' the butler reminded her. 'You get paid for housekeeping, not being governess to the children.'

'There's a woman being interviewed tomorrow for the post,' Mrs Glover informed them. 'Let's hope she stays longer than the last one.'

'Only if she's old and toothless,' Cook snorted.

Nancy Tomlin had a face stuffed with cake, but was so

intrigued she had to ask and set them all laughing, 'Why would the mistress want to tek on somebody who were old and toothless? And anyway, wouldn't she frighten the children?'

'Yer a joy, Nancy Tomlin,' Cook told her in a fit of giggles. 'Yer might be daft as a brush, but yer a joy all the same.' And Nancy beamed so wide that all you could see was mangled cake. Until Cook told her to close her mouth, 'Before yer put us off our tea!'

Subdued by the ensuing laughter and feeling a bit of a fool, yet not really knowing why, Nancy closed her mouth and didn't speak again for an hour; much to Cook's delight.

<hr />

AFTER LEAVING PETERSON's office, Geoff Matthewson did a quick tour of the spinney; he followed the path to the river and here he came across two men. One of them was Connie Blakeman's brother, Steve. 'What are you doing here?' Taking his gun off his shoulder, Matthewson held it loosely over his arm. 'This is private property. Be off with you!' Still smarting from the confrontation with Peterson, his tone was sharp. His job was at risk, and though he could soon get other work, he preferred to stay where he was. He had no liking for his employer but Elizabeth was another matter. While he worked here, he was close to her, and that was important to him.

Steve was quick to reply. 'Sorry, mate, we were just taking a short cut home. Me an' me mate here, we work at the mines – or we did till an hour back when we were given our cards and told to piss off. We ain't got no work at all now.' He paused. 'Don't suppose you've got work we could do, 'ave you?' he asked innocently.

'No,' said Matthewson curtly. 'And don't let me catch you here again,' he added.

The two men made their way off Peterson's land. 'By! That was close!' The older man, whose name was Ned, had been persuaded to the river against his will. 'If he knew we'd skipped work just to fish the river, we'd have had our collars felt an' no mistake. All the same,' he went on, 'we were caught on private property. Funny that gamekeeper didn't march us up to the house, don't you think?'

'Naw. He could see we were honest blokes,' quipped Steve. 'And anyway, he'd have to be a heartless bugger to haul us in when we've just lost our jobs.'

Ned laughed. 'How you came to think that one up, I'll never know.'

'Well, I weren't about to tell him that we were skiving work and fancied making a bob or two off the poacher's back.'

When Steve took another turn, away from the river and deeper into the woods, Ned was alarmed. 'Christ, Blakeman, where the hell are you going?'

'I fancy a fat rabbit for me tea.'

'Don't be so bloody daft, man. The gamekeeper can't be far away. He's probably watching us right now.'

'You're free to go.'

'You'll get us both hanged, you bugger.' But the prospect of a rabbit stew was too tempting, so he stayed. 'I've heard Peterson is a bastard.'

Steve nodded. 'You heard right.'

'From what I understand, he likes his women fresh and young. Treats 'em like dirt under his feet, so I'm told.'

Steve stayed quiet for a time, remembering his sister confessing how Peterson had bedded her time and again, and what was more she'd bloody well enjoyed it. Well, now she knew what he was like, and served her right. But what about his mam? Been a whore in her day, she had, and kept it quiet all these years. That had really got to him. Filled with contempt and disgust, he would never feel the same way towards either of them again. Yet he didn't altogether blame his mother and Connie. He blamed men like Peterson. Men who had it all, and still wanted more. Jealousy crept through him, trembling in his voice. 'That bugger Peterson needs teaching a lesson.'

'Maybe he does, but I'll leave that to others. It's all right for you, taking risks like this. You're footloose and fancy-free, but I've a wife and kids to worry about.'

Steve wasn't listening. 'If you knew your sister had been taken advantage of by a man who should know better, what would you do?'

'Cut his balls off, an' no mistake.' He'd hardly got the words out of his mouth when the sound of footsteps caused them to dive behind a shrub. 'It's a woman,' Ned whispered. 'By! She's a bit of all right an' all.'

'Ssh! It's Peterson's wife.'

'How do you know that?'

'Well, just look at her, man. She ain't the bloody gardener's wife, is she, eh?'

They ogled her from their hiding place. Her hair was loose and blowing in the breeze and the sun lit her face. She was enough to tempt any man, but Ned was nervous. 'Jesus Christ. Peterson's wife. And only an arm's reach away.' Trembling with fear, he clutched Steve by the arm. 'What if she sees us?'

'She won't.'

Ned wasn't convinced. 'I should never have listened to you in the first place. I must want my brains tested, coming on to Peterson land.'

'Ssh!' Elizabeth had stopped to look around. 'She must have heard you,' hissed Steve.

While the men crouched low, their hearts beating for fear of being discovered, Elizabeth remained quite still, her quiet eyes searching the immediate area. She had not heard them, but they didn't know that. Neither did they know that in fact she was afraid of being discovered herself and was only satisfying herself that she was not being followed. Presently she moved on, quickening her footsteps.

'That were too close for comfort, Blakeman.'

'Curious, weren't it?'

'What d'you mean, curious?'

'I mean she seemed to be looking for somebody.'

'Aye, she bloody were! She were looking for *us*. I'm off, mate, and if you had any sense, you'd do the same.'

Steve shrugged. 'Bugger off then.' He smiled. 'And mind how you go. I hear Peterson has mantraps set all over these woods. They'll tear your leg off like it were a twig.'

He watched Ned until he had disappeared from sight. 'Now then,' he muttered, his shifty eyes peering in the direction Elizabeth had taken, 'why would Peterson's wife be skulking about in the woods, I wonder? What if she's playing him at his own game, eh?' The thought was very satisfying. 'While he was bedding my sister, what if his lovely wife was being bedded by some other bloke?' He chuckled. 'Happen I should find out what she's up to.' With that he softly made after her and soon caught sight of her a short distance ahead. 'Easy, boy,' he told himself. 'Don't scare her off now.'

⊰━◆━⊱

ELIZABETH KNEW THE way by heart. Through the fringe of trees that bordered the woods, then down into the valley where the shepherd's hut nestled with its back to the trees and its face to the land. There was a time when the hut was used regularly, but not any more. Not since Robert had sold off all the sheep and concentrated on crops.

Her face lit up when she saw Geoff Matthewson standing at the door, and she ran to meet him. 'Oh, Geoff, Geoff, I do love you so.' She laughed like a child as he swung her round. Then he wrapped his arms round her and kissed her long and passionately.

'I'm so glad you're here,' he whispered. 'I was afraid you wouldn't be able to meet me.'

'Nothing would keep me away. Don't you know how much I love you?'

He held her to him. 'It's just that he was in such a foul mood, I thought he might take it out on you and somehow keep you from me.'

She shook her head. 'Never.'

'Are you ready to go inside?' He was ready. He was always ready.

'Can we go for a walk first?'

'We have to be careful, Elizabeth.' He glanced nervously about. 'We mustn't be seen. At least not until we've finalised our plans.'

'I know, but it's such a beautiful day, and I need to talk.' She gave him a little smile. 'I talk better when I'm walking.'

'Sounds serious.'

'It is.'

'About us?'

'Yes – and him, and the children.' A deep frown creased her pretty face. 'What we mean to do, and when. We have to be clear about it, Geoff. I need to talk it through.'

His face lit up. 'Are you saying you're ready to come away with me?'

'Yes, but I'm not sure what to do about the children.' She turned and started to walk away. He followed. 'I know I told you I didn't want to take the children, but now I'm not so sure. He's such a cruel man, and he hates the boy. He has an unhealthy obsession with Kathleen, and it frightens me.' She shivered. 'The children are so young, Geoff, so vulnerable. I don't know if I could bear to leave them with him.'

He caught her to him. 'Oh, Elizabeth. It's only right you should bring the children. They'll have a better life with us, you know that.' He smiled. 'Adam will make a fine young man, and Kathleen is such a delightful little soul.'

Shame suffused her face. 'I'm not a good mother,' she murmured, unable to look him in the eye. 'It shames me to say so, but I have no talent for it.'

'I'll help you.'

'I'm afraid.'

'Don't be.' Taking her by the hand, he led her back to the hut. 'You know I would never let any harm come to you or the children.'

They moved out of earshot, but Blakeman had heard enough to have his suspicions confirmed. 'Well, I'm buggered!' He was beside himself with delight. 'So they're planning to clear off, eh? And take the kids an' all. By! I shouldn't think Peterson will take very kindly to that, no sir.' Going carefully so as not to be discovered, he backtracked towards the river. 'We'll have to see what the big man has to say about all this, won't we, eh?'

Laughing out loud, he began running and rounded the river bend straight into the arms of the man himself. His face coloured with fear. 'Mr Peterson!'

Robert Peterson was taller and far stronger than his quarry. He was also enraged at finding a stranger on his property. 'What the blazes are you doing on my land?' He grabbed Steve by his jacket. 'Who the hell are you?'

Filled with the knowledge of what he had just seen, and feeling the taste of revenge so close, Steve grew bolder. 'I'm Connie Blakeman's brother,' he said arrogantly. 'And I know all about you and her.'

Startled, Robert almost let him go, but then he tightened his grip and gave him a shaking. 'Blackmail is it? Well, you can go to hell. Your sister knew what she was doing. She got what she wanted, and no more. She's just a whore, like all the others, and as for you, you're trespassing on my land.' His eyes glinted with malice. 'I'd be well within my rights to shoot you. I mean, you're a poacher, you ran away, I had no choice but to stop you.' With a sudden movement that took Steve by surprise, Robert flung him to the ground, dropped his gun from his shoulder and took aim. 'The only good poacher's a dead one,' he muttered.

Afraid for his life, Steve cowered before him, arms crossed over his face, babbling, 'It's not my sister who's the whore. It's your own wife. I've just seen them, her and the gamekeeper.'

There was a moment of silence, during which Steve didn't dare look up. Then pain exploded in his groin as Robert's booted foot slammed into him. 'You're a liar!'

'I'm not. I swear to God.' Still he didn't have the courage to look up. 'I'll take you to 'em if you want. Honest to God, I saw the two of 'em with me own eyes, kissing and canoodling, talking of runing off an' taking the kids with 'em.' He felt the cold bore of the gun against his head and for a long, terrifying moment he thought Peterson would shoot him anyway. But then the gun was pressed into his back and he was viciously propelled forward.

'Move!' ordered Robert.

And move he did. As fast as he could, Steve led the way to the hut, every now and then glancing back at the gun which stayed unnervingly close, pointing right at him. He had never been so near to the barrel of a gun before and it was a terrifying experience. More than once he wished he'd gone with Ned when he ran off. But it was too late now, and he had to use his wits or never see his mam again. Suddenly that was important. He thought he was a man, but right now, in the face of losing his life, he was just a shivering, pitiful little wreck.

As they approached the hut, Steve pointed. 'There,' he said excitedly. 'They were just there.'

'Well, they're not there now.' Robert was past patience. 'I did warn you,' he said, and his meaning was clear.

'No! They're inside!' As there was no immediate sign of the woman and her lover, it was all he could think of. 'I swear! They were making plans and he said they should take the children, that you were a cruel bugger, and it would be wrong to leave them with you. She was afraid, but he said he would never let any harm come to her.' His life was at stake, and he had nothing to lose by telling the truth now. 'He asked her to go inside and she said she wanted to walk. But they're inside now. They've got to be!'

As if in answer to his prayers, the soft, pleasant sound of a woman's laughter rang out.

Robert was visibly shocked. 'Elizabeth!'

'I told you!' Steve was jubilant. 'I said they were inside!' Seeing how Robert had dropped his guard Steve broke away, and ran like the wind. 'You won't shoot me, you bastard!' he shouted bravely. 'If you're itching to shoot somebody, shoot them!'

It was only a matter of minutes before he heard two distinct shots. 'Jesus!' Gasping for breath, he stopped to look back. All around him the trees gave cover, but he felt naked and threatened. 'He's shot 'em!' He ran on, ignoring the flailing branches that cut and bruised him as he fled, dodging and weaving, getting deeper and deeper into the woods and growing more fearful with every step. 'He shot 'em!' he kept saying, over and over. 'The bastard shot 'em!' He knew how close he had been to the very same fate, and his soul quivered.

Suddenly his heart was almost stopped by the sound of Robert Peterson's voice calling, '*Blakeman, listen to me!*'

It was close. Too close. 'God Almighty, he means to kill me an' all!' He had seen too much, he couldn't be allowed to live.

'I only want to talk. I won't hurt you.'

Steve had no intention of stopping to 'talk'. He made himself go faster, his lungs burning. He had no doubts whatsoever that Peterson meant to shut his mouth once and for all.

'Blakeman, don't be a bloody fool, man. I only want to know what they said.'

God, but he was close.

'Blakeman?'

Visibly shaking and dripping with sweat, Steve flattened himself against the trunk of a broad oak tree, silently praying. 'Don't let him find me. Dear God, don't let him find me.' In all his life he had never been so frightened.

'We can do a deal. What do you say?' An eerie silence, then, 'Money in your pocket, Blakeman. More money than you've ever seen. What do you say to that?'

Steve was shaking so hard he thought Peterson must find him.

Robert feverishly hunted the area, poking his gun into the undergrowth and softly swearing under his breath. He came so close to where Steve was hiding that one sound, one breath too loud, and it would all have been over. But he didn't see him, and was eventually forced to conclude that Steve had run off, and was still running. 'Damn his eyes!' he cursed, and angrily strode away, leaving Steve almost collapsing with relief.

'Don't count your chickens,' he told himself. 'The bastard could be waiting anywhere for you.'

He was. Coming to the edge of the woods, Steve was shocked to see him patrolling up and down, obviously hoping he might still catch a glimpse of his quarry. 'The bugger ain't giving up easily,' he mused. 'I'd best keep down and go by way of the river.'

But in that moment when he believed he had cheated death, greed got the better of him. 'More money than I've ever had,' Peterson had said. '*They'll* have money on them, I'll be bound, her and her fancy man. What's more, if I remember right, the gamekeeper were carrying a very 'andsome shotgun. Happen I'll need it if I come face to face with the big feller again.' The prospect of being able to defend himself by the same means as his enemy was too tempting. 'Once I'm safely home, that shotgun should fetch a pretty penny, I'll be bound.'

Without delay, he turned and made his way back to the hut.

What he found sickened him to his stomach.

The man had obviously been shot first; he was at the far end of the hut and partway covered by the woman, who lay on her back with her arms flung wide, as though trying to shield him from her husband. They were both partly unclothed, not completely naked. Blood patterned the wall, and for a moment Steve was morbidly fascinated by Elizabeth's dress on which small splashes of blood had caused the tiny rosebuds to blossom into full-blown red roses.

'Can't blame him for wanting you,' he murmured, admiring her beauty. 'If I'd known you were going for the asking, I might have made a play for you myself.'

He bent to ease her aside and turned back the gamekeeper's jacket. Dipping into the pocket, he sighed with satisfaction. Just as he thought, the wallet was bulging. Quickly, he slipped it into his own pocket and was about to turn away when he was startled almost out of his wits as Elizabeth's hand reached out to take hold of his trouser leg. 'Help . . .' she whispered, her stricken eyes looking up. 'Please . . . bring help.'

Frantic, he didn't know what to do. Snatching away, he stared down at her. 'You brought it on yourself,' he croaked miserably. 'I had to tell him or he'd have shot me. I had to tell him, I had to!' Tears ran down his face at the sight of her. She wasn't dead, like he thought. She was still alive, and he couldn't bear it. 'All right!' As bad as he was, he couldn't desert her altogether. 'I'll get help. I'll find somebody. Hang on, missus. Just hang on.'

He shifted her gently to one side, where he made her as comfortable as he could. Then he took off Matthewson's coat and laid it over her. 'Just hang on,' he said again. 'I'll be quick as I can.' Her eyes closed and he feared she was slipping away.

As he departed, he caught sight of the shotgun propped against the wall by the door. 'Don't suppose the poor bugger could get to it in time,' he remarked, snatching it up. 'But he'll pay. Me an' the woman in there, between us we'll see Peterson dangling on the end of a rope an' no mistake.'

Only then did he fully realise how much he needed to keep her alive. 'Jesus! If she croaks before I get back, it'll be my word against his. If I'm not careful, it'll be *me* dangling on the end of a bloody rope!'

Chapter Four

THE SOUND OF their boots echoed down the corridor. Silent and grim, the two officers made their way to the ward where Elizabeth Peterson lay, gravely ill and as yet unable to confirm or deny the account given by Steve Blakeman. 'If she dies without talking, we'll never know the truth,' Inspector Larch remarked as they approached the room. 'One of them is guilty. Which one, though? That's the thing. Which one?'

'For my money it's Blakeman,' his sergeant replied. 'Guilty as hell if you ask me, sir. Comes of a troublesome family, and he's been had up many a time before.'

'Minor things though.' Larch had his own strong beliefs. 'Nothing like this. Good God, man, we're talking about murder! Blakeman might be a bloody nuisance, and he'll fight with all and sundry, but murder? No, I don't reckon that. He's too much of a coward.'

'There's a first time for everything, sir. Blakeman had a run-in with the gamekeeper earlier, he admitted as much. Peterson himself said he caught Blakeman poaching on his land. And what about the sister? When Peterson sacked her because she was no good at her job, she threatened to send her brothers round. What's more, the servants heard her make the threats.'

'I'm not denying Blakeman was poaching. That's about his style, and his workmate admitted that. But I still don't think he's guilty of murder.'

Then you're a bloody fool, thought Sergeant Armitage.

'What about his claim,' Larch went on, 'that Peterson's wife was having an affair with the gamekeeper? It has to be true. I mean, they were found together, weren't they? And why would Blakeman try and save her if it was him who shot her in the first place? It doesn't make sense.'

'It does if you're a cunning bugger like Blakeman. He probably didn't realise she was still alive and ran for help to make himself look good. As for finding the two of them together, who's to say Blakeman didn't somehow arrange all that, just to support his story? Who's to say he didn't shoot her elsewhere and then carry her to the hut? And think on this. If he did stumble across them, what was he doing so far into Peterson land? And what was he doing with the gamekeeper's gun?' Armitage shook his head, a smug little smile on his face as he concluded, 'He's as guilty as they come.'

'He told us why he took the gun. He said Peterson was after him, to shut him up because he'd seen too much. And what makes you assume Peterson had no motive for killing them both? What makes you think they *weren't* having an affair, just like Blakeman claims?'

'Because Blakeman's a liar, sir, and Peterson's not. I know which man I believe. I've dealt with his type before.'

'There's something strange about this whole business. When Blakeman burst into the police station, he was still carrying the gamekeeper's gun. He made no attempt to hide it, which makes me believe his story, that he took it for his own protection. Besides, we know now it wasn't that particular gun that fired the shots. So where's the weapon that did the damage? We've searched everywhere but we've still not been able to turn it up – unless Peterson's got it hidden away. If you ask me, that gent is making fools of us all.'

'If the murder weapon is hidden away, then it's *Blakeman* who's hidden it.' Sergeant Armitage was a man who looked at the immediate facts, made a fast opinion, and clung to it. 'Blakeman did it all right, but his dirty little plan backfired and now he's locked up where he should be. If there's any justice, he'll be hanged and we'll all be well rid of him.'

In the three weeks since she was brought to Blackburn Infirmary, Elizabeth Peterson had received the very best of care, and still she showed no sign of recovery.

'Please make it very brief,' the nurse instructed the officers as they entered the private room. Then she left them alone. She went no further than the corridor, where she chatted to the constable on duty. 'A terrible thing,' she commented. 'With the poor woman at death's door and her husband spending every minute God sends by her side.'

'I don't know what the world's coming to,' the constable replied. More than that he was not allowed to say.

'He's a creepy sort, though, don't you think?' She was glad Peterson wasn't *her* husband.

The constable coughed politely. 'Under the circumstances, I don't think it's wise for me to pass an opinion on the gentleman.' In truth, though, he didn't care much for Peterson. He didn't care much for Blakeman either. As far as he was concerned, the world would be a better place without both of them.

The sound of footsteps in the corridor made them turn.

'Well, I never,' said the constable under his breath. 'Talk of the devil,' and he gave the nurse a wink, to imply nothing she had said would be repeated.

Pale and gaunt, Robert Peterson looked in need of sleep and sustenance. The nurse went to meet him. 'Excuse me, sir, but the police are in with your wife.'

'Police?' Robert stiffened. 'You had no right letting them in to see her!'

'I had no choice, sir. It's only for a moment and I was never far away.'

'Out of my way.' Rudely shoving her aside, he burst into the room, demanding that the two men leave immediately. 'What kind of people are you?' he said angrily. 'My wife is seriously ill. You can't just barge in here. I'll have your jobs for this!'

Inspector Larch tried to calm him. 'I'm sorry, sir, but we're not here to disturb your wife in any way, only to sit quietly and hope she may be able to tell us something.'

'How the hell can she do that? Talk sense, man!' After nights without sleep, his nerves were frayed, but he had to be careful. One slip and he might give himself away. 'You've no idea how distressing this is for me,' he said more calmly.

'We do understand how you feel, sir. But you have to understand our situation too. We're in the middle of a murder inquiry. The doctor informs us that your wife is not beyond regaining consciousness, if only for a moment or two. Anything, the smallest detail, might throw light on what happened.'

'You already know what happened. Blakeman and his sister did this, to teach me a lesson.' Robert bowed his head and ran his fingers through his hair. 'God Almighty, haven't we suffered enough,' he groaned. 'I want you out of here. I need to be alone with my wife.'

'Of course, sir.' Larch nudged his sergeant. 'We'll be just outside.'

Robert followed them to the door. 'I want to see the doctor,' he told the nurse. 'According to these gentlemen he told them my wife might regain consciousness. Why wasn't I told that? I want to see him. Now!'

'I'll see what I can do.' Arrogant man, she thought. Outside she told the officer in charge, 'I won't be long. I'm sure he wouldn't mind though, if you peeped in now and then.' It was just an instinct but it made her feel more comfortable to know he was being watched.

Robert closed the door and turned to the bed. For a long moment he stared at Elizabeth's face, at the deathly pallor and the closed eyes, and he feared the awful secret that lay behind them. 'Why don't you die?' he muttered. 'You shouldn't be here. You were meant to die with him, with your lover.'

A look of hatred coloured his features. 'You and him,' he hissed. 'You little whore! I ought to finish you off here and now.' Instead he bent to kiss her. 'See?' He was half crazed. 'You might prefer him to kiss you but he can't. He's dead, and so are you. It's only a matter of time.' Exhilarated by the power he had over her, he kissed her again. 'Do you hate the touch of my mouth on yours, eh, my darling? Want it to be him, do you? Oh, I am sorry. But you see it doesn't matter to me how you feel. If I want to kiss you, I will. If I wanted to make love to you, I could climb right in beside you.' Soft laughter issued from his throat. 'I can do whatever takes my fancy and there isn't a single thing you can do about it.'

He became maudlin. 'You should never have done it, you know. You should never have taken a lover. You insulted me, and I can't allow that, can I?' He took a deep breath and the words came out in a quiet rush. 'I wanted you dead then, and I want you dead now. Only I have to be careful. There's always somebody watching. They're outside right now.'

He put her limp hand in his. 'Day and night I've been here. Day and night, guarding you, afraid you might open your mouth and tell them what really happened.' He closed his eyes. 'Oh, I'm so tired, so very tired. Everything's being neglected. The farm's crying out for me to be there, it's harvest time, there are a thousand and one things I should be seeing to, but I don't care. Let it all go to pot. I'll start again somewhere. Once you're gone, I'll take off and make a new life. Put it all behind me . . . put *you* behind me.'

Suddenly he drew back. Her hand had been loosely resting in his, but now her long, fine fingers gripped his with such startling strength that it put the fear of God in him.

Just then the door opened and in came the doctor, followed by the nurse. One look at Peterson's horrified face and he said, 'What is it?' Bending to examine Elizabeth, he was astonished to see her eyes flicker open. 'Mrs Peterson, can you hear me?' he asked urgently. 'Don't worry. You're safe.'

'Tell her to let go!' Panic-stricken, Robert was struggling to release himself from her iron grip. 'Tell her,' he cried, 'for God's sake, tell her to let go!' He was trying to prise her fingers off but she had the grip of death on him and wouldn't let go.

'Nurse!' The doctor beckoned, then gave an instruction. An injection was administered. Still, Elizabeth would not let go of her husband's hand. 'She's in spasm,' the doctor explained. 'A moment longer, that's all.'

When Elizabeth looked up at him, he realised she was trying to say something. Bending his head to hers, he listened intently. On the other side of the bed, Robert could not move, held there by his wife's unrelenting grip. 'What's she saying?' he demanded nervously.

Outside, the officers patiently waited. Then the nurse opened the door to usher them in. 'She's awake,' she informed them. 'Please, you must be very quiet.'

Inside the room, the atmosphere was electrifying, with Robert, frozen with fear, and Elizabeth relating the tragic events to the doctor in painful, broken whispers.

It was all over in a matter of minutes. Her last words were for her husband. 'God forgive you,' she said, and long after her eyes closed for the last time, she held on to him. It took both doctor and nurse to release him from her clutch.

Inspector Larch read Peterson his rights. Quickly and quietly, he was escorted from the room, quivering like a child. Six weeks later he was hanged, the bruises made by Elizabeth's fingers still on his flesh, 'Like the mark of Cain,' one officer said.

For years following his execution, there were those who claimed his greatest fear on going to the gallows was that Elizabeth would be waiting for him on the other side. There were also those who thought it highly unlikely, because the gentle Elizabeth had gone one way, while he, with his wickedness, had gone another.

Chapter Five

THE LONG, HOT summer clung, until it seemed it might last for ever. But now, in the first week of October, the brown and rust of autumn began to show in the hedgerows. The sun dipped lower in the skies and in the evening the breeze took a chilly edge. But autumn had its own special beauty, and though it was sad to see the summer leave, the onset of winter brought its own comforts.

'By! There's nothing like a cheery fire to warm the soul.' Mabel rubbed her hands and settled down after a fine dinner of baked fish and home-reared asparagus. 'The company appeared to enjoy the meal,' she told John who was seated beside her. 'I've never seen food disappear so quickly.'

John agreed. 'They certainly had some good appetites and that's for sure.'

'The plates were so clean and shiny, Nancy could have saved herself the trouble of washing up. If she'd put them plates straight into the cupboard as they were, I'd never have guesed.'

'Oh, yes, you would,' Nancy contradicted her from the other side of the table. 'You'd have known and I'd have got a terrible beating for not doing my job properly.'

Mabel was offended. 'When did I ever give you a terrible beating, my girl?'

'Sorry, Cook,' Nancy muttered. 'Yer ain't never done that, even though there's been times when I've deserved it.'

'Think before you speak, my girl,' Mabel reprimanded. 'I'll

thank you not to make me look like an ogre.' She gave John a sidelong glance. 'Especially not in front of Mr Mason here.'

'Oh, don't worry,' he remarked, smiling from one to the other. 'I know very well you're not an ogre. You've always been kind and fair, and generous to a fault,' he gushed, always trying to get into her good books.

'Hmm. It's a pity Nancy doesn't think so.'

The sound of Nancy crying startled them. 'Whatever's the matter?' Getting out of her chair, Mabel went to the girl's side. 'You mustn't take it to heart, I meant nothing by it. You know me, I were just letting off steam.'

'It ain't that,' wailed Nancy.

'What is it then?' asked John.

'I'm worried about me job.' The tears fell thick and fast, and Mabel had to dip into her pocket for a hankie which she pushed into Nancy's hand; though instead of drying her tears with it she screwed it over and over in her fist, until Mabel was obliged to take it from her.

'You never have appreciated good things,' she chided gently. 'This was a present from Mr Mason.' Holding it up, she pointed to her initials embroidered in the corner. 'See? He had it done specially.'

Nancy had other, more pressing matters on her mind. 'I don't want to lose me job,' she wailed. 'Oh, Cook, I'm that worried.'

'We're all worried about our jobs,' Mabel said stiffly. 'It's worrying times but we'll just have to make the best of it.'

Nancy wasn't reassured. 'Whatever will I do?'

Straightening her back, Mabel put her hands on her hips. 'We'll know our fate tomorrow. Until then it's not a bit of good you fretting.'

'You don't understand,' Nancy wailed. 'Me mam says if I lose me job I'm not to show me face at her door again.'

'What?' It was enough to make John get out of his chair. He knew Nancy was the eldest of a large and poor family, but surely she would still have a home to go to. 'That's not fair,' he said. 'It's not up to us. With the master and mistress gone and the whole place going to pot, doesn't your mam know we could all be given our marching orders and through no fault of our own?'

'I've told her that but she don't care. She says it ain't no party with so many young mouths to feed and a man who don't like to work, an' if I think I'm coming back to be another burden on her then I've to think again, because she don't want me nowhere near.'

'Then you'll just have to get another live-in position.' Mabel was ever optimistic.

'Who's gonna set me on, eh? I ain't no good at nuffin'.'

'What are you talking about?' Mabel exclaimed. 'Who told you such a thing?'

'You did.'

Mabel was shocked into momentary silence. Guiltily she recalled the many occasions on which she had indeed called the girl good for nothing, but that was then and this was now. 'Nonsense!' she spluttered and bristled with indignation. 'I must say, girl, sometimes your imagination runs away with you.'

'She has a point,' John intervened. 'I wonder if any of us will find another place after what's happened in this household. I mean, there's been both of 'em carrying on outside their marriage, then murder committed, then a hanging, and now it seems that he ran up bad debts all over the place.'

'Hearsay,' Mabel replied promptly. 'Until someone in authority tells me otherwise, I shall treat those nasty little rumours with the contempt they deserve.'

'Come now, Mabel,' John persisted. 'You know as well as I do, the man was no good.'

Being the superstitious soul she was, Mabel softly warned, 'Mustn't speak ill of the dead.' And all three made the sign of the cross. 'All the same, you're right,' Mabel conceded. 'These past months the estate has been going downhill fast. I blame the solicitor myself. When the manager took off, he should have got someone else in the very next day. Instead the crops were left to rot and now the creditors are queuing up.' Nancy started crying again but this time Mabel took no notice. 'I wonder, when the debts are settled will there be enough money left to pay what *we're* owed?'

John had been thinking along the same lines. 'I've always guarded against something like this,' he said proudly. 'A few shillings here and there over the years. I'm pleased to say it's mounted up to a pretty penny.' To Mabel's extreme embarrassment, he eyed her curiously. 'I imagined you might have been doing the same.'

'Maybe I have and maybe I haven't,' Mabel retorted. 'If I haven't, I dare say it's my own fault, and if I have, it's no one's business but my own.'

John felt well and truly put in his place and there followed a moment's silence while each of them reviewed their own particular situation.

It was Nancy who broke the silence. 'Yer lucky to 'ave a nest egg,' she said. 'I ain't got a farthing to call me own.'

The other two stared at her.

'Not even tuppence to get you from here to any position you might be offered?' Mabel asked.

Nancy shook her head. 'Not a farthing. Not a penny. And even if I were offered a position, I couldn't present meself, 'cause I ain't got no decent clothes, nor money to buy 'em.' In fact she thought the best solution was for her to climb on Blakewater Bridge and throw herself over.

'Where's all yer wages gone then?' John was so frugal he couldn't believe anyone could squander everything they earned.

'Gone to me mam.'

Mabel was shocked. 'What? All of it?'

'Every penny. Every week, reg'lar as clockwork, and now, if I can't send money, she don't want me.'

'She don't deserve you!' Mabel had a mind to pay Nancy's mother a visit, and she said as much. But Nancy was filled with such horror at the idea that she had to promise not to do it.

'Right then.' Taking charge, John began pacing the floor. 'This is the situation as I see it.' He took a deep breath. 'As Cook rightly said, the manager went some time back and since then many of the farmhands beside. We've lost old Tom the gardener, who struck lucky and was offered a place with the Henshaws in Langho. And then there's Mrs Glover who's staying only out of loyalty to the children. Little by little this household is falling apart. It's been dragging on for weeks, but now, what with the gathering of officials, it seems some sort of decision is about to be made.'

'D'yer think they'll throw us out?' Nancy was still in a fright.

'There's no telling.' He didn't want to alarm the women but felt it his duty to point out the possibilities. 'Anything could happen. We shall just have to hope they want the household to remain intact. No doubt we shall be the last to know. We might be fortunate, Nancy, so don't go worrying yourself half to death. The solicitors might decide in their wisdom to keep the house up and running for the sake of the children – though who will be in charge of it all, God only knows. On the other hand, if the rumours of bad debts are true, the children might be taken away and the house sold. If that turns out to be the case, every man jack of us will have to fend for himself.' He smiled at Mabel. 'Of course there are those who will never want for a home or someone to take care of them.'

Embarrassed, she looked away, her face pink.

'So there you are,' John concluded. 'That's the way I see it.'

'I do wish we knew for sure, one way or the other,' Mabel said quietly. 'It's so unsettling.'

Squaring his narrow shoulders, he tucked in his chin and sounded very official. 'It's out of our hands. We should get a good night's sleep and hope tomorrow brings favourable news for us all.'

'It's them children my heart goes out to.' Mabel shook her head forlornly. 'Poor little buggers. With both their parents gone and the house filled with strangers to decide their future, heaven only knows what they're going through.'

UPSTAIRS, SEATED BESIDE Kathleen on the window seat, Adam tried not to let her see how afraid he really was. 'They won't let us come to any harm,' he told her. 'We'll be taken care of, you're not to worry.'

'I don't like that man.'

'Which man?'

'Mr Ernishoam.'

Adam smiled. 'You mean Mr Ernshaw.'

'Yes.'

'Why don't you like him?'

'Because he'll take you away from me.'

'I won't let him!' The idea that he and Kathleen should be separated was unthinkable. 'He and the others are here to see how they can keep us together.'

'Who are those men, Adam?' So much had happened so quickly, Kathleen's young mind could hardly grasp the implications.

'Mrs Glover already told you.' So many questions, and so much to think about.

Tears trembled in her eyes. 'Don't be cross with me.'

He put his arm round her shoulder and drew her close. 'I'm not cross.'

'Are you afraid?'

'Of course not!' Yet he was only a boy, and it was hard, being strong enough for both of them.

'Who are they, Adam?'

'Mr Ernshaw is Father's solicitor. I don't know who the others are.'

'I want them to go away.' Small and frightened, the only time she felt safe was when Adam was here.

'They'll all be gone tomorrow.'

'And will they never come back?'

'I don't suppose so.'

'Will Father ever come back?'

The question took him by surprise. 'Do you want him to?'

'No.'

'Then he won't.'

'Why are those men here, Adam?'

In as kind and careful a way as possible, Mrs Glover and Mr Ernshaw had outlined the situation to Adam. Not the true situation, however. No one had had the courage or seen any reason to explain that his mother had taken a lover and when his father had discovered them together he had killed them both. Instead, the boy was told a simple tale. 'Your parents were killed in an accident on the highway,' they said. 'Nobody's fault. Just one of those dreadful things.'

Once again, Adam explained it to his sister in the same careful way he himself had been told. 'So we're orphans now. The men are here to decide our future.'

Kathleen was too young. 'If Father comes back, we'll have to run away, won't we, Adam?' In her mind she could see the rage on her father's face. She could feel the cruelty and loathing; smell it, as if it was a perfume that clogged the brain. It was something she would carry with her all her life.

'He *won't* come back,' Adam promised. 'People can't come back if they're killed.'

'He hurt you.' Another image, another reason to be afraid.

'He can't hurt me any more.'

'Mummy was pretty, wasn't she, Adam?'

'Yes.' But she was distant. They could never love her.

'Why did she never cuddle me?'

'Maybe she didn't know how.' He felt her tremble. 'Are you sorry she's not coming back?'

'I think so.' Raising her face, she looked at him; a small, trusting little face, the sad eyes filled with confusion. 'Adam?'

'Yes?'

'Are *you* sorry?'

'What about?'

She shrugged her shoulders. 'I don't know.'

He thought for a moment. Yes, he was sorry. He was sorry he could never reach his father. He was sorry his mother had been like a stranger to them. He was sorry for his little sister.

79

'I'm sorry they wouldn't let us go to the funeral,' he said; that bothered him more than anything.

'Why?'

'Because they were our parents.'

'Mrs Glover didn't want us to go, and Cook didn't want us to go either. I heard her telling Nancy.'

'Nobody asked *us*.' That was the bit that hurt. He was the man of the house now, and nobody had asked his opinion about going to his own parents' funeral. 'We should have been there. It was our place to be there, Kathleen.'

'I'm tired, Adam.'

'Get into bed then.' He walked across the room with her. 'I expect we'll have to be up early in the morning. Mrs Glover said we might be sent for.'

Kathleen was too tired for all that. 'Goodnight, Adam.'

'Goodnight.' He gazed down at her, then softly left the room and went to his own bed.

But he didn't sleep. With both his parents gone and strangers in charge, he didn't know what to expect. 'I'm frightened too, Kathleen,' he murmured. 'Frightened of what might happen to us. Frightened they might send us away from each other.'

It was a terrible, crippling fear.

Morning broke in a blaze of glory. 'By! What a day for the sun to shine,' Mabel exclaimed. 'It should be pouring with rain, and a sky so black and thick you'd think it were a pie crust over the world.'

Nancy nodded in fervent agreement.

'Away with you!' After a sleepless night, John looked ragged. 'We must look on the sunny side, Mabel. It won't do to get ourselves in a state before we even know what the verdict is.'

'I had bad dreams, an' now I'm fit for nuthin'.' She dropped into the armchair. 'If they think I'm cooking breakfast, they can think again. I'm not budging from this chair until someone tells me whether I'm safe enough here or whether I'm out on the street.' She folded her arms and set her features.

John was unperturbed. 'Is that freshly brewed?' he asked, pointing at the big brown teapot.

'Course it is!' She had no patience, not even with him.

He took a moment discreetly to regard her. She didn't look her usual self, he thought. There were bags beneath her eyes, and a tight line to her mouth that suggested she meant every word she said. It was plain she needed something to distract her from the matter that was to be finalised in the drawing room after breakfast.

With this in mind, he went to the table and poured himself a cup of tea. With great deliberation, he took a mouthful, immediately grimacing. 'I thought you said this tea was freshly brewed?'

Both Nancy and Mabel stared at him in astonishment. 'What's the matter with you?' Mabel demanded, ready for a fight. 'I made that tea meself not two minutes afore you walked through that door.'

Taking his life in his hands, he bravely confronted her. 'All I can say is, you must be losing your touch. This tea's stone cold.' To underline his point, he strode to the sink and threw the offending liquid into it. 'In fact it might be as well you're not cooking breakfast for our guests or you might poison them before they've a chance to secure all our jobs.'

'You devil!' Mabel was beside herself. 'In future you'd best stay outta my kitchen. D'you hear?'

As he left he could hear the pots and pans being slammed down. 'I've never known anything like it,' Mabel complained loudly. 'Coming into my kitchen and telling me I can't make tea. The very idea!'

Unable to resist a peek, John inched open the door and poked his head round it. Mabel was standing at the range, sleeves rolled up as she arranged the bacon rashers in the pan. Nancy stood at the table, slicing bread and looking like the tousle-headed mop that stood outside the back door.

She looked up, and was so startled by the sight of John's face she gave a squeal. The squeal startled Mabel, who splashed herself with hot fat and flew into a tantrum. 'What have you done now, you silly, useless girl?' she shrieked. 'Get over here and see to the bacon. I'd better slice the bread afore you cut your skinny arm off.'

As she exchanged places with Mabel, Nancy shot a look at John, who winked at her. 'Cook?'

'What now, for heaven's sake?'

'I think the butler fancies me.'

'What?' Swinging round, Mabel glared at her. 'How did that foolish notion get into your silly head?' Mimicking the girl, she said, '"I think the butler fancies me." Good grief, girl, have you lost your mind?'

'Just now,' Nancy revealed, 'he was at the door and he winked at me.'

'Winked at you?'

'He were there, I tell yer. He were the one who made me squeal. I didn't mean to do it, only he winked, d'yer see?'

Mabel was indeed beginning to see. 'Are you saying he was watching from the door?' she asked softly. 'That he never really went after he threw away his tea?'

'That's right, Cook. An' he were smiling, like he were really pleased about summat.'

Mabel burst into laughter. 'Why, the crafty little bugger! The tea weren't cold at all. It were just a ruse to get me in a temper so I'd feed the devils out there.'

And feed them she did, with tureens filled to the brim with bacon and sausage, and mushrooms and tomatoes. There were kippers and porridge, and freshly squeezed orange juice; piping-hot coffee and tea, and thick slices of toast dripping with butter. All in all, it was a feast for kings.

'Splendid!' After such a meal, Mr Ernshaw was ready for battle. 'If you've finished, gentlemen, shall we retire to the drawing room?' He looked round the table, taking in the stern expression of a rival solicitor who was here to represent irate creditors who were demanding the sale of all land and property. There was also an appointed judiciary to weigh up all the considerations and arbitrate as necessary, and finally there was Mr Ernshaw's own partner who was here to lend support to the unlikely prospect that maybe the house and lands could be saved and thereby perhaps secure the future of the unfortunate children.

It was a very delicate situation, and one which would tax all their skills.

Impatient to get started, Mr Ernshaw beckoned to Nancy, who was attending table and looked quite presentable in a clean white apron over a dark frock, with her hair firmly pushed under a pretty cap.

'Yes, sir?'

'Please advise Mrs Glover that we will expect her in the drawing room in one hour from now.'

'Yes, sir.'

'And kindly bring a pot of tea through.' He patted his rotund stomach. 'We've thirsty work ahead.'

'Yes, sir.' Nancy knew what thirsty work he was talking about. When these men came out of the drawing room, she and everyone else would know the worst, or the best.

───────➤◉◀───────

MRS GLOVER WAS in the kitchen, talking to Mabel and John. 'You'd think they might have come to a decision yesterday,' she was saying. 'Half the day walking the grounds, taking notes and looking into every nook and cranny, then another four hours locked in the drawing room. Four long hours talking it through, and not one of them prepared to give way.'

'What makes you so sure they'll come to a decision today?' John's anxiety was echoed on everyone's face.

'Because I've been told as much.'

They all turned as Nancy entered. 'Mr Ernshaw says you're to see him in the drawing room in an hour.'

'There you are then,' said Mrs Glover. 'One hour. They must have thrashed out most of the business yesterday after all.'

Nancy brought some shocking news back with her when she returned from taking in the tea tray. 'Mr Ernshaw was saying how the children were orphans now, and there was a danger of them being sent to the orphanage.' She was so upset she could hardly talk. 'If they don't care about the children, why should they care about us?'

John calmed her down. 'I expect they were looking at the worst possibility,' he said. 'It wouldn't surprise me if Mr Ernshaw was just being clever. He's the one who wants to keep the house and land, don't forget.'

'Will it be all right then?'

'Of course it will,' he assured her. 'Now then, get about your work and put it all out of your head.'

While the servants waited inside the house, the children sat in the orchard with Mrs Glover who was reading a favourite storybook to them. 'I have to go inside now,' she told them when Nancy came to remind her of the time. 'Adam, read to your sister while I get back, will you?' Adam read well, and Kathleen, too, had an excellent grasp of the written word.

When Mrs Glover walked into the kitchen she found Mabel, Nancy and John lined up by the hallway door, looking at her as if silently pleading for their jobs to be saved. 'I'll do my best,' she murmured as she swept by; for wasn't her own position at stake too?

A sharp tap on the drawing-room door and she was quickly summoned inside. 'Ah. Mrs Glover.' Ernshaw gestured to a chair. 'Please, sit down.' When she did so, he went on in sombre voice, 'We have finally managed to reach agreement,' he informed her, 'but I'm afraid it isn't the news you might have hoped for.'

Suddenly, to her shame, she had thoughts only for herself. 'Tell me at once,' she said boldly. 'Is my position safe here?'

He studied her for a moment, thinking how human nature could be so disappointing. He had truly believed that Mrs Glover, above all people, would want to know how the children were to fare in this dreadful situation, and here she was, concerned only for her own situation. 'The decision we have reached affects everyone in this house,' he said sternly. 'Perhaps it might be as well if you were to sit quietly and listen to what I have to say.'

While Mrs Glover listened in silence in the drawing room, Mabel sat without speaking at her big kitchen table drinking tea, Nancy nervously bit off every fingernail, and John paced the floor, hands behind his back and a look of determination on his face.

Some time later, Mrs Glover went to fetch the children. 'You're to see Mr Ernshaw in the drawing room,' she told them, and when they had gone, she silently wept. 'I let you down,' she whispered. 'You trusted me, and I let you down.'

By the time she came into the kitchen, she was composed enough to impart the news. 'The house is to be sold to satisfy the creditors, and I'm afraid we are all out of work.'

Nancy cried, and Mabel looked at John with sorry eyes. 'What about the children?' he asked, voicing the question that was on everyone's lips. 'Surely to God they won't send those two bairns to the orphanage?'

'You may recall a visitor here some time ago, not long after little Kathleen was born. A small, wizened old dowager, who was sent packing by the master after only two days.'

'Widow Markham!' Mabel cried at once. 'I remember. She was the strangest little thing I've ever clapped eyes on.'

Even Nancy recalled the odd visitor. 'She just turned up one day and never left her room until the master kicked her out.' She rolled her misty eyes. 'She were ninety if she were a day. I expect she's dead and gone by now.' Even in her misery she had to chuckle. 'When she were going, she told the master how she'd be back and then he'd have to pay what he owed her. Shouted at 'im all the way to the carriage, she did. What a funny little thing she were.'

'No funnier than you, my girl!' Mabel remarked. 'By! You've got a lot to say for yourself all of a sudden, haven't you? Sit still and be quiet while we hear what Mrs Glover has to tell us.'

Mrs Glover continued, 'It seems that Widow Markham was

Mrs Peterson's aunt, and consequently the children's great-aunt and only living relative.'

The news came as a great surprise to one and all. 'Mind you, we shouldn't be all that surprised,' Mabel decided. 'If I remember rightly, she arrived as if she were part of the family. There was a lot of arguing, like families sometimes do, and when the old dear left, Mrs Peterson did seem upset.'

'So the children have a great-aunt,' John said. 'Does that mean they won't be going to an orphanage after all?'

'No orphanage,' Mrs Glover confirmed. 'According to the solicitor, there won't be much money after all the debts are paid, but apparently enough to satisfy their modest needs should their great-aunt agree to have them.'

'I bet she won't!' Mabel was convinced. 'I mean, the master threw her out of here so she ain't likely to want his childer, is she?'

'Time will tell.' John always tried to be optimistic. 'And what will you do, Mrs Glover?' he asked politely.

'I expect I shall find a post. Mr Ernshaw says he'll give me the highest references.' She hadn't expected that after showing that streak of selfishness. 'What about you?'

'Oh, I have plans,' he said cagily with a twinkle in his eye. 'I mean to get married and open a guesthouse by the seaside.'

Mabel was astounded. 'Married?'

'That's right,' he confirmed, 'if you will please do me the honour, Mabel my love.'

She went all shades of red. Nancy screamed out loud, and Mrs Glover beamed with pleasure. 'Oh, how romantic,' she sighed, thinking it could never happen to her.

Flustered and thrilled, Mabel accepted and everyone had a drop of best sherry. 'Here's to us,' John said, raising his glass.

The only one with a frown on her face was Nancy. 'I wish I were going with yer,' she muttered.

John put the matter to his betrothed. 'What do you think, Mabel? Will you need someone to change the beds in your little guesthouse?'

'I dare say I will,' she chuckled. 'There'll be rugs to beat and washing to be done, tables to be waited on and all manner of household duties to see to.' Winking at Mrs Glover, she said wryly, 'I'm not sure Nancy has it in her. I mean, she's such a little thing, don't you think?'

Everyone laughed when Nancy jumped up to show off her muscles. 'I can fetch and carry better than *anyone!*' she protested, then burst into simultaneous tears and laughter when Mabel told her she'd better start getting her bags ready, 'If you're coming with us.'

PART THREE

1855
THE LEAVING

Chapter Six

———⊷∘⊷———

K ATHLEEN WAS AFRAID. 'I don't want to go,' she sobbed
as Mr Ernshaw hurried her along the hallway to the front
door. 'I want Adam! Where's Adam?'

Impatient to get the difficult task over and be on his way,
Mr Ernshaw gave her a little shake. 'Behave yourself, child!'
he reprimanded. 'You know very well Mrs Glover has gone to
fetch him.'

'Poor little bugger.' Peering from the kitchen door, Mabel
wiped the tears from her own face. 'She's only a bairn,' she
muttered to John, who was standing beside her. 'She's lost her
mam and dad, and now she's being shipped off to some strange
old woman she's never met in her life afore.'

As always, John looked on the bright side. 'Let's be thankful
they're not being shipped off to some awful orphanage. At least
they'll be with blood kin.'

Nancy joined them. 'That ain't allus a good thing neither,'
she told them. 'See how me mam's turned on her own daughter. Since I lost me job, she'll not even look at me in the
street.'

'Aye, but you'll be all right,' John replied kindly. 'God willing,
you'll have a good home with me and Mabel.'

Mabel had something to say about that. 'Mebbe. So long as
she keeps her nose clean and earns her keep,' she said. 'At our
age, we can't afford to carry no lazy good-for-nothings.'

Nancy was indignant at the slur on her good character. 'That ain't fair, Cook,' she replied sulkily. 'I ain't *never* been a lazy good-for-nothing.'

'Aye, well, think on you never are,' Mabel warned.

Suddenly Kathleen broke free from Mr Ernshaw and flung herself at Mabel. 'I want to stay here,' she cried, holding on to her skirt for dear life. 'Me and Adam don't want to go away.'

Deeply moved, Mabel swallowed her tears and painted on a smile. 'You'll be fine, bless yer,' she told the child. 'You're going to yer Aunt Markham's house, and you'll have Adam there with you. Be a good girl now, won't you, eh?'

'I don't want to go,' Kathleen wept. 'Don't want to go.'

Pulled away by Mr Ernshaw, she cried all the more. 'You're a bad girl!' he declared, marching her to the front door. 'It took time and a great deal of effort to squeeze enough money out of this estate to see that you children were well placed.' Red with anger, he let his temper get the better of him. 'I've a good mind to send you to the workhouse. You'd have something to cry about then, I'm sure.'

John stepped forward. 'There's no need for threats,' he said angrily. 'Can't you see, the child is frightened enough.'

Furious, Mr Ernshaw drew to a halt, keeping a firm hold on the struggling Kathleen. 'I'll thank you not to interfere, my good man. Especially as you have not yet received your severance pay.'

It was enough to silence them all. Without their severance pay it would be difficult trying to build a new life elsewhere.

'Shame on you, sir.' Mrs Glover had not heard the warning but she'd heard the child sobbing, and she'd heard Mr Ernshaw shouting at her to stop. 'I did warn you. It would have been kinder to bring the children down together.'

'I'm here to carry out my duty,' Mr Ernshaw told her acidly. 'With other urgent business to attend to, I have no time to waste. I want the children away so we can finish up here before the auctioneers move in.'

His words had a deep effect on all those present. Whether he meant it to be or not, it was a stark reminder that their work here was finished and, like the children, they were about to embark on an uncertain future.

'Lord help us,' Mabel muttered and scurried into the kitchen to shed more tears. Nancy followed and sat dolefully at the table. John remained where he was, head bowed and heart heavy. 'Before this is over,' he said, 'we'll all need a slice of good fortune.'

Adam ran downstairs to his sister. 'Don't cry, Kathleen,' he urged. 'We'll look after each other.' He took hold of her hand and, with great dignity, walked her to the waiting carriage.

When the luggage was loaded, Kathleen looked at Mrs Glover. 'I wish you were coming too,' she said forlornly. 'I wish Cook was coming, and Nancy, and everyone.' While she spoke, she held Adam's hand so tightly her knuckles ached.

'Bless you.' Mrs Glover's voice wavered with emotion. 'Remember what Adam said,' she urged gently. 'You can look after each other.' Cupping the child's face between her hands she tenderly kissed it. 'Your aunt will love you both,' she promised. Yet deep down she wondered. Would their lives be any better for their change in fortunes? Or would they be worse?

The other servants gathered round and said their goodbyes. 'God luv 'em,' Mabel trembled as the carriage drew away down the drive. 'Let's hope they're going to a better place, eh?'

'Aye.' John knew exactly what she meant. 'They've not known much love in this house, that's for sure. Let's hope to God they'll be cherished by their aunt, however strange she may be.'

Nancy had been thinking about her own particular situation at home. 'If there's any justice in the world, they will be,' she said with such feeling that they were all subdued.

They made their way back into the house and a moment later Mr Ernshaw joined them in the kitchen. 'Now then,' he said, seating himself at the table and unfolding a large leather file, 'let's get this over with.'

Half an hour later he rose to leave. 'You have your dues,' he said, pointing to the envelopes each one clutched, 'and you have your orders. The house is to be left spotless from top to bottom, and all of you are to be gone by four o'clock today. Mrs Glover, you are to oversee the leaving and then to deposit the keys at my office.' He looked from one to the other. 'Be warned, I've taken an inventory of everything, so I shall know if even the smallest item goes missing.'

There was a chorus of protest.

'Are you calling us thieves?'

'You've no call to say a thing like that!'

He was unmoved. 'So long as you understand what I'm saying.'

When they silently glared at him, he grunted. 'Right. I'll be off then. Good luck to you all.'

After he'd gone, they all remained in their seats for a moment. 'The house seems dead with the children gone,' Mabel mumbled, and Nancy shivered.

The first to rise was Mrs Glover. 'We might as well get on with it,' she suggested. 'I'll check the upstairs, if you'll check downstairs,' she told John. 'Once that's all done, we can pack our bags and meet back here in an hour.' She glanced at Mabel. 'Is that all right?'

'Sounds fine to me. There's nothing to be done that I know of. I had Nancy cleaning the upstairs all morning, and there isn't a speck of dirt or dust in my . . .' She stopped. 'It isn't *my* kitchen any more, is it?' she whispered brokenly.

John put his arm round her. 'Come on now,' he said fondly. 'We've a number of guesthouses to view, so with a bit of luck and some canny bargaining on my part, you'll have your own kitchen soon enough.'

'Not before I've a ring on me finger!' she told him.

'And that will be taken care of before you can say Jack Robinson,' he promised.

The house was checked and nothing was amiss.

One hour later, they each returned to the kitchen carrying their bags. 'Well, this is it.' Mabel looked round the kitchen and her heart sank. 'I shan't see this again,' she said. 'I hope the next person to come in here takes care of it. I couldn't bear to think of it all going to rack and ruin.'

Overcome, Nancy muttered, 'I'll wait outside,' and made good her escape.

There was nothing more to be said, so the others followed her outside. Mrs Glover locked the doors. They all shook hands, wishing each other well, and then went their separate ways – John, Mabel and Nancy to the bottom of the lane to catch the bus to the railway station and a train to Blackpool, to view the first guesthouse on their long list, Mrs Glover to the offices of Ernshaw, Trial and Bottomley, Solicitors, where she would deliver the keys and wash her hands of the Peterson place for good and all. Once her duty was done, she meant to go straight to the agency on King Street; they had promised to find her a place with a suitable family in Manchester.

Just before she turned out of Penny Street, she glanced back, to see the others waving her off. 'Goodbye,' she murmured, waving back. 'And good luck.'

As she continued on her way, two other faces entered her mind; small, innocent faces with young, sad eyes. 'Mr Ernshaw should have let the children meet their aunt before packing them off,' she muttered. 'But then she wasn't interested in meeting them, was she? If you ask me, all Widow Markham wants is the money that Mr Ernshaw enticed her with.'

It was a very worrying situation, but not one she was paid to worry about, she reminded herself. She had her own uncertain future to cope with. All the same, she couldn't help but wonder what sort of life was awaiting the children. How would they be received? Most important of all, would they be given the love they so desperately needed?

Mrs Glover sighed. It was all very unsettling and worse, she would never know what became of them.

Chapter Seven

THEY WERE LEAVING.

Kathleen and he would never again climb the aged oak trees in the grounds of that big old house. They would never again see the new lambs being born, or play in the corn when it was so high they could hide from the world. They wouldn't sit at Cook's table, eating the delicious tarts that spilled over with warm raspberry jam. Nor would they be taken into town by Mrs Glover, to gaze at the shop windows and later stop at the pretty little café in the railway station for a plump muffin and a glass of dark-brown sarsaparilla.

All that was gone. But then, so were the beatings and the fear. So were their parents; the pretty mother with the cold heart, and the father with his hatred and obsessions. All were gone.

'Where are we going, Adam?' The small, familiar voice broke into his mind. At least she's still here, he thought. We still have each other.

'You know where we're going.' He tried so hard not to be impatient with her. She was only a baby, and he had to take care of her now. 'We're being sent to Lytham St Anne's.'

'What's the lady's name?'

'Great-Aunt Markham.' Very carefully, he pushed aside a lock of hair that was falling over her dark eyes. 'She was Mummy's aunt, and so she's our great-aunt. Mr Ernshaw says she's promised to look after us.'

'She's never seen us.'

'She did, once, when we were small. I think Father threw her out.' It was only a dim memory. He remembered being woken by angry voices, and when he started down the stairs, this little woman was being bundled out of the door. 'Mummy was crying, and Father was in a really bad mood. When he slammed the door shut, he told Mummy her aunt was never to visit the house again.'

'I don't remember that.'

'You were too small to remember. I was nearly six.' He didn't go on to tell Kathleen how his father had found him hiding on the stairs and he had received a terrible beating.

'What if she doesn't like us?'

'Why would she not like us?' He shrugged his shoulders. 'It wasn't us who threw her out.'

'What if we don't like *her*?'

'We *have* to like her, Kathleen. Mr Ernshaw said if it wasn't for Great-Aunt Markham, we might have been sent to the orphanage.'

'Oh.' The very word 'orphanage' made her shiver. 'We won't have to go now, though, will we, Adam?'

'No.'

'Does she live on a farm?'

'No. She lives west of here, at the seaside. Mrs Glover says we're very lucky.'

'I'd rather live at home.' With the fields and the trees, and the pretty flowers all around. She could see it all in her mind's eye. She would always see it.

Adam knew what she meant. 'We have each other,' he said, and that brought back the smile to her face.

Lost in thoughts of what had been and what might be, the children fell silent, sombre faces turned to the rear window, gazing out as the familiar landscape disappeared into the distance.

The carriage took them through the lanes and into the smoky grime of Blackburn itself, past the many inns and churches; cobbled streets and long rows of tiny houses; cotton mills and factories that rose up like great monsters, belching smoke and fumes across the sky.

As they went, the wheels played a merry tune against the cobbles, clickety-clack, clickety-clack, almost as though they were singing.

Suddenly, the landscape was changing. The autumn sun shone down, the road opened up, and suddenly, there were green fields on either side.

Soon they were travelling through the fringe of the Ribble Valley. All around were lush fields and sparkling brooks, and trees with wide-spreading branches, beneath which the many cattle rested. The land rose and fell like a green ocean, and the autumn sun bathed it in a special glow. 'I like it here,' Kathleen whispered, and Adam promised they would come back again one day. 'When we're grown up,' he said, and Kathleen couldn't wait.

The journey took a little over an hour. The children talked themselves out, and slept awhile. When they were woken by the driver, they realised with a sinking feeling that they had arrived at their new home.

'Where's Great-Aunt Markham?' A long, lazy yawn showed Kathleen was still sleepy. 'Do you think she's run away?'

'She's very old,' Adam said wisely. 'Maybe she's having a little nap – you know, like Cook used to do.'

'Cook said she was only resting her eyes.'

'Nancy told me Cook said that because she didn't want people thinking she was getting old.' He climbed out of the carriage and helped Kathleen down. 'Be on your best behaviour,' he warned. 'Mrs Glover said we have to make a good impression.'

'Is Great-Aunt Markham *very* old?'

'I heard Mr Ernshaw telling Mrs Glover, "Widow Markham must be going on eighty."'

'How old is that?'

'Older than Cook, I think.'

'Will she be able to play with us?'

'I don't suppose so.' His eyes lit up. 'But she might have a dog. Father would never let me have a dog but, oh, if only I could have one now.'

'Why do you want a dog when you've got me?'

He laughed out loud at her. 'It's not the same,' he told her. 'Every boy wants a dog.'

'I do too.' If Adam wanted a dog, then so did she.

While the driver unbuckled the luggage from the rear of the carriage, the children stood side by side, looking towards the sea. It stretched as far as the eye could see, vast and endless. There were little ships bobbing up and down, and a stretch of golden sand beyond the promenade where laughing couples strolled and looked into each other's eyes. 'Can we go to the beach, Adam?' Kathleen felt better already.

'We shall have to ask Great-Aunt Markham.' He swung round to look at the house, and Kathleen did the same.

'It's scary,' Kathleen declared, and Adam was inclined to agree.

A grand old place, the house had seen better years. The stonework on the three steps up to the door was crumbling at the edges. The timber on the gable was flaking with age, and there were several tiles missing from the roof. There was a big, panelled oak door, with a lion's head knocker in the middle, and eight long windows across the front of the house, all dressed with faded lace curtains; like the house, they were past their best.

From the top step to the pavement and along the width of the house ran a rusty old wrought-iron railing. At the far end of this was a stairway leading down to a small wooden door. 'Where does that go, Adam?' Nervous though she felt, Kathleen was filled with curiosity.

'I expect it goes to the cellar,' Adam answered.

They were both startled when a high-pitched voice called out, 'That's right, young man, and if either of you give me any trouble, I shall lock you in there till kingdom come.'

The woman was small and wizened, with a pointed face and a wild halo of silver hair. She carried a silver cane with splayed feet and a large eagle on its top, its big glittering eyes staring down as though it was about to swoop on something tasty.

Instinctively, Kathleen took a pace backward. 'That bird wants to eat me,' she whispered, much to the amusement of her brother.

'It can't eat you,' he assured her. 'It's not real.'

'Is that Great-Aunt Markham?' she asked tremulously.

'I think so,' Adam answered softly. 'I can't be sure.'

'I don't like her, Adam. Tell her to go away.'

The high-pitched voice shrieked out, 'You! Driver! Put that luggage down. I'm not giving you good money to carry it in when there's a perfectly healthy boy here.'

Affronted by such treatment, the driver boldly gave her a piece of his mind. 'I weren't looking for no money,' he protested. 'I were paid at the start of the journey, by a Mr Ernshaw, so yer can keep yer money in yer pocket, missus.' Under his breath he added, 'Bleedin' little shrew!' He kept hold of the bags, one in each hand and two tucked under his arms. 'Well? D'yer want the luggage or don't yer? I ain't got all day.'

'I want you off my pavement!' she squealed. 'Leave the bags there. The boy can fetch them in.' Pointing to Adam, she ordered, 'Hurry up then, before he thinks to charge me waiting time. It's hard enough making ends meet without paying for a job twice.'

'I already told you, I don't want yer bleedin' money.'

'Clear off, you scoundrel, before I set the dogs on you.'

'Hang on a minute, missus.' He wanted to see the children safe inside, as was his duty. What's more, he didn't think the lad was strong enough to carry all the luggage, and he said as much.

Unperturbed, the little woman turned away, flung open the door and yelled, 'Here, boy! Here, Jake. See him off!'

Not wanting to be torn limb from limb, the driver dropped the bags and leaped into the carriage. Urging the horse away, he was soon careering down the street, cursing. 'Off yer rocker, missus, that's what you are, off yer bleedin' rocker! I pity them kids having to stay with an old bat like you.'

With the driver gone and the baggage lying on the ground, an odd silence remained. Silently, the widow regarded the children, and the children regarded her. Kathleen remained half hidden behind her brother, who was trembling in his shoes.

For what seemed an age, the silence continued, and so did the mutual regarding, until at last the little woman pointed a bony finger at Kathleen. 'You, girl! Come out of there!'

Far from coming out, Kathleen shifted further away, with only her big, dark eyes peering round Adam.

Adam stood firm, one hand by his side, the other holding Kathleen safe. 'Leave her alone,' he pleaded. 'She's afraid of you.'

Suddenly, a shrill peal of laughter sent the seagulls soaring with fright. 'Look at the brave little man,' she pointed at Adam, 'protecting his sister as though his life depends on it.' Wagging a finger at him, she added, 'You'd better be warned, young man, I won't stand for any disobedience. And I won't have you talking to me like that. How dare you raise your voice to me? Noisy, and insolent too. Whatever will the neighbours think?'

Always brave when her brother was under attack, Kathleen stepped out from behind him and confronted the little woman. 'It wasn't Adam being noisy,' she said quietly. 'It was you.'

For a dreadful minute Kathleen thought she might be given a spanking there and then. Instead, much to the surprise of both the youngsters, the old woman threw back her head and roared with delight. 'You're right,' she spluttered. 'I do tend to make a lot of noise. But then I'm entitled. I live here. What's more, I've lived here a lot longer than anyone down this street.' She eyed Kathleen with interest. 'They're a curious lot of devils. The best thing is to pretend they're not there.'

Kathleen gave her her answer. 'We don't want to stay here.'

'Oh?' Widow Markham wasn't quite so amused now. 'And why's that, young madam?'

'Because you're not nice.'

'Not nice, eh?' Keeping her beady eyes fixed on Kathleen's

face, she made her way down the steps towards them. 'I'm not paid to be nice. Unfortunately, I'm your only living relative and it seems you are now my responsibility. Nice or not, you're stuck with me, and I'm stuck with you. As for me being nice, as I'm the one who's been put upon, I shall be whatever I choose to be.' Quickening to anger, she turned to Adam. 'Don't just stand there, boy. Fetch the luggage, and be quick about it.'

The little woman led the way and with great difficulty Adam struggled up the steps after her with the bags. Kathleen walked behind him.

'Not nice indeed!' rambled the widow. 'I don't suppose you think I'm pretty either,' she said, her voice falling to a softness that was strangely pleasant. 'It doesn't matter though. I don't really care what you think. I stopped caring what people think a long time ago.'

Kathleen was sorry she had made the remark, and she said so. 'I didn't mean to offend you, Great-Aunt Markham, only you shouldn't blame Adam when it isn't his fault.'

'I shall blame whom I please, young know-all!' Anger coloured her face. 'It's no good you being sorry either. You said what you said and you can never take it back. What's more, I don't think *you're* nice – you *or* your brother. I suppose it's not your fault you happen to be children. The thing is, I don't like children. I don't want children in my house. But I was approached by Mr Ernshaw and he reminded me I have a duty towards you. I explained how I couldn't possibly take such young children into my care, but he was persuasive, told me how you would otherwise be taken away and deposited in some institution.' She tutted and shook her head. 'After the way your father treated me, I ought to let them take you away. What should I care? But, because of your poor, foolish mother, I couldn't say no, and now I'm stuck with the pair of you.'

At the door she swung round. 'Your mother was a silly creature, with no thought for anyone but herself. She married that man against my advice. I warned her, but would she listen? No, she would not.'

Gazing at the children, she suddenly saw how tired they seemed, how weary and small, and afraid. She saw the look on Adam's face, a look that said, 'You can send us away if you like, and we'll manage.' She saw Kathleen's tortured little face and realised that here was a tiny soul with a big heart. She looked at these two remnants of a terrible situation and knew instinctively that they were made of much sterner stuff than either of their parents, and for one, aching moment they melted her heart; a quiet, lonely heart, which until now she had determined to harden against them.

Drawing in a deep breath, she let it out noisily through her narrow nose. 'Unfortunately, your mother was my niece, and now she's gone and left me with a problem. That's what you two are, a problem to an old woman who doesn't care tuppence for you.'

Adam remained silent, but Kathleen was outspoken. 'If you don't care tuppence for us, why are you looking after us?'

Widow Markham thought about that for a moment, her gaze roving the girl's lovely features. There was something about Kathleen in particular that touched her old, mad heart. She had been intrigued by a letter from Mr Ernshaw that had arrived that very morning, and now she was intrigued by the girl. She was tempted to hurt her by revealing the letter's contents, but she didn't.

Instead, with a crafty little smile and a wink of the eye, she answered, 'Because, like the man said, I must be "off me bleedin' rocker", and because Mr Ernshaw paid me to have you – though not as much as I deserve.'

Adam muttered something under his breath, and her mood immediately changed. 'Bring the bags inside,' she snapped, turning away to enter the house.

Inside the gloomy hallway, she pointed to the wide stairway. 'Up there,' she told Adam. 'You're in the first room on the right.'

Kathleen's voice piped up, 'Where's the dog?'

'What dog?'

'The one you wanted to bite the man.'

The old shrew regarded Kathleen with amusement. 'That was just to get rid of him,' she confessed. 'I can hardly afford to keep *myself* at times, let alone a dog.' She turned to Adam. 'The girl's room is on the left, two doors down. Next to mine.'

Alarmed, Kathleen appealed to her. 'I don't want to be next to you,' she pleaded, her face white. 'I want to be next to Adam.'

'That's too bad, my girl, because I've made up your room, and it's the best one, after mine of course. It's at the front of the house, and if you press your face to the window, you can see the sea.'

'I don't want to see the sea.' She did, but not if it meant sleeping next to someone who was 'off 'er bleedin' rocker'.

'You're an ungrateful girl. I've a good mind to let Mr Ernshaw collect you straightaway.'

'She doesn't mean to be ungrateful.' Adam felt the need to intervene. 'It's just that she's really very frightened. Please don't send her to an orphanage, Great-Aunt Markham.'

'Why not?'

'Because she will sleep in the room you've got ready.' He stared at his sister. 'Won't you, Kathleen?'

'If you say so, Adam.'

The little woman bristled with satisfaction. 'Good!' She looked from one to the other. 'One more thing before you take your bags upstairs.'

Adam looked her in the eye. 'Yes, Great-Aunt Markham?'

'There! You're doing it again. Great-Aunt Markham this and Great-Aunt Markham that.' A deep frown swallowed the many wrinkles in her tiny face. 'What idiot told you to call me that?'

Kathleen giggled. 'Mr Ernshaw.'

'Hmm! Well, I don't like it at all. I haven't got time for all that nonsense. Kindly address me as Markham. It's short and quick, and I won't have to wait half an hour before I know what you're trying to say.'

The children couldn't make head or tail of her. She was odd, and weird, and a little scary, yet she was sweet and funny, and already they were beginning to like her, just a tiny bit.

'Right then. Off up the stairs, and get a move on. We have things to do before the day is out.' As they went away, she ran after them, clapping her hands and crying, 'Come on! Come on!'

Never having met anyone quite like her before, and not knowing what else to do, the children looked at each other and giggled.

They had gone only a short way up the stairs when Adam had to stop and shift the luggage. No sooner had he put down the bags than the little woman was scurrying up the stairs. 'What next?' she shrieked. 'Have I to carry the things myself? Have I to unpack them and treat you like babies?' Taking two of the bags she marched ahead. 'Quick now,' she called, 'before I throw you and the bags back out on the pavement.'

Carrying the remaining two bags between them, the children dutifully followed, across the dingy landing and along the passage, until they came to Adam's room. It was a large room, with bulky dark pieces of furniture: a dresser with six drawers and big wooden knobs; a tall fearsome wardrobe, and a wide iron bed. The dark tapestry curtains at the window were moth-eaten and ragged. 'You're in here,' she told him. 'Once a week you take out the rugs and beat them. You keep the furniture dusted and the room generally clean. Right. Which bags are yours?'

'The brown one and this one I'm carrying.'

Markham slung the bags on to the bed. 'Follow!'

She went out of the room, down the corridor, and into a smaller, prettier room, with a narrow brass-headed bed, a small light-wood wardrobe and a dressing table with an oval mirror. 'You do the same,' she told Kathleen. 'Keep the room clean, and everything in it. There are no servants in this house.'

With that she marched out, leaving Adam to unpack Kathleen's things and then his own.

'You really can see the sea,' Kathleen said, with her nose squashed against the windowpane.

'There you are then.' Adam knew they had to make the best of it here. 'She might be crazy, but she doesn't tell lies.' In fact, if anything, she was too truthful.

Downstairs in the drawing room, with its heavy old furniture, yellowing lace and smell of lavender, Markham listened a moment at the door. 'Hmm. That should keep them busy for a while,' she muttered. Fishing out a long silver chain hanging round her neck, she selected one of the small ornate keys hanging on it and unlocked the bureau. She opened the flap and took out the letter that had arrived this morning from Mr Ernshaw. The neat handwriting filled two pages.

This letter is formally to execute my duties as instructed.

Adam John Peterson, and his sister Kathleen Beth, being the surviving children of Robert and Elizabeth Peterson, are to be given into the care of their great-aunt, Judith Markham, until they come of age.

Should Judith Markham die or, for whatever reason, become unable to continue her duties with regard to her wards, then it falls upon the writer of this letter to seek other guardianship; or, if deemed to be the only solution, to place the children in a suitable institution.

The sum of fifty pounds has been paid over to Judith Markham, to be returned in the event of her not carrying out the appointed duties.

Yours faithfully,

Frederick Ernshaw

OFFICE OF SOLICITORS

The letter had a postscript, and it was this that had caused Markham to regard Kathleen with interest.

Some years ago, the writer of this letter was made party to a confidence he would rather not have been entrusted with.

In a state of distress, Elizabeth Peterson told how

she had taken a lover, and that she was carrying a child fathered by this man.

The man in question was the same man who, together with Elizabeth Peterson, was later shot and killed by Robert Peterson, for which crime he was hanged. The bastard child was named Kathleen Beth.

Having kept this secret for too long, the writer of this letter takes the opportunity to unburden himself of it.

This privileged information is now entrusted to the girl's appointed guardian who, in turn, must do as her conscience bids.

'Stupid, foolish woman!' muttered Markham. Hearing the children approach, she quickly thrust the letter back into the bureau and slipped the silver chain inside her blouse. There was a tap on the drawing-room door. 'Come!' she called, making an effort not to look guilty. 'Finished, have you?'

'Yes, ma'am.' Adam led the way into the room.

'No! No!' She shook her head vigorously. 'Not ma'am, not Great-Aunt Markham. Have you forgotten already, damn you? What have I told you, boy?'

'We're to call you Markham. I'm sorry.'

'Sorry is not good enough.'

'No.'

'I'm sorry too.' Kathleen did not want to be left out.

'Be quiet, girl.'

Kathleen did as she was told.

'Close the door.'

Kathleen ran and closed the door.

'Come over here. I have something to show you both.' Markham beckoned them to the far side of the room, to where a piano stood. 'Shift it,' she told them, and they stared at her in disbelief. 'It's got wheels on,' she informed them. 'You just need to get your backs behind it and push,' and she illustrated the action for them.

They obeyed and it was as she said, it was no great effort to move the piano aside.

'That's far enough,' she said. 'Now you, boy, turn the rug back and raise the floorboard beneath. You'll find a box hidden there.'

It was a small, iron cash box.

She took it from Adam's hands and carried it to the table. 'This is a small fortune,' she told them, revealing a wad of bank notes and a cache of coins. 'Part of it was given me by Mr Ernshaw to take care of you, and part of it I've managed to save over the years. I'm an old, old woman,' she confided, 'and I won't live for ever. If there should come a time when I'm very ill, or taken away to die, I want you to take this box and run – run as far and as fast as you can. Because if they ever find you, you'll be locked away and might never be seen again.'

Kathleen was alarmed. 'Don't die, Markham,' she pleaded. If she had to choose, she would rather stay with Markham than be locked away and never seen again. 'I don't want to live in an orphanage.'

'And you won't.' Markham was adamant. 'Why do you think I let myself be persuaded into taking on a pair of brats like you? I'll tell you why. It was because of your mother. She may have been stupid and fickle, and she may not have loved you like she should have, but she was my only kith and kin, and I know my duties.' She wagged a finger at them both. 'It was a pity she didn't know *her* duties or none of this would ever have happened. Now look what she's done. Both your parents gone, and the pair of you farmed out to a mad, crotchety old woman who should know better. The plain truth is, after what your mother did, she should have been hanged, along with the other culprit. I, for one, will never forgive her.'

Realising she was saying too much, she briskly changed the subject. 'That's enough of that,' she snapped. 'Just remember what I said about this box, if anything should happen to me.'

Adam had always suspected there was more to their parents' deaths than they had been told. And now the old woman had as good as confirmed his suspicions. 'What did Mummy do?'

'Never you mind.'

'Please. I need to know.'

Slamming shut the box, she handed it to him. 'Put the box back.'

When the box was safely tucked away and the piano returned to its place, she led the children to the cellar. 'Down you go,' she said. Thinking she was about to follow, they went ahead, jumping with fright when she shrieked from the top of the steps, 'Markham does *not* like to be questioned. Your mother's mistake was marrying that oaf of a man, and that's all there is to it.' As she closed the door she could be heard shouting, 'I warned you the cellar was for naughty children, and now you can stay there until I think to let you out!' With that she turned the key in the lock and stormed off.

———❖———

IT WAS A long night. 'When will she let us out?' Like her brother, Kathleen had slept fitfully, wary of the dark, and shivering with cold in that damp place.

'Soon.' Maybe never, he thought, and there was no way out, because he had searched while Kathleen slept.

'I don't like it in here.'

'Try not to think about it.'

'Will it be morning soon?'

'I think so.'

'Will she let us out then?'

'Maybe. When daylight comes, and she's punished us enough, she might be sorry.'

Adam was wrong in one way and right in another. She did arrive with the daylight, to let them out. But she was not sorry. 'Just remember,' she told the wary pair, 'Markham will tell you as much as she wants you to know, and no more.'

She ordered them to wash and change, and when they came

downstairs, she put a dish of hot porridge before them. 'Mind you eat it all up. This is good, wholesome food.'

When their dishes were scraped clean, she told them to wash up, while she fetched her hat and coat. 'You don't need to wrap up,' she told them, eyeing the cardigans they both wore. 'You'll do as you are. Your bones are not as thin and worn as this poor old woman's, and anyway there's still a bit of warmth in the sun.'

Out in the street, a group of boys shouted obscenities. 'Ignore them,' Markham said. 'They don't like me, and I don't like them. I've learned not to take any notice.'

Adam was all for giving them the same treatment but Markham told him that would make him as bad as they were. 'You're a gentleman,' she said. 'Hold your head high and walk right by, as if you can't even see them.' And, remembering the cellar, that's what he did, much to the louts' frustration. There was one boy, however, who stood aside from the others. Tall and well built, with fair, unruly hair, he smiled at Kathleen who, taken by surprise, smiled back.

'Where are we going?' she asked Markham.

In that unpredictable manner they had already come to know and respect, the frown disappeared from Markham's face and an impish grin lit up her features. 'Why, we're going to the beach,' she answered. 'You took your punishment well, and now it's time to enjoy yourselves.' She tutted at their puzzled faces, her eyes wide and surprised as she asked impatiently, 'Isn't that what children do . . . enjoy themselves?'

And that was exactly what they did. In fact they had the best day of their lives. In spite of the slight chill in the air, they rode the brown-eyed donkeys and ate the largest ice-cream cornets they had ever seen. They played on the beach and buried Markham up to her waist. And afterwards, tired and weary, and very happy, they made their way home.

At the end of that eventful day, two things were clear.

Great-Aunt Markham was like no one they had ever known. Peculiar and frightening, she was also funny and childish and, in spite of their ordeal in the dark cellar, the children were already beginning to warm towards her.

It was clear, too, that for as long as Adam and Kathleen remained in her dubious care, no two days would ever be the same.

Chapter Eight

NANCY WAS LIKE a dog with two tails. 'Oh, Cook! Is this where we're going to live?' Her eyes were like saucers in her head. 'Oh, I do want to live here, I really do.'

Mabel was in no mood for Nancy's silly banter. 'Be quiet,' she told her. 'You're driving me mad with yer chatter. All the way up on the train yesterday, and then in the hotel lounge all evening long. And now, here we are, looking round the first house of many and all I can hear is you and yer bleedin' chatter.'

Nancy was downcast. 'I'm sorry, Cook,' she muttered. 'Only it's the first time I've ever been anywhere, and I've allus wanted to come to Blackpool. Now here we are, an' I'm that excited, I can't stop meself from talking.'

John chuckled, but Mabel was not amused. 'You'd better stop yerself,' she warned, 'or I swear to God, I'll gag yer.'

'Sorry, Cook.'

'Sorry nothing. Don't start that again, and don't keep calling me Cook. I've left all that behind. Besides, I'm a married woman now, so you'd best call me Mrs Mason.'

Nancy giggled. 'Funny, ain't it?'

'What?'

'You, being called Mrs Mason.'

'There's nothing funny about it. You're a silly, brainless girl!'

'Sorry, Cook.'

'God help me if I won't strangle yer with me own hands, Nancy Tomlin!'

Nancy hung her head and shuffled her feet.

Mabel looked at her husband, and he shook his head, as if to say, 'Don't let the girl suffer too long.'

Dropping her weight into the nearest chair, Mabel sighed. 'Don't sulk, Nancy,' she chided. 'Look at me.'

Nancy raised her head.

'I didn't mean to bite yer head off, only you do go on. You must learn how to contain yer excitement.'

'Yes . . . Mrs Mason.' She nearly said 'Sorry' and she nearly said 'Cook'. And the fright showed on her face.

John chuckled again. 'I think it's all too much for her, Mabel,' he said kindly. 'Would it really matter if she went on calling you Cook? After all, you'll still be doing the cooking here, won't you?'

'Well, I'm certainly not trusting *her* to do it, that's for sure. Anyway, she'll have her own work cut out.'

'Well then?'

Seeing she had an ally, Nancy made the most of it. 'Please,' she pleaded. 'I'm used to calling yer Cook, d'yer see? I can't never get used to new-fangled ideas.'

'Oh, all right then. I've been Cook for most of me life, an' I expect I shall still be cooking the day they carry me off.' She looked up at John. 'I can't think straight,' she complained. 'I'm hot and bothered, and gasping for a decent cup of tea. There's half the day gone already, and still four houses to be looked at.'

'It's my fault,' John said, concerned. 'I haven't given you time to get your breath. We got married in a hurry, and now I'm rushing you into making other important decisions.' He felt guilty. 'If you like, we can leave it until tomorrow. Tonight, we'll sit and discuss whether we really want Blackpool or whether we should look at other seaside places.'

'No.' Mabel was having none of that. 'Whatever we've done, we've done with our eyes wide open and I don't regret one single thing.' Giving him an encouraging smile that lifted his heart, she went on, 'I always hoped you and me would get wed, and now

I'm proud to be yer wife, John Mason. As for looking elsewhere, what's wrong with Blackpool?'

'Nothing, as far as I can see.'

'Right, then. Blackpool it is. What's more, we'll look round this partic'lar house, and if we like it, we'll look no further. What do you say?'

'I say that's a grand idea.'

'And then we'll find a café for a cup of tea and an Eccles cake. What do you say to that?'

'Even better.'

'Come on then, you two.' Struggling up, she stretched her back and groaned. 'Might as well make a start upstairs.'

The house was lovely. A grand old place built in 1800, it was situated on the promenade, overlooking the sea. In its lifetime it had been a gentleman's residence, a home for retired folk, and, more recently, a small hotel catering for holidaymakers who thronged to Blackpool in the summer months.

Painted white, and with every room beautifully decorated, it was a spacious and desirable property. Catching the sunlight for most of the day, the rooms were bright, with tall ceilings and pretty cornices. There were good carpets on the floors, handsome lightshades hanging from the ceilings, and all the furniture was of a tasteful, sturdy kind. 'Some of this stuff's for sale with the house, ain't it?' Mabel stared round the sitting room, her mind leaping ahead with ideas. Particularly attracted to a long walnut sideboard with a mirrored back, she commented thoughtfully, 'This would be more useful in the dining room.' She fingered the deep carving on the drawers. 'The top is big enough to take any number of tureens, and the bottom cupboards could house all the usual paraphernalia – plates, condiment sets and suchlike.'

John thumbed through the details. 'Yes, this one is open to offers,' he informed her, 'but we might have to lower our sights, love. I mean, the house is more than we thought to pay, and there are other things we have to get. Besides, we don't really know how the business will go at first, so we need to keep back a bit for a rainy day.'

Mabel didn't agree. 'If you ask me, we have to start out right,' she said. 'It's no good scrimping and scraping and ending up with only half what we need, or the cheap, nasty stuff got from down the market. We need good stuff, like this. First impressions are important, and if we're to build up reg'lar customers, we need to offer comfortable beds, good food, and a feeling of wellbeing. It has to be the kind of place where folks will want to come back again and again. I say we should throw caution to the winds and jump in with both feet. Sink or swim, that's what I say.'

John was impressed. 'You really think we can make a good business, don't you?'

'If we don't, then we don't deserve the chance.' When they had first learned that they were to lose their jobs, Mabel had been worried, but now she truly believed they would never look back. 'It's just under four weeks to Christmas,' she said. 'Do you think we could be installed in time for Christmas? Oh, I know we won't be up and running, but we could have our own Christmas in our very own place, and in the New Year we could start the decorating and planning. Oh, wouldn't that be wonderful?' Her eyes sparkled.

'Sounds to me like you've set your heart on this place.' John glanced round the room. 'Don't you even want to see the others?' He hoped not, because he, too, had taken a fancy to this grand old place.

She shook her head. 'This is the one,' she replied decisively. 'It has a good feel about it.'

It was settled. 'Right then, Mrs Mason,' he beamed at her with affection, 'make a list of the bric-a-brac you want and we'll get straight back to the agent's office to thrash out a deal.' He winked mischievously. 'I've a feeling that cocky young feller behind the desk won't know what's hit him.'

Nancy was overjoyed. 'We might even bump into the children one day.'

'Why do you say that?' Mabel asked.

'Because I heard Mr Ernshaw tell Adam that they were going to the seaside. Blackpool isn't far away, that's what he told him.'

'Well, I never!'

'Wouldn't it be grand if we came across them one day?'

'It would, Nancy,' Mabel agreed. 'It'd put my mind at rest to know the children were happy enough in their new life.' A great sigh seemed to travel from her boots to the top of her greying head. 'Lord knows they deserve a bit of happiness.'

Chapter Nine

IT WAS TWO days before Christmas 1861.

Six years had passed since the orphans were delivered to Markham's door, and with the passing of the years, the boy had matured with confidence, the girl had grown tall and softly beautiful, with a nature as lovely as a summer's day. The old aunt, however, was madder than ever, unpredictable as the English weather, and shrivelled with age.

Perched on the edge of her seat, she gazed at Adam. A handsome fellow, with a tall, capable figure and blue honest eyes, he made the old woman proud. She had learned to respect him as someone who knew his own mind and did not hesitate to say what he thought, even if it got him into hot water, as it so often did. Between the boy and herself there reigned a constant, silent tussle for supremacy.

Mr Ernshaw was seated beside Markham and directly opposite the children. 'Everything is most satisfactory.' He smiled at Markham with approval. 'The girl is an independent, intelligent creature, while the boy has made good at school, so much so that it seems he may qualify for a higher education.' His smile broadened. 'Well done, Mrs Markham, the children certainly seem to have prospered under your care.'

'I do my best.'

Addressing the children, he informed them, 'I have received several complimentary notices from your school. It seems you both have a remarkable ability for learning.'

Adam felt obliged to speak for himself and his sister, who was unusually quiet. 'Thank you, sir.'

Mr Ernshaw rose to leave. 'You're a young man now. Sixteen years old, and I have no doubt you have a fine future ahead of you. I see I shall have no more cause to visit. My duty is ended.' Very grandly, he shook Adam by the hand.

He was less gracious to Kathleen, recalling how she was not a true Peterson but a bastard, born out of a tawdry affair between her wayward mother and the gamekeeper. 'You do as your great-aunt instructs,' he said sternly. 'You're out of my hands now.' Thank God, he thought.

'Yes, sir.' Kathleen had not forgotten how he had man-handled her out of the old house and made her cry. She hadn't liked him then and she found no reason to like him now.

Sensing her animosity, Ernshaw was abrupt. 'Goodbye then. It's time I was on my way.'

'Just a minute,' said Markham. 'I'd like a word before you go.'

'Of course.' He was impatient to depart, and it showed. 'But please bear in mind I do have a train to catch.'

Dismissing the children, Markham got right to the point. 'I need more money,' she said bluntly. 'With the children being older, everything costs more – clothes, food. The boy may have prospects but the girl has a few years left at school. She's required to wear a uniform, and there are other expenses which try my allowance to the limit.'

'I'm sorry, but there are no more funds,' he informed her coldly. 'You must either manage or commit the girl to an orphanage.'

'Never!'

'Then I'm afraid there is nothing I can do.'

On that sombre note, he departed.

Later that evening, when the three of them were seated round the kitchen table drinking tea, Adam wondered how he should broach a particular, thorny matter – the matter of Christmas and a certain promise made by Markham, which she appeared to have conveniently forgotten.

'I was wondering, Markham,' he began, 'whether we shouldn't start to look for a tree.'

Markham took a nibble out of her scone. 'No tree,' she said, and a blob of red jam landed on her chin. She snaked out a long narrow tongue and flicked the jam into her mouth. 'Don't bother me, boy.'

'But a tree isn't much to ask for,' he coaxed, 'not when it's Christmas, and you promised Kathleen we could have one this year.'

The old woman was stubborn as ever. 'There'll be no tree in this house, young man. In all the time I've lived here, I have never seen the need for a tree, and I don't see the need for one now. You've done without one these past six years. What's so different about this year?'

'Please, Markham,' said Kathleen. 'You said we could have one, as long as it didn't dirty the carpet. The man at the market said if we put it straight into a bucket, there wouldn't be a mess, and if the needles fall, I'll clean them up, I promise.'

'There'll be no mess, girl, and there'll be no needles because there'll be no tree, even if it means me going back on my word.'

'That's not fair.' Kathleen had set her heart on a tree. When she had first mentioned it to Markham, the old woman had not seemed to mind. Now, though, as always, she was going back on her promise. 'Cook used to say if you told lies, no one would ever trust you.'

Markham regarded her through narrowed eyes. 'You may be coming up twelve years of age and growing wiser by the minute, but don't get too big for your boots, young lady. I don't give a tinker's cuss for what Cook said. What's more, I can see I've let you two get away with far too much. I won't have you talking back to me, and I will not have you telling me what I can or cannot do in my own house.' She wagged a bony finger at the girl. 'You've got far too much to say for yourself, young madam.'

Kathleen certainly had come out of her shell. It had happened about the time that rascal from Adelaide Street had started hanging about the house, and Markham had had to send him on his way. 'I knew it was wrong to let that young ruffian come to your birthday party,' she said now. 'Murray Laing comes of a poor family. There was a time when they had money but the father gambled it all away when his pretty wife ran off with some sailor. As far as I can tell, the lazy fellow hasn't done a day's work since. There was talk at one time that he sent the boy out thieving in the dead of night, breaking into houses and the like, and I for one am quite ready to believe it.'

Kathleen held her head high. 'Well, *I* don't believe it,' she declared. 'Murray would never break into people's houses.'

Murray Laing was the tall, fair-haired boy who had smiled at Kathleen that first day when she and Adam had left the house to go to the beach with Markham. After that, Murray had often loitered near the house, waiting to give her a smile whenever she left the house, and she had begun to look forward to seeing him. She had begged Markham to let him come to her eleventh birthday party, and to her surprise and delight the old woman had eventually agreed. He brought her a present, the prettiest thing Kathleen had ever owned – a small bone comb, edged with mother-of-pearl. 'I didn't steal it,' he told her earnestly. 'I saved hard to buy it for you.' And Kathleen never doubted him.

The old woman shook her silver head. 'Murray Laing is five or six years older than you are,' she tutted, 'and he's charmed you with his beguiling smile. Where does he get his money if he doesn't steal it, tell me that? He told us here in this very house that he was sixteen years of age, and if that's the case, why isn't he working, eh? I'll tell you why. It's because he finds it easier to pick other folks' pockets, that's why. He wants to pick your pocket too, I dare say. I've no doubt the boy's father put him up to getting to know you. He probably thinks you're worth a penny or two, and that he can get his hands on your money through his son.'

'I haven't got any money.'

'He'll be disappointed then, won't he?' These past weeks the old woman had felt closer to her maker than she would admit, and when her time came to face him, she meant to see that the children would not be left penniless. Though she would rather they had not been placed in her care, she had come to rely on their company in a way she never envisaged. There was a brightness about this old house that had not been there before. These two unfortunates had taught her how to laugh again. They had brought sunshine into her empty life, and not a day went by when she didn't thank the good Lord for sending them to her.

All the same, she must not let the children get the better of her. They seemed to grow taller by the minute, they were strong, capable characters she had secretly grown proud of, and she was sometimes tempted to lean on them in her times of need, when she felt so old and tired she could hardly put one foot before the other. But that must not be allowed to happen, she thought. She couldn't let them feel responsible for her. It wouldn't be right. She had her pride, and young as they were, they still relied on her. She must be strong. For all their sakes, she must always be seen to be in charge.

'If you ask me, that young fellow is not to be trusted. He's too much like his father ever to make good, he's lazy and ignorant, and you've got too keen an eye for the blackguard, my girl.'

'I like Murray, and I want to see him again.' In fact Kathleen had taken him to her young heart. He was warm and funny, and he made her laugh. Moreover, he was the first real friend she had ever known, and she couldn't bear the thought that she might be forbidden to see him again.

Her affection for the boy only strengthened the old woman's determination to take a firm line. 'You'll do as you're told,' she snapped. Her manner was unyielding, but still her heart was sorely touched by Kathleen's young, generous face.

It was a face to turn any boy's head, she thought bitterly. The girl had the makings of a beauty, with her long dark hair and those dark, desperate eyes. She was tall and slim, and filled with a zest for life that made the old woman feel breathless just watching her. 'And don't tell me I made promises when I didn't,' she said angrily though she clearly recalled doing so in a moment of weakness. 'I've an idea you and your brother would like me to think I'm growing senile. And anyway, even if I did promise, it doesn't matter because I've changed my mind. I'm an old woman. I can change my mind whenever the fancy takes me.'

Kathleen would have argued the point, but Adam saw the danger signs. 'Leave it, Kathleen,' he warned. 'We'll talk about it later.' Over the years, he had come to recognise the old woman's moods and knew when not to press a point.

Kathleen was bitterly disappointed. It was going to be such a wonderful Christmas, and now it was being spoiled, like all the other times. 'We need a tree to put the presents under,' she said sadly.

'Presents?' the old woman shrieked. 'What presents?'

'Adam and I have bought each other a present, and we've bought you one as well.'

'Where did you get money for presents?' Markham sat up, her whole body bristling.

'We bought them out of the pennies you paid us for doing the housework,' Adam explained.

'Then I've paid you too much. "Presents" indeed! From now on you can do the housework for your board and keep, and you can go without supper tonight. That'll teach you to argue with me.' Aching for her afternoon nap, she closed her eyes. 'Now go away.'

Obediently, they went upstairs to Kathleen's bedroom. Later, as she gave herself up to sleep, the old woman thought of the children and was filled with a warm and wonderful sense of belonging. In the space of a heartbeat, the sensation became a feeling of deep down love which, in all her lonely existence, she had never known before.

'Markham's crazy, isn't she?' Kathleen said, setting herself on the window seat. Adam sprawled on the bed.

'Mad as a hatter,' he smiled. 'But she's harmless enough, though I sometimes wonder if she's ill.'

'Why do you say that?'

He shrugged his shoulders. 'Sometimes, when she thinks no one's looking, she holds her side and her face is filled with pain.'

'Is that why she's so grumpy?'

'Maybe.'

Kathleen felt bad about that. 'If Markham's ill, I don't really care if we have a tree or not,' she lied. A terrible thought occurred to her. 'Markham won't die, will she, Adam? I know she's cruel sometimes but I don't want her to die.' Her voice shook with emotion.

'She won't die,' he answered. 'She'll probably live to be a hundred. Maybe we should have let her sleep before we asked her about the tree. When she's tired, she gets irritable and stubborn.'

Kathleen's mind turned to something else Markham had said. 'Adam, do you think Murray Laing is a thief?'

'I don't know,' he answered truthfully. 'He seems decent enough to me, but we don't know whether his father might bully him into doing something he doesn't want to do.'

'He's not a thief,' she insisted. 'And I will see him again, whatever Markham says.'

The next morning they woke to the smell of freshly cooked omelettes and sizzling bacon. Kathleen leapt out of bed and beat Adam to the bathroom. 'Brr! She's filled the jug with cold water,' she gasped as she splashed her hands and face.

She emptied the used water into a bucket while Adam waited patiently, before refilling the bowl from the water jug. Gingerly cupping a generous measure into his hands, he threw it over his face, spluttered loudly, then briskly rubbed himself dry. 'That'll do,' he declared, leading the way downstairs.

Markham greeted them suspiciously. 'Did you wash thoroughly?' she demanded, hands on hips and guarding the table. 'Did you scrub yourselves clean, you dirty pair? Did you use the soap?'

'Yes, Markham.' Kathleen could hear her stomach rumbling.

'Let me see your hands, young lady.'

Stepping forward, Kathleen held out her hands, palms up, then turned them over. 'See,' she said boldly. 'Satisfied now?'

'Not yet.' Markham swept back Kathleen's hair and examined behind her ears. 'All right,' she said. 'Sit at the table. But don't start until I say.'

She put Adam through a more vigorous inspection. 'You don't look to me as if you've had a thorough wash,' she said, stretching up and sniffing his face. 'You don't smell as if you've used the carbolic either.'

'I did,' he protested. 'Ask Kathleen.'

The old woman looked at Kathleen and got an affirmative nod. 'All right,' she relented. 'Sit down.'

Relieved, Adam drew out a chair and sat opposite his sister. She gave him a little smile that did not go unnoticed by Markham's small, busy eyes. 'What are you grinning at, young lady?'

Fearing she might be sent from the table, Kathleen put on her most innocent manner. 'I'm not grinning.'

'You *were* grinning.'

'I didn't mean to.'

'And don't talk while you're having breakfast.'

'No, Markham.'

'And no leaving food. It's a sin and a shame to leave food when I can hardly make ends meet.'

'Yes, Markham.'

In spite of Markham's constant chirping, breakfast was hugely enjoyable. There were fluffy omelettes and crispy bacon; delicious shop-bought scones and heapings of strawberry jam. And to top it all, Markham produced two glasses of dark sarsaparilla. 'Just this once,' she said, 'as a special treat.' In fact the whole breakfast had been a special treat. Normally, they were fortunate if they had toast and jam.

Their pleasure and contentment lasted only as long as breakfast did because for the next three hours Markham made them earn the food. First they had to wash up while she paced the room, pausing occasionally to make sure they were doing it properly. Then they had to take out every rug and mat in the house, which, under strict instructions, they hung over the line and beat until their arms ached. Next they had to take down every ornament in every room, only returning them to the shelves when Markham was satisfied that each one had been polished until it shone.

Finally, when the house sparkled from top to bottom, Markham ushered them into the drawing room. 'Think yourselves fortunate,' she told the suffering pair, 'you're about to hear me play the piano for the first time in many a year.'

This was the worst 'punishment' of all, because, while Markham's piano playing gave her immense pleasure, it was half an hour of sheer purgatory for the children.

'There!' Having played herself into a frenzy, she slammed down the piano-top and turned jubilant to smile on their crestfallen faces. 'Right! Coats on, you two.'

'Where are we going?' asked Kathleen wearily. She felt exhausted and just wanted to sit somewhere quietly out of reach of Markham's constant demands.

Markham grinned. 'We are going out for some fresh air and exercise.' She paused, and Adam groaned inwardly. The last thing he felt like was exercise, after all that running about the house. 'And while we're out,' Markham went on, 'we'll buy a Christmas tree.'

'Oh, Markham!' Delighted, Kathleen ran to fling her arms round the little woman's waist. 'Thank you!' She could hardly believe it.

'Not a big one, mind,' Markham warned. 'The big ones are far too expensive.'

IT WAS GROWING dark and still they had not found a suitable tree. Now they were standing outside a shop with numerous trees displayed on the pavement. Wearied by a long, tiring day, Markham lost no time in choosing one she thought could be easily carried home. 'This one looks all right to me,' she announced. She was tired. Her old legs ached, and she longed for the warmth of her cosy fire.

The short, round shopkeeper had been watching the little group. 'That's a good choice, missus,' he told Markham. 'It's stout and full, with more at the bottom than the top, so it won't fall over when you stand it in a barrel.'

Giggling, Kathleen whispered to Adam, 'It sounds like him,' and Adam had to agree.

Markham eyed the fellow with her birdlike stare. 'How much is it?'

'A shilling.'

'Too much.'

'Ninepence then.'

Markham was having none of it. 'Come along, children. There are plenty of shops who'll be glad to get rid of their trees so near Christmas.'

''Old on, missus!' The shopkeeper stepped in front of her. ''Ow much then?'

'Threepence, and not a penny more.'

'Daylight robbery!'

'Is it a deal?'

'Go on then.' He scratched his head and looked bemused. 'I must be losing me bleedin' marbles,' he groaned.

Adam hoisted the tree on to his shoulders and they made their way home. 'It's a lovely tree,' Kathleen exclaimed. 'And we don't have to buy any trimmings because I've made some paper chains and rag balls. They'll look ever so pretty, you'll see.' It made her feel that at long last they had a proper home, and a real parent to care for them.

She thought of her mother and father, and her heart grew heavy. But it was only momentary. They had never loved her or Adam. Not really. They only looked after them. Like Cook looked after Nancy. She thought about them, and realised how much she still missed old Cook and the rest of the servants. Markham had made up for a lot though. She did some strange and frightening things, but she did love them and in spite of the times when she and Adam were locked in the cellar or were sent to bed hungry, Kathleen dearly loved the old woman.

'Don't loiter, girl!' Markham was eager to be off the streets. 'It's late. We should have been back home ages since.' Gathering up her skirt hem, she stepped off the pavement, almost under the wheels of a carriage and four.

'Yer want to look where yer going, yer silly old bugger!' came the shout from the driver's seat.

'That's no way to speak to an old lady!' Markham yelled back. 'I should get my man here to teach you some manners.'

The driver looked at Adam and roared with laughter. 'I'd 'ave more trouble fighting the bleedin' tree!'

'Ignorant devil!'

Markham's mood was not improved when they were confronted by the louts who habitually jeered at her when she ventured out.

'Well now!' It was the same big, untidy fellow, with the same big, loud mouth. 'If it ain't the crazy old bag who thinks she's better than the rest of us.' He and two others barred her way. 'Cat got yer tongue, 'as it?' Pressing his face to within an inch of hers, he hissed, 'Give us yer purse and we'll be on our way.'

Kathleen had been lagging behind with Adam, but now she ran forward. 'Leave her alone!' she cried. 'Get away from her!' A swift kick on his shins made him cry out, more with astonishment than pain. Markham laughed in his face and Adam dropped the tree and ran forward too.

'You'd best be on your way. Now!' He glared at the offender, who squared his shoulders and glared back.

'That yer sister, is it?' he sneered.

'I told you to clear off.'

'Bit of all right, ain't she?' He grinned nastily at Kathleen. 'Wouldn't mind 'aving an armful o' that.'

Adam lunged forward and in a moment the two were rolling about the ground, with Kathleen kicking the lout at every opportunity and Markham urging her on in the background. But then the other two joined in, and it was soon obvious that Adam was getting the worst of it. One lout grabbed hold of Kathleen. 'Give us a kiss then,' he demanded, holding Kathleen's arms tight by her sides.

Suddenly a young man sprang on the lout's back. 'Get yer dirty paws off her!' Murray Laing had been keeping his distance, but the lout's treatment of Kathleen had incensed him. Adam, meanwhile, had been kicked to the ground, momentarily stunned.

Concerned at the developments, Markham suddenly began shouting, 'Police! Police! Oh, there you are, officer.' She seemed to be addressing someone in the shadows. 'The ruffian's after my purse. Grab him, officer, before he gets away.'

Alarmed, the ruffians took to their heels with Murray in pursuit. All four were soon lost in the dark.

'There!' Markham pointed after them. 'Did you see who that was? That was your friend Murray Laing. Did you see him? Did you?'

'He was trying to help.' All the same, Kathleen had to admit to herself that he had seemed to be part of the gang, until the lout took hold of her.

'He was one of them, I tell you! In fact he's their ringleader. If that lout hadn't threatened you, Murray Laing would have stood by while they took my purse.'

'We don't know that for sure.' Kathleen didn't want to believe it, but she had lost some of her faith in Murray. She would have to confront him when next their paths crossed.

'You must have nothing at all to do with that ruffian, do you understand?'

'Was there really a policeman?' Kathleen asked, hoping to distract her aunt.

'Course not,' said Markham. 'I was just pretending, and it worked a treat. Ran off like the cowards they are,' she chuckled. 'They're not so big, letting an old lady hoodwink them. They'll not get the better of me.'

T HAT NIGHT KATHLEEN lay sleepless in her bed for what seemed an age.

The muted chiming of the downstairs grandfather clock filtered through the house. It chimed the evening out and the morning in, and still she couldn't sleep. 'Maybe he really is bad,' she mused. 'Maybe he's everything Markham says he is.' The thought of Murray as a thief and rogue made her young heart ache. So much so that she had to get out of bed and sit by the window, her sad, dark eyes searching the night.

At first she thought it was a trick of the dark. Then she realised there really was someone moving about outside, directly beneath her window. Anxious, she quickly stepped back and hid behind the curtain.

He called out to her. 'Kathleen. I need to talk to you.'

'It's Murray!' Her heart soared. 'I was thinking of him and now here he is.'

'Kathleen!'

Quickly now, before he woke the others, Kathleen opened the window. 'Go away, before Markham hears you.'

'I'm not part of that lot,' he said, 'I swear to God.'

'I saw you.'

'I know, and I'm ashamed. I didn't think they were out for trouble, but after tonight I'll steer clear of 'em, I promise.' He smiled his easy lopsided smile. 'I've brought you a present.' He placed a small package on the wall.

'Markham says I'm not to see you ever again.'

'I'll talk to her.'

'It won't do any good. She's made up her mind.'

'What about you, Kathleen? Have you made up your mind?'

'You should never have gone with them.'

'I know that now.' He dropped his head and stared at the ground, his next words only just audible. 'Believe me, I didn't know they were out for trouble.'

'How do I know you're telling the truth?'

'I am!' He flung out his arms in frustration. 'Look, Kathleen, I know why your aunt doesn't like me, and I don't blame her. I'll not deny I've been running with a bad lot, and I'm not surprised she tars me with the same brush. On top o' that, she doesn't like it because I'm five years older than you, and you're too young. But I need to see you . . . until we're old enough to court proper. I'll wait, Kathleen, for as long as it takes. We've got a lifetime to find out about each other, ain't we?'

In the lamplight from her bedroom, his face shone with affection. 'Yer do like me, don't yer, gal? I mean, just to be friends, till we know what we want. I swear to Gawd I ain't never looked at any other girl. Me dad says I should be looking, on account of me coming up seventeen and close to being a man.' He grinned. 'If he had his way, I'd be married with a dozen kids as quick as the drop of a hat.' The grin faded and he was penitent again. 'I'm really sorry,' he apologised. 'I wouldn't have let them hurt her.'

'My aunt says you're the ringleader. Are you?'

There was a pause. 'I *was* the ringleader,' he confessed, 'but that was a long time ago. Now I just hang around sometimes 'cause there's nothing else to do, but I don't go along with them. Not any more. It's different now. I've changed, Kathleen. I've changed because of you.'

'Have you, Murray?' Her voice was kind. Her heart was warmed by his declaration though she couldn't understand the deeper implications. 'I'm glad.'

'Tomorrow I'm going for a job in the market. I'm gonna work hard and save every penny I earn, for when we get married.'

He might have said more but he was grabbed from behind and shaken like a rag doll. 'Get away from here!' Enraged, Markham had heard every word. 'Married indeed! She's only eleven years old. And even if she were a grown woman, I'd give her to a travelling circus before I'd see her with a ruffian like you.' Swiping him hard across the ear, she yelled, 'Now be off before I set the authorities on you!'

'All right, missus, I don't want no trouble.' He moved off down the street. 'But I meant what I said. One day I'll prove meself, and if she'll have me I mean to marry 'er.'

'Over my dead body!' Markham's words echoed in the night. 'Keep away from her, do you hear me?'

'All right,' he promised, 'but only until she asks for me.'

Markham marched upstairs to confront Kathleen. 'I blame you, my girl!' The old lady shook with anger. 'You deliberately defied me! You talked to him after I ordered you not to. That scoundrel came here like a thief in the night, and you encouraged him.'

'He's not a scoundrel,' Kathleen protested. 'He's changed. He's even going for a job in the market tomorrow.'

'I heard what he said.' She was done with arguing. 'There will be no tree. No rag balls or paper trimmings. And no more mention of Christmas in this house.' Until then she had kept her right arm behind her back, but now she brought it forward, to show the cane clutched in her hand. 'It's such a shame, I have to punish you now when you were doing so well.'

The punishment was cruel.

Made to stand with her face to the wall, Kathleen tried hard not to scream when the cane cut into her legs time and again. But she was only a child, and soon she was crying out in pain.

Her cries brought Adam from his bed, but by the time he burst into the room, it was all over. Quietly sobbing, Markham was cradling Kathleen in her arms. 'I had to punish her,' she said brokenly. 'It was for her own sake.'

Later, when Kathleen was sleeping, she ordered Adam to take the tree outside and burn it. Reluctantly, he did as he was told. There were things here beyond his understanding. He couldn't be sure who was in the right, Markham or his sister, but there was no denying Kathleen had an unhealthy liking for Murray Laing.

Inside the house, Markham found Kathleen's trimmings and destroyed them. 'She has to learn,' she told the shocked Adam. 'The whipping hurt me more than it hurt her. But I know I've done right, and in your heart you know it too.' Wiping the back of her hand over her brow, she sounded weary. 'When the Lord sent you to me, he sent me a heavy burden,' she said. 'I've never had children, and maybe I'm not very good at being a parent. But I do love you both.'

It was an admission that shook him. 'You've never said that before,' he responded quietly.

'And I'll never say it again,' she told him.

Chapter Ten

CHRISTMAS CAME AND went. Kathleen's wounds healed, and her fondness for Markham was not wholly diminished by the treatment she had suffered at the old lady's hands. Markham, however, was not her usual, commanding self.

'What's wrong with her, Adam?' It was plain to them both that their aunt was not well. 'When I ask her she tells me it's nothing and that I shouldn't worry.'

'Then don't.' Adam wouldn't admit that he, too, was concerned. 'You know what she's like. She hates to be fussed over. If she needs a doctor, I'm sure she'll send for one.' Head down, and pushing against the bitter wind, he hurried across the yard. Having just spent half an hour in the bitter cold tipping coal into the coal hole, he was eager to get back inside. But he paused to glance up towards the old lady's bedroom window. 'All the same, it's not like her to lie in bed day after day.'

'What did you say?' Kathleen had been hanging washing on the line. She turned to look at him with a frown. 'Adam, what did you say?'

He walked on. 'I said hurry up with that washing before you catch your death.'

Kathleen's mind was still on Markham. 'It's New Year's Eve. She's stayed in her bed for almost a week. It's not like her. Do you think it's my fault? Do you think she's ill because of what happened with those louts, and then afterwards, when she saw fit to punish me? You told me yourself she said it hurt her more than it hurt me.'

'I dare say it upset her.' He knew it was more than that. He'd seen the way the whole series of events had affected the old lady, and yet he had not entirely forgiven her for whipping his sister like that.

'I should have listened to her about Murray Laing. I shouldn't have riled her like I did.'

'There's no blame.' The cold reached his bones and made his teeth chatter. If anything, the blame lay with his parents, he thought, for doing what they did and saddling a tired old lady with two children she never wanted. 'Markham is a tough old bird, but she's very old. It's to be expected that she might have an off day or two. She'll be fine. Finish what you're doing, then you can take her tray up. She'll feel better with some hot food inside her.'

Ramming the last peg home, Kathleen let go of the line which instantly sprang upwards in the wind. Markham's nightshift billowed like a cloud and her bed socks did a comical tap dance one against the other. 'Wait for me, Adam.' Collecting her wicker basket from the flags, she followed him into the kitchen.

'I wish she would eat some hot food,' she remarked, dropping the basket to the floor. 'This morning, I made her two soft-boiled eggs, and she didn't even touch them.'

'Like I said, she'll be fine.' Placing the coal bucket in the hearth, he began banking up the fire. 'I'll go up and have a word with her when I've done this.'

'And I'll serve up a good helping of that baked fish. I've done it exactly the way she likes it.' Markham had shown her how to bake a cake and cook a ham, and do all the things her mother had never taught her. 'I'll have it ready in half an hour. You tell her that, Adam. And tell her I'll never talk to Murray Laing again, if only she'll get better.'

'Don't make rash promises, Kathleen.' He stood up, his face rosy-red from the heat of the fire.

'It's not a rash promise,' she protested. 'I really mean it.

That's what all the trouble was about. That's why it's all my fault.'

Washing his hands at the sink, suddenly he knew how enormous a responsibility Markham had taken on, because now it was his responsibility. Kathleen had no one but him to rely on if Markham should die. He daren't let himself think about it.

Kathleen noticed his preoccupation. 'Adam, you will tell her what I said, won't you?'

'Tell her yourself,' he answered impatiently.

A small voice startled them both. 'Tell me what?'

Kathleen was thrilled to see the old lady standing by the door. 'Oh, Markham!' Running to her, she put her arms round the frail shoulders. 'Are you better?' Carefully, she helped the old soul forward.

Adam pushed the armchair nearer to the cheery fire. 'You look better,' he lied. He wished it was so, but in truth Markham looked grey with pain.

'I'm perfectly all right. Stop fussing.' Her small face crumpled in a smile. 'You're worse than a pair of old hens,' she chuckled.

'It's good to see you out of your bed, Markham.' Greatly relieved, and certain now that her aunt was on the mend, Kathleen was close to tears.

Markham saw how anxious she was. 'I smelled the fish baking,' she declared with a sly wink at Adam. 'I remember the last fish your sister put in that oven. It started out as a fat, juicy trout and ended up looking like a roasted sprat.'

'I think you'll be pleasantly surprised with your supper tonight,' Adam said with a smile. 'You've taught her well.'

He was right. Supper was delicious: slowly baked fish steeped in cider and slightly browned, small potatoes in their skins, and dark green cabbage lightly done. A dish of jelly topped with custard followed.

Having eaten a good measure, Markham gave her approval. 'You've done me proud, my girl,' she said, and Kathleen blushed with pleasure.

The evening was spent leisurely, with Markham tucked up in

a blanket in front of the fire. Kathleen sat at her feet, and Adam reclined in the chair beside them. 'This last lot of coal is really good,' he remarked, shoving his chair back a way. 'It throws out more heat than the scrapings we had delivered last time.'

Markham loved the heat on her face. It made her feel safe and cosy. 'Since old Laurence gave up the coal round, it's not been the same,' she said. 'He's been delivering coal round these parts for nigh on fifty years, and now any old Tom, Dick or Harry turns up on the doorstep.' The long drawn-out sigh made her physically shrink, until she seemed like a doll in her chair. 'They say he'll not last long, poor thing.'

All this was news to Kathleen. 'What's wrong with him?'

Markham shrugged her narrow shoulders. 'No one seems to know for sure. I heard people talking in the grocer's shop the other week. Some say he's crippled, and others say he's too tired to work any more. I'm not surprised. Years of carting heavy sacks of coal on his back can cripple a man.' She liked old Laurence. When he called to collect his money on a Friday night, he'd always have a broad smile and a word of cheer. Another familiar face gone for ever, she thought sadly.

'I wouldn't mind being a coalman,' Adam confessed. 'Nobody to tell you what to do and a wage in your pocket every week.'

Kathleen sat up and stared at him. 'I thought you wanted to be a rich farmer. With land and cattle and everything.'

He shook his head. 'That was when I was young. I know better now.' He was thinking of his father, and of how the land had not brought his family happiness.

Markham smiled at his worldly comment. 'You're still young now,' she laughed. 'Sixteen is a prime age. I wish I was that young again.'

She let her mind wander over the years, to when she was Adam's age and loved a young man who went away and left her lonely. All her life she had never forgiven him for it. If she was young again, she would not make the same mistakes. She would not end up old and alone. But she wasn't young. She was crotchety and ancient, and her old bones creaked when she walked. Still, she couldn't complain. There were always people worse off than she was.

She looked at her companions and her spirit brightened. Because of these two, she thought, her quiet life would not end in loneliness.

'*I* wouldn't want to be a coalman,' Kathleen piped up. 'And I don't care if I'm not rich. I want a pretty cottage with roses round the door, like that one on the way to the church. I want a white pony and trap, who'll take me where I want to go. Two big dogs to play in the garden, and six noisy children – three boys and three girls.' She swept her audience with a wonderful smile. 'You two could come and stay for as long as you wanted, and when the circus comes to town, Uncle Adam could treat us all.' Funny how she hadn't mentioned her husband. But the shadowy figure at the back of her mind resembled a young man she had been forbidden to see ever again.

Adam smiled at her daydreams. 'I hope you get what you want one day, sis,' he said, 'but I don't know if I'll have the money to treat six children to the circus. I'm not interested in making a fortune. All I want is enough money never to have to beg, steal or borrow.'

Markham nodded approval. 'Your brother's right.' She knew how money brought its own curses. 'Making a fortune isn't everything. It's far more important to be content in your work.' She regarded Adam with affection. 'You may find yourself making a fortune without meaning to,' she said. 'You're a very bright young man. The headmaster says you have a natural aptitude for figures and, if you wanted, you could have a brilliant future in the business world.' She thought it a pity for him to waste such talents and said so. 'Having money isn't always an evil,' she concluded. 'It depends on the man.' She thought of Adam's father, and it was obvious that Adam had him in mind also.

'We'll see,' he mused. 'I haven't really made up my mind what I want to do with my life.'

'What about me and Markham?' Kathleen suddenly felt left out of her brother's future. 'When you're a businessman and you travel the world, you won't forget about us, will you, Adam?'

He gazed at her and the love lit his face. 'How could I ever forget about either of you. You and Markham are all I have.'

Markham's next words were sobering. 'Whatever happens, you must always watch out for your sister. Once you're out in the big wide world, anything can happen. Kathleen, too, will have a life of her own, but you two must always be close, Adam. You've been through so much together.' Leaning down to stroke the girl's long dark hair she went on softly, 'Don't worry about me. I'm old. I won't always be around.'

At eleven o'clock Markham bade them goodnight and made her way upstairs. 'No, I'll be all right,' she told them as they offered to help. 'And you two should get off to your beds. It's very late, and I've kept you talking too long.'

Half an hour later, Kathleen went upstairs and soon after-wards she heard Adam close his bedroom door. She knew it was his door because it was ill fitting and when it scraped the carpet it made a swishing sound.

Contented, she turned on her side and went to sleep.

Outside, the night thickened.

It was in the early hours when they arrived; three burly louts who had not forgotten their confrontation with the old lady. They had been seen off shamefaced and empty-handed, and now they were out for revenge.

'Seems quiet enough to me.' The dark-haired fellow with big, crooked teeth edged forward. Looking up at the bedroom windows, he whispered, 'No lights. Not a sound to be heard. Seems to me like the little darlings are all asleep.'

'Which room is the girl's, d'yer reckon?' The ringleader couldn't get Kathleen out of his mind. He'd been cheated last time, but this time he meant to have a taste of her. 'Once we find her, she's mine. Understand?'

Tongues hanging out like a pair of curs, the other two nodded. 'We can watch though, can't we?'

'Don't see why not. So long as yer keep yer hands to yerself.'

The third one had his mind on other things. ''Ow much d'yer think the old bat's worth?'

'Don't know for sure, but we'll soon find out.'

'What makes yer think she'll 'ave it tucked under her mattress?'

''Cause that's where they all hide it.'

'Fair shares when we find it then?'

'That's what we agreed, ain't it?' Pointing to the thin fellow, he told him, 'You keep watch while we ransack the place for anything worth taking. Stay hidden, and be quiet about it. If you hear anybody coming, whistle like I said.' Addressing the one with the crooked teeth he hissed, 'Any sign o' trouble, and we leg it outta there. Understood?'

'What if the bloke sets about you?'

'He'll be sorry, won't he? Last time he had help from that traitor, Murray Laing.' His features thickened to a scowl. 'I'll deal with that one when the time comes. As for the bloke here, he'll soon find out he ain't no match for me on his own.' With that he put his fingers to his lips and crept forward. Used to entering other people's houses, he soon had the back door open, and the two of them crept inside.

———⊰•⊱———

THE FIRST INDICATION Markham had that someone was in her room was when thick, rough fingers gripped her face and covered her mouth. 'Do as you're told, yer old bugger.' A face leered at her from above; in the moonlight from the window it looked like the devil himself.

The lout pulled her to the floor and, with surprising ease, tore two strips from the bedsheet. One he fastened tightly about her mouth, the other he used to bind her to the foot of the bed. With her hands and feet secured, and her mouth cruelly gagged, she was unable to move or call out.

Helpless, she watched with wide, angry eyes while he ransacked the room. She saw him turn the mattress over and rip it from top to bottom, growling like an animal when he found nothing valuable. He searched beneath the bed; he emptied the drawers and turned out the wardrobes, all done softly, so as not to wake anyone. 'Where d'yer keep yer val'ables?' he demanded, grabbing her by the throat and raising her from the floor. 'Tell me, or I swear to Gawd I'll tear yer limb from limb.'

As the neck of her nightshift tightened on her throat, the old lady feared she might be murdered there and then, leaving Kathleen and Adam at the mercy of this foul creature. Trembling, she nodded and he let her loose. 'Where is it? And you'd better not lie to me, old woman.' Quickly, he loosed her hands and feet and thrust her forward. 'Get it!'

Seeing a cradle of matches and a candle on the bedside cupboard, he ordered, 'Light the candle.' With stiff, shaking fingers, she did as she was told. He kept hold of her while she went slowly across the room.

Going to the chimney breast, her mouth still tightly gagged, she reached inside and drew out a small dirty bag. 'There ain't but a few guineas in 'ere!' he growled, throwing the contents into a chair. 'Don't tell me this is all you've got! Where's the rest of it?'

The old lady shook her head.

Enraged, he hit her.

She shook her head once more, her eyes now wide with fear.

'Useless old biddy!' He hit her again, so hard her nose was broken and the force of the blow sent her in a heap to the floor. 'Happen this is all you've got.' Sniggering, he gave the small limp figure a spiteful push with the toe of his boot. 'I don't think you'd take a battering like that for nothing.' Reaching down, he grabbed her by the hair, grinning in her face. 'No matter. There's bits and pieces downstairs might fetch a bob or two. I'll be off in a minute, yer old bag, but first I've a date with a pretty dark-eyed beauty. You might have liked to watch, but I can see you're not up to it.'

Stretching to his full height, he chuckled, a low, grating sound that stirred her senses. 'Which room is she in, eh?' he mused, thoughtfully stroking his chin while he glanced this way and that. 'Never mind, I'll find her. And if I should come across the feller-me-lad, happen I'll teach him a lesson he's not likely to forget in a hurry. If it hadn't been for that traitor Laing, I'd have dealt with him afore. Laing's gone all soft on that gal o' yours. Because of her, 'e wants no part of his old pals. Mind you, 'e were never any good at stealing. He's a fighter though, I'll give him that. Got a pair o' fists like sledgehammers, an' knows how to use 'em. But he ain't got the killer instinct, not like me.'

After stashing the money into his pockets, he bent down and caught hold of Markham's hair. Summoning all her courage, the old lady kept her eyes tightly closed and her body perfectly still. Her face beneath the blood was as white as chalk. Momentarily frightened, he whispered, 'Yer ain't dead, are yer?' In the candlelight he stared hard at her face, but then a smile crept over his rough features. 'It's no matter if yer 'ave snuffed it. The buggers won't catch me, not in a month o' Sundays, they won't.'

Snorting angrily, he let her fall to the floor. 'To hell with yer! A few minutes with the girl an' I'll be on me way.'

Unaware that the old lady had partly regained her senses and was catching snippets of what he was saying, he bound her hands again, muttering all the while. 'Can't have yer waking up an' making a fuss, can we, eh? Can't 'ave yer waking the feller neither, though I'm not frightened of him, I can tell yer that. But y'see my dilemma. I've got certain business to attend to, and I wouldn't want nobody finding their way into the girl's room just when we're enjoying ourselves.'

Eager for her to hear what he was saying, he bent closer. 'Laing says you've told the girl she ain't to 'ave no truck with him. Well, yer might be sorry about that, 'cause now she's anybody's, ain't she, eh? I dare say 'e won't like it when he finds out I've had her before him. But then he wouldn't take her against her will. Like as not he'd hold her hand and whisper sweet nothings in 'er ear.' His expression hardened. 'But then he's pretty an' I'm ugly, an' the ladies don't take kindly to me whispering in their ear. Don't matter to me, 'cause I ain't got time for such—'

A hard fist came crashing down like a hammer blow to his head, knocking him to the ground and stunning him.

Murray Laing's first thought was for the old lady. Stooping, he quickly released her. 'It's all right,' he murmured when she looked up at him with stricken eyes. 'You're safe now.'

Returning to the other man who was still dazed, he pulled him up by the neck of his shirt. 'Think yourself lucky you won't be swinging on the end of a rope. Another few minutes and it might have been a different story, you bastard!'

Murray Laing had left the other two beaten senseless downstairs, and now he intended to teach this one a lesson. He covered his mouth with one hand while with the other he twisted his arm up his back. 'I warned you about the girl,' he whispered. 'I said I'd do time if you laid one finger on her, and I meant every word.' Forcing him forward, he told him, 'It seems you're hard of hearing. Outside! We'll sort this out, once and for all.'

As they went out on to the landing, Adam came running down the passage, with Kathleen behind. On seeing the two men, Adam launched himself at them while Kathleen ran to check on Markham.

In the uproar that followed, the lout managed to get away. Realising he might be implicated, Murray Laing, too, made good his escape. The two he had laid into downstairs had scarpered as soon as they'd regained their senses.

Adam chased after Murray and the other thug, but they knew every alleyway and escape route and soon disappeared from sight. 'I know who you are!' Adam called out. 'You won't get away with it!'

Dejected and bruised, he returned to the house and went upstairs to the old lady's room.

'She's badly hurt.' Kathleen was on her knees, her arms round the small, frail figure. 'Oh, Adam, I'm frightened.'

He knelt by her side and lifted Markham into his arms. 'I'll stay with her,' he told Kathleen. She was too young to see this, he thought, too dear and vulnerable. It would be better if he stayed and Kathleen went. 'Run and get help. Quickly!'

The sound of his familiar voice filtered through the old lady's pain. She had to tell him how that young man had helped her, how he had saved Kathleen from terrible harm.

Opening her eyes, she looked up at him, her lips moving, but no sound emerged.

'What is it, Markham?' Tenderly, Adam took hold of her hand and bent to hear what she was trying to say. Kathleen paused at the door.

'Murray . . . Laing,' Markham managed.

'It's all right. He can't hurt you now.'

She shook her head. He didn't understand. Wearied, she closed her eyes and was silent.

Kathleen heard her say his name, and her heart hardened against him.

When help arrived and Adam heard them hurrying up the stairs, he assured the old lady she would be all right.

'Don't . . . leave me,' she pleaded.

'We won't leave you.'

'The young . . . man . . .'

'Murray Laing? He'll be caught, don't worry, and he'll pay for this. They *all* will.'

As the ambulance men came into the room, her hand tightened on his. 'No! He . . . helped me . . . saved Kathleen . . . Not him . . . Not him . . .' She saw the look of realisation dawn on his face and knew he had heard. Contented now, she rested.

Kathleen heard her frantic whisperings but was not near enough to decipher the words. She saw the thoughtful look on her brother's face. 'What did she say, Adam?'

Markham was being carried out on a stretcher and the two of them followed close, Kathleen anxiously waiting for an answer, Adam struggling with his conscience.

He knew what Markham had been trying to say. He knew that it was not Murray Laing who had done this terrible thing to her. And yet he wondered whether he should keep the information to himself. There had been awful arguments in this house because of that fellow.

He made up his mind. Kathleen's admirer might not have been guilty of anything here tonight, other than being in this house where he had no right to be, but one way or another he had caused a lot of trouble and deserved to be punished.

'Hush now, Kathleen.' Winding his arm round her shoulders, he drew her close. 'There'll be time for questions later.'

F OR TWO DAYS and nights, the old lady remained oblivious of all around her. 'Your aunt's very ill.' The doctor was brutally honest. 'She may not last another day.'

From the same, uncomfortable chair where she had slept and sat and guarded the old lady, Kathleen gazed up at him. 'Don't let her die,' she pleaded brokenly. 'Please, don't let her die.' She put her hands over her face and quietly sobbed. Adam gently held her. 'I don't want Markham to leave us,' she whispered.

Though he, too, was heartbroken, Adam knew he must be strong for her sake. 'There must be *something* you can do,' he entreated the doctor.

He shook his head. 'I'm sorry.' He looked at Kathleen, and his heart went out to her. 'When do your parents return?' The astonished look on Adam's face puzzled him. 'Before she lost consciousness, your aunt told me you were staying with her for a short time. Until your parents return from abroad, she said.'

Adam did some quick thinking. Of course! Bless her old heart. Right to the last she only had thoughts for them. If the authorities knew they were orphans, they might be taken away. 'That's right, sir,' he lied confidently. 'Our parents are due back soon, and then we'll be going home.'

'Your aunt said it was not possible to contact your parents. Is that right?'

'Yes, sir.'

Eyeing Adam with concern, he asked, 'How old are you?'

'Eighteen, sir.' It was what the doctor needed to hear.

'I see.' Certainly he sensed nothing untoward here. Indeed, the young man and his sister seemed more capable than a good many older people who had frequented this infirmary. 'And are there no other relatives?'

'No, sir.' Adam stood up, a tall, fine young man with an air of proud confidence. 'Our parents would want us to be here with our aunt,' he assured the doctor. 'She has no one else.' That much at least was true.

The doctor was humbled. 'Of course.' At times like these, he felt like an intruder. 'I understand.' More relaxed now, he asked with a smile, 'And are the nurses looking after you both?' His question was put to Kathleen.

'Yes, thank you, sir.' She wiped her eyes. He must not think her a baby.

'Good. That's good.' He spoke to Adam now. 'Your sister looks washed out. Why don't you and – Kathleen isn't it? Why don't you go and stretch your legs for a while? Your aunt will be in good hands, I can assure you.'

Adam wasn't convinced. 'What if she needs us?'

'If your aunt needs you, we'll find you quickly enough,' he promised. 'Meanwhile, it will do you both good to walk in the fresh air. In fact, if you go by way of the office, I've no doubt Sister will have a pot of tea in the making.'

Adam nodded. 'Thank you, sir.' He glanced at Markham's quiet face. 'Don't leave us, Markham,' he murmured. Then he led Kathleen away down the ward.

<hr />

Tired though she was, Markham could not rest. There was still so much to do. 'The children?'

'The children have been sent for.' The nurse was a homely soul, small and prim as her patient. 'Are you sure there's nothing I can get you?'

Markham shook her head. 'I need . . . the children.'

'The children will be here any minute.' Plumping up the pillows, she caught sight of them. 'Here they are now.'

The nurse pulled the screen round the bed and left them alone.

'Oh, Markham, you're going to be all right!' Kathleen was filled with hope.

Markham smiled sadly. 'I don't think so,' she whispered. 'But you mustn't be sad.' Pausing to gather her strength, she went on to tell Adam, 'The house was never mine, just rented. But you know where I keep the money. It's yours, yours and Kathleen's. Take it and go away, before anyone gets suspicious.'

Adam was taken aback. 'We don't want your money, Markham,' he told her gently. 'I thought the thieves made away with everything anyway.'

'That's what . . . they thought too.' A coughing bout took hold of her and brought the nurse running. 'I'm all right,' she argued. 'Please . . . leave us alone . . . a minute longer.'

Reluctantly, the nurse did as she was asked, remaining close by, in case she was needed.

Hard though it was, Markham went on, occasionally pausing to take a deep, grating breath. She had to make certain the children were safe. 'Mr Ernshaw must not know,' she told them. 'Take the money. Get away . . . don't let them put you in . . . an institution.'

Kathleen could hold her grief no longer. 'No, Markham, don't leave us!' Sobbing, she wrapped her arms round the dear soul. 'Don't die,' she pleaded, the tears rolling down her face. 'Please, Markham.'

Tenderly, Adam put his hand on Kathleen's shoulder and drew her aside. 'Come away,' he murmured. 'We have to do as she says.'

Helpless in his arms, Kathleen kept her stricken gaze on the old woman's face.

'Come here, sweetheart,' Markham bade her. 'Come here, child.'

When she was close again, Markham stroked her young face. 'You know I love you both . . . don't you?' A little chuckle escaped her throat. 'I've locked you in the cellar, and I've had to punish you time and again, but you must know . . . I always loved you.' In Kathleen she saw herself as a child. She felt a deep empathy with the girl, this poor little bastard who, thankfully, would never know the truth. 'Do you love old Markham?' she asked.

Kathleen's tears blinded her, but not to the abiding love she had come to feel for this woman. 'Yes,' she said firmly, 'I do love you.' She always would, even if tomorrow Markham was not here. Even if she never saw her again, she would always love and remember her.

'Will you do . . . what old Markham wants then?' She felt her life ebbing away. It was not a sad thing, but for these two who had come to lean on her, it would be hard. It was in her power even now to help them, and help them she would, or be ashamed to meet her maker. 'Go with your brother now,' she said. 'Will you do that?'

Filled with emotion, Kathleen could only nod. The tears burned her eyes, blurring her vision. When she was able to see Markham more clearly, it was with the stark realisation that the little woman was struggling to breathe. 'Adam, quick!' Instinctively, she stepped away.

The nurse came running at Adam's call. 'Best you wait outside,' she told the children. 'I have to get the doctor.'

She hurried away, and Markham grabbed Adam by the arm. 'Get away!' she urged. 'Now!' When he hesitated, she shook her head. 'Please go,' she begged, her gaze going to Kathleen's sad face. 'Take her . . . away from here.'

'I won't go!' Kathleen said stubbornly. 'I won't leave you.'

Markham appealed to her goodness. 'You promised.'

Adam knew they had to leave. 'You did promise,' he told his distraught sister. 'You said you would do what Markham asked.'

Markham closed her eyes. 'Take her. Quickly.'

As they left, passing the doctor and nurse on the way, Markham murmured after them, 'God go with you.'

⎯⎯➤◆◀⎯⎯

ADAM FOUND THE money beneath the floorboard under the piano.

'It's like stealing,' Kathleen said. 'When Markham gets better, she'll need it herself.'

Adam sat her down. 'Kathleen.' He ran his fingers over hers, his heart heavy. 'Markham won't get better. That's what she was trying to tell us, to get away from here, before news gets to Mr Ernshaw and he comes looking for us.'

'I don't care.'

'Don't you care if he puts you in an orphanage? Markham cares. That's why she's helping us.'

'I want to go back.'

'Back where?' For a moment he thought she meant to the old house, to where they had lived with their parents. The thought made him shudder.

'To the infirmary. I want to be with Markham.'

'We won't be able to stay.'

'Why not?'

'Because they'll start asking questions. Because Markham doesn't want us there.' He swallowed hard. 'Because, whether we like it or not, Markham is leaving us, and we have to get away.' For the first time he couldn't hold back the tears. 'We have to do as she asked.'

Distressed to see him crying, she promised, 'I just want to see her once more.'

'All right, but then we must leave.'

'I know.'

By the time they got back to the infirmary, it was too late for goodbyes. 'I'm sorry,' the nurse said, 'but there are forms to be filled out. The police have questions, and we need more information.' She spoke briefly to the clerk at the desk, before hurrying away. 'I'll only be a minute,' she told Adam as she went. 'Then we can talk in Sister's office.'

Fearful that they might be detained, Adam told Kathleen, 'We have to go.'

Kathleen, too, was keen to leave, but first there was something she had to do. Going to the desk, she told the clerk, 'It was Murray Laing.'

The round-faced woman smiled and it seemed as if the full moon had risen. 'Pardon, dear?'

'The people who robbed Markham and hurt her, it was Murray Laing and his three friends.'

'Did you tell this to the police?'

'No. But I want you to tell them. Murray Laing and his friends broke into my aunt's house and attacked her. Tell the police to find them. They have to pay for what they did!'

To the woman's surprise, Kathleen turned and ran out of the building. Adam thrust a fistful of money on to the desk and told her, 'This is to bury Markham.' Then, without another word, he hurried after his sister.

Outside, he caught her by the shoulders and spun her round to face him. 'Why did you say it was Murray Laing who attacked Markham?' Up until now, no names had been mentioned, not even when the police asked them a number of questions.

'Because it was. You heard Markham say so, didn't you? She said it was Murray, didn't she?'

With a rush of shame he recalled how Markham had in fact cleared Murray of the crime, but that he had let Kathleen believe she was accusing him instead. What had happened to Markham was a wicked and evil thing, but by not telling Kathleen the truth, he himself had done something even more wicked. But they couldn't go back now. It would raise too many awkward questions about their circumstances.

'Adam!' Kathleen's anxious voice disturbed his thoughts. 'Markham said it was Murray, didn't she?'

'You know she did,' he assured her. 'You were there, weren't you?' He felt angry. Guilty.

'They killed her. I hate them! I hate *him*!'

'Come on,' he said, urging her forward. 'Let's get out of here.'

<hr />

A S THE DARKNESS closed in and weariness overwhelmed them, they found refuge in an old warehouse in Blackpool's back streets. 'Where will we go, Adam?'

'We'll decide in the morning.'

Curling up in a corner, she drew her coat tighter about her and settled down to sleep.

Fishing in his pocket for the brown paper bundle he'd found in Markham's hiding place, Adam took out an official-looking envelope. Opening it, he began to read.

The letter was from Mr Ernshaw. It revealed how Kathleen was conceived by her mother in an illicit affair with the game-keeper. It also revealed exactly how his parents had died. He could hardly take it in. His senses reeled as if he'd been punched repeatedly. 'Kathleen, not my full sister but my mother's bastard! And my father! Hanged as a double murderer! It can't be true,' he cried out.

Kathleen stirred. 'What's wrong, Adam?' Peering through the half-darkness, she saw the letter in his hand. 'What's that?'

'Nothing,' he managed to say. 'It's nothing.' As she watched, he tore the letter into shreds. It was too much to bear. He felt utterly drained. He was the son of a murderer, and his sister – his *half*-sister – was the bastard daughter of a gamekeeper. He couldn't come to terms with it.

He gazed at Kathleen, this delightful creature who looked up to him, loving him with an innocence that tore at the heart, and a great compassion and strength filled him. She was no more responsible for the circumstance of her birth than he was. A piece of paper with some words written on it didn't change anything; it didn't suddenly turn her, or him, into a creature to be shunned. 'It's all right,' he told her, more composed now. 'It's just an old letter, of no consequence.' Standing up, he resolutely stuffed the torn pieces through the broken window. 'Go to sleep,' he said, watching the bits of paper disperse in the breeze. 'We've a long day ahead of us tomorrow,' he reminded her. 'I need to get work.'

'Me too,' she replied.

He smiled. 'We'll see,' he said. 'We'll see.'

Curled up on the floor, Kathleen's thoughts went to the woman they had left behind, and she wept softly

She wondered about the future. She thought of Murray; that tousle-haired young man who had wormed his way into her young heart; she thought of his winning smile and the mischievous way he would wink at her. She recalled how they had talked, and laughed, and shared their foolish, childish dreams.

These were the good things.

Then she thought of Markham, and sorrow swept over her like a dark, suffocating blanket.

KATHLEEN WAS THE first to wake. Something had stirred her out of a restless sleep, and now she saw the reason. Far from alarming her, it brought a smile to her face. 'Hello,' she said, winking sleepily at the tiny mouse perched on her arm. 'Where have you come from?'

Its beady little eyes stared back at her, its face so near she could see the silky whiskers twitching. 'I've got nothing for you to eat,' she apologised, 'so you'd better go and look elsewhere.'

The creature cocked its head to one side, as if to say, 'I can wait.' And for a while they looked at each other, the mouse studying Kathleen and she studying the mouse. 'You're a pretty little thing,' she murmured. When it sat back on its haunches and brought up its tiny fists to wash its face, she reached out to touch it, half fearing it would scurry away. But it stayed, even when her gentle fingers stroked its small, smooth back. 'I won't hurt you,' she smiled. 'You know that, don't you?'

It was Adam who scared it away. Hearing her voice, he woke with a start. 'Who's there?' Sitting up, he rubbed his eyes. 'Are you all right, Kathleen?'

'I didn't mean to wake you.'

He scratched his head and looked around. 'I thought I heard you talking to someone.'

'We had a visitor.'

Alarmed, he glanced around. 'Where is he?'

'Stop worrying,' she chuckled. 'It was only a mouse. The poor little thing was hungry.'

He laughed. 'Talking to a mouse! Whatever next.' More serious issues filled his mind. 'Come on, Kathleen. We've a lot to do. We need somewhere to live and I need a job.'

Scruffy-headed and still yawning, she stood before him. 'But how?'

'I haven't made up my mind. Maybe we could find work in a Blackpool hotel. That way we would have a wage and a roof over our heads. Or we could go south, into the country. Get work with lodgings, in one of the big farmhouses.'

Kathleen shook her head. 'I'm not going anywhere until I've seen what they do with Markham.'

'Have you gone mad? It was Markham who told us to get away. There's nothing we can do, Kathleen. I know you loved her, and so did I, but she's gone now. I left money for her to be buried, and there's nothing more we can do.'

'If there was no money, what would happen to her then?'

He shrugged, trying hard to recall what happened when people had no money to be buried. 'I'm not sure. I think they put them in a pauper's grave.'

'What's a pauper's grave?'

'It's a place outside the church grounds. Sometimes, if people don't have money, the authorities open up somebody else's grave and put them in there.'

She fell silent, obviously troubled, and he did his best to reassure her. 'But that won't happen to Markham. I left more than enough money.'

'What if somebody steals the money?'

'Who would steal it? These are doctors and nurses.' The idea that they would steal a person's burial money was unthinkable.

Kathleen was not satisfied. 'I'm not leaving until I know what they're going to do with her.'

He knew that when she had made up her mind about something she was stubborn to the last and there was little anyone could do. 'All right. But don't blame me if it all goes wrong.'

In a way he felt the same as Kathleen, but not for the same reasons. He just wanted to see the old lady put to rest. 'We're taking a risk,' he reminded her. 'If they find out Markham was all we had in the world, they'll want to put us away, and they might separate us. Do you understand what I'm saying, Kathleen? If that happens, we might never see each other again.'

The idea made her feel physically sick, but the thought that Markham might be put in a pauper's grave was too shocking. 'We'll have to be careful, that's all,' she said. 'We'll have to stay out of sight. Afterwards, we'll go wherever you want.'

He paced the floor, thinking. 'How can we find out what's happening? I mean, we can't go in and ask, can we?'

'We could ask that nice nurse.'

He shook his head. 'She'd call the authorities.'

'What about somebody who works there, like a cleaner, or one of the women who take away the bed linen?'

'We could try, I suppose. They must know what's going on. Just as long as nobody else sees us.'

'They won't. Especially if we wait until dark. I expect the cleaners and laundry women leave the infirmary by the back. We could wait there.'

He regarded her with admiration. 'You've given this a lot of thought, haven't you, sis?' Calling her 'sis' came without thinking, but to his dismay he was reminded of the contents of that letter. He thrust it away. 'I don't expect they waste much time once a person's dead, so let's hope we can sort this out tonight. We'll have to spend another night here but with any luck we'll be able to get away tomorrow.'

'Thank you, Adam. But we don't have to hide in here all day, do we?'

'No, we don't. We must get something to eat, too. I'm starving.'

The day was cold and crisp, with a keen wind and a biting chill, but they were well wrapped up and didn't feel the cold. They bought some buns at a baker's shop and spent the day on a deserted beach, losing themselves in memories of when Markham had taken them to Lytham.

Balancing precariously on the narrow wall which protruded into the ocean, Kathleen looked back at Adam who was lying on the sand, his long legs crossed, his face towards the sky and his eyes tightly closed. 'Are you thinking, Adam?'

He didn't move. 'Yes.'

The wind was gaining strength, forcing her to raise her voice. '*What* are you thinking?'

'Things.' Still he made no move and his eyes remained tightly closed.

'What things?'

'None of your business.'

'I've been thinking too.'

'Oh?'

'About Markham.'

'What about her?'

'I'm just remembering Lytham. We ate our ice cream, and we buried her up to her waist in the sand. It made us all laugh.'

'I remember.' He blinked, stared at the sky and closed his eyes again.

Kathleen's voice trembled just a little, and her eyes grew moist. 'People stopped and stared.'

'I remember that too.' He gave a little laugh.

The wind was raging around them, so strong that Kathleen had to cup her mouth in order to be heard. 'That man with the bowler hat thought she was a crazy old woman let loose from the asylum. He said people like her ought to be locked up.'

'It's people like him who should be locked up.'

The wind receded a little. The sea calmed and everything became eerily quiet for a moment. She watched the sea awhile, frothing and raging and seeming like an angry, tortured soul. 'I'm afraid of the sea,' she murmured, but Adam didn't hear. Her dark eyes grew troubled. 'Remember how she told us the sea was alive?' she said more loudly. 'How we should never be afraid of it but must always be respectful?'

'Did she say that?'

'She said the sea could think. That it could be kind, and angry, just like a person. She said if it grew angry, it could rise up and take you, and you would never be seen again.'

Forced to shout above the elements, he replied, 'I don't recall Markham saying that. But then you only hear what you want to hear. You're a lot like Markham. You have strange ideas about things.'

'I think she was very wise.' She had learned more from that old lady than from anyone else she had ever known. 'Markham said this was a world of mystery, and that nobody would ever know what secrets it held.' Kathleen had been fascinated. 'Do you believe that, Adam?'

Adam could hardly hear her. Wondering why she sounded so far away, he opened one eye and was horrified to see her balancing on the far end of the wall, waves battering at her feet. 'For God's sake!' Darting forward, he grabbed her by the hair and pulled her off the wall. 'Have you no sense?' He was shaking with fear. 'You could have been swept in and drowned!'

Rubbing her sore scalp, she retorted, 'I was safe enough.'

'Stronger people than you have been dragged under. Stay off the wall or we'll leave right now.'

'Can I dip my feet in the water?'

'No!'

'Please, Adam. Just for a minute.'

'I said no!'

'Just to paddle, that's all.' She gazed longingly at the ocean. 'It might be years before we come to the seaside again.'

'One minute,' he conceded. 'Then we'll have to go.'

She took off her shoes and socks. Mindful of how defiant she could be, he went with her to the water's edge and stayed close by. 'Don't go in higher than your ankles,' he warned, catching hold of her skirt hem and keeping her in check. 'There might be undercurrents.'

Bravely, Kathleen dipped in a toe. 'It's freezing!'

She squealed and paddled, and splashed the water in his face. 'You're mad,' he told her with a laugh. 'And look at the pair of us. We're soaked.' But it didn't matter. For that one precious moment in their young, innocent lives, nothing else mattered but that they had each other, and a whole life's adventures before them.

Soon it was time to leave. 'We'd best make our way to the infirmary,' Adam said, and they retraced their steps along the beach and up the steps near the windmill. Here, Kathleen sat to put on her shoes and socks.

'I didn't realise it was so late,' Adam said, glancing at the darkening sky. 'Move yourself, Kathleen. It's a fair walk to Lytham.'

By the time they had walked the length of the promenade, the night was closing in fast. Adam was striding out, with Kathleen running behind, trying to keep up. Every now and then she would call and he would wait, but soon he was striding ahead again. 'It was your idea to wait outside the infirmary,' he reminded her. 'By the time we get there they'll all have gone home. Hurry up, Kathleen!' It was dark and cold and he was impatient.

As he walked he twisted round yet again to check how far behind she was; he didn't see the woman who got up from the bench and bent to pick up her bag. He walked straight into her and sent her and her bag sprawling.

'Get off, yer scoundrel!' she yelled. Scrambling to her feet, she attacked Adam with her umbrella, forcing him to fold his arms across his face to protect himself.

When he gallantly tried to pick up her handbag for her, she smacked him hard across the head with the butt of the brolly.

'Thief!' she cried. 'Knock a woman down and steal her bag, would you?' Angry and indignant, she tore into him.

'Adam's not a thief!' Kathleen threw herself between them. 'He's only trying to help. He didn't see you, he was looking out for me.'

In an instant the woman stopped, brolly held high and an expression of astonishment on her face. In the yellow halo of lamplight, she stared at Kathleen, then she stared at Adam, astonishment giving way to uncertainty.

Kathleen wasn't certain. The years had marked the woman's face but the features were still scraggy and the body still thin and waif-like. 'Nancy?' She could hardly believe it. 'Nancy Tomlin!'

Nancy screeched with delight. 'It *is* you! Oh, my God!' To Adam's relief, she threw down the brolly and flung her arms round them both. 'Wait till Cook finds out. I told her we might see you one day, on this very promenade.' She cried and laughed, and there was so much to talk about, but they couldn't stand there in the dark and cold. 'Come on,' said Nancy. 'Cook and Mason are waiting back at the house.'

As they hurried along the street, Kathleen and Nancy chattered excitedly. Adam kept silent. He was pleased to see Nancy again, and meeting Cook would be wonderful, but he couldn't help wondering how this would affect their plans.

The guesthouse was only a short walk. 'I can't wait to see Cook's face,' Nancy said as she opened the door with her key. 'She won't believe her eyes.'

When the three of them came into the parlour, a cosy domestic scene greeted them. A cheery fire warmed the room and on one side of the fireplace John Mason was slumped in a big flowered armchair, fast asleep with his mouth wide open and the newspaper spread out on his lap. Mabel's chair had its back to the door, and as Nancy entered, her voice sailed from its depths, 'Is that you, Nancy Tomlin? Where've you been till this time? I've told yer time and again not to stroll that promenade after dark. There are rascals out there as 'd cut yer throat for a shilling.'

Glancing at Kathleen and Adam, Nancy put her finger to her lips. Trying hard not to giggle, she said sombrely, 'You're right, Cook. I should've listened to you, 'cause I came across a pair o' rascals tonight. I even had to fight one of 'em off with me brolly.'

'What!' Mabel leaped out of her chair. 'Are yer all right, yer silly woman?' Being a big lady and not given to leaping, it took a moment before she was steady on her feet and looking Nancy in the eye. 'Yer just won't listen . . .' Her gaze went to Adam first. 'Who the devil's this?'

From Nancy's side, Kathleen stepped forward. 'Hello, Cook,' she said softly. 'Don't you know us?'

Mabel stared at her. As realisation came, her hand flew to her mouth and the tears sprang to her old eyes. She gazed into Kathleen's dark eyes and the years fell away. 'Oh, my goodness.' That was all she could say. 'Oh, my goodness.'

Nancy was beaming from ear to ear. 'These are the rascals I were telling you about,' she said proudly. 'I thought you'd want me to bring 'em home.'

Unable to contain her emotion, Kathleen ran forward to fling her arms round that familiar, podgy figure. Overwhelmed by the occasion, she couldn't speak.

Adam was more restrained. 'I'm sorry if we're intruding,' he apologised. After all, it wasn't Cook who had invited them into her home.

'Intruding?' Mabel was flabbergasted. 'By! Yer a sight for sore eyes, that's what yer are.' Having recovered from the shock, she caught hold of him and, much to his embarrassment, crushed both him and Kathleen to her ample bosom. 'Yer can't know how glad I am to set eyes on yer again,' she cried. 'It does me old heart good to know yer both all right.'

Nancy was glad she'd done something right after all. 'I knew you'd want to see 'em.' With a dark shawl flung haphazardly over her shoulders and flyaway hair framing her thin, bony features, she resembled a scarecrow.

'Tidy yerself up, woman,' Mabel told her. 'Yer enough to frighten the dead.'

With the hugging done for now, Mabel proudly regarded Kathleen and her brother. 'By! Just look at the pair of yer,' she said. 'All growed up and looking more handsome than ever.' She saw how Adam was a young man now, and how Kathleen was on the verge of changing from child to woman. 'You'll break a few hearts along the way, I'll be bound,' she observed. 'Oh, my goodness!' She sniffed and wiped her eyes, and startled everyone by yelling at the top of her voice, 'Mr Mason, wake up. We've got visitors!'

Through sleepy eyes he peered at the little group. It took a moment, but soon he was on his feet and greeting them with excitement. 'I never thought we'd clap eyes on you two ever again,' he said, his own eyes popping with astonishment. The questions fell thick and fast, until Mabel put a stop to it. 'There's time enough for all that,' she reprimanded. 'Let them get through the door first.'

Taking charge as always, she settled Adam on the settee, with Kathleen beside him, and then she sent Nancy off to the kitchen. 'We'll have a pot o' tea, an' some o' them little scones I baked today,' she ordered, and Nancy went away in great excitement.

'Are you still with your great-aunt?' John asked Adam. 'We weren't told all that much, only that you'd gone to live with her, and that Mr Ernshaw would be keeping an eye on things. Still, I expect you're at that stage now where you'll be deciding whether to go to college or look for suitable work.' He was amazed at how confident a young man Adam had become; it was heartening to see, especially when he'd had such a bad start.

Adam was saved from having to reply because John turned to address Kathleen.

'And you look lovely as ever, my dear,' he said. 'I hope you've been happy. You seem to have been well looked after and all that. But whatever were you doing in Blackpool after dark? And won't your aunt be wondering where you are?'

Mabel was exasperated. 'For heaven's sake, John,' she exclaimed, 'leave the children alone.' Nancy came into the room and she gestured for her to set the tray on the low table between them, and to sit herself down on a chair. 'We've a lot to talk about,' she said. 'It might not be good manners, and I dare say the old aunt wouldn't approve, but we'll enjoy our tea as we talk.' Handing round the scones, she informed Kathleen, 'I made these special, for the guests, you understand.'

Kathleen wondered about the guests. 'Won't they mind?' Normally she would never eat a scone belonging to someone else. But then again, she and Adam had been out all day and she was so hungry her stomach was playing a tune.

Mabel chuckled. 'I made the scones and I say who eats them. The other buggers can 'ave crumpets instead.'

Kathleen took a bite out of her scone. It melted in her mouth. 'You make the best scones in the world,' she said, and Mabel's face lit like a beacon.

Adam had one eye on the clock and the other on Mabel. 'I'm sorry, Cook,' he apologised, 'we didn't realise you had guests.' Like Kathleen, he was starving hungry. Biting eagerly into the scone, he sent a shower of crumbs down his front.

'Oh, bless yer! They ain't guests like family or friends, nor anything like that. They're more like lodgers that come and go. This is a guesthouse, y'see. I'd like to call it a small hotel, but in truth it ain't that grand.' She shrugged her shoulders and smiled easily. 'Still, it's a fine little place, and it gives us a living.' She was rightly proud of her business. 'I'll show yer both round when you've had yer tea.'

Adam didn't know how to excuse themselves without sounding ungrateful, especially when he dearly would have liked to stay and talk, and learn what Cook and the others had done with their lives. 'Thank you,' he answered, 'but we'll have to be going quite soon.' He shifted his gaze to the mantelpiece clock. 'It's quarter to six,' he said, and he gave Kathleen a swift, knowing glance, discreetly reminding her of their urgent errand.

John had been quietly watching and listening. He was wondering about these two: what were they doing wandering Blackpool in the dark? Where was the aunt, and why did they seem loath to mention her? Moreover, they looked unkempt, as if they hadn't washed or changed in days.

When he saw the glance that passed between them, his suspicions heightened. 'There's something wrong here,' he remarked, at the same time gesturing for Mabel to remain silent when she seemed about to protest. 'Are you two in some kind of trouble with the old lady? Have you deliberately stayed out and now you daren't go home, is that it?' He smiled. 'You can tell us. You're among friends here.'

The colour drained from Adam's face. He was tired, and a little afraid, but it was his problem and these kind people must not be dragged into a bad situation. 'We have to go, sir.' More than that he wouldn't say.

Mabel wasn't having it. In that firm, authoritative voice they knew so well, she declared, 'Yer neither of yer leaving this house till somebody tells me what's going on.'

Silence greeted her.

Undeterred, she addressed Kathleen in a warmer voice. 'Is Mr Mason right, luv? Have yer stayed out too long, and now yer worried what yer aunt might say when yer get back?'

Kathleen glanced at her brother. 'Tell them, Adam,' she pleaded. 'They might be able to help.'

'Of course we'll help,' Mabel said firmly. 'Isn't that what friends are for?'

Since Kathleen had already given the impression that they needed help, and since he was unsure whether her plan would have worked anyway, Adam felt he could do a lot worse than trust these people who had played such an important part in their childhood. 'We haven't done anything wrong,' he began, 'but you're right, we are in a bit of trouble.'

John nodded, his smile reassuring as he regarded them. 'You really are among friends here,' he affirmed. 'A trouble shared is a trouble halved.'

When Adam hesitated, Mabel prompted him. 'Whatever kind of trouble you're in, I promise we'll do all we can to help.'

Kathleen was nervous. 'You won't go to the police, will you?'

'Never!'

'And you won't take us back to the house?'

'I can't promise that. Let's hear what you have to say first, then we'll decide what's best to do.'

She and John and Nancy sat, quiet and thoughtful, as Adam told how they had been unhappy with Markham when they first arrived, but then they had come to love her. 'Even though she was a little bit crazy,' Kathleen added, her young heart filled with pain.

Mabel chuckled. 'I knew that already,' she told them. 'Right from the time she stayed at the big house and the master threw her out.' Realising she had said too much, and being silently chided by a fierce look from John, she apologised. 'Sorry. Go on, luv. If yer came to be fond of her, why is it yer don't want to go back?'

Adam took a moment to compose himself. In his mind's eye he could see Markham lying in that hospital bed, and he ached with loss. If only he had been able to do something. If only he'd heard those thugs earlier, she might still be alive.

He told of how the thugs had victimised Markham long before he and Kathleen had come to stay with her. He explained how Markham treated them with contempt and how that only seemed to make them worse. He described how, on that fateful night, he was woken by a commotion. When he went to investigate, he found the thugs had attacked the old lady. He fought them, and they ran out of the house, himself in pursuit. But they escaped, and the old lady was rushed to hospital where she had died.

Mabel was appalled and Nancy chewed her bottom lip to stop from crying. John stood up and came to where Adam sat. 'I'm sorry,' he said. 'If there's anything we can do, you've only to ask.'

'We need to make sure she has a proper funeral,' Kathleen told them. 'We left some money, but somebody might steal it and I don't want her to go in a pauper's grave.'

'Bless your heart, child,' Mabel cried. 'We won't let them do that to such a fine old lady.'

Adam confessed how they meant to waylay one of the hospital

cleaners or a laundry woman to try and find out what had been arranged for Markham.

'First of all,' said John, 'do the authorities know she was your great-aunt and that you've got no one else in the world except her? Do they realise you're left as orphans? And secondly, you said you left money for her funeral. Where did you come by that? And what's happening to the old lady's belongings – her house and suchlike? Did she make a will, and if so are the two of you mentioned as beneficiaries?'

'Really, John.' Mabel thought he was being insensitive. 'The children have just lost the only person left to care for them, and here you are talking about wills and such.'

'I'm being practical, that's all,' he protested.

'She didn't own the house,' Kathleen piped up. 'It was rented. She told us that. She said she owned nothing worth selling, just bits and pieces, and furniture that was past its prime even when she bought it.'

'She hid some money away and told us where to find it,' said Adam. 'I have what's left of it here.' He tapped his jacket pocket. 'It should be enough to keep us from starving while I find work.'

'Work, eh?' John looked at the young man, thinking how he was too fine to be a manual worker. 'What have you got in mind?'

'I don't care what it is. I'll do anything, as long as we have a roof over our heads as well. Maybe a labourer on a farm, or a porter in a hotel.'

'If I remember rightly, you had a particular leaning towards numbers.' John winked at Mabel. 'You could add up a shopping list before Cook got to the second column.'

'I might go into accounts later, when Kathleen is older. For now, I'll have to take what's on offer and be grateful. I've got Kathleen to think of now. We'll need to get away from these parts, in case the authorities find us and tell Mr Ernshaw we're on our own again.'

'If he finds us, he'll put me in an orphanage.' Kathleen's voice trembled.

'He'll do no such thing!' Mabel declared. 'Mr Ernshaw won't know, 'cause we won't tell him. And as for having a roof over yer heads, you need look no further.'

Excited and appalled by the turn of events, Mabel had let her tongue run away with her. If they were to let these two stay, it meant turning away other, paying guests, and that meant a considerable drop in income.

The same thought had crossed John's mind. Alarmed but not surprised by her outburst, he gave her a warning look. She knew he was concerned, but she had made the promise, and now she must keep it. 'We'll work it out 'atween us,' she said, and when Kathleen ran to her, overjoyed at the prospect of staying here, John had no choice but to agree.

As for Nancy, she was so thrilled, she danced on the spot. 'We'll have such fun,' she told Kathleen. 'Adam can get a job, and I'll meet you every day from school.'

Adam was still worried. He was sure the only way to keep out of Mr Ernshaw's clutches was to leave Blackpool. 'It's very kind of you,' he said, 'but we couldn't put on you like that. Besides, we've made our plans, and please don't worry, I'll see Kathleen comes to no harm.'

'We'll discuss all that later,' John told him. 'Right now I'd best get down to the infirmary and see what's being done. I'll say I'm a neighbour of your parents or something, and have just heard the news about Markham.'

⇒►◉◄⇐

THE NURSE AT the desk was most helpful. 'I'm very glad the children are back with their parents,' she said. 'Of course, the authorities did question them but they couldn't throw much light on the matter.' She paused. 'Although, come to think of it, later on the girl did point a finger at someone, and she must have been right, because he's been arrested.'

She leaned forward as if to impart a secret. 'Mind you, the old lady did say to the nurse who tended her that this particular young man had tried to help, but what I'd like to know is, what was he doing in the old lady's house? Tell me that? Up to no good, that's what. If you ask me, he's every bit as guilty as the others.'

'I dare say.' John knew nothing of this, and didn't want to know. But he had information to ferret out, so must show a degree of interest. 'Terrible thing, though.'

'Still, she had two good friends in those children. They even brought money in, to pay for her funeral.'

'So the old lady is to be given a decent burial, is she?'

'Good enough. At least she'll be laid in consecrated ground.'

'Where?'

'I'm not sure.'

'Do you know when?'

'I'm not sure about that either.' He was asking too many questions. 'Surely the children's parents can tell you.'

'Yes, of course,' said John quickly, 'but I've only just heard what happened, and since I was passing the infirmary I thought I'd get the details here. I'd like to pay the old lady my respects, and I don't want to trouble the relatives at this sad time.'

The nurse nodded in understanding. 'You'll need to speak to the chaplain.' She pointed along the corridor. 'To the end, then turn left. You'll see his office there.'

—————⇒•⇐—————

FOUR DAYS LATER, beneath a flurry of snow, Markham was laid to rest in a pretty old church close to the railway. 'She'll like it here,' Kathleen said. 'She always enjoyed standing on the bridge, watching the trains go by.' Somehow it made losing her more bearable.

'Let's get home out of the cold,' Mabel urged, her shawl flying in the wind. 'This is no place to linger.' She felt the need to sit by the fire and feel the warmth on her face. At that moment, after laying the old woman in the ground, she felt her age and it weighed heavily upon her. 'I'll have a lazy evening,' she declared, 'with the fire up the chimney and a spot o' gin in me tea.'

The small party of mourners made their way out of the churchyard. 'Tired, are you, me dear?' Linking his arm with Mabel's, John walked her to the waiting carriage. 'We'll have an early night, eh?' he suggested.

'I don't fancy an early night, thank you. I'm in no hurry to climb the stairs tonight,' she informed him.

'Well, I am.' Nancy had a bad habit of butting into their conversations. It was an irritating habit which Mabel had failed to cure. She glared at her, sending out a message that anyone else might have taken note of, but not Nancy, who was delightfully unaware of her own shortcomings. 'It's been a long day. I need to put my feet up,' she groaned. 'They feel like two swollen loaves.'

'That's too bad,' Mabel snapped. 'There's work to do.'

There were three paying guests staying at the house; an old man by the name of Jed, and a recently married couple with eyes only for each other. These two stayed in their room most of the time, and came down for meals looking bleary-eyed and in a kind of trance. 'Young love!' Mabel said, wishing she was thirty years younger, and much to John's amusement old Jed would wink at her in a suggestive manner.

This evening was no different from any other, except for Kathleen and Adam's presence. They all sat round the table and enjoyed one of Mabel's special meals: a grand stew of meat and vegetables with her own homemade gravy, so thick you could stand a spoon up in it. There was jam tart and cream for afters, and a pot full of piping-hot tea to swill it down.

Afterwards the guests retired to their rooms, where the couple would cavort for a while until they were so exhausted they'd fall into a state of unconscious rapture. The old man would read until his eyes began to close, then he would climb into bed and wake only when the smell of Mabel's sizzling bacon teased his hairy nostrils.

When the dishes were washed and returned to the cupboard,

Adam, Kathleen and Nancy went off to their beds too. Mabel sank into her favourite chair in the parlour, beside a banked-up fire, with the warmth playing on her face and the gin playing on her senses. John read the newspaper for a while, then he sat, watching her and thinking.

'I need to talk to you,' he said eventually. 'About a certain matter that's been worrying me.'

Mabel sat up. 'Then get it off yer chest,' she urged. 'We've never kept things to ourselves, and we mustn't start now.'

A few moments later, Adam made his way downstairs for a glass of water. The stew had given him a raging thirst. The parlour door was ajar, and hearing an intense conversation taking place between John and Mabel, he tactfully turned to retreat. He paused, however, on realising that the conversation concerned himself and Kathleen.

'We can't just turn the poor little devils out, not after what they've been through.'

'But you must know they can't stay here indefinitely. They're taking up two rooms, and we've already turned guests away because of it. That's money out of our pockets. Money we can ill afford.' John felt guilty, but the running of this household was ultimately his responsibility, and he had never been afraid to make difficult decisions when duty called. 'Much as I'd like to keep them here, they're not our responsibility,' he insisted. 'We've helped them out of a sticky situation, and now they'll have to look after themselves. After all, Adam is of an age when he can earn a living. By the same token, he's old enough to look after his sister.'

Mabel was not easily persuaded. 'The lad's already been out looking for work. He's bound to strike lucky this coming week, and when he does, I'm sure he'll pay his dues.'

'It won't be enough.' John sounded exasperated. 'At his age he'll be paid a pittance. Even if he does contribute to his board and lodging, it can't possibly make up for what we lose. And we'll still have to keep the girl for some years before she's earning.'

There was a pause in the conversation, during which John could be heard pacing the floor. 'It's not what we planned, Mabel. We're getting on in years, and we neither of us know how to raise children, even if wanted to.'

'I don't think I've the heart to ask 'em to leave.' There was a pitiful break in her voice. 'I'm sure the lad can take care of himself, but what about the girl? She's only a child.'

'Exactly.'

'Oh, John. She's such a trusting young thing. It would be a crime to turn her away just when she's found some kind of security again.'

'I'm not denying she's a lovely girl, and I no more relish the idea of turning her away than you do, but I don't see what choice we have. We can't run this place as a charity home. It's hard business that puts the bread and butter in our mouths.'

'God forgive us. The poor lass.' Mabel was on the verge of tears. 'Do you think she knows?'

'How can she? I've said nothing to her. I wanted to discuss it with you first.'

'No, I don't mean what we've just been talking about.'

'What then?'

'Do you think she knows that Peterson wasn't her father?'

'I shouldn't think so. The secret went to the grave with her mother. As far as I know, there's only you and me left who has an idea of what was really going on in that house.'

'I hope you're right, John. It would be a terrible shame if the truth got out. Being born out of wedlock is a bad thing. It can scar a body for life.'

'We none of us know for certain,' John reminded her. 'A little knowledge can be a dangerous thing. It might be wise not to mention it ever again. Not even among ourselves.'

Adam was dismayed by what he'd heard. He had thought nobody but himself and Ernshaw knew about Kathleen's parentage, now that Markham was dead. He toyed with the idea of telling Kathleen before anyone else did, but then he wondered how she would take it. Maybe she would be happy to know that Peterson was not her father, but how would she feel about being born a bastard? How would she cope with the knowledge that he was not her full brother? Wouldn't she feel that he was under no obligation to take care of her? Would she believe him if he told her differently? He was all she had to cling to. And she was about to be turned out on the streets.

Adam knew he couldn't tell her.

As he turned to creep back up the stairs, his heart stood still. John was at the parlour door. Standing on the stairs directly opposite, Adam could go neither up nor down without being seen. He stood quite still, holding his breath, praying John would not glance up. He did not. He quietly closed the door and returned to his conversation.

Adam had heard enough to know that he and Kathleen must leave that very night.

Upstairs, he gently shook his sister awake. 'Get dressed,' he whispered. 'We have to go.'

She stared at him through sleepy eyes. 'Why?'

'Do you trust me?'

'You know I do.'

'Then get dressed and move quietly. We don't want anyone to know we're leaving.'

'Has something happened?'

'Ssh!' He looked anxiously towards the door, convinced he'd heard footsteps. 'Get dressed,' he urged. 'Quickly.'

While Kathleen did as he asked, he went to the dresser and scribbled out a note. He wouldn't leave without a word of thanks or reassurance for Mabel.

A moment or two and Kathleen was ready, with more questions. 'Adam, what's happened? Why do we have to leave?'

'Later,' he answered softly. 'Keep quiet or they'll hear us.'

As they approached the door, he suddenly halted, putting his finger to his lips. There *was* someone out there, he was certain. With a sudden movement he flung open the door, and there was

Nancy, hand over her mouth and her eyes wide with shock.

'Ooh! You gave me a terrible turn,' she cried. 'I've been waiting for you.'

'What do you mean?' Quickly, in case they were overheard, Adam took hold of her arm and unceremoniously pulled her inside. 'Why were you waiting out there?'

Nancy's gaze fell to the floor. 'I was in the kitchen,' she explained. 'I saw you come back upstairs and I knew you'd be leaving tonight.' Tears rolled down her face as she looked up. 'I 'eard what they said. Yer mustn't be too 'ard on 'em. They do love yer. Only this little guesthouse is all they've got, and it's terrible hard to make a living. Honest to God, I know they'd keep yer if they could.'

Now Kathleen understood. 'Are they turning us out, Adam?' She looked at him and the truth was written on his face.

Nancy was distraught. 'Whatever will yer do? How will yer manage?'

Kathleen took hold of her hand. 'We'll manage all right, Nancy,' she said softly. 'Please don't worry.'

Adam was impatient to be gone, but first he had to be assured of one thing. 'You won't let them know I overheard, will you, Nancy?' he pleaded. 'I'd rather they thought it was our decision to leave. That way they won't feel so bad.'

Nancy's gratitude was obvious. 'Course I won't tell 'em,' she whispered. 'And I'll not forget you – either of you. God bless yer, and take care, eh?'

Adam folded the note into her hand. 'Give this to Cook,' he said, and she promised she would.

She watched them go softly down the stairs and past the parlour, like a pair of thieves in the night. 'Look after yerselves,' she murmured. 'God willing, happen we'll meet again in better circumstances.'

The door opened to let the night in. Then it closed, and they were gone.

In the lamplight, Nancy unfolded the note and read it through a blur of tears:

Dear Cook,

    Thank you for having us.

    We're very grateful for all you've done, but now we have to move on. I must find work where we're provided with board and lodgings.

    Once we're settled, Kathleen will need to finish school. I'll look after her, don't worry, and we'll be in touch when we've found a suitable place.

    Thank you again for all you've done.

    Adam

Outside, the night closed in around them. There was a coldness in the air that pinched at the face and stiffened the fingers. 'Stay close to me.' Adam kept to the houses as they hurried along; the walls were a welcome buffer against the elements.

They had dressed sensibly and so were protected from the biting wind, but there had been no time for anything else. They had no food, or change of clothing, and the money Adam had would not last for ever.

'We'll make for the railway station,' he told Kathleen. 'It'll be warm there, and we can decide what best to do.' He had an idea to go south, but he needed a plan of sorts and, before deciding, he wanted to talk his ideas through with Kathleen.

Kathleen was feeling sad at leaving Cook and the others behind, but she tried to look eager and even managed a smile. 'All right,' she answered. 'I'm hungry. Maybe the hot-potato man will still be there.'

'You had a huge helping of Cook's stew,' he reminded her. 'You must have hollow legs.'

Two lost souls, they hurried through the night, heading towards the station and a promise of warmth.

The snow was falling thickly now, driven by a fierce wind that made it difficult to see. 'Keep close to me,' Adam urged as they crossed the main road. Even at this time of night there was a steady flow of traffic through the town.

Blinded by the snow and pushing hard into the wind, they

didn't see the carriage and four as it came careering towards them. In that last split second before it sent Kathleen hurtling backwards, Adam lurched forward to grab her, but he was too late.

While pandemonium broke out, with passers-by chasing after the carriage, shaking fists and abusing the driver, Kathleen lay on the ground, white-faced and still. 'Gawd Almighty, he's killed the poor lass!' one shocked woman uttered.

Adam was on his knees, talking to his sister, rubbing her cold hands and trying to ease her back to consciousness. In the lamplight she looked as grey as marble. For one awful minute he feared the woman might be right. 'Kathleen. Look at me, *Kathleen. Please.*' He had to believe she would be all right.

'Help is on its way,' a man in the crowd promised. There were others, though, who thought she was beyond all that.

'Kathleen.' With the tears blinding him, Adam continued to call her name. 'Kathleen . . .' When he sensed she might be responding, he urged in a stronger voice, 'Open your eyes, Kathleen.'

Suddenly, someone was pushing through; a tall gentleman, clad in cloak and hat, and with a look of anxiety on his handsome face. 'Let me through,' he ordered authoritatively, and people instinctively moved back. There was even a mark of respect for him, until an onlooker called out, 'It's the gent from the carriage! The murdering bleeder!'

There was a fierce scuffle. The man's hat was knocked into the gutter and, if it hadn't been for the burly carriage driver who accompanied him, the distinguished gentleman might have been rolled in the gutter with his hat. In the event, the carriage driver put out his big arms and held back the crowd, and in a moment anger was replaced by apprehension, and a morbid curiosity.

'Let me take her to my house,' the man said to Adam. 'I know a good doctor. I can have him with her in a matter of minutes.'

Incensed, Adam turned on the man. 'If she dies, I'll kill you!' he yelled. 'I swear, I'll kill you!'

'She won't die if we get help quickly. My home is only a short distance away. Please. Let me help.'

His anger spent, Adam nodded numbly. Carefully he picked up Kathleen and carried her to the carriage. The gentleman ordered his carriage driver to take them home, telling him sharply to watch his speed. In a few minutes they reached their destination, a grand house, situated high above the town in a row of fine houses, with long, small-paned windows and heavy curtains keeping out the night. A broad run of four stone steps led to the front door; it was an impressive door, of solid oak, with four deep panels and a huge brass knocker in the shape of a lion's head.

As Adam carried Kathleen up the steps, he was only vaguely aware of the house but sensed an air of grandeur and opulence here. As they approached, the door inched open and then swung back to reveal a small man of advancing years, with a thick mop of snow-white hair and a round, protruding belly that looked as if it had been stuffed for the Christmas table. His face wrinkled with curiosity. 'Whatever's happened, sir?' His eyes were on Kathleen. 'Shall I get the doctor?'

'Straightaway, James.' The urgency in his voice sent James rushing into the house and out again, with his long coat on and wearing a pork-pie hat that sat on his head like something dropped from a great height. He made off down the street, heading for the big house at the end where the doctor resided.

'Take her into the front room,' the man instructed Adam. He would have taken Kathleen into his own arms but Adam held her fiercely to him. As he laid her on the couch, she opened her eyes. 'Hello, sis.' Adam tenderly raised her to a sitting position. 'Easy now.' To see those lovely brown eyes alive and inquisitive was an indescribable joy to him.

'Adam?' Dazed and confused, she could recall nothing of the accident. She had been walking along, there was a lot of shouting, and now she was here, aching from head to toe. Her unsteady gaze reached beyond Adam to where the gentleman was standing. Who was he? Was this his house? Why was she here?

By the time it was explained that she had been involved in an accident, the doctor had arrived, together with the butler who was wheezing and gasping and seemed to be more in need of medical attention than Kathleen. 'For heaven's sake, man,' snapped his employer, 'go and get yourself a nip of brandy. It'll warm you up.' The gentleman turned to the doctor, who was tending Kathleen. 'I was a passenger in the carriage that knocked her down,' he explained. 'The driver's had a roasting but I dare say it won't end there.' He addressed Adam. 'Say the word, young man, and I'll have him reported to the police station.'

Kathleen heard all of this, and her first thought was that if the driver was turned over to the police, then so too might they be. If that happened, the authorities might ask all sorts of awkward questions. 'I'm all right, sir,' she said, though she felt as if she really had been run over by a carriage and four. 'Please, I'd rather you didn't cause a fuss.'

Somewhat bemused by this, and fascinated by Kathleen who he thought was an extremely attractive girl, he smiled at her. 'I'm sure your brother thinks differently.' Shifting his attention to Adam, he wondered about these two. The young man was what? Sixteen, seventeen? And the girl probably no more than twelve years old. They appeared to be hiding something. Certainly they were nervous, frightened even, and if he knew anything about human nature, it was little to do with the accident.

He was intrigued, especially when Adam gave the same answer as Kathleen. 'We don't want any trouble. As long as Kathleen's all right, that's all that matters.' He knew why Kathleen had answered the way she did, and he was proud of her.

'You surprise me. Anyone else would want that man punished.'

Kathleen answered for them both. 'We can't stay in these parts,' she told him. 'Reporting the incident would only hold us here. Besides, I should think the man's learned his lesson. I expect he'll drive more carefully in future.'

'I see.' Yes. These two were definitely afraid of something. 'Let's hear what Dr Jarvis has to say first.'

What he had to say put all their minds at rest. 'Like all young things, she must have rubber bones because there appears to be nothing broken, and apart from a few bruises and a bump on the head where she hit the pavement, I'd say she's had a very lucky escape.'

Adam was relieved. 'We'll be on our way, then, just as soon as she's able.'

'I'm able now, Adam.' Suppressing the discomfort she felt, Kathleen struggled to stand up, but when she almost lost her balance, it was plain to all that she was far from able.

'You've had a nasty shock,' the doctor reminded her. 'If you value my advice, you won't attempt any travelling for a day or two at least.'

'I suggest you stay here the night.' The gentleman stepped forward. 'There are enough rooms in this house to sleep an army.' He smiled and Kathleen thought him very handsome. He looked to be in his early thirties. Tall and lithe, he had a commanding presence. His face was proud but kind, and his blue eyes seemed to shine with goodness. She felt he could be trusted. After all, he'd brought them here to safety, hadn't he?

Similar thoughts were running through Adam's mind and after only a moment's hesitation he graciously accepted the gentleman's hospitality. 'Thank you, sir,' he said.

'Wonderful! James will take good care of you. Chief cook, bottle-washer, and wicked wizard in the making, he knows what I'm thinking even before I do.' He laughed out loud; it was a warm, pleasant sound. 'There are times when he thinks I'm the servant and he's the master, but I don't mind telling you I wouldn't know what to do without him.'

Adam held out his hand. 'I'm Adam Peterson,' he said. 'This is my sister Kathleen. We're in your debt, sir.'

The gentleman shook hands with them both. 'Glad to help,' he said. 'Westerfield is the name, Maurice Westerfield. I dabble in anything that makes money, and I must be doing something right because I'm disgustingly wealthy. I import mostly – buy cheap, sell at a profit, that's the way I work. I'm also a widower, with a son who thinks work is for fools and a daughter who spends money faster than I can earn it.' When James coughed meaningfully, he chuckled. 'My butler thinks I talk too much.'

'I'm sorry, sir.' Behind James's apology lay a stern tone of disapproval. 'I was only wondering whether you would like refreshments now.'

'Of course, and I hope you'll join us, Dr Jarvis. Though knowing you, I shouldn't be at all surprised if you'd prefer a drop of good brandy.'

The good doctor accepted the brandy, knocked it back in one gasp, then took his leave. 'I left an important dinner engagement,' he explained. 'Now we know the young lady is all right, I'll make my way back. Will I see you before you return south?'

'What? Afraid I might make off with your fee?'

The doctor rolled his eyes. 'God forbid! Then how would I afford my brandy?'

Later, the other three sat round the small table, enjoying the hot tea and sandwiches James brought. The atmosphere was friendly and relaxed. They exchanged small talk, until Maurice's curiosity got the better of him. 'Have you no parents?' he asked.

Adam shook his head. 'We've been staying with an aunt but she died recently.' He glanced at Kathleen. 'I won't let them put Kathleen in an orphanage. That's why we have to keep travelling. I must find work.'

Maurice regarded them both with interest, particularly Kathleen; he could hardly take his eyes off her.

'Are you good at figures, Adam?'

'So I'm told.'

'And are you ambitious?'

'I like to think so.'

The next question was put after some quiet deliberation. 'Would you be interested in working for me?'

Adam thought quickly. 'We must have a place to live, sir.'

'And so you shall. I have a house and land in the south, not too far from London. You and your sister could live there. You'd be paid according to your work, with free board and lodging until you feel the need to find a home of your own.' His smile was warm and honest. 'Does that suit you, young man?'

'It sounds wonderful!' Exactly what he wanted.

Maurice's warmest smile was bestowed on Kathleen. 'Good. That's settled then. As soon as you're up to it, the three of us will travel south.'

Chapter Eleven

MAURICE WESTERFIELD WENT to great lengths to ensure that Kathleen was well cared for on the journey south the next morning, with blankets tucked round her legs and a pillow on which to rest her head. He ordered a picnic hamper to be set inside the carriage and, to Adam's irritation, personally took charge of her wellbeing.

They stopped twice along the way, each time at a reputable inn where every assistance was lavished on them. At two o'clock on a bright, cold day, they arrived in Ilford. Kathleen was mesmerised. 'Why, it's beautiful!' she cried, and while she gazed out of the window at the sights that greeted them, Maurice Westerfield gazed at her. And as he gazed, his heart was filled with a sadness he could hardly bear.

'Look, Adam!' Kathleen pointed to the street name. 'Beehive Lane,' she read. 'There was a street named Beehive Lane next to Markham's house.'

Maurice was interested to know about their past. During the journey Kathleen had referred to Markham several times. 'This Markham seems to be an important person in your life,' he observed. 'Was this the aunt you told me about?'

Adam replied. 'Yes,' he said shortly. They had trusted Maurice with the information that they were orphans but Adam was reluctant to divulge any details that might lead to Mr Ernshaw. If things didn't work out with Maurice Westerfield the less he knew about them, the better. 'I think we should forget the past and start afresh. That's what Markham would have said.'

'Of course,' Maurice conceded. 'And I should mind my own business.'

There was an uncomfortable silence until they came into Cranbrook Road overlooking the wash and Kathleen spotted two puppies playing on the bank. 'Oh, look! Aren't they lovely?' She smiled straight into Maurice Westerfield's watching eyes and his heart turned over.

'You'll be pleased to know I have two dogs,' he told her. 'They're not puppies, I'm afraid. I bought them from the meat market six years ago. It was the end of the day and, being unsold, they were about to be put down.' He shook his head. 'I couldn't leave them to such a fate.'

In that moment, he grew tenfold in Kathleen's estimation.

At the bottom of Cranbrook Road the carriage came to a halt. 'This is it, guv.' The driver jumped down and opened the door. Maurice climbed out and helped Kathleen down; Adam followed, a little peeved.

'I thought you said you had land.' He glanced up and down the road. All he could see were grand houses. One thing was for sure, he thought, there's a deal of money in these parts.

'The land lies beyond here. At the moment, the only access to the house is along the lane.' Maurice pointed to a narrow gap between the last house and a small wooded area. 'Unfortunately it's impassable to vehicles in winter.' An impish grin creased his handsome face. 'Mind you, that can be a Godsend,' he declared. 'It keeps out the undesirables.'

'Such as us,' Adam quipped. He felt irritated, jealous even. And he couldn't understand why.

'Oh?' Maurice gave him a curious look. 'Are you and your sister undesirables then?'

Adam was saved from having to reply by Kathleen.

'Why did you buy this house if you can't get a carriage up to it?' she asked, ever curious; he was obviously wealthy enough to buy whatever he wanted.

While the driver unstrapped the cases from the back of the cab, Maurice directed them towards the lane and, as they walked, he explained, 'I searched far and wide for a house I could spend the rest of my days in. Although the access was not altogether suitable, I liked the place. I was not told that the lane was impassable during winter; I found that out for myself. This is my first winter here. Mind you, it's only a temporary obstacle.'

'What will you do?'

'Fortunately, a parcel of land between the road and one of my meadows came up for sale and I snapped it up. I can now build my own driveway straight to the house. The workmen began constructing it about a month ago. It winds through the cherry trees up to the house and then branches off to the stables at the back.' He waved his hand in a grand gesture. 'There are two hundred and sixty acres all told.'

Kathleen was glad they had come, it sounded lovely. 'Are you a farmer then?'

'I don't have time to farm. The land is all leased. It brings in a great deal of money and I don't have to lift a finger. There are two cottages, but they're kept for my house servants. The handyman lives in one, the other is vacant. When the drive is finished, I'll take on a driver for my own carriage and four. The cottage will be his, rent free. I did have a driver when I first came here but he went away to be a sailor. God knows how anyone could prefer the ocean to the land.' He smiled directly at Kathleen. 'Still, each to his own, that's what I say.'

'Do you have horses?' Kathleen had visions of herself leaping over fences on a black stallion.

'Why do you ask?'

'You mentioned stables.'

'Yes, we have four carriage horses and a large grey gelding belonging to my son.' A dark frown crossed his face as he thought of his son, Christian. That young man had been a heartache for too long now.

Quiet in their own thoughts, they trudged towards the house, Kathleen with the blanket wrapped securely round her shoulders,

Adam with his arm round her to keep her steady. The driver brought up the rear loaded down with baggage.

As they rounded the bend, Adam stopped in his tracks. 'Is this your house, sir?'

'It is.'

Kathleen stared, and couldn't believe her eyes. 'It's like a palace!' she cried, and felt very foolish when the driver gave her a sidelong glance.

The house was a mansion. Built of white stone, it was wide and high, with many large windows and round bays, and numerous chimneys reaching to the sky. The walls were criss-crossed with sleeping ivy. The wide steps that led up to the entrance were flanked by tall stone urns, spilling over with the sad remains of autumn blossoms.

For all its great size and presence, there was something about the house that exuded a welcome, and also a certain calm in spite of the uproar of work going on. Immediately before the house, the ground was in upheaval, but it was possible to discern a wide, sweeping track taking shape.

'Why don't you live in the house up north?' Kathleen asked. 'Nobody needs two houses, do they?'

He led the weary party up the steps to the front door. 'I have business interests in the north as well as in the south. Besides, much as I love the north, this is home.' He sighed, reflecting on the way it used to be. In a quiet voice, heavy with emotion, he murmured, 'They say the heart is where the roots are, and that's certainly true in my case.'

At the door he turned to survey the scene before him, the ravaged earth and the beautiful, untouched land beyond. 'From here you can see the rooftops of Ilford. This is where I belong. I was born in Ilford and I've no doubt this is where I shall die.'

On seeing Kathleen's face fill with horror, he laughed that warm, engaging laugh that set everyone at their ease. 'Not for some years yet, I hope,' he said. 'I'm not yet forty, and there is still so much I want to do.'

He turned and fumbled in his waistcoat pocket, eventually

producing a key that opened the front door. 'Leave the bags in the hall,' he told the driver as they went inside. 'My son will see to them later.'

While he paid the driver, Kathleen's interested gaze went round the hall. There was the usual rack for umbrellas and cloaks, a tall and beautiful grandfather clock, a dark-wood dresser as high as the ceiling, and rugs beneath their feet that were soft and mellow.

Through a high, wide arch, she could see another richly furnished room, with crystal and silver ornaments, and plush, red velvet curtains framing floor-to-ceiling windows. There were tapestries on the wall, and deep floral-covered armchairs. In the marble fireplace, a roaring fire threw out warmth and cheer. Altogether, Kathleen felt that this was a good place, a place where she and Adam might find contentment.

Adam, too, felt this was a good house. One thing puzzled him, though, and while Maurice was busy with the driver, he voiced his concern to Kathleen. 'It's strange,' he whispered. 'Where are the servants?'

No sooner had the driver been shown out than there was a loud, excited shriek. 'Daddy! Daddy!' Along with two dogs and a woman, the girl raced down the stairs, her arms stretched wide. She was a pretty thing, aged about twelve, with long fair hair and huge blue eyes. 'I didn't know you were coming home today,' she cried, throwing herself into his arms. 'You said you wouldn't be home for a week.'

Catching hold of her, he swung her round. 'And *I* thought the house would be empty,' he laughed. 'You were supposed to be staying in London – shopping and all that.' He fondled the two dogs jumping up at him, one a big black creature with drizzling mouth and floppy jowls, the other a tall, thin animal with sad red eyes and feet the size of meat plates.

'Down!' The woman's voice intervened, a sweet, invasive voice which had the dogs running to sit obediently at her feet. Addressing Maurice, she explained. 'The trip to London was planned for tomorrow,' she said, 'but now that you're home, I don't suppose I'll be able to drag her away. No matter, we can visit London another time.' The woman was slim and attractive, and obviously very much in charge. Her voice was disturbingly familiar to Adam, though he couldn't immediately place it.

She stepped closer. 'It's good to see you, sir,' she said, smiling into Maurice's eyes. 'Melinda does so pine when you're away.'

'It's good to see you too, Emma, my dear.' Yet he seemed less happy to see her than she was to see him. 'I concluded my business early.' He gestured for Adam and Kathleen to come forward. 'I've not returned alone. This is Adam and his sister Kathleen.' A wave of regret flitted across his features. 'I'm afraid we didn't meet under ideal circumstances. I had the misfortune of choosing a maniac for a driver. He lost control of his carriage and four, sending Kathleen hurtling across the pavement.' He stroked Kathleen's hair, a simple, instinctive action marked by all of them, with varying unease. 'Thankfully, she wasn't too badly hurt,' Maurice went on. 'However, I feel a certain amount of responsibility so I want our guests treated very well while they're under this roof.' He looked at his housekeeper. The nod of her head and the ready smile on her face suggested she was happy to comply with his wishes. His gaze shifted to his daughter, who also smiled back at him. 'That's settled then.' He was satisfied. Yet the minute he looked away, the girl's smile was replaced by a sour expression. Adam noticed it, and his unease increased.

Maurice completed the introductions. 'This is my daughter Melinda, and Emma Long, my housekeeper and Melinda's governess.' He gave her an appreciative glance. 'She's only been with me since I bought this house, but I really don't know how I ever managed without her.'

Emma had been paying particular attention to the visitors. When she had first laid eyes on them, she had had a feeling they were known to her. Now, after hearing their names, she was positive. She was shocked to her roots but she managed to keep calm, and even to appear delighted. 'I'm so glad you weren't badly hurt,' she told Kathleen. In truth, she would rather the girl had been trampled to death.

'They'll be staying here with us,' Maurice told her. 'Kathleen will be taught alongside Melinda, and Adam is to be trained under my guidance.'

'Very well, sir.' She turned to them. 'I'm sure you'll be happy here,' she smiled, but there was a glint in her eye that said otherwise.

Kathleen shrank from her. Something about Emma disturbed her.

The housekeeper took a moment longer to stare at Adam. He was so like his father, it was unnerving. 'I'm sure we're going to get on very well.'

Introductions over, Maurice led the way into the drawing room. As they filed in, with Adam and Kathleen bringing up the rear, Adam suddenly realised who the woman was. 'I know her!' Gripping Kathleen's arm, he held her back. 'And so do you.'

'There is something familiar about her,' Kathleen replied softly, 'but I don't know anybody called Emma.'

'Anyone can change their name.'

At that point Emma turned, her small, beady eyes enveloping them. She lingered, her gaze going from one to the other. It was obvious she had overheard their conversation.

'She knows,' Adam whispered, horrified. 'She knows I've recognised her.'

Emma smiled and placed her fingers to her lips as if to say, 'It's our secret.' In a moment she had turned away and was chatting to Melinda as if nothing had happened. 'You have two new friends, Melinda,' she said. 'We must make them feel at home.' Out of the corner of her eye she glanced back. And winked.

That bold, intimate wink and the easy, arrogant way she walked were unmistakable. 'It *is* her!' Adam muttered. 'It's been years now, and she's changed. She's cut her hair and got herself a new name, but it's her all right.'

Kathleen was alarmed. 'Who, Adam?'

'Connie Blakeman. She was—'

'Our nanny from the big house, before Father threw her out,' Kathleen finished for him. 'I remember now.'

AFTER BEING SHOWN their rooms, which were situated in the east wing of the house, they were taken to the kitchen and fed. Connie, or 'Emma' as she was known to the others, did the cooking, and it was a filling, wholesome meal.

'We don't have a cook yet,' Maurice explained. 'Before buying this house, my children and I travelled a great deal. I bought it on the spur of the moment. I do that sometimes, buy on the spur of the moment. It's in my blood, you know. You might not believe it, but I used to be a barrow boy in my youth.'

Adam was astonished. 'You? A barrow boy?' And here he was, with a mansion to live in and all the trappings of a gentleman. In an instant, Adam saw himself in the same situation. If a former barrow boy could do all this, then so could he.

Maurice laughed. 'It's hard to believe, isn't it? But it was easy enough really. I'm not ashamed of my background, and I'm not a proud man, although having said that, I am proud of what I've achieved. I could say it was hard. I could claim that every step of the way was a nightmare, but I'd be lying.' His face clouded. 'I might be a lot of things but never a liar.'

Leaning back in his chair he surveyed the faces before him: his own daughter who was more ashamed of his background than he was; his housekeeper, an attractive, secretive woman who pretended to be genteel but in fact was no more a lady than he was a gentleman. She was good with Melinda, however, and she had also proved herself to be a very competent housekeeper. He had a sneaking suspicion she fancied being the mistress of this house, but that would never happen, not in a million years.

Then there were his two house guests: the young man, Adam, who, he could tell, had the hard-nosed makings of a good businessman; and the girl, Kathleen. Oh, the girl! The dark, intense eyes, and that long flowing hair that he ached to run his fingers through. But he mustn't. He must never frighten her away. She belonged in this house, and if he had his way she would stay here for as long as he drew breath.

'Daddy?' Melinda's voice shook him back to the present moment. 'Are you all right?'

'I'm sorry, I let my thoughts carry me away.' He finished his tale. 'I've always had an instinct for buying at the right time and selling for a profit. I do the same now, only on a grander scale. I import goods at a bargain price and sell them on at a profit. There's no secret to it. No matter what you have to sell, if you're prepared to travel, you'll always find a ready market.' He wagged a finger at Adam, who was listening intently. 'But you do need money to get started, and you need the courage to buy when everyone else is looking the other way.'

'How do you mean, sir?'

'Here's an example. Last summer a business acquaintance mentioned that he'd been offered a consignment of trees from Norway. He turned it down because we were enjoying a heat wave and, like many other traders, he was too busy concentrating on parasols, garden furniture, and suchlike.'

He took a moment to savour the memory. 'I made extensive inquiries, bought the timber consignment at rock-bottom price, and stored it until the winter when I made a very handsome profit. Like I said, I have an instinct for buying at the right time and knowing when to sell. It's important to read the market for months ahead. Not everyone can do that. I can. That's why I'm a wealthy man. Some say I'm an entrepreneur, others say I'm a very clever, shrewd businessman. In actual fact I'm still a barrow boy, but dealing in larger quantities.'

Realising he had wandered off the point, he shook himself mentally and told them in a crisper voice, 'As I say, I've travelled a great deal, and have only recently acquired this house. I am in the process of hiring servants and by the end of the week, we should have a full complement.'

He dabbed at his mouth with his napkin, his gaze falling to the table. For a long, awkward moment he seemed to be far away, but then in a soft voice he continued. 'I'm afraid I've been a little neglectful, disorganised even,' he confessed. 'You see, I lost my dear wife after a long illness.' He looked at Kathleen, and his eyes were pleading. 'After that, I couldn't settle. I couldn't think, and I couldn't work. So I sent my son away to college and took my daughter to see the world; of course she had a governess to tend to her schooling, so I did not fail in my duty on that count.' He took hold of his daughter's hand. 'I sold my previous house before we sailed for America. I lost the heart to live there – too many memories.'

While he was speaking, Connie sat with her hands crossed on the table, listening closely.

Adam and Kathleen were embarrassed and surprised that he should confide such private matters to them, while Melinda sat protectively by her beloved father's side, her blue eyes bright with malice as she looked at the two guests he had brought home. She did not take kindly to their presence, and she did not think that her father should entrust his life story to these strangers.

Unaware of the tension, Maurice went on, 'I'm home now, and life must go on, as they say.' He straightened his back and sat up. 'Eat and drink,' he urged. 'We'll talk again later. You must be wondering what I expect of you, Adam. You, Kathleen, will work hard at your schooling, I hope.' The smile slid from his face, and his gaze became more intense. 'I have great plans for you, my dear,' he told her. 'You have no parents or relatives to take an interest in your welfare other than your brother, of course, who must be commended for the way he's looked after you.' Sensing Adam was about to protest, he added quickly, 'But now your brother's of an age when he needs to concentrate on his own future.'

'Kathleen is my future, sir,' Adam retorted sharply.

'Of course. All I am saying is, your sister will be cared for in every way, while you may pursue a career and look forward to a secure future. You seem a bright young man, and I mean to do everything in my power to see you reach your full potential. I do hope I haven't offended you.'

Adam was bone-tired. They were all tired, he reasoned, and Maurice Westerfield did seem genuine enough even if he was rather high-handed in his assumption of responsibility for Kathleen. Adam wondered about that, and he resented having his own place in his sister's welfare brushed aside so lightly.

Nevertheless the fact was, Westerfield was offering them both a unique opportunity, and for that they should be immensely grateful. 'No, sir,' he answered. 'You haven't offended me.' But Maurice's words had created a small barrier between them.

'Good.' Maurice rubbed his hands together, as though ridding them of something unpleasant. 'Finish your meals, and then I suggest an early night. Tomorrow, my son will be home. The day after that it's back to business, and I can assure you that next week this house will be bustling.' Again his brightest smile was for Kathleen. 'There is much to look forward to,' he promised.

They all heard his promise. But it was not meant for them. It was meant only for Kathleen.

<hr />

A T NINE THIRTY, they went to their rooms. The housekeeper led the way. At the top of the stairs she turned to glare at them, the real Connie Blakeman shining out of her eyes. 'If you've any sense you'll keep your mouths shut,' she hissed, her face looking garish in the halo of lamplight. 'I've worked long and hard to get where I am, and I don't mean to lose it all because of you two brats.' Leaning forward she held the lamp forward to look at them more closely. 'D'you understand what I'm saying?' She spat out the words.

Adam was not afraid. 'We understand.'

She looked him up and down. 'Quite the little gent, aren't you?' she sneered. 'And look at madam here.' She eyed Kathleen with a surge of grudging admiration. 'I'm buggered if she hasn't turned into a right little beauty.'

Kathleen met the hostile glare with indignation. 'We won't tell him about you,' she said, 'if you don't tell him about us.'

'What could you tell him about me, eh?'

'That you were our nanny and Father threw you out because you were no good.'

Adam knew more. 'I heard Cook say you and Father were

"dancing a pretty tune together". I didn't know what it meant then, but I do now.'

'Then you know enough to finish me here, don't you?'

'I think so.'

'And is that what you have in mind?'

'Not unless you give us reason.'

'I won't give you reason, you little bastard.' Her face was contorted with rage. 'Since your precious father threw me out, I've suffered some terrible times. I've travelled the length and breadth of this country, and I've skivvied in many a big house. I've cleaned boots belonging to people no better than me; I've scrubbed the spit off kitchen floors and I've taken care of brats that should have been strangled at birth. There have been times when I've almost starved.' She threw back her head and stared at the ceiling, and for one awful minute Kathleen was convinced she was crying.

The minute seemed to go on for ever. Just as Kathleen was about to ask if she was all right, she lowered her head and looked at them. 'I've had some bad times,' she said, her voice not quite steady, 'but I've picked myself up and I've done well. I've got prospects here. Mr Westerfield has respect for me. He pays me well, and who knows . . .' Suddenly she was the old Connie, grinning wickedly and making plans that once before had proved to be her downfall. 'One day, I might even fill his late wife's shoes and be mistress of this place.' She flicked a glance up and down the stairs. 'So think on, you two. I can be a good friend, or I can be a bad enemy. Give me trouble and you'll get more back than you can handle. Do you hear me?'

'We don't want trouble either,' Adam said.

'What about you, young madam?' She glared at Kathleen. 'Is he speaking for you as well?'

Kathleen nodded. 'We won't tell.'

IN THE EARLY hours, Adam was awakened by a commotion downstairs.

He got out of bed, flung on the robe which Connie had draped on the chair, and in a minute he was out on the landing, peering towards the stairway and thinking all hell had been let loose. There was a fierce row raging downstairs; shouting and swearing, and the sound of things being knocked about.

He was about to investigate further when a sound behind him startled him. When he saw that it was Kathleen, he visibly relaxed. 'What are you doing out of your bed?'

Tousled-haired and bleary-eyed, she was relieved to see him there. 'The dogs are going mad. It sounds like somebody's fighting down there.'

'I don't know what's happening. Go back to bed. I'll go and see.'

He might as well have saved his breath. Kathleen was not the sort to lie in bed while her brother investigated the row. She was too curious. Too rebellious. 'I'm going with you,' she stated, and he knew nothing he could say would change her mind.

Cautiously they made their way towards the head of the staircase. There was the sound of scuffling. 'Don't be a bloody fool, man!' That was Maurice Westerfield's voice, and he sounded furious.

Creeping along the landing, they stretched their necks to see over the top and down into the hallway. There were signs of a struggle: a vase smashed on the floor; a picture hanging crooked on the wall; and, directly beneath the picture, red stains on the wallpaper.

'That's blood!' Kathleen instinctively recoiled. 'Adam! There's *blood*. On the wall.'

'*Ssh!*' Putting a hand over her mouth, he drew her back. 'Be quiet. I don't want them to know we're watching.' Her big brown eyes stared back at him. She nodded, and he let her go.

At that moment there was a screech of laughter and a man's voice said, 'Don't care much for me, do you? Think I'm no good, don't you?' Another screech of laughter, followed by a curious silence. Even the dogs were stilled.

Connie Blakeman's voice could be heard asking, 'What do you want me to do, sir?'

Maurice answered, 'Help me get my son to his bed. There's little else we can do tonight.' In the background the barking of dogs could again be heard. 'Keep hold of him,' he said. 'I'd better quieten the dogs before they wake the whole house.' It took only a moment, and he was back. 'I've given them some food,' he said. 'That should keep them quiet.'

Up on the landing, Adam drew his sister away. 'Get back,' he whispered. 'They're coming up here.'

Crouched down against the balustrade they could see without themselves being seen.

Three people emerged from the drawing room; between Connie Blakeman on one side and Maurice Westerfield on the other slumped the limp form of a young man not much older than Adam. His head lolled and his thick mop of brown hair obscured his face. His jacket was open and his shirt smattered with blood.

'So that's his son,' Adam whispered. 'Doesn't amount to much, does he?'

'Is he dead?'

'Either that or he's so drunk he can't walk on his own two feet.' Disgust marbled his voice.

The trio were mounting the stairs now. 'Keep still,' Adam warned. 'Don't say a word.'

They had climbed only three steps when the young man suddenly threw out his arms and turned to face the hallway, as if performing to an audience. Loud and abrasive, he launched into a bawdy music-hall medley.

The awful racket made the dogs start barking again and Connie Blakeman smile, but Maurice Westerfield was beside himself with rage. Grabbing at his son's arm, he pulled him onwards. 'Have you no shame?' He glanced up, towards the bedrooms, his eyes momentarily closing in anguish when he saw his daughter standing at the top of the stairs. 'Go back to bed, Melinda,' he pleaded. 'There's nothing for you to worry about.'

Melinda's expression stiffened. Her brother's behaviour made her angry.

'Do as I say, Melinda,' Maurice called. 'Go back to your bed.'

She made no move, and continued to watch as, in a sudden convulsion, her brother threw himself towards the banister and spewed up the contents of his stomach.

While Connie ran to the kitchen to collect a mop and bucket, Maurice fought with his son, telling him what a useless being he was and wondering how he ever came to spawn such a creature.

Having seen enough, Melinda turned away, a look of utter disgust on her face. She had seen it all before and no doubt she would see it all again.

Out of the corner of her eye she caught sight of the two figures crouching there, shame-faced and at that moment wishing the earth would open and swallow them whole.

They waited for the recriminations, but there were none. Instead, Melinda softly laughed, regarding them with sly eyes, before walking away, quietly smiling.

Closing his eyes and gritting his teeth, Adam groaned. 'Damn! I wish she hadn't seen us.'

'She doesn't like us, does she?' Kathleen had sensed that from the first moment they met. 'She wants us out of here.'

'Well, she'll have to want on. This is her father's house. He was the one who invited us here, and so he should after almost killing you.'

'I've got a gash and a few bruises, that's all,' Kathleen reminded him.

'That's not the point. You could have been killed.'

'All the same, I'm not sure I want to stay here. If she put her mind to it, she could make our life a misery.'

'She could, I suppose. But we've got nowhere else to go,

and no one to help us. Maurice Westerfield has given us a roof over our heads. He's offered me a job, the chance to earn money and better myself. He's also promised to give you a good education. I'm buggered if we'll turn it all away because of that spoilt brat!'

Shocked to hear him swear, Kathleen regarded him with amazement. 'You *like* her, don't you?'

'Don't be silly.' All the same, he couldn't look Kathleen in the eye. 'She's about the same age as you are.'

'What does that mean?' She was remembering how much she had been drawn to Murray Laing. She recalled how her heart had lifted whenever she saw him, and how devastated she was when Adam had confirmed he was partly responsible for Markham's death.

'It doesn't mean anything in particular.'

'If you mean younger people can't be attracted to someone older, then you're very wrong.'

He knew she was thinking of Murray, and the guilt tormented him. 'Come on, sis.' He nodded down the stairs, where the trio were making headway. 'We'd better get back before anyone else sees us.'

Suddenly all hell broke loose. The young man began to yell and shout, fighting like a tiger when his father tried desperately to urge him forward. Barking frantically, the dogs sprang from nowhere. The big black one bounded up the stairway. Launching itself through the air, it landed with a thud on the young man's chest.

Startled, he lashed out at the dog, screaming abuse. With one mighty sweep of his arm he sent the poor animal flying through the air to land in a crumpled heap in the hallway below. The other dog trotted over to it and nudged it with its head, then sat, whimpering, beside it.

'You bastard!' Flinging his son aside, Maurice went down the stairs two at a time, but it was no good. He knew the dog was dead before he reached it.

White as a sheet, he made his way back upstairs. 'You drunken swine, you've killed the dog. He didn't deserve that.'

But there was no regret in the young man's eyes, no trace of compassion. 'One of these days, you'll get your dues,' Maurice vowed, and roughly shoved his son up the stairs as if he could hardly bear the sight of him.

Horrified, Adam and Kathleen crept swiftly to their rooms. 'Don't cry,' Adam said, seeing the tears flowing silently down his sister's face. He gave her a hug. 'We'd best stay clear of that one. He's as bad a lot as I've ever seen.'

Kathleen nodded.

'Don't think too much about what we've seen tonight,' he suggested. 'You have to try and put it out of your mind.' He smiled into her sad brown eyes. 'All right?'

She nodded again.

'Quickly then. Get to your room.'

'Goodnight, Adam.'

'See you in the morning, and remember what I said, try not to think about it.'

She hurried away. Witnessing that poor animal's death had made her sad and angry. Besides that, memories of Murray were breaking her heart.

Safe in her room, she climbed into bed and closed her eyes, but it was a long time before she gave herself up to sleep. In her mind's eye she could see the dog lying on the floor. She thought of the young man responsible. She wondered how he could have done such a terrible thing, and she recalled what Adam had said. 'He's as bad a lot as I've ever seen.' Adam was right. Adam was always right.

Her mind shifted back, to Markham, and Murray, and how he had left that helpless old woman lying on the floor, just like that young man had left the dog there. In that moment she wished Murray was here so she could tell him what a bad lot he was. Just like Maurice Westerfield's son.

'You lied to me, Murray,' she whispered. 'You're wicked too, just like they said.' She cried for a while, her heart hardening. 'I hate you for what you did to Markham,' she murmured. 'I'll never forgive you, as long as I live.'

Adam, too, was struggling with his emotions. Torn by his feelings, he paced the floor. 'How can I tell Kathleen?' he asked himself. 'Especially when I deliberately let her believe Murray was guilty? Because of it, she even gave his name to the authorities? Good God! It must have torn her apart to do that! If she was to find out what I'd done, she would despise me.'

Another thing plagued him. He was only just beginning to realise there was a very real possibility that Murray might be hanged.

There was no contentment for the master of the house, either.

After seeing his son to his room, Maurice Westerfield left his trusted housekeeper to undress him and put him to bed. 'I must bury the dog,' he told her. 'I'm very grateful for your help. I hope the events of this night will stay within these four walls.'

She smiled at him in that sly, seductive manner she had. 'You can trust me, sir,' she said.

And he did.

He fetched a spade and dug a grave for his dog beneath one of the cherry trees. Its companion stayed there, howling its lament into the night. When the task was done, he led the sorry animal into the house and then went back outside, to sit by the naked lady, a statue that had come with the house. Tall and elegant, with perfect limbs and coiled hair that resembled sleeping snakes, she looked down on him with cold arrogance.

'You're lucky,' he told the silent stone lady. 'You have no feelings. You can't be hurt, or shamed, and you'll never feel the loss of a loved one. You don't know what it's like to have a longing that you can't shake off, or to want affection so badly you can't sleep or work.'

His soft voice touched the night but had no effect on her; hard and unyielding, she continued to look down on him with unseeing eyes. The night closed in, deeper and darker, echoing with strange sounds, the clicking, whispering sounds of another world. A weird and wonderful world that came alive when humans slept.

He wondered what it might be like to feel nothing, to survey the world and not be part of it; never to be hurt, never to love, or hate.

He laughed softly. 'No,' he murmured. 'I'm the fortunate one.' He touched her hand, the stone fingers like ice against his skin. 'I'm alive. I don't envy you, because however hard life can be, it is also immensely precious.'

He moved away, walked awhile, and eventually returned to the house. He took the lighted lamp from the hallway table and carried it up to his room. On the landing, he paused to listen. There was no sound to disturb him. Satisfied, he went into his room and closed the door.

Inside the sanctuary of his own quarters, he went directly to the dresser where he looked at the painting above. It was of his late wife; young and strikingly beautiful, with her long, chestnut hair, pixie face and dark, smiling eyes.

Gazing on her face was a torment to him. 'I miss you, my love,' he murmured, his long, sensuous fingers reaching up to stroke her features.

The pain of remembering was too much. He put his head in his hands. 'I'm so alone,' he groaned. 'I have wicked thoughts, and I'm so ashamed.'

Sighing, he looked up at the portrait once more. In the halo of light from the lamp, she seemed almost to be alive. 'Have you seen her?' he asked softly. 'Have you seen the girl?' A small smile flickered over his face. 'When I first saw her, I thought I was looking at you. And when she spoke, she so reminded me of you, I could hardly breathe. She has that same soft manner, and a certain way of looking at me, with those familiar dark eyes. Oh, you can't know . . . It's as if I've been born again. It's as if you've come back to me. I can hardly wait for her to grow up. But I will wait. I can't let her go. I *won't* let her go. I'll make her happy. She'll learn to love me, I know. And I won't neglect our daughter, or turn out the son we brought into this world, though God knows he deserves nothing from me.' His voice grew hard. 'I have to love him because he's our son. But I can't like him.'

Thinking of Christian brought a shadow to his face. 'He shames us, my love. Our own son is like a stranger to me.' His kindly eyes glinted with unshed tears. 'I've been so sad,' he confessed. 'But now I've found a reason to go on. I look at the girl and my heart sings like a bird.'

He gazed on the face, as if waiting for it to smile, or answer, or give approval of some kind. But it remained passive, and in his heart of hearts he knew she would never smile on him again, or talk to him, or look at him with approval. He had never been able to accept that before, and it was something of a shock to him now.

'I know you're gone from me,' he murmured. 'And I will never forget you.' The smile lit his face. 'But if I have the girl, she can bring you closer. That's why I can't let her go.' He touched the features again; the eyes, the mouth, his fingers lingering there. 'Fortune sent her to me.'

Turning his back on the painting he looked out of the window, into the dark night. Into the future. For the first time in ages, he felt a surge of real hope.

PART FOUR

1868
THE LOVER

Chapter Twelve

THE SOUND OF her laughter sailed across the lawn, making him laugh too. 'It does my heart good to hear it.' Stroking the old dog at his side, he raised his eyes to a blue, unblemished sky. 'I'm a happy man,' he mused, 'and it's all because of her.'

Maurice Westerfield couldn't recall a time when the sound of Kathleen's laughter didn't echo round this house, or fill his heart with joy. 'It will soon be time,' he told the old dog. 'Next Saturday is Kathleen's eighteenth birthday. It shouldn't be too long after that before we're man and wife.'

The thought of putting a ring on her finger and the two of them exchanging marriage vows was a dream he had cherished ever since she had come to live here. More than that, the idea of her lying beneath him, naked and yielding, was enough to take his breath away. 'She knows nothing of my plans,' he murmured. 'Not yet. Soon though, very soon.'

At that moment, Kathleen came running round the corner, with Melinda hard on her heels. Screeching with laughter, they fled across the lawn towards the house. 'You cheat! You're not having it!' Kathleen called, and Melinda ran all the faster.

'Give it back!' she cried. 'It's mine!'

Excited by their antics, the dog scrambled to its feet and chased after them. He'd gone only a few paces when he decided it was all too much and lay down beside the willow tree. 'Come back, you silly old thing.' Maurice laughed aloud. 'I'm afraid you're a bit like me, too old and dignified for such carrying-on.'

Connie Blakeman's voice made him turn towards the house. 'The dog might be old,' she said kindly, 'but not you, sir.'

'Oh, I don't know. I'm in my fortieth year. Soon my bones will start to creak.'

'Your bones will never creak, sir,' she told him. 'You head a thriving business, and your energy outpaces many a younger man's.'

Maurice smiled and gestured for her to be seated. 'All the same,' he said, 'I must seem old to those young ladies, Kathleen and Melinda.' The thought worried him, and he was looking for reassurance. Connie's response did not really supply it.

'I hope you won't think me bold, sir,' she said, 'but I'm sure there are plenty of women who would give their eye teeth to have you walk beside them.' She certainly would. She would give her right arm if it meant she could have him and all his fortune. But she was no fool. The passing years were sapping her beauty. Her mother had been a beauty when she was young but she had aged before her time. Connie felt she was going the same way. In her early thirties, she thought she looked much older. Her breasts were not so round, not so firm. Her waist was beginning to thicken, and there were permanent shadows beneath her eyes. The days were long gone when she could count on her looks to snare a man. If she was to build a nice little nest egg for the future, it would be through her brains and cunning. Thankfully, these had not been dimmed by the flow of time.

Maurice was silent for a while. He seemed to have gone into a little world of his own. 'Would you like me to leave, sir?' Connie felt uncomfortable. She also realised he was looking at Kathleen with the eyes of a man in love. But then, she had seen him look at Kathleen like that before. At first it had bothered her, but not now. Now, she saw it as an advantage to herself. After all, if she couldn't snare the man, why not let Kathleen do it for her?

He returned his attention to her. 'I'm sorry. I was deep in thought.' When he smiled, like now, the years fell away from his handsome face. His gaze found Kathleen again. Having settled their differences, the two young women had resumed their croquet match. 'She's grown into a beautiful woman.' He spoke softly, almost as though he'd forgotten anyone else was there.

'Your daughter or your ward?' Connie asked slyly.

Startled, he jerked round. 'Well, of course they're both lovely, but in fact I was referring to Kathleen.'

'Yes, sir. She is a beautiful woman, with a quick, intelligent mind too. She does you proud, sir.'

'So do you, my dear.'

'Beg your pardon, sir?'

'Over the years, I mean. You've been with me ever since I bought this house, and I don't know what I would have done without you. There have been times when I've been at my wits' end, times when I might have thrown my son out bag and baggage and you dissuaded me.' He grimaced. 'Though, God forgive me, I often wonder whether I shouldn't have done it anyway.'

'Christian is stubborn, but I don't think he's bad, sir. Some children just take longer to grow up. I'm sure he'll make you proud of him one day.' Connie didn't believe that would ever happen. Christian Westerfield was not of the same mould as his father. He was clever, but the cleverness was of a devious, mercenary kind. Much like myself, she thought with amusement.

Maurice didn't believe it would ever happen either, and he changed the subject. 'I was thinking about Kathleen in particular,' he explained, 'because I was just now recalling the dreadful scenes when she first came here. For a long time, Melinda refused to accept her into this household, yet you managed to persuade her that the two of them could become good friends. I don't know how you did it, but you were right.' The two young women were now seated on a bench, deep in conversation. 'Look at them,' he remarked. 'Whoever would have thought it?'

Connie was delighted. 'You have a soft spot for Kathleen, don't you, sir?' Her best bet was to encourage it. In the long run, his infatuation with Kathleen might work to her advantage.

'Oh yes,' he answered. 'She means a great deal to me.'

'I can see that, sir.'

He looked at her consideringly, then took a deep breath and confessed, 'I mean to marry the girl.'

Connie could hardly contain her excitement. 'I'm not surprised, sir,' she said carefully. 'I've seen the two of you together, and I've always thought you would make a wonderful couple. It's plain you adore her, and, if you don't mind me saying so, sir, I believe she feels the same way about you.' What a liar you are, Connie Blakeman, she chided herself. Kathleen would run a mile if she knew what he had in mind.

He beamed with delight. 'Do you really think so? I honestly thought you would be shocked. I think most people would be if they knew I meant to marry her.'

'People will always stand in your way if you let them, sir,' she chirped. 'I mean, I've no doubt your own son and daughter might be against the idea.'

'Quite so. And probably Adam won't take kindly to it either. I'm sure he has ambitions for his sister, and they don't involve marrying her off to a man more than twice her age.'

'But surely, sir, such an important decision has to rest with you and Kathleen, doesn't it?' She laid the seed and watched it grow. 'I mean, a man like you makes powerful decisions every day. I wouldn't have thought you were likely to let others make this particular decision for you.'

At that moment the dog came ambling back and dropped at Maurice's feet. Bending forward, he tickled its ears, and Connie couldn't see his expression. 'I suppose it was very remiss of me to confide in you like this,' he said awkwardly.

'Not at all, sir. Not a word of it will ever be repeated.'

'I meet people every day, all kinds of people in all kinds of places. I travel the world and I'm never alone. But I'm always lonely.' He looked at her and smiled that wonderful smile of his. 'Does that make sense to you? Don't you think it odd that a man can be surrounded by people and yet still be lonely?'

'I'm a little like that myself, sir.' He had touched a raw nerve with his sad remark.

He sensed her pain and was immediately concerned. 'I hope I haven't upset you, my dear.'

'No. It's just that sometimes we forget old friends and family. A chance remark can bring it all back.' She was thinking of her estranged mother who had died some years back. She was thinking, too, of Kathleen's father, and how it had been between them. In her foolish girlish dreams, she had really believed he would always look after her. She must never make that mistake again.

'You know this family as well as I do,' he told her. 'I look on you more as a friend than a housekeeper.'

'Thank you, sir.' She knew now. Being a 'friend' was all she could ever hope for. To be a 'lover' would have been better. To be a 'wife' better still. However, a small bone was better than a big nothing. For now, anyway.

Seeing Kathleen and Melinda coming towards them, they stood up. 'I'm proud of them,' Maurice said. 'Considering they had no mother to raise them, they've turned out quite well, wouldn't you say?'

'They're a credit to you, sir.' There had been times during the past six years when she had hated the sight of them both. But that feeling had mellowed, and another took over; a feeling of superiority. She knew things they would never know. She had experience of life, and they were innocent babes. She soon learned she had no reason to fear them. Instead, she saw how she might worm her way into the master's good books by nourishing these two. And, to her satisfaction, it had worked. Maurice Westerfield valued her. He valued her opinion and, according to what he had just now said, he valued her as a friend. It wasn't much, and it wasn't what she had hoped for, but if she kept her wits about her, it offered a measure of power over them all.

'They're also a credit to you,' he told her. 'You have guided them well through some very difficult times.' He looked at her with a warm smile. 'You can't know how grateful I am.'

Oh, I do, she thought cunningly. And there'll come a time when I take my reward.

They watched the two young women approach, and he had eyes only for Kathleen. Connie saw this and secretly smiled. Through Kathleen she would get what she deserved. 'They look hot and tired,' she commented. 'Would you like me to arrange a cool drink for all of you, sir?' Always the good servant, always at hand, she thought slyly.

'That's an excellent idea,' he said, and she hurried away to her tiresome duty.

His face glowed with pleasure the closer Kathleen came. She was so beautiful. It wasn't a glamorous beauty, or a bold beauty. She was warm, and kind, and lovely at heart. Her long chestnut hair flowed behind her as she ran, and her eyes sparkled with the joy of life. When she laughed, as she did now, her teeth shone white and perfect in the summer sunshine, and her face lit with happiness. And yet, for all her generosity of heart, Kathleen had a fiery temper. She loved all animals and hated to see a less fortunate being hurt or used in a way that might cause pain or distress. When that happened, her temper caused sparks to fly.

Only that spring she had found Christian shooting rabbits caught in his traps; the wicked snares had maimed two baby badgers, one with its leg hanging off, the other spiked across its back. In danger of being shot herself, Kathleen released them and carried them back to the house. Maurice ordered Christian not to set any more traps, and he was furious at being slighted by the girl.

Lovingly, Kathleen tended the badgers until they were recovered enough to be returned to the wild. They never did completely leave her though. Even now, she would sometimes sit and wait by the kitchen door in the early hours, and the three of them would meet and renew their acquaintance. Once, Maurice saw them from his bedroom window, and he was captivated.

She championed the underdog, and he loved her for it. He loved her temper, and he loved her laughter. There was nothing she could do that would ever stem his love for her. Rightly or wrongly, he believed Kathleen was everything a woman should be. She was his late wife, his lover, his partner and his friend all rolled into one. The intensity of his devotion sometimes frightened him, for Kathleen had become his very life.

Melinda, too, delighted and surprised him. As a girl she had been too possessive of him; too quick to turn on anyone who threatened to come between them. Now she was more tolerant. She had taken to Kathleen, as he had. As everyone did. It gladdened his heart to see how they were the best of friends. Melinda was pretty in her own way, like a small, precious doll with her blue eyes and golden hair. Yet beneath that babyish appearance she could be hard and tough, even a bit of a bully when the occasion warranted. She was a good daughter, though.

'If only my son had turned out half as good as his sister,' he mused. 'But he's not like her, not like any of us. He's hard and peevish, with a wicked, selfish streak.' He sighed deeply. 'God only knows what's going to become of him.'

As the girls came on to the porch, he smiled and kissed first Kathleen, then his daughter. 'Sit with me,' he invited. 'Tell me what you've been up to.'

'Women's talk.' Bright with sweat, Melinda flopped into a chair.

'Your daughter's a cheat,' Kathleen teased. 'The ball wouldn't go straight for her, so she moved the course.' Hitching herself on to the rail, she winked at him, and his heart quickened.

'It's the only way I can win,' Melinda protested. 'She's too good for me.'

A small, brown-haired maid arrived with a tray on which was a huge jug of cordial and three glasses. Carefully she placed it on the low table before the chairs. 'Will there be anything else, sir?' As she looked up at Maurice, her face grew a peculiar shade of grey. It was all she could do not to burp in his face. That morning she'd had too much porridge, and it weighed on her stomach like a sack of coal.

'Are you all right?' Kathleen had seen the colour drain from the girl's face.

'Yes, miss. Thank you.'

Maurice gave her a curious look. 'A plate of sandwiches, I think,' he said, 'and three big slices of Cook's gooseberry pie.'

'With lashings of cream,' Melinda added. 'I've worked up a huge appetite.'

The maid hurried away, heading straight for the outer loo, to throw up the contents of her stomach. The thought of sandwiches and gooseberry pie, with lashings of cream, was the last straw.

From his comfortable wicker armchair, Maurice regarded the two young women. 'So.' He looked at his daughter but his mind was on Kathleen. 'Women's talk, eh? I don't suppose I'm allowed to know what it was about.'

Melinda tutted. 'No, you're not.'

'It was about my birthday,' Kathleen volunteered. 'Melinda wants a big, glamorous party, and I don't.'

'I see.' He was disappointed because his plans coincided exactly with those of his daughter. On Kathleen's eighteenth birthday, he wanted the biggest and finest party this house had ever seen; not least because he had another little surprise in mind. 'And what do you want, Kathleen?'

'Family,' she answered without hesitation. 'I just want my family round me. You and Melinda and Adam . . .' She hesitated. 'And Christian of course.' Even the mention of his name made her cringe. 'I thought maybe the servants could have a little party too.'

Melinda was horrified. 'Servants are for serving,' she retorted. 'Giving them a party would only embarrass them.'

Maurice seized on the idea. 'No, she's right,' he declared. 'Let them have a party.'

Kathleen was delighted. 'Do you mean it?'

'On one condition.'

'What's that?'

'You let me organise a big, wonderful party for you, and we'll invite everyone who wants to come.'

'I don't want a big party.' She hated crowds. If all the others could be here, she would not have hesitated – Markham, and Cook, John Mason, Nancy. But Markham was long gone. She had no idea whether the others were still in Blackpool. Adam had written to them, as he had promised, to reassure them that he and Kathleen were well and living in the south in some comfort. But he hadn't included a return address in his letter. Finding Connie Blakeman at Westerfield House had made him more cautious.

Maurice persisted. 'I thought you wanted the servants to have a party.'

'I do.'

'Well then. It's up to you.'

Kathleen thought of all those in the past who had cared for her. She hadn't been able to give them a party but there were others, here and now, who had also been kind; good, ordinary people who might never be fortunate enough to attend a party except as servants. Now she was being given the opportunity for them to have something special, away from their daily grind. 'All right,' she conceded. 'You can plan my party if Melinda and I can plan the servants' party.' She looked at her companion. 'You will help, won't you?'

Melinda was tempted to refuse, but then she changed her mind. 'I think you're mad, but it might be fun.'

Maurice was not convinced about the servants' party. In fact he was against it. But if it was the only way he could persuade Kathleen to have the party he wanted, where he could show her off to the world and maybe make that special announcement, then so be it.

'When shall we have this splendid party?' Melinda asked excitedly.

'When Adam comes home,' Kathleen said wistfully. These days he seemed always to be travelling and she missed him so.

Maurice came to stand beside her. 'He should be home by mid-August,' he said, placing a hand on her shoulder. 'I know it's hard for you when he goes away, but there are vast untapped markets abroad. Adam has taken to merchandising as if he was born to it. Tea, tobacco, silk or calico, it doesn't matter what cargo he buys, he makes us all a handsome profit.' If only my own son was as enterprising, he thought. But he wasn't, and never would be.

'Mid-August it is then.' Kathleen was beginning to look forward to it. 'Who will be your partner, Melinda?'

Melinda twirled on the spot, pretending to hold someone in her arms. 'I don't know yet,' she replied. 'But whoever he is, he'll be tall and impossibly handsome, and he'll dance like an angel.' She threw a look at Kathleen. There was mischief in her face, but also a hint of serious rivalry. 'And you'd better keep your eyes off him.' The trouble was, with Kathleen around, nobody looked at her. It was a sore point. 'What about you?'

Maurice froze. Did Kathleen have an admirer he knew nothing about? She had never shown any interest in any of the young men she had met through his business acquaintances.

Kathleen laughed. 'Don't be silly, Melinda. What do I want with a partner at my own birthday party?'

Maurice breathed a silent sigh of relief. I shall be your partner, he thought. For life.

Chapter Thirteen

I T WAS ALL ready.

On this glorious summer's day, the rhododendrons and hydrangeas provided a galaxy of reds and blues down the west side of the sweeping lawns. Placed along the east side and shaded by the old cherry trees were five long tables. Each was spread with a white cloth which hung to the ground and was laden with all manner of sumptuous food: whole fishes baked in their own juices; joints of pork and plump chicken; slices of ham off the bone, piled high and decorated with segments of orange. Strategically placed among the main dishes were dishes of nuts and sweetmeats, and little titbits to whet the appetite.

On the centre table stood a remarkable selection of desserts – jellies, trifles, scones aching with currants straight out of the oven that very morning, and the daintiest, prettiest fruit pies.

The beverage table boasted a splendid display of fresh fruit and a long array of silver coolers housing fine wines, some of which Adam had acquired on his travels, others brought from the wine cellars beneath the house. There was a huge crystal bowl filled to the brim with punch and hung with crystal cups. Beside this were numerous fruit juices, and, set aside on its own small table, a large urn with china cups and saucers for anyone who fancied a cup of tea.

'Wonderful!' Maurice had watched the preparations all day. 'All we need now is the music and the guests.' He looked at

Kathleen with adoring eyes. 'And you, my dear, the star of the evening, looking as lovely as ever.'

'I don't know about that.' Kathleen had been anxious about such a big event, but now her excitement grew with every passing minute. 'I've hardly had a wink of sleep this past week, what with Adam being caught up in rough seas and not knowing from one day to the next whether I'd ever see him again.' The fear momentarily shadowed her dark eyes. 'I was so afraid.'

'Understandably so.' He placed a comforting arm round her shoulders. 'When the report came in, I was afraid too,' he confessed. 'The sea is unpredictable. One minute it can be calm and beautiful, lulling you into a false sense of security, and in the next it can be wild and mountainous, and you know in your heart that your life is in her hands.'

'It sounds terrifying.' The thought of crossing vast oceans had always frightened her.

'It is.' He smiled, that handsome, winning smile of his. 'But there's something wonderful about the sea. She's magnificent and alive. Sometimes wild, yes – like any woman.'

'You love travelling, don't you, Maurice?' For a long time she had felt uncomfortable calling him by his first name, but that was what he had insisted on, and now she addressed him like an old friend. 'Doesn't the sea ever frighten you?'

'I'm a born sailor,' he replied, 'and after the thousands of miles he's travelled these past five years, your brother is as fine a sailor as any man I know.'

She was proud of Adam, and she said so now. 'You gave him a future, and I'll always be grateful to you for that,' she told him. 'We both owe you so much.' She laughed aloud. 'Oh, he does love the sea. He always comes home excited and raring to be away again. Last night he told me such wonderful tales, of India and America. He told me about the people there and the way they live, and oh, it sounds so wonderful.'

'Don't you ever want to see for yourself?' Lately he had been thinking of a honeymoon at sea. It would be wonderful to take her to those new and exciting lands.

She shook her head. 'No, thank you.' She was emphatic. 'You and Adam may love sailing the oceans, but I mean to keep my feet on firm ground. I wish I had Adam's pioneering spirit, but I'm just a homely girl at heart. Sails in the wind and a horizon that never seems to come closer is not really my idea of heaven.'

'What is your idea of heaven, Kathleen?'

For one strange, nostalgic moment Murray Laing came into her mind. Murray, with his laughing eyes and lopsided grin that filled her with joy. She would have given anything to have him near. But then she thought of Markham, and the image was gone.

'My idea of heaven is four walls about me and a floor that doesn't roll about when I move. It's a garden filled with flowers that waft their scents on a summer's breeze; where the bees flit from one blossom to another, where I can stroll and sit, and quietly think of the future. Heaven is sitting on a fallen tree in the woods and watching the animals at play. Heaven is a house to come home to, with a roaring fire in the winter and the windows flung open to the breeze in the summer. Above all, it's having the people I love all about me.' She moved away, her dark eyes thoughtful. 'It's not worrying about whether the sea will take someone away from you for good.'

He was deeply moved by her words. 'Are you really that afraid?'

'Of the oceans, yes.'

'You never told me.'

'I'm telling you now.' Suddenly her mood changed, and her smile was bright and bold as ever. 'I'm glad you've given Adam something that satisfies him. He has such a wonderful sense of adventure.'

'So have you.'

'Maybe.' Her mind flashed back to when she and Adam had had to fend for themselves, sleeping rough, wondering where the road would lead them. Those unhappy times would live with her for ever. Maybe it was the uncertainty of her past that made her want a certain future. Yet there were times when she felt like taking off and going where her heart led her. Unfortunately, her heart might take her straight to Murray Laing, and that would never do. 'I'm content enough for the moment,' she said. 'Adventure can wait.'

She laughed. 'Look at me! The guests will be arriving all too soon, and I'm not even ready. Adam and I stayed down talking well into the early hours. I expect he snored like an old dog when he went to bed, but I could hardly sleep for thinking about the party.' She tweaked her hair and grimaced. 'I'll probably look like a wreck by the time the first guests arrive.' Kissing Maurice fleetingly on the face, she ran indoors. 'See you later.'

Upstairs, she bathed, washed her hair, dried and brushed it until it shone. Then she hunted through the wardrobe, choosing a gown of darkest blue, with a slim neckline, pretty ruffled sleeves and a hem that danced when she walked. She brushed her cheeks with the merest flush of rouge and touched her lips with warmest pink. Finally she fastened a single string of pearls round her neck and slipped her small feet into her favourite blue shoes. Then she regarded herself in the mirror. 'Shadows under your eyes,' she tutted, 'but you'll do.'

With that, she ran out of the room and all the way down the stairs. 'What do you think?' she asked Melinda, who was ready before her.

'You look as if a good night's sleep wouldn't hurt,' Melinda answered flippantly.

'I ought to say the same to you,' Kathleen chuckled. 'But honestly, you do look lovely.' Her own dark-brown locks hung loose about her shoulders, but Melinda's golden hair was piled up and fastened with a silver comb. She wore a burgundy gown which fitted her dainty figure perfectly and showed more ankle than her father might think proper. 'Has anyone arrived yet?' Kathleen asked nervously.

Melinda shook her head. 'One or two early birds, but Father is keeping them entertained, I think. It would serve you right if they all arrived in a rush,' she teased. 'Imagine a hostess who wasn't there to greet her guests. The social circle would talk about you for weeks.'

Kathleen shrugged carelessly. Leading the way outside, she stood on the verandah, viewing the scene before her. 'I got ready as quickly as I could.'

'You're a fool, Kathleen.'

'Oh, and why's that?' She knew what was coming.

'If you hadn't insisted on the servants having a day off for this ridiculous party of theirs, Maisie would have been there to help you get ready.'

'I'm perfectly capable of getting myself ready.'

'It's so mean. I had to bring a stranger in to do my hair, and I really missed having my back scrubbed.'

'You should have called me.'

'And have the skin taken off?'

'Oh, stop moaning.' Kathleen looked on Melinda as a sister now. In the early days it had been very difficult, and at one stage she despaired of ever befriending her. 'Look.' She pointed to where servants were busy putting the finishing touches to the tables. 'The domestic agency sent us some good people, so everything's turned out all right.'

'Well, I agree with Father. The idea of servants having a party is shameful. On the same day as you have yours too! Whatever will the guests think?' The matter of the servants' party had been a bone of contention between them since it was first mentioned. 'We'll never live it down.'

Under constant pressure from Melinda, Kathleen had conceded one point. 'Since you insisted they should have their party two miles down the valley, our guests won't even know.'

'I should hope not!'

'Aren't you even the teeniest bit curious to know how they're getting on?'

'I have more important things on my mind.'

'Such as?'

Melinda hesitated, but she had to say something or burst. 'I have a secret.' Her devious smile alerted Kathleen.

'I knew it!' she cried. 'I just knew you'd been up to no good. Going out night after night when your father was away on business, and sneaking back at all hours. It's a man, isn't it? Come on! Own up, Melinda, you've got yourself a man, and he's such a bad lot you daren't let your father know about him.'

'Don't be silly.'

'What then?'

'You know what Father's like. He thinks there's no man on earth good enough for me.'

'This man, what's he like?'

'You'll meet him later.'

'Who is he?'

'Wait and see.'

'Is he here?'

'Not yet. About nine thirty, he said.'

'Is he good-looking? How old is he? He's not one of your father's pot-bellied friends, is he? What does he do for a living?'

'I said, wait and see.' Melinda giggled. 'I'll introduce you when he arrives. Meantime, I'm off to enjoy myself. There was a good-looking fellow down by the food tables just now. I might go and say hello.'

She never ceased to amaze Kathleen. 'Wait a minute! So you're not serious about this other mysterious man then?'

Melinda appeared to be shocked. 'I adore him,' she said softly. 'He's everything I want in a husband. He's wealthy and handsome, and he's generous with it. But, apart from all that, I really do love him. I've loved him for months now, from the first minute I saw him.'

'Months!' Kathleen wondered how she'd managed to hide it for so long. 'You've been seeing him as long as that?'

'It seems like for ever.' She smiled dreamily. Kathleen had never seen her like this before. 'He bumped into me when I rushed for cover in that dreadful rainstorm – middle of March, you remember, the wind blew some of the rooftops off and I was caught out in it. He took me into the hotel and bought me a drink to calm my nerves.'

'He sounds like a real gentleman.'

'He is.'

'If he is, and you love him, like you say you do, why in God's name are you still making eyes at other men?'

'It doesn't mean anything.' She was taken aback by Kathleen's condemnation. 'And anyway, tonight will be my last fling before I settle down. It frightens me, but once we're married, I won't cheat on him. Honest, Kathleen, I really do love him, and when I'm wearing his ring on my finger, I mean it, I'll never deceive him.'

'I know how to keep you out of mischief. Let's go and see how the others are getting on with their party.'

'What?' Her mouth fell open. She stared at Kathleen with horror. 'You mean the servants?'

'I want to make sure they have everything they need.' Cook had been working like a slave but, like everyone else, she was thrilled they were having their very own party. No one had ever given them such a treat before.

'You must be mad!' Melinda had no intention of making sure the servants had everything they needed. Her horror was replaced by relief when she saw a carriage approach. 'You can't go, your guests have started arriving. You'd better go and greet them. And do try and behave like a lady.'

'Yes, ma'am.' Kathleen gave a wonky curtsy.

Melinda had to laugh. 'Now, where's that good-looking fellow got to?' Kathleen's concern showed on her face. 'One last fling,' Melinda promised. 'That's all it is.'

'I wish you wouldn't. What if he arrives before you get back?' She had a bad feeling about Melinda's last fling.

'Don't worry. I'll be back before he gets here.' She took hold of Kathleen's hand. 'You'll like him, Kathleen. When you meet him, you'll see why I want to spend the rest of my life with him.'

Kathleen realised that Melinda really was serious. 'He must

be very special,' she said wonderingly. No man had come into her life that she cherished in such a way. Only Murray, and he was long gone.

'He is. Later on tonight, we mean to speak to Father and ask for his permission to be married. I know he'll say I'm too young and that we should wait, but I'm not a child. It's time I was married and responsible for my own life. I want my own home, and lots of children – we both do.'

'It sounds as if you've made your mind up, whether your father agrees or not.'

'I won't take no for an answer.' Winding her arm in Kathleen's, she said softly, 'I've found the man I want, and I won't let anyone or anything take him from me. He wants the same things I want, and I'll be happy with him, Kathleen, I know I will.' She sounded sure. Desperate even.

'Then don't go chasing after other men.'

'Just this once.' Bending forward, she whispered wickedly, 'In the long years ahead I might need a memory or two to keep me going.' She giggled like a naughty schoolgirl. 'I like to compare the men – if you know what I mean.'

Kathleen choked back her laughter. 'I know what you mean, and I think you're wicked.'

'Tonight will be the last time, cross my heart.' Making the sign of a cross on her breast, she rolled her eyes to heaven, as if offering a prayer.

They left the house and crossed the lawn, Kathleen to her guests, and Melinda to the Irish musicians who were still setting up with their fiddles and bows. 'We want soft music, until the wine starts to flow,' she ordered. 'After that, we'd like music to set the feet tapping.'

They knew what she meant, and exchanged a merry word or two when she departed. 'Be Jaysus! There's young stuff here.' One of the men caught sight of Kathleen talking to her guests. 'Sure, I wouldn't mind a dance with that little beauty.'

His colleague looked to where Kathleen was and he, too, was struck by her presence. With the sun playing on her long dark-brown hair, her tall, slim figure and lovely, laughing face, she was a desirable and sensuous woman. 'Hands off, Seamus,' the little flute-player muttered. 'Sure, she's a lovely lady but she's not for the likes of us.' And he should know, because hadn't he tried time and again to make it with the ladies?

'If you've been turned down afore, it's because yer an ugly ol' bugger,' Seamus quipped. 'I'm young and handsome, and there's where the difference lies, me ol' mate.' He puffed out his chest and drew in a noisy breath. If he did strike lucky today, it wouldn't be the first time he'd had his arms round a good-looking lady.

'Keep yer eyes on the job, Seamus, me ol' son.' That was the old fellow again. 'Sure, you'd be wise not to poke yer fingers – or anything else – where they don't belong.'

The young man laughed. He shrugged his broad shoulders, picked up his fiddle and started to play.

The music was enchanting. Music was his first love. Women came a close second.

Soon the party was in full swing, and much to her disappointment, Kathleen had no chance to see how the servants' party was faring. Deciding to slip away later, she poured her boundless energy into playing the dutiful hostess.

The music played and the wine flowed, and soon everyone was in high spirits. 'Are you glad I persuaded you to have a party?' Keeping an eye on the needs and pleasures of the many guests, Maurice's watchful gaze followed Kathleen wherever she went. He was never far away and once again she found him at her elbow when she turned.

'Oh, I am! I am! You were right, and I was wrong.' She hadn't had such a good time in ages. There were people here she had never met, and others whom she'd met at Maurice's business dinners. He liked to gather important men around him and show off his family.

Kathleen's eyes roved over the many people gathered for her party. 'How did you manage to persuade them to come?' she asked with interest. 'I don't know any of them well, and they don't know me.' Some of them looked as if they were ready for their last, long sleep. Yet there were others young and lively enough to make the party fun.

'Everyone loves a party,' he answered. 'And I wanted to make certain you were noticed.'

What he really wanted was for them to see his future wife and be filled with envy. He wanted them to know how beautiful and intelligent she was, and how excellent his judgement. But even if, for whatever reason, they disapproved of her, it would make no difference. He was painfully aware of the difference in their ages, and he knew she could probably have any man she wanted. The fact that she didn't seem interested in men in that way only fired his confidence. He knew also that his own son would be the first to condemn a marriage between himself and Kathleen. To hell with them all if that was the way they felt, he thought bitterly. He loved Kathleen too much to let anyone ruin his plans. He would take her for his wife, come what may. Even if Kathleen herself had her doubts, he would overcome them, somehow.

Kathleen's voice interrupted his thoughts. 'They're a mixed bunch, and no mistake.' When she was a child and Cook was preparing a dinner party for her father, Kathleen had heard the old dear make the same remark. Now here she was saying it herself. Strange, how you subconsciously mimicked someone you had lost, she mused.

Remembering was painful. Amusement turned to regret, and her spirit was dimmed for the moment.

'Kathleen?' Maurice had sensed she was a million miles away, and he felt left out. He didn't like that. 'What are you thinking, my dear?'

She forced a smile. 'Nothing. I was just looking at the guests, wondering who they all were.'

He chuckled. 'You're right,' he admitted. 'They are a mixed bunch.'

There were young merchants dressed in long coats and bright cravats; old men with young things on their arms and wallets bulging under their coats. There were a number of attractive, middle-aged women, all dressed to the nines, obviously on the loose for a man, and two newcomers to the merchant line, who, so Maurice informed Kathleen, 'had great promise'. They all threw themselves into the spirit of the party. The more they enjoyed themselves, the more Maurice smiled. While they were entertained, he could stay beside Kathleen – except now and then some daring young scoundrel would infuriate him by taking her on to the lawn to dance to the strains of an Irish ballad.

As the evening wore on, Kathleen became anxious. Adam had gone out to look for Christian and they weren't back yet. She sought out Melinda, to see if she knew anything.

'They're old enough to take care of themselves,' Melinda said haughtily. 'What's more, I'm enjoying myself too much to care about anybody else. Before too long my future husband will arrive, and I'll have to behave myself. Until then, I mean to make the most of it.' And, without further ado, off she went with a young man in tow.

Kathleen went in search of Maurice. 'Adam and Christian still aren't here, are they?'

'I shouldn't worry,' Maurice told her. 'Adam's a sensible young man. I'm sure he'll find Christian without getting himself into any kind of trouble.' He didn't say so, but he was in fact concerned about the kind of places his son frequented and the shady people he seemed to know. He glanced at his pocket watch. 'It's almost nine,' he said. 'I'll give them an hour. If they're not here by then, I'll go looking for them.'

'I'll come too.' It wasn't like Adam to miss her birthday party. She was worried about him.

'You'll do no such thing!' Maurice glanced around at the many people chatting, laughing and dancing, all of them happy to be here. 'In half an hour you must stop the music and send the people towards the food tables. It's your birthday party, Kathleen, and your place is here. As I said, if your brother and Christian aren't back in an hour, I'll go and find them. On my own. All right?'

Kathleen nodded, but she wasn't reassured.

At a quarter past nine, she decided to take her mind off Adam by going to see how the servants' party was faring. 'I'll walk you there,' Maurice said at once.

'No. I'd prefer to go on my own,' she said gently. 'I'll only be gone a short time. I can run there and run back, and while I'm gone you can make sure no one misses me.' She needed to get away. She needed a few moments' peace and quiet, under God's quiet sky.

'As you wish.' Clearly, he was disappointed. 'Later, when your brother and Christian appear, I'll find a moment to pay a call myself. After all, it's only courteous.'

Her answer was a peck on the cheek, and before he could say anything else, she lifted her hem and set off at a run. In a moment she was gone from his sight. 'Hurry back,' he whispered.

Kathleen sped over the meadow and across the small brook that ran between the two fields. Here she sat and caught her breath, feeling exhilarated and happy, and wonderfully free. 'It's not that I don't like parties,' she told a curious water rat disturbed by her arrival. 'It's just that sometimes I feel hemmed in.' Leaning back on the wooden strut of the bridge, she wished Adam hadn't gone looking for Christian. 'That one is bad, through and through.'

There it was again, that awful sense of dread. 'I'd best get a move on,' she muttered, taking off again. 'Whether Maurice likes it or not, I'm going with him to find Adam.'

She could hear the music ahead of her, and she could hear the music behind. The two different, distant strains of melody made a weird, haunting sound.

Quickly now, she ran past the big barn, pausing when she thought she heard something inside. 'Rats,' she muttered, going on across a field. 'The little devils are everywhere.'

Inside the barn, Melinda giggled. 'You'd best hurry up,' she told Seamus. While he took down his trousers, she slipped the silver watch out of his pocket. In the light of the moon through the open window, she could just make out the time. 'It's quarter past nine already. I must be back by half past.'

'Won't take me long,' he panted. 'Open yer legs, there's a good girl.'

'Don't be too quick, though, will you? I don't want it to be over before I've had my money's worth.'

'Will twice do you then?'

'Three times if you've the energy.' She laughed out loud, and then sighed with pleasure as he rolled on to her. A series of groans and squeals was followed by a long, exquisite, shivering sigh.

***

K ATHLEEN WAS WELCOMED with open arms. 'Oh, miss, it's wonderful!' Cook was merry on cider. 'I ain't never had such a rousing time since we buried Uncle Willie.'

Accepting a glass of Cook's homemade rhubarb wine, Kathleen was glad to stay awhile. She emptied the glass and was warmed through. She ate a generous helping of chocolate cake and tapped her foot to the tune of an accordion. With regret she realised she ought to get back. 'Mr Westerfield will be calling on you later,' she said, though they were too merry to care. 'I'll try and get back too.'

With that she was off again, running across the field, though maybe not as fast as when she came because now she was full of rhubarb wine and chocolate cake. 'Serves you right,' she chuckled, resting by the big barn. 'You shouldn't have had such a big slice.'

Suddenly she was aware of noises coming from inside the barn. 'That isn't rats,' she whispered. 'There's somebody in there.'

Softly, she crept up to the window and stretched her neck to see over the ledge. The sounds intensified. She could tell there were two people, one groaning as if in pain and the other making small unintelligible sounds. 'Sounds as if some poor devil's being murdered.' Afraid yet determined to help if she could, she put her two hands over the ledge and drew herself up. Peeping over the top, she couldn't believe her eyes.

The man was facing her but he was too far gone to know she was there. Rising and falling in a frenzy, he pushed in and out of the woman, holding her legs wide apart while she gripped his bare buttocks. As his movements grew more feverish, the sweat dripped down his face on to her bare breasts, his face creased with arousal.

Suddenly he reared up, pushing hard into her with the whole of his body, and as he did so his eyes opened and he looked straight into Kathleen's shocked eyes. 'Jaysus, Mary and Joseph!' In an instant he was on his feet, his member sticking out like a ramrod, his eyes bulging with disbelief. 'It's a Peeping Tom! Sure, we've a bloody Peeping Tom looking through the window!' Panic-stricken, he snatched up his trousers, and while he hopped about trying to get them on, his still-swollen member getting in the way of his buttons, Melinda swung round.

She gasped with shock to see Kathleen at the window. 'What the hell are you doing here?' she demanded. 'Bugger off!'

Kathleen had no intention of 'buggering off'. 'Get out of there this minute!' she cried, and ran round the side of the barn to the door. 'I don't know who your man is,' she yelled, 'but he'd better be the one to bugger off and quick, because your husband's on his way.'

The man came rushing out, carrying his coat and shoes. 'Run for your life!' Kathleen cried. 'Her husband's got a temper like a mad bull, and a loaded shotgun too. If he catches you, you'll never be able to enjoy another woman, I can promise you that.'

By the time Melinda emerged, red-faced but fully dressed, Seamus was out of sight. 'You bitch!' She wasn't pleased. 'You spoiled it all. What did you want to do that for?'

'To stop you from going to your "special man" carrying someone else's baby.'

'That won't happen.'

'How can you be so sure?'

Melinda wouldn't meet her eyes. 'That woman on Albert Street has potions,' she said evasively.

'Oh, Melinda! Things like that are no good. They might even do you harm. What if they don't work?'

Melinda was silent.

Afraid for her, Kathleen pleaded, 'Please, Melinda. Promise me you won't use anything like that again.'

Melinda straightened her corset. 'I don't need to promise,' she replied slyly. 'I've already told you, from now on I'm saving myself for my future husband, and we both want a whole lot of children.' She regarded Kathleen warily. 'He's not really looking for me, is he?'

'Not as far as I know.' Putting her hand beneath Melinda's elbow, she propelled her forward. 'But he will be if you don't get back.' As they hurried away, Kathleen glanced over her shoulder. 'Who was that man, anyway? The last time I saw you, you were with one of your father's promising young men.'

'Not my cup of tea.' Melinda grinned. 'The Irishman knew what I wanted.'

'I know I've seen him somewhere before. Who was he?'

'Seamus, the musician.'

'Of course.' Now she remembered. 'I saw him earlier, making eyes at the women. Just now, though, it was hard to recognise him. I mean, it was difficult to look anywhere else but . . . down.' She had to ask, 'Are *all* men as big as that?'

Melinda turned to stare at her. 'You mean you've never seen a man's . . . *thing* . . . before?' When Kathleen shook her head, she gasped. 'Good God! You don't know what you're missing!'

The image was still alive in Kathleen's mind. 'I couldn't very well miss *his*, could I?' she chuckled. The chuckle grew into a laugh, and suddenly the whole incident seemed wildly funny. Soon she was bent double, tears of laughter streaming down her face. 'Did you see him trying to get his pants on?' she cried.

The humour of the situation hit Melinda too, and as they went on their way, the sound of their laughter echoed across the valley.

In the far field, Cook took another swig from her cider jar. 'Did you hear that?' Trying desperately to keep her balance, she informed anyone who was interested, 'That was the first cuckoo.' She then keeled over and had to be carried away to sleep it off.

M AURICE DIDN'T HAVE to go out after Adam and Christian. 'They turned up five minutes after you'd gone,' he told Kathleen.

Melinda's attention was on the milling guests. 'He isn't here,' she said distractedly, 'and it's gone half past nine.'

Maurice was curious. 'Who isn't here?'

'A friend,' she said. 'Someone very special to me, Father, and I so much want you to meet him.'

'Him?' This was the first he'd heard of it. 'And who is this friend?'

'You'll like him,' she answered warily. 'You'll all like him.'

'I think you and I had better have a talk. Who is he, and when did you meet him?' He could recall no mention of a young man in Melinda's life; though she had so many friends, it was difficult to keep track. However, this one sounded different.

'You can ask him all your questions when he gets here,' Melinda said. 'Please be patient, Father.'

Hoping to distract Maurice, Kathleen said, 'I can't see Adam and Christian anywhere.'

'They're both inside,' Maurice told her. 'Unfortunately, Christian is hopelessly drunk and Adam is freshening himself up. I'm afraid there was a skirmish. Christian was with some undesirable people. Apparently he owes them money – gambling debts or some such trouble. Adam insisted they turn him loose and was caught up in a fight.'

Kathleen turned, intending to hurry into the house. She stopped at the sight of her brother emerging from the drawing room. 'Adam! Are you all right?'

He came and hugged her, just like he used to when they were small and she was frightened. 'Still worrying about your big brother, sis?' Adam had grown into a very attractive young man. He hadn't changed much, except he was taller, and broader, and his thick, fair hair was longer than he used to wear it. His eyes especially hadn't changed. They were still the same darkest blue, clear and honest, and now they crinkled in a smile. 'Haven't had a good fight in ages,' he laughed. 'It never ceases to amaze me where Christian finds these people. They're all muscle and mouth.'

'You shouldn't keep putting yourself in danger for him.' Kathleen found it hard to feel charitable towards Christian. She still hadn't forgotten their first night at this house when Christian had caused the death of that lovely dog. 'Just look at you.' She reached up to the swelling on his face.

'It's just a bruise.'

Melinda met his gaze. 'You could have been knifed, or kicked to death in the street,' she said. 'He wouldn't have cared.'

Adam looked at her for a long, intimate moment. He loved Melinda. He had always loved her, even that first night when she saw them hiding on the stairs and looked at them with contempt. But she didn't love him, and so he kept his silence. 'Christian is Christian. Bad as he is, we can't leave him to the wolves.'

'You may not be prepared to leave him to the wolves, but I am,' Melinda retorted. 'It's what he deserves. He's a no-good drunkard, and he doesn't care what happens to any of us, especially Father, and God knows he's caused him enough pain over the years.'

Maurice hated to see what his own son was doing to his family, but he had given up. He had tried everything and now he found it easier to turn a blind eye. 'Don't think like that,' he begged. 'It doesn't solve anything.'

Melinda's eyes blazed with anger. 'What am I supposed to think?' she demanded. 'I'll tell you, shall I? I think he'll never be any good, and I think he'll drive you into an early grave, that's what I think. And I wish to God he was dead. Do you hear me, Father? I wish he was dead!' Breaking into a sob, she ran into the house.

Kathleen would have followed but Maurice caught hold of her arm. 'No,' he murmured. 'Stay with your guests.' He turned to Adam. 'Please, Adam.' He felt old, and haggard. Christian always did that to him. 'Will you go to her?' Adam was more of a son to him than his own. It had been his dearest wish that Adam and Melinda might get together. But it didn't seem as if that would happen now. He consoled himself with the thought that at least they were the best of friends.

Adam nodded and went after Melinda.

'They didn't see Christian,' Maurice told Kathleen. 'The guests, I mean. They didn't see him drunk. I managed to get him out of sight and up the stairs before anyone realised.'

Kathleen's heart went out to him. 'I'll talk to him tomorrow,' she promised. 'Maybe he'll listen to me.'

'My son listens to no one.'

Kathleen had seen the truth of that time and again. Always at the root of any trouble, he seemed beyond redemption. 'I'm sorry,' she said, and she really was.

'You're a good person, Kathleen.' Taking hold of her hand he softly kissed it. 'What would I do without you?' The answer, he knew, was that he would shrivel and die.

She smiled brightly. 'No frowns please. It's my birthday party and I want everyone to be happy.' She was immensely fond of this kindly man, and it hurt her deeply to see what his son was doing to him.

'I wouldn't spoil your party for the world,' he said.

'Come on then.'

'Lead on, my beauty.'

They went down the steps and across the lawn to the dancing area, where Maurice caught her to him in a waltz. All eyes turned to them. 'Look at them,' he said, his head high, his handsome face wreathed in a proud smile. 'There isn't a man here who wouldn't swap places with me now.' Winking at her, he chuckled, 'Let them wait.' He swung her round with panache, declaring firmly, 'It's *my* turn to dance with the birthday girl.'

As they danced, Kathleen caught sight of a group of women watching them. And *they* wouldn't mind changing places with *me*, she thought wryly.

U P IN HER ROOM, Melinda stared out of the window, watching her father dancing with Kathleen, and wishing she could be out there enjoying herself too. Her father had been very attentive towards Kathleen this evening. He always was, but tonight Melinda couldn't help but notice his love for her shining in his face. She had long suspected that her father's feelings towards Kathleen were more than simply paternalistic; now she was convinced. She was both shaken and pleased. It might be a good thing if her father's attention was taken up with Kathleen, especially just now.

She gazed miserably out of the window. Oh, where was he? *Why* wasn't he here? 'Maybe he doesn't want me any more,' she mused worriedly. 'Maybe he's changed his mind about getting married.' The thought was unimaginable.

There was a tap on her open bedroom door. 'Am I welcome?' Adam asked, poking his head round. 'Or would you rather be left alone?'

Melinda wiped her eyes. 'Of course you're welcome,' she said. 'Come in, Adam.'

He entered the room but kept his distance. This was the first time he'd been in her room, and he felt stupidly self-conscious. 'I came to take you back to the party.'

'In a moment,' she said. 'Come and stand beside me.'

He crossed the room and stood so close she could feel his warm breath on her face.

'What's wrong?' he asked. He had come to know her very well, and he sensed her unhappiness wasn't only because of Christian. 'If there's something troubling you, I wish you'd tell me.'

She laid her head on his shoulder, taking him for granted, as she had done ever since he had come to live in her father's house. 'You're a good friend, Adam,' she murmured. 'You're always there when I'm in trouble.'

'Are you in trouble now?'

She drew away. 'No, of course not. Forget I said that.' She pressed her nose to the windowpane, her blue eyes still searching. '*You* wouldn't let me down, would you, Adam?'

'Never!'

'You wouldn't arrange to meet me and then not turn up?'

'You know I wouldn't do such a thing.' He swallowed hard. 'Is it a man?'

She nodded but didn't look at him.

'Is he special, Melinda?' He held his breath, letting it out in a gasp when she answered truthfully.

'I love him, Adam. I really love him.' She turned to him and her eyes were shining. 'Oh, Adam, I can't wait to be his wife.'

He took a moment to compose himself. 'Does he feel the same way about you?'

'Oh, yes. He was coming to the house this very night, to ask Father if we could be married.' She didn't see how her words tore him apart. 'But he isn't here. He told me half past nine, and he still isn't here!' She gabbled on, 'Oh, Adam, if he doesn't want me any more, I'll throw myself in the river. He has to come for me. He *has* to!'

She would have gone on, but she glanced out of the window and there he was, striding towards the house. 'Oh! He's here! Adam, he's here!'

Screaming with delight she ran out of the room and down the stairs, alight with joy, laughing as she ran into his arms.

From the window, Adam saw it all. 'I've lost you,' he whispered brokenly. 'I've missed my chance.'

He lingered there a moment longer. 'You're a lucky fellow,' he murmured, his gaze falling on the man below. 'I hope you know how to take care of her.'

Suddenly his face paled. 'My God!' He pressed closer to the window, his eyes wide as he took in the man's face; older, yes, and more lined with experience, but there was no doubting who it was.

The man Melinda was walking towards the house with was Murray Laing.

Chapter Fourteen

MELINDA GATHERED HER father and Kathleen together in the drawing room. 'Stand there, and don't move,' she told them. 'I've got a surprise for you.' As she ran out, the sound of her laughter made them smile.

'What's she up to now?' Maurice wondered.

'Whatever it is, she's happier than I've ever seen her.' Kathleen suspected she was about to produce her boyfriend. 'Be kind to him,' she whispered to Maurice. 'She really likes this one.'

Maurice smiled. 'I see. It's him, is it? All right, I'll be kind, but he'd better be good enough for her. I'll soon know if he's not.'

They were still smiling when Melinda came back in. 'This is Murray Laing,' she told them. 'We've been courting for two months.'

Kathleen heard the name and her heart skipped a beat. The smile slid from her face and she could hardly breathe. She was looking straight at him, and still she couldn't believe what she was seeing: Murray Laing, the man who was responsible for Markham's death, right here, in this house, looking at her as if he, too, couldn't believe what was before him.

'Murray?' Her whisper was heard only by Maurice, who glanced curiously at her.

'Do you two know each other?' he asked, addressing Kathleen.

Kathleen opened her mouth to speak, but Melinda answered first.

'Of course they don't!' she said. 'It's the first time Murray's been to this house.' Neither Kathleen nor Murray corrected her. 'Well? Aren't you going to welcome him, Father?'

'I think you both owe me an explanation.' He was a man of principle, a man who valued the old traditions and who expected his daughter to do the same. 'You say you've been courting for two months. I don't recall anyone asking my permission.' His back stiffened. 'What have you to say for yourselves?'

His question was directed at Murray, who met his gaze coolly. 'We owe you an apology, sir.' Before he could say more, Melinda again intervened.

'It's my fault, Father. Murray insisted I should tell you, he even threatened to call on you without my knowledge, but I begged him not to.' She looked at her father with those big blue eyes. 'Please don't be angry,' she begged. 'I do so want you to like each other. You *must*. You really must!' There was desperation in her voice.

'Oh?' Maurice raised his eyebrows. 'And why is it so important that we like each other?'

'Tell him, Murray. Please tell Father what we planned.'

Hesitating now, his glance going nervously to Kathleen who stood white-faced and motionless, he confessed, 'Melinda and I had a mind to be married, sir, with your permission of course.'

'I see.' Maurice's voice was authoritative, his manner stern, though in truth he had taken an instinctive liking to Murray who appeared to be prosperous and well mannered. It was painful, but he had come to compare every young man with his own son.

'You have to say it's all right.' Melinda was growing nervous. 'Please, Father.'

Maurice's face stiffened. 'You'd better come through to the library.' He ushered them both towards the door. 'Excuse me, my dear,' he said to Kathleen. 'I'm sure this won't take too long.'

The moment before he left the room, Murray glanced at Kathleen. It was a forbidden moment but later, when the shock of seeing him subsided, she held that moment in her heart, and, through all the years to come, it never left her.

———•◦•———

CONNIE BLAKEMAN WATCHED Kathleen slowly leave the drawing room and go into the garden. Connie hadn't joined the other servants at their party; somebody had to oversee the people the domestic agency had sent, and as she had made no real friends among the other servants she was quite happy to do so. She had spotted Melinda run out of the house to throw herself into the arms of a stranger. Her curiosity aroused, she had followed them back inside, where she had seen and heard everything from her vantage point in the shadows of the hall. She was delighted to learn that Melinda was hoping to be married. It all fell in very nicely with her own plans. With Melinda out of the way, she would have a freer hand. But she was puzzled by Kathleen's reaction.

'Strange,' she mused, a look of cunning on her still-attractive face. 'She didn't seem too delighted by Melinda's happy news. I should have thought she'd be overjoyed because, when all's said and done, they have turned out to be the best of friends.'

In her mind, she ran over the scene she'd witnessed. 'Come to think of it, there was a moment when Maurice thought Kathleen and that fellow knew each other.' A devious little smile crept over her features. 'I wonder.'

———•◦•———

ADAM FOUND KATHLEEN standing apart from the party guests, beneath the cherry trees. Drawing close, he saw how distressed she was; her face was turned to the sky and tears were rolling down her cheeks. He took her hand in his. 'Come and sit with me here.' As she meekly followed him to a bench beneath the trees, he breathed a silent sigh of relief. It seemed Murray had not yet said anything which might cause

235

Kathleen to question the circumstances surrounding Markham's death. 'I'll get us a drink,' he suggested. It wasn't just his sister who needed a drink. 'We have to talk. Stay right there.'

Adam had waited upstairs in an agony of suspense and turmoil while Melinda introduced the man she intended to marry to her father and Kathleen. Pacing up and down, he had prayed that whatever happened, Kathleen would not find out he had deceived her about Murray's role in Markham's death. How in God's name had the man found them? Did Melinda know he was an ex-convict? No, surely not. That wasn't the sort of information he'd be likely to divulge to anybody, let alone the daughter of a wealthy household he was hoping to marry into. Did he want revenge? Of course he did, but was he using Melinda as a means to achieve it, to gain her father's trust and then tell him he'd taken a couple of liars into his house, hoping they'd be thrown out in disgrace? Or did he just see Melinda as a route to easy money? In his well-tailored suit and polished brogues he didn't look short of money. Adam shied away from the thought that Murray might genuinely love Melinda. There was harsh justice in the fact that he should lose the woman he loved to a man he had wronged so utterly. And there was cruel punishment in the knowledge that if Kathleen found out the truth, he would lose her, too. What he had done to Murray, and to Kathleen, was unforgivable. But Murray didn't know Markham had cleared him of all blame. And in that, Adam thought, lay his only hope.

Seated on that bench, in the twilight of a beautiful evening, Kathleen tried to come to terms with seeing Murray again. Alone in that quiet corner, she thought how far away her childhood seemed. She recalled growing from child to woman, a slow, surprising change, when powerful emotions seemed to chase away all else. She remembered when she first saw Murray, the tousled-headed boy with the wide, cheeky grin and laughing eyes.

In all her memories one thing stood out above all others. She believed she had put it all behind her, but now it rose before her like a phantom from the past. Her love for the boy who was now a man was stronger than ever. Now, that man was in love with Melinda, and Kathleen was bitterly torn between the two.

Could she let Melinda marry him? Or should she tell her the dreadful thing Murray had done? If she came between the two of them, Melinda would hate her. Then again, if she didn't tell Melinda and later it was discovered that she had known all along that Murray was responsible for an old woman's death, Melinda might still hate her. Love was a powerful thing. It made people blind to the faults of others. Kathleen knew that better than most. She had named him as a murderer to the police and yet, God forgive her, she still dreamed of being in his arms.

Adam returned with a cordial for her and a whisky for himself. He sat beside her and told her he had seen Murray with Melinda in the garden. 'I've never said anything, but I had hoped Melinda and I . . .' He took a gulp of his drink. 'I'm a bloody fool!'

Kathleen laid her hand on his. 'I've always known you love her,' she murmured. 'I'm so sorry, Adam.'

'What are we going to do about *him*?' He jerked his head towards the house.

Kathleen knew what she must do. Despite her own feelings, she was determined not to flinch from it. 'There's only one thing we can do,' she said sternly. 'Melinda has to be told. We owe her that much at least.'

He was afraid. 'Wait until he's gone,' he pleaded. 'Don't tell Melinda in front of him. He might lie, worm his way out of it.'

'What's wrong with you?' She couldn't understand him. 'There's no reason to wait. He can lie all he likes, but the truth will out, and Melinda will know the kind of man she wants to live with for the rest of her life.' She recalled Melinda saying those very words. 'Come with me or stay here. It's up to you.' She put her glass on the ground and stood up. But she had no chance to carry out her intention because Melinda came running across the garden.

'Father said yes!' she laughed. 'Murray and I are to be married, as soon as it can be arranged.' She threw herself into Kathleen's arms. 'Oh, Kathleen, isn't it wonderful?' Running to Adam, she kissed him full on the mouth. 'Be happy for me, Adam,' she said. 'Say you'll be best man. Please.'

Taking her by the arms, Kathleen made her sit down. 'Are you really saying your father has agreed you can be married?' She couldn't believe it. Maurice had been so guarded when he went into the library with the two of them. 'I was sure he'd insist you court a while longer before making any decision.'

Melinda shook her head. 'He was all for it. Murray and I are to be married as soon as arrangements can be made.'

Suspicions were already stirring in Kathleen's mind, but it was Melinda's secret little smile that gave it away. 'Oh no!' Kathleen closed her eyes in anguish. 'You're with child, aren't you? *That's* why your father's agreed. That's why he wants it done as quickly as possible.' Her heart sank. How could she tell Melinda now?

'The doctor says I'm almost two months pregnant.' She proudly stroked her stomach. 'And you can't even notice.'

Adam was so shaken by the news, he stared at Melinda as if seeing her for the first time. 'You shame yourself,' he said coldly. 'You shame us all.'

Melinda pouted. 'I'm sorry you feel like that. I was sure you of all people would stand by me.'

Kathleen drew her aside, whispering so only Melinda could hear. 'Is Murray really the father?'

'I swear! If it wasn't Murray's, I wouldn't be marrying him.' She looked the picture of offended innocence. 'You do believe me, don't you, Kathleen?'

Against her better instinct, Kathleen nodded. Her reward was a hug and a kiss. 'I must get back to him,' Melinda declared, and ran off as merrily as she had arrived.

'Maybe you deserve each other,' Kathleen murmured.

The knowledge that Melinda had been fornicating with another man that very evening even though she was already pregnant by Murray nauseated her. But then, she wasn't at all certain that Melinda was telling the truth when she swore that the baby was Murray's.

'Well,' said Adam bitterly, 'you can't tell her now, can you? The bastard's made her with child, and there's nothing we can do.' He drank his whisky and went for another, leaving Kathleen alone.

She wasn't alone for long. Soon a group of guests joined her, and for the next hour she was caught up in their laughter and chatter.

Midnight came, and the guests began leaving, each one searching out Kathleen to thank her for a lovely evening. Maurice was nowhere to be seen, and she explained he had been unexpectedly called away on a family matter.

By one o'clock the guests had all gone, and still there was no sign of anyone emerging from the library. 'Now the work really starts.' Connie Blakeman marched by with her little army of servants in tow. 'You there, and you, clear the tables and then fold the cloths,' she instructed quickly organising the clean-up.

Kathleen went in search of Adam. She hadn't seen him since Melinda had told them her shocking news. She eventually found him by the brook, seated on the grass, his back to a tree trunk, his head in his hands. Beside him was a half-full jug of ale. 'Adam!' She ran down the grassy bank to him. 'I've been looking everywhere for you.'

'Well, now you've found me.' He looked up at her and his face was haggard in the moonlight. 'I know she has lovers and I'm insanely jealous, but I was sure in the end I would have her all to myself. She's a bitch, isn't she?' His voice rose and the words slurred. 'No! She's wonderful and lovely, and I want her so much it hurts. Can you believe that, sis? Can you believe I would still want someone like that?'

Kathleen believed it, for didn't she feel exactly the same way about Murray?

Folding herself beside him, she entreated, with a world of love in her voice, 'I know exactly how you feel, but it won't help to get drunk. Come inside, Adam. Get a good night's sleep. In the morning you might see things differently.'

He was crying like a child now. 'Oh, sis! I've lost her. Sleeping or waking, nothing can change that. Melinda's gone, and I want no one else.'

She put her arm round him and he laid his head on her shoulder. 'Tell her,' Kathleen suggested. 'Tell her how you feel.'

'No. I can't do that. Not now. Maybe I should have done it a long time ago, but not now. Not when she's carrying another man's child. Besides, if she had ever loved me, I'd have known. I suspect the plain truth is, Melinda sees me only as a substitute brother.' He laughed wryly. 'God knows, she needed a better one than Christian.'

He drank deeply from his ale jug. 'Leave me. I don't want anyone near me right now, not even you, sis.' Especially not you, he thought, because now I know how you must have felt when you lost Murray. 'I have things to sort out in my mind.'

'What things?' She didn't want to leave him here, so close to the brook, in his sorry condition.

He waved the jug in the air. 'The wedding, of course! I need to think about Melinda's wedding. Have you forgotten I'm to be best man?' He laughed and spluttered, choking on his words.

'There may not be a wedding.' The cool firmness of her voice made him stare.

'What do you mean?'

'Being the kind of man he is, Maurice is bound to make inquiries into Murray's background. He'll dig deep. Money won't matter, you know that. Melinda is precious to him, and there won't be a stone left unturned. Once he learns the truth, he'll know what to do for the best, I'm sure.'

'Does he realise we knew Murray before?'

'I don't think so.' As far as she could tell, Murray had kept silent about that, and no wonder, she thought bitterly. 'But it's bound to come out. There are records – he'll know I turned Murray in. I'm not ashamed of that.'

'I am,' Adam muttered, turning away.

'What did you say?'

He mentally shook himself. 'I'm tired, that's what I said,' he snapped. 'You'd better take me to the house before I fall in the brook and drown.' He groaned as she helped him up. 'It would solve everything though, wouldn't it, eh? If I were to drown, we'd all be better off.'

'Don't talk like that.' Supporting his considerable weight as well as she could, she led him back to the house. 'Things really will seem different tomorrow,' she promised. But she didn't believe it, and neither did he.

M AURICE STOOD BY the window, listening to an account of Murray's life. 'That's all I can tell you, sir,' he finished. 'I learned how to be a commercial broker the hard way. There have been times when I've had to be ruthless, but I have never gone out of my way to harm anyone.' It was the truth as he saw it.

'I see.' Not altogether satisfied, Maurice stared out of the window, hoping he might see Kathleen. The party was over and he still hadn't declared himself to her. He had so wanted to be able to announce their engagement tonight. Instead he was being forced to agree to his daughter's. My God, the girl ought to be whipped. He turned back to Murray. 'I won't deny I've heard of you, and as far as I can tell you have a decent reputation.' He raised an accusing finger. 'But it's a pity you weren't capable of being decent where my daughter was concerned.'

'I won't shirk my responsibilities, sir,' Murray said boldly. 'I never have.' Not even when he was sent to prison for harming that old lady when in fact he had not touched a hair on her head. He had followed the others, suspecting they were up to no good and concerned for Kathleen. If only he'd dealt with them earlier, all might have been well. For that he accepted part of the blame. The others were never charged. The police knew he had not been alone in the house but they didn't have any names, and Murray hadn't enlightened them, reckoning that it was safer not to. Those thugs would only have tried to save their own necks by pointing the finger at him. Without any witnesses to prove he had been the one actually responsible for attacking the old lady, he had calculated – and prayed – he would be spared the hangman's noose. And so it was.

Murray shook off the memory of that time and looked at Maurice levelly. 'I'm always prepared to face the consequences of my actions, sir.'

Maurice was impressed with his sincerity. He returned his attention to the outside, his eyes lighting up when he saw Kathleen coming towards the house with Adam, though Adam appeared to be leaning rather heavily on her. 'Excuse me a moment,' he told the other two.

He went out of the room, closing the door behind him. Hurrying to Kathleen, his worried gaze went to Adam who was swaying slightly, his eyes half-closed and the remnants of a song issuing from his lips.

'I'm afraid he's drunk.' Straightforward, without excuses; there was no other way to say it.

'Drunk? I've never seen Adam drunk before.'

'Neither have I,' Kathleen said. 'I expect we all fall from grace once in a while.' She didn't mean anything by it, but Maurice obviously assumed she was alluding to Melinda.

'She told you then. I saw her run across the lawn to where you and Adam were sitting.'

'Yes, she told us, and I'm very sorry. I know it isn't what you wanted for her.'

'What do you think of the young man?' He valued her opinion. 'Do you think he would make a suitable son-in-law?'

She could have told him everything, but wisely decided not to. There was no need to alienate Melinda when Maurice was bound to find out anyway. 'It's what you think that matters,' she said diplomatically. 'Anyway, if I know you, you're already planning to have him thoroughly investigated.' She hoped so.

'I have that in mind, yes.' He felt better for having talked to her. 'Here.' He slid Adam's weight on to his own shoulder. 'I'm sure we can get Adam to his room without bothering the servants.'

'He'll have a roaring headache in the morning,' Kathleen said, 'and it'll serve him right.'

Between the two of them they got Adam to his bed. Then Kathleen went to her own room while Maurice returned downstairs. As he went he smiled fondly at her. 'Goodnight, my dear,' he said. 'Don't worry about Adam. I'm sure he'll be full of remorse in the morning.'

'And so he should be,' Kathleen said, though her heart went out to him.

In the privacy of her room, she looked at herself in the mirror. Surprisingly she appeared as fresh as a daisy, her face glowing with health and her eyes sparkling. 'Must be the fresh air,' she told herself. 'Poor Maurice. I wonder what he'd say if he knew how much Adam loved his daughter?'

She knew what he would say: he would much prefer Adam as a son-in-law.

She undressed, washed all over, and brushed her long hair. That done, she put on her pretty blue nightgown and climbed into bed, wanting to put the whole business out of her mind.

It was impossible. When she lay awake it played on her mind, and when she slept it haunted her dreams.

There was a lovely church, bedecked with flowers and ringing to the sound of bells. Melinda and Murray, arm in arm, were walking back down the aisle. He saw her there, he smiled, and suddenly it was her walking arm in arm with him, it was her wearing the wedding ring. Then out of nowhere came the small, familiar figure of Markham, and suddenly it was snowing; there was no church, no Murray, and even Adam had deserted her.

Twice she woke with a start, and each time she turned over, desperate for sleep. Finally, when she could fight the tiredness no longer, her mind relaxed, the images disappeared, and she slipped into a deep, sound sleep.

I N THE FURTHEST wing of the house, Connie Blakeman was also restless. She lay on top of the bed, the lamp still alight on the cupboard, and her eyes wide open, counting the wrinkles in the curtains. Behind the eyes was a shrewd, mischievous mind. Almost all her life she had lived by her wits, until now she was as sharp as a tack.

'The buggers must be asleep by now,' she reasoned. Still, she mustn't be hasty.

Five minutes passed.

Getting off the bed, she tucked her feet into soft slippers. Her elbow knocked the lamp, making it rock. 'Whoa!' Carefully she righted it. 'Quietly does it. Mustn't get caught.' Taking her robe from the back of the chair, she put it on and tied the belt tightly. Then she took up the lamp and made her way across the room. Softly she opened the door, peering out to make certain there was no one about.

Satisfied, she went along the landing, down the back stairs and through the house towards Maurice's study. She had done it so many times before, she knew the route by heart. That's why she was now able to quench the light from the lamp and leave it safely on the hall table.

She pushed open the study door and went inside. She lit the table lamp and made sure the curtains were closed. Then she pulled out the bottom drawer of the desk, placed it on the carpet and stretched her arm into the gap it had left. 'Ah!' There was a small click as the hidden door sprang open. 'I still haven't lost my touch.'

Drawing out the wad of notes, she counted them. She liked nothing better than counting money – unless it was having a well-endowed man roll on top of her. She was disappointed. 'Only twenty-five pounds! Why doesn't he keep more money hidden here? The bigger the wad, the more I can sneak away without him suspecting.'

How much should she take this time? A daring thought presented itself, and not for the first time. 'Why not take the lot?' she asked herself. 'With this, and the notes I've already stashed away, I could live comfortably.'

It was a temptation, but there was more to be gained by staying, she reasoned. 'Another year and I could have enough trickled away to see me right into my old age. Then again, if I can get him and Kathleen together, I could name my price. Once the old fool's tied the knot, I can tell him a few home truths that would rock him in his shoes. Like how his pretty bride comes from a mother who was nothing better than a whore, and a father who was hanged for two murders. On the other hand, once she's wed to him, the lovely Kathleen will have the keys to more money than I'll ever see in a lifetime. Happen she'd be prepared to pay more for me to keep my mouth shut than he'd pay for me to open it.'

It was intoxicating to think of being in such a fortunate and powerful position. 'I'll take two of these here notes now,' she decided. 'I'll put the rest back and wait for my chance of a bigger pot.'

Deftly she tucked two notes inside her slipper, replaced the drawer and blew out the lamp. Departing the room, she headed in the opposite direction from which she'd come.

Whenever she went robbing, it gave her a crippling thirst. Just now the roof of her mouth was so dry, her tongue was sticking to it. 'A drop of cool sarsaparilla, that's what I need, and then I'll be away.'

In a moment she was in sight of the main kitchen. There was no light on. The house was quiet. She felt safe enough.

She entered the kitchen. The curtains were open and the moonlight broke the darkness just enough for her to see where she was going. Careful as a mouse, she took the sarsaparilla jug from the pantry and popped out the cork. It rolled away across the floor. Leaving the cork, she raised the jug to her parted lips. 'Mmm!' The rich, brown liquid slithered down her throat, warming her all over. Her thirst not yet quenched, she took another drink. Sheer heaven. A drip escaped from her mouth. She wiped it away, then licked the tips of her fingers.

From his seat at the table, Christian watched her, his face creased in an evil smile.

He, too, had come down to quench a raging thirst; it was always the same when he'd had too much to drink. The booze got in his blood and the blood boiled, until he cooled it with a hair of the dog.

He let her drink, and made not the slightest move. There was something very gratifying about watching someone who had no idea you were there. Especially when that someone was not bad looking, with tousled hair that hung down and a figure not too displeasing to the eye.

As she moved, her legs parted. The night sky filtered through her robe, silhouetting her figure: small-waisted, with breasts that were still round enough to cup in the palm of a man's hand. Her face was upturned, her mouth open to the spout of the jug.

His avaricious eyes took in every wonderful, tantalising detail.

He could wait no longer. Silently, he rose from his chair and stepped away from the table. Like a cat he went towards her, his loins burning with desire. In all the time she had been in this house, he had never seen her in such a way before, never wanted her like he wanted her now, nor thought she was worthy of his attention. But he was still giddy from a night of revelling and wasn't thinking straight.

When he was just an arm's reach away, she stooped to retrieve the cork from the floor. This was his moment.

With surprising agility he lunged forward and grabbed her, one hand over her mouth, the other sneaking up her nightgown. 'It's all right,' he whispered. 'It's me, Christian.' When the horror had died from her eyes, he took his hand from her mouth. The other hand continued to caress her warm, smooth flesh. 'I saw you. Just now, in the moonlight, I *saw* you.' He smiled knowingly. 'I never realised you were so beautiful.' Lies would get him what he wanted. Tomorrow, he would be lying to someone else. To him, women were all of a kind.

She was passive in his arms, delighted by his attentions, knowing that he was yet another means to a small fortune. 'What do you want with me?' Her voice was the smallest whisper, but her eyes shone with triumph. Bastard! she thought. Take me, and I'll make you pay! She knew what he wanted all right, and she was more than prepared to oblige. Yet it might pay her to behave like a lady, or at least not to appear eager. To that end she struggled, but not very effectually.

'I don't want to hurt you,' he said, stroking her hair. She wasn't struggling now. 'I wondered if you were lonely, like me.' His hand crept to her thigh, to that soft, warm, pulsing corner. 'Are you? Are you lonely, like me?'

She nodded, but remained silent.

He kissed her then. It was a moment before she kissed him back with any passion, but when she did, it was all he needed. Sometimes when he'd been drinking he could not be aroused easily, but now he was as hard as he had ever been.

When she wrapped her legs round him and drew him in deep, he laughed softly. 'Bitch! You want it too, don't you?'

She didn't answer. She was too busy kissing him, licking him, moulding herself into his body.

It was a wild and hungry coupling. Two people gratifying themselves for their own selfish reasons. Fast and furious now, he brought her to a climax, before he too was satisfied, the pleasure coursing through his senses.

When it was done, he rolled away and left her there on the floor. 'Keep your mouth shut,' he warned. 'One word of this and you'll wish you'd never been born.'

When he'd gone, she made her way back to her own quarters. Once inside, she twirled round and round, softly giggling, as if demented. After a moment she fell on the bed, pressing her hands over her face to muffle the laughter. 'You've done a good night's work, Connie, you clever thing,' she flattered herself. 'One way or another, Christian Westerfield will be made to pay for his naughty little pleasures.'

ADAM WAS WIDE awake. He was sitting by the window in his bedroom, deep in thought. Slowly and painfully he came to a decision.

Once the decision was made, he lost no time in carrying it out. It didn't take long to throw a few things into an overnight bag. He checked his wallet. It was enough. Over the years he had amassed a considerable bank balance. 'The days are long gone when I might go hungry.' It gave him a great deal of satisfaction to know that every penny he owned had been earned by the sweat of his brow.

Seating himself at the desk, he took up pen and paper and wrote a long, careful letter. This he sealed into an envelope, addressing it to 'My sister, Kathleen'.

He wrote a second, shorter letter, this one for Maurice.

As he sealed it, his resolve faltered and for one weak moment he almost tore the letters up. But he knew that the alternative was worse. Stay and watch Melinda marry another man, see it tear Kathleen apart? He couldn't do it. And he couldn't go on living a lie. His immediate reaction on seeing Murray had been how best to keep Kathleen from suspecting the truth. Recalling that now, his shame only increased. His sole option was to make a clean breast of it.

He made his way to Kathleen's room where he slid both letters beneath her door. 'God bless you, little sister,' he murmured. 'We've been through some bad times, you and me, but you'll be fine now. You don't need me any more.'

This was the worst moment of his life. He lingered there, making the agony last, touching the door and wishing he had the courage to tell her face to face. 'Forgive me,' he whispered. Then he departed, leaving behind everything that made life worth living.

K ATHLEEN WOKE FEELING refreshed. A moment later her spirits dipped as she recalled Murray's presence in the house last night, and the reason for it. 'Leave it to Maurice,' she decided, shutting her mind to it all. Even so, it wasn't easy.

She selected a sage green blouse and white skirt. 'First a brisk wash at the basin, then dress for breakfast.' Yet she couldn't shake her mind free of the knowledge that soon Melinda and Murray would be married. And before long there would be a child. 'Put it out of your mind,' she told herself in the mirror. 'No matter how much you might wish it, the child isn't yours. However much you love him, he was never for you, and never could be.'

A short time later she was washed and dressed, and ready to meet the world. She threw open the window on the August sunshine, then quickly made her way to the door. 'Best foot forward, Kathleen, my girl,' she declared. 'You may not fancy breakfast, but you'll have to show willing, for Melinda's sake, if nothing else.'

She almost stepped on the letters. They lay side by side half under the door, half out. She picked them up, turning them over in her hands. 'Looks like Adam's writing.' Her insides grew cold. 'Why would Adam be writing letters when he's just down the corridor? And why put this one under my door?' she wondered, reading Maurice's name on the second letter.

She rushed out of the room and down the corridor. The door to Adam's room was open and the maid already tidying the room. 'Yes, miss?' Startled by Kathleen's unexpected arrival, the maid looked up from making the bed.

Kathleen sensed the awful emptiness of the room. 'I'm sorry,' she said lamely. 'I'm looking for my brother. Have you seen him this morning?'

The maid shook her head. 'No, miss.' She gathered the laundry and excused herself. As she went, she muttered under her breath, 'No wonder I'm late doing me chores, with folks rushing about all over the bleedin' place!'

With the letters still in her hand, Kathleen went out on to

the landing. Seating herself on a tall, upright chair beside the jardinière, she opened the letter addressed to her.

My dear Kathleen,

I hope you will forgive me for what I'm doing, but I see no other way. I have to leave this house and find work abroad. I don't have the kind of courage to stay and see Melinda married to another man.

There is something else, Kathleen. Something I've kept to myself all these years, though it has haunted me every minute.

I know how much you liked Murray, right from the very first day you saw him. I know, too, how the liking turned to love, and how it broke your heart to name him as Markham's attacker.

The shameful truth is, I did you, and Murray, a terrible wrong, and now I can't keep silent any longer. I feel I owe it to you and Melinda, for he is not the devil he appears to be. You see, Kathleen, it wasn't Murray who attacked Markham. In fact, she told me herself how he tried to save her from the others.

I didn't tell you because I thought it was for the best. I know now I had no right to let you go on believing he was the cause of her death. It was wrong of me to keep the truth from you. It was wrong of me to stand by when you gave his name to the nurse at the hospital. Because of me, Murray must have served a long term of imprisonment.

I wouldn't blame you if you told him and sent him after me, but I know it isn't in your nature to do such a thing. Maybe he already knows anyway. Maybe he's a more honourable man than I could ever be.

I had no right to do what I did, and I offer no excuses.

A better man might have stayed and told you both face to face. It's ironic that I should lose Melinda to a man I wronged. That is my punishment.

I know this will be a terrible shock for you. I only hope there may come a time when you can feel it in your heart to forgive me.

I'm going far away. By the time you read this, I will be aboard a ship bound for foreign parts. It will be many a year before I see these shores again, if ever.

Please, Kathleen, don't think of me too harshly.

Take care of yourself.

Your loving brother,

Adam

Kathleen fell back into the chair, anguish flooding her soul. Her eyes were tightly closed and her hands lay loosely in her lap. The letter fluttered to the floor. Dear God, Adam had stood by while she had labelled Murray a murderer. *No!* Oh no!

'Oh, Adam. How could you?' She covered her face with her hands and cried bitterly, wishing herself a million miles away. But she was still here, having to face them all while he was gone, run away like the coward he was. 'It was *me* who put Murray away for all those years. I daren't even think about it. What if they'd hanged him? Oh, dear God!'

The thought was horrifying. 'You're right, Adam,' she muttered harshly. 'I wouldn't send him after you, though God knows you deserve it. But I can never forgive you. Not as long as I live.'

Shakily she dried her eyes and picked up the letter. The other one was tucked in her skirt pocket. She took it out and stared at it for an age. 'I expect you've told Maurice the truth. I hope you have. But the truth won't erase the years Murray spent in prison.' She couldn't begin to imagine what he must have gone through. She had heard tales of the cruelty meted out to prisoners. 'The truth won't give him back the peace of mind he lost. Nor will it clear the way for Murray and me to find each other again.' That was what cut most deeply. She had lost him, and in such a wicked, wicked way.

A feeling of disgust came over her. 'Shame on you, Adam! You may have run from it all, but I won't. Someone has to stay and face him. Someone has to say sorry, futile though it sounds, and as you're not here, it falls to me.' She shivered at the prospect. 'God help me, I'll do what's right, with as much courage as I can muster.'

A strange calm settled over her. She stood up and went down the stairs straight to Maurice's study.

'He's in the breakfast room, miss.' It was the same maid she'd encountered earlier, in Adam's room.

'Is Miss Melinda with him?' She had things to explain to them both.

'Yes, miss.' A little grin crinkled her homely features. 'With her young man, miss. They're having breakfast with the master.'

'Thank you, Sally.'

On her way to the breakfast room, she paused, her heart beating wildly. For one faltering moment she was afraid she might not be able to go through with it.

The moment didn't last long. She carried on, and the nearer to the breakfast room she came, the stronger grew her courage. She had to be brave. Adam had left her little choice.

When she entered the room, Maurice stood to greet her. 'Kathleen, my dear. As you see, we have a guest. Do come and join us. I'll get you some fresh tea.' He turned to the maid. 'A pot of fresh tea, if you please, and some hot muffins.'

Kathleen remained standing at the head of the table. Maurice was on her right, the other two on her left. Her gaze went from Maurice to Melinda, who was too interested in Murray to notice anyone else. Then, with a heart-rending effort, she brought her gaze to Murray. He smiled at her, slowly, fondly, looking at her with those wonderful sincere eyes. Kathleen's heart turned over. What she felt for him was reflected in his gaze. The same love. The same regrets. The same memories and longing. The realisation shook her. His love for her had survived the years, in spite of everything, just as hers had for him. It made her task all the more painful.

Maurice was puzzled. 'What's wrong, my dear? Please, come and sit down.'

Kathleen said, 'There is something I have to tell you.' She

was looking at Maurice but was acutely aware that the other two were paying close attention. 'Adam has left this house for good.' Before they could respond to the startling news, she went on, 'He had things to tell you but was afraid he might never be forgiven. Now I have to tell you these things. Afterwards, I too may be asked to leave this house.'

'You will never be asked to leave,' Maurice assured her. 'For pity's sake, Kathleen, what is it? What's happened?'

'I can't believe Adam's gone!' Melinda's impatient voice broke in. 'Why would he do that?' Her small fist banged the table. 'I want him at my wedding. He promised to be best man.'

'Quiet, child!' A stern glance from Maurice and she was instantly sullen.

Shifting her gaze briefly to Murray, Kathleen said quietly, 'What I have to say mostly concerns you.'

She took a deep breath. 'I've no doubt that Murray was preparing to tell you this himself.' She had to keep all possibility of blame from his shoulders. 'Adam and I knew Murray years ago, when we were children. After our parents died, Adam and I were sent to live with Great-Aunt Markham. We saw Murray often on our walks across the park or along the beach, but he only ever came to the house once. All the same, we might have been very good friends, only . . .' She gulped, choking back the tears.

'Murray used to hang around with a gang of young hooligans, but then he left their company for good and got himself a job. He meant to do well, that was what he said, and I always knew he would. Right from the start, I knew he didn't belong with those people. Aunt Markham told us his father was a bully; it wasn't surprising he got mixed up with a bad lot because he was not encouraged to do anything else. He had faith in himself though, and I was proud of him.' I loved him, she thought. I believed in him even then.

At that moment the maid arrived. 'Not now!' Maurice was totally absorbed by Kathleen's tale.

'These same hooligans broke into Aunt Markham's house. We don't know exactly what happened but she was badly hurt and later died from her injuries.' Once again she had to swallow the rising emotion. 'Murray was there, but I didn't know until this day that he was trying to save Markham. I know now he wasn't involved in the break-in, and had nothing to do with the attack on my aunt.' When she glanced at him, he looked away, his eyes downcast.

She went on, 'My brother knew this because Markham told him before she died. For reasons I won't go into, I was never told of Murray's innocence, and so, to my undying shame and in a fit of rage, I gave his name to the authorities. Needless to say, he was arrested and imprisoned, for something he didn't do.'

'My God!' The colour had drained from Melinda's face. Maurice sat rigid in his chair, speechless with shock.

Kathleen felt Murray's eyes on her, and faced him with courage. 'There is nothing I can do or say to make up for what I did or to convey how sorry I am. All I can say in my defence is that I had no idea you were innocent until this morning, when I found this letter from Adam beneath my door.' She held up the letter for them to see. 'He knew Melinda's father would search into your past. He was afraid I might find out that he'd deceived me all along. That's why he went away, because he couldn't face the consequences of what he'd done.'

She made no mention of Adam's love for Melinda, or that he couldn't bear to stay and see her married to another man. Nor did she confess how she loved Murray with the same passion. There was nothing to be gained from revealing all this. Instead, she said simply, 'I'm as guilty as my brother. I'm so very sorry.' The shame and heartache threatened to suffocate her. 'I should have known you weren't capable of such a thing.'

The silence was profound.

She gave the second letter to Maurice. 'He left you this,' she explained. When he opened the letter and began reading, she quietly left them. She had no right to stay. How could any of them want her there?

KATHLEEN WAS OUT in the garden when Maurice came to her. 'No one blames you,' he said. 'And please, Kathleen, don't ever talk of leaving. This house would be empty with you gone.'

He sat beside her on the bench and put his hand over hers in a gesture of friendship. Above them the boughs of the cherry tree were heavy with fruit. In the clear blue skies birds swooped and from the woods came the plaintive sound of animals calling. Yet Kathleen could find no solace in the beauty that surrounded her.

'Will you let them marry?' She prayed her confession had not spoiled Melinda's life. At the same time, she wished those two had never met. Maybe then, somehow in the future, there might still have been a chance for her and Murray.

'I have no choice,' he answered. 'You know Melinda is with child. Even if she were not, and I truly believed those two were in love and wanting to marry, I think I might still agree. He seems a good choice. Melinda is strong-willed but I don't think she'll get the better of him. He's a good man. Intelligent and ambitious, and in view of his background his success is all the more remarkable. We've talked at great length. I like him.'

'Will you investigate him?'

'Of course. I wouldn't be doing my duty as a father if I didn't probe into his past. But now that I know the worst I doubt whether I'll find anything but good.'

'I'm glad you won't stand in their way.' She wasn't glad. She was desperately unhappy.

'Adam going like that.' He shook his head. 'I never would have believed it. One of the things I admired most about him was his courage.'

But you don't know, she thought bitterly. You don't know how much he loves your daughter, and how devastated he was when he discovered she was to be married – and to the man he'd wronged all those years ago.

'Why didn't he come and explain his mistake?'

'It wasn't a mistake. He let me send Murray to prison and he knows I will never forgive him for it.' She wondered if he really would never return.

'Never is a long time not to forgive someone.' He sensed something here that was too secret, too deep to be spoken about, yet he had to ask. 'Tell me, Kathleen. Was there ever anything between you and Murray?'

'We were only children,' she prevaricated. 'When Melinda brought him here it was the first time I'd seen him in all those years.' It wouldn't do if Maurice thought Murray meant anything special to her.

'I'm sorry, my dear. It was a foolish thing to ask.' He tucked his fingers under her chin and raised her gaze to his. 'Kathleen, promise me you'll never again speak of leaving.'

She smiled, and for the briefest moment she forgot the pain. 'As you said, never is a long time.'

Feeling foolish, he stared at the ground. 'With Adam gone and Melinda leaving soon for a home of her own, I can't imagine being here without you.'

'I thought I might take up secretarial work or something useful like that. I won't waste my life.' For some time she had been considering asking Maurice if she might be involved in his work. Now, though, she wouldn't be so direct.

'If that's what you want, we can talk about it, but promise me you won't leave, at least until after Melinda's wedding.'

It wasn't much to ask. 'All right.' But she must find work. Only busying herself would keep her sane.

'Thank you, my dear.' Realising she needed to be alone, he made his excuses and returned to the house. There would be time enough later to put his ideas to her. This was not the moment.

The old dog came to sit at her feet. 'Hello, old feller,' she murmured, stroking his head. 'Are you lonely too?' Until that moment, she had never known what it was to feel utterly and completely alone.

Another voice answered, a voice she knew immediately. 'I'm lonely,' it said. 'Even more so since I came to this house and saw you again.'

Her heart leaped. 'Murray!'

'Don't run away,' he begged, sitting down beside her. 'I only want you to know I don't hold you responsible, or your brother come to that.'

'But it was Adam who let me believe you were responsible for Markham's death, and it was me who gave your name to the authorities. For God's sake, Murray, you were innocent.' She was crying now, hot, burning tears streaming down her face. 'How can you not hold us responsible?'

He gazed at her for a while, his warm, anxious eyes quietly regarding her every beloved feature. 'Don't cry.' Raising his hands, he thumbed away her tears. 'I did a lot of bad things before I realised what a fool I was – stealing and fighting, halfway to being a thug every bit as bad as the others. If it hadn't been for you, I might have gone on to be even worse. Oh, I won't deny the long years in prison were sheer hell, but they taught me a valuable lesson. I've become a good citizen. I earn my living through legitimate means, and I'm a very wealthy man.'

'Oh, Murray. Will you ever forgive me?'

'For sending the authorities after me, yes. For sending me away from you, no.' There was a world of regret in his voice.

His warmth and tenderness moved her deeply. 'I missed you,' she confessed. 'After we went away, and even though I thought you were to blame for Markham's death, I couldn't stop thinking of you.' She laughed, embarrassed. 'Isn't that silly?'

He held her gaze, his voice trembling with emotion. 'No, Kathleen, it's not silly. In that prison, and ever since, not a day has gone by when I haven't thought of you.' Taking hold of her hand he pressed it to his face. 'Oh, Kathleen, Kathleen. You can't know how much I still love you. When I came out of prison, I searched far and wide for you. I asked everywhere. But it was as though you'd vanished into thin air. When I saw you here, I thought I was going mad. I still love you, Kathleen. I've never stopped loving you.'

Fearful now, she drew her hand away. 'It's too late,' she reminded him. 'You're marrying Melinda. She's carrying your child.' She would have given anything for that not to be so, but it was. And nothing could turn the clock back.

'There's no love there. I was lonely, at my lowest ebb. One night Melinda was there, lovely, willing, and I was weak.' He shrugged, as if casually dismissing the episode. 'It was just one encounter, short-lived and quickly forgotten. It meant nothing, not to either of us, I thought. Just two unhappy souls comforting each other.'

He drew in a long breath. 'Now she's having my child. Oh, I'll do the right thing by her. I hope I haven't lost my sense of decency altogether. I helped make that innocent child, and a child needs its father. I'll care for Melinda, and I'll give her all she wants.' He paused, his voice a soft caress. 'But it's you I love, Kathleen. It will always be you.'

He loved her! She wanted to shout it from the rooftops. Instead she remained silent, and more than a little afraid. 'You'd better go. She'll be wondering where you are.' She wanted him to stay, or go away with her. But that was impossible, she knew.

'Melinda and her father are in the library.' His smile was mischievous, delightful. 'No doubt they're discussing the shocking news you dropped in their laps just now.' He stood up. Leaning easily on the trunk of the cherry tree, he remarked kindly, 'I'm sorry about your aunt. She was a strange little thing, but she was always a lady.'

'Yes, she was always a lady.'

'Life couldn't have been easy for you after she died.'

'We had plans, me and Adam.'

He sat down beside her again. 'Tell me about your plans,' he urged. 'I want to know everything about you.'

In the years to come, he would remember these precious moments.

MELINDA WAS ADAMANT. 'No, Father! I won't forgive her. And I won't forgive Adam for going away.' The truth was, she had always been fond of Adam, and the idea that she might never see him again was too upsetting.

Maurice was equally adamant. 'I will not have bad feelings in this house. Kathleen has been a good friend to you. Either you show her some compassion now, or I might have to think again about this young man of yours!'

Stamping her feet, Melinda showed a fierce temper. 'You heard what she said, Father. Murray was innocent of the charges against him.'

'Exactly. And if it hadn't been for Adam confessing to that, and Kathleen having the courage to tell us, I might have discovered Murray's prison sentence and that would certainly have put an end to any marriage between you.' Taking her by the shoulders, he warned angrily, 'Your shame, and mine, would have been tenfold. Think of that, my girl, and be grateful to her.'

She fell silent, realising that what he said was the truth. But the truth was, she was wildly jealous that Kathleen had known Murray first, all those years ago. And from the way Kathleen had spoken about him, they had obviously formed a close bond. Why didn't Murray tell her last night that he knew Kathleen? Was he hiding more than just his prison sentence? Whatever her father said, and however unreasonable it might be, she would never again be able to feel the same about Kathleen. She blamed her too for not stopping Adam from leaving. That distressed her more than she liked to admit.

'Go to her now.' Maurice turned her to face the door. 'Kathleen must not leave. Where would she go? How would she live?'

'She's capable enough. Anyway, why should you care?' She knew the answer to that well enough, and her jealousy deepened.

'It's enough that I do care, and so should you,' Maurice said, exasperated. 'You must let her know she still has a friend in you. Tell her you don't blame her for any of this.' His patience at an end, he thrust her forward. 'Go on, child! Do as you're told.'

She wasn't sure, but as she approached Kathleen and Murray, Melinda felt they were sitting too close together, talking too quietly and, when they got up on seeing her, looked almost guilty. 'What are you up to?' she asked, painting on a smile. To Murray she said, 'Father would like a word with you. He's waiting in the library.'

As he came close, she took hold of him and bent his head to hers. 'He won't bite you,' she murmured. Then she kissed him on the mouth, her eyes open and looking over his shoulder at Kathleen. Embarrassed, Kathleen stood up.

'It's getting chilly,' she said. 'If I'm wanted, I'll be in my room.'

Taking Melinda by the shoulders, Murray stood her away from him, his eyes on her but his message for Kathleen. 'I think Melinda would like you to stay awhile.' His voice was firm as he then addressed Melinda. 'Isn't that so?'

Realising she had no option, Melinda ran and linked her arm with Kathleen's. 'We need to talk,' she said. 'I don't want you to think we can't be friends any more.' Gritting her teeth, she sat down on the bench and waited for Kathleen to do the same.

When, just before entering the house, Murray glanced back, it was to see the two of them deep in conversation. 'At least I haven't come between you,' he murmured. 'God willing, we won't be strangers over the coming years.' Though, in a way, it might have been less painful if they were never to see each other again.

He would have been less easy in his mind if he'd heard what his future wife was saying.

'You won't tell, will you?' Melinda was pleading. At first, when her father had insisted she should show compassion to Kathleen, she hadn't considered the possibility that Kathleen might be the one to withdraw her friendship. 'I know I've had too many men friends, I'm not denying that. But that's all over now. I'm in love for the first time, and I'll be a good wife.

I'll never again cheat on him. He's a wonderful man, rich and handsome, and he knows how to take care of a woman.'

Her words cut into Kathleen's heart.

Unaware, Melinda went on, 'Murray is the kind of man any woman would die for. If he should find out how many men I've had before him, he wouldn't feel the same way about me any more. He'd call off the wedding, I know he would. You won't tell, will you, Kathleen?' She wished to God she hadn't boasted about her many conquests. Now, if she wanted to, Kathleen could cause her untold hardship. 'Please, Kathleen, promise you won't tell.'

Grateful still to have Melinda's friendship, Kathleen said warmly, 'It isn't for me to tell. If anyone should tell Murray about your previous lovers, it ought to be you.'

'Never!'

Kathleen wondered if Melinda was right to be so afraid that Murray would desert her if he knew the truth about her. He might still go ahead with the wedding, if only for the child's sake. But if he did choose to walk away, Melinda would be left a mother with no husband. The scandal might persuade Maurice to send her from this house for good, though he would undoubtedly see she never wanted for anything. That gentle, kind man had already suffered one shock after another: his only daughter carrying a child out of wedlock; the revelations about Murray; the bitter disappointment of Adam going away. For his sake, as well as Melinda's, Kathleen knew she could never betray Melinda, though she couldn't help but wonder whether her silence wasn't a betrayal of Murray. 'You must do as you see fit,' she told Melinda quietly. 'I won't tell, you have my word.'

Melinda hugged her. 'I knew you wouldn't turn your back on me,' she laughed, secretly triumphant, 'and I won't turn my back on you. It must have taken a lot of courage to admit how you sent Murray to prison,' she grudgingly admitted, and then, with astonishing arrogance, 'it was a wicked thing you did, but I forgive you.' A sly grin curled the corners of her mouth. 'We all have our little secrets. In a way, you're no different from me.'

Kathleen burned to wipe that smirk off her face with the

sharp edge of her tongue, but she let it go. 'Tell me one thing, Melinda.'

'Ask.'

'The child, is it really Murray's?'

Melinda laughed softly. 'Like I said, we all have our little secrets.'

'Are you saying Murray *isn't* the father?' Damn Melinda and her games.

Melinda replied warily, 'I'm not saying any such thing, and even if I was, it can never be proved either way. All I am saying is, I slept with Murray, and we made love like I've never known before.' Bunching her fists and thrusting them out before her, she sighed ecstatically. 'It was wonderful!'

Kathleen's silence urged her on. 'Seriously though, there's no doubt in my mind that Murray is the father. When our child is born, you'll see for yourself.'

It occurred to Kathleen that maybe Melinda herself did not know who the father was. God knows the girl had had enough lovers.

Melinda sprang to her feet. 'I'm going inside, to make sure Father isn't bullying my husband-to-be.' Reluctantly, she added, 'Are you coming?'

Kathleen shook her head. 'I think I'll stay out here for a while. I have a lot of thinking to do.'

'Father says you're not to leave. He won't stand for it, and neither will I.' At least, not until I'm safely married to Murray, she thought. 'You're not planning to leave, are you?'

'I haven't got as far as making plans.'

Satisfied, Melinda touched on another issue. 'Do you know where Adam went?'

'No.'

'Will you make an effort to track him down?'

'No.' Her heart was hardened against him.

'I'll miss him.'

'I expect you will.' It struck her that Melinda might have been more fond of Adam than she'd ever admitted. A rush of spite drove her to say something she instantly regretted. 'Was Adam one of your little secrets?'

For a moment Melinda was shocked, yet she knew it might have been true, if only Adam had shown her the way. 'If you're asking whether he was a lover, no, he wasn't.'

'I'm sorry. I shouldn't have said that.' She recalled what Adam had written about his love for Melinda, and she was overwhelmed with shame.

'Can I tell my father we're friends again?'

Kathleen began to understand. 'Did your father send you out here?'

'Of course not!' Melinda was an accomplished liar.

'Go on in, I'll follow in a while.'

'Just now, when I came out, what were you and Murray talking about?'

'Oh, nothing much.' Everything, Kathleen thought.

'It didn't look like it was nothing.'

'Oh? What did it look like then?'

'Like two lovers whispering.' Bristling with jealousy, Melinda demanded, 'You wouldn't be keeping something from me, would you?'

'Like what?' Anger rose in Kathleen.

'I don't know. Something.'

'Please, Melinda. We've made our peace, and now I'd like to be left alone for a while.'

'I'm sorry if I've made you angry.'

'You haven't.'

'I'll see you later then?'

'Yes. Later.'

Connie Blakeman had witnessed the meeting from an upper window. Intrigued, she watched Melinda as she walked back to the house. She could see the young madam's dark expression. 'Nastier piece of work than I'll ever be,' she muttered. 'Smiles on one side of her face and spits on the other.'

Bringing her gaze to Kathleen who sat dejected on the bench, she warned, 'Watch her, my beauty. She knows her dad's fond of you. Whether she marries her rich young man or not, it'll never be enough. If she thought for one minute you might get your hands on her father's fortune, she'd cut your throat soon as look at you.'

After a while, Kathleen made her way to the house.

As she passed the library, she could hear voices, intense, deep in discussion. Probably making plans for the wedding, she thought, going on up the stairs.

Suddenly the door opened and Melinda came out, her arm linked with Murray's. He seemed preoccupied but she appeared to be bubbling over with happiness.

As Kathleen paused, looking down, her gaze met Murray's and, for a moment, time stood still.

She turned away and carried on to her room. As she closed the door, her heart was like a clenched fist inside her.

Chapter Fifteen

I T WAS THE sort of day any woman would wish for her wedding. The September sun shone gloriously, the gentle breeze was wonderfully refreshing, and everything was ready for the big event.

From the upper reaches of the house came Melinda's shrill, peevish voice. 'If only I wasn't so fat!' She was now almost three months pregnant and it was beginning to show. 'Everyone will know,' she wailed. 'They'll stare at me.'

Kathleen had been up since five o'clock that morning, helping where she could and soothing Melinda's frayed nerves. 'Nobody's going to stare at you.' Laying Melinda's beautiful wedding dress on the bed, she tried hard not to wish it was hers. 'Honestly, Melinda, you're never happy unless you've got something to moan about.'

'But what if they *do* stare?'

Kathleen rolled her eyes. 'They won't! And even if they do, it'll only be your lovely dress they're looking at.'

'Oh, thank you very much!' She gave Kathleen a disdainful stare. 'You're not much help. I think you'd better go and see what's going on downstairs.'

'Gladly,' Kathleen replied, and she hurried off before Melinda could change her mind. She could hardly bear to be actively involved in preparing another woman to wed the man she herself loved so desperately. As she went, she could hear Melinda shrieking at the two unfortunate women who had been summoned to make her beautiful for her big day.

Kathleen shut her ears to the angry cries. Today was going to be enough of an ordeal without Melinda doing her best to be a miserable, obnoxious little pig! She ran down the stairs, pushing all upsetting thoughts out of her mind. 'You're on trial, Kathleen,' she told herself. 'Don't let yourself down.'

Connie was downstairs, checking that everything was in order. Over the years she had honed her skills as a housekeeper until now she excelled at her job. When Kathleen came into the dining room, she was alone there, setting out the crystal. 'Chased you away, has she?' Flicking an indignant stare towards the ceiling, she muttered, 'It's a pity she can't realise how much of a friend she has in you.'

'What exactly do you mean by that?' Kathleen asked. She was always uncomfortable in Connie's presence, hating the familiarity she had shown to herself and Adam from their first day here. And she always seemed to be watching and listening.

Every word she uttered, every look and insinuation suggested this woman knew more about what went on here than she ever revealed.

Connie shifted her attention to the flower display. 'I'm not trying to say anything,' she said. 'I'm simply remarking on what an ungrateful, selfish devil she is.'

'She's nervous, that's all. Any woman would be.' Feeling the need to defend her, Kathleen put her own feelings aside, though they were remarkably close to those of the housekeeper.

'Would *you* be nervous?' Connie didn't look up, but the sly smile still shaped her mouth.

'I suppose so, yes.'

'Of course you would.'

'I'm not sure what you're trying to get at but I don't like your attitude very much.'

'I'm sorry.' Unusually contrite, Connie stepped back to admire the flowers. 'Maybe you'd better go and get ready, leave me to my work.'

'You're right. It wouldn't do for the bride to be without her maid of honour.'

She was halfway across the room when Connie's next remark stopped her in her tracks. 'I expect you'd rather be the bride.'

She swung round. 'What did you say?'

'I saw you last night. You and him.'

Stiff with anger, Kathleen clenched her fist and for one awful moment was tempted to slap that sly, brazen face. 'If you have something particular to say, you'd better come right out and say it.'

Connie fiddled with the flowers. 'I can't imagine why you're getting in such a state. I only said I saw you and him – having a chat as far as I could tell.' Facing Kathleen now, she said softly, 'Isn't that how it was?'

'You know perfectly well that's how it was. If I hear you saying otherwise, you'll answer to me.'

'Such a temper,' Connie remarked casually. 'Anyone would think you had something to—' Suddenly she clutched her stomach, her face as white as a sheet.

Kathleen stared at her, wondering whether she was genuinely ill or just playing some bizarre trick. But when she groaned and slumped forward across the table, her legs buckling beneath her, Kathleen darted across the room. Putting her arms round Connie's shoulders, she helped her up into a chair. 'Sit here,' she said. 'I'll get you a drink. Will you be all right?'

Connie nodded. 'But please,' she gasped, 'don't say anything to the others.'

'I won't,' Kathleen promised, hurrying out of the room.

The house was a hive of activity as servants rushed about putting the finishing touches to the preparations. In their best bib and tucker, they went about their duties with a smile on their faces. Even if Melinda wasn't the nicest person they'd ever worked under, a wedding was always cause for celebration. Besides, she and her husband had bought a house in Kent. After today, the master's daughter would be far enough away not to bother them.

Kathleen went swiftly towards the kitchen. The hallway was filled with flowers – a beautiful, trailing rose bouquet for the bride, a smaller, less formal one for the maid of honour, and a selection of corsages for anybody in need of one.

'My goodness, miss!' exclaimed Cook as Kathleen entered the kitchen. 'I would have thought you'd be upstairs, getting ready. Maisie's been up and down wondering where you are. Look at the time, miss!' She waved a hand at the clock. 'In a few hours the carriage will be here to collect you.'

'When it comes I'll be ready – done up like a princess, don't you worry.'

Maisie was bold enough to remark, 'You're always like a princess, miss.'

'Why, thank you, Maisie, and so are you.' Wasting no time, she poured a glass of water from the jug. 'Nerves,' she explained coolly, and pretended to take a sip.

As she left the kitchen, the glass still in her hand, Maisie ran after her. 'Are you going upstairs now, miss?'

'You go on up, Maisie. Get everything ready, and I'll follow you up in five minutes.'

'Very well, miss.' And off she went, softly singing to herself.

When Kathleen made her way upstairs ten minutes later, it was by way of the back stairs. Connie leaned heavily on her arm. 'Thank you for getting me past without anyone seeing,' she said. 'I don't want them thinking I can't do my job.' Connie had two rooms in the upper reaches of the house, at the front and some way from the servants' quarters.

'Are you sure you'll be all right now?' Kathleen wasn't certain she ought to leave her. 'I could send Maisie,' she suggested. 'She's a good girl, not prone to gossip.'

Connie sat in the chair, her colour slowly returning, and her breathing almost back to normal. 'No, no. I'm better on my own. I'm not ill . . . as such.' She seemed to blush a little. 'You go on. You've got to be ready when the carriage comes. Maisie will be waiting.'

'If you're sure.'

'Just one thing. Why did you help me after the way I goaded you?'

Kathleen smiled. 'Because I'm not sure you meant anything by it. And anyway, shouldn't we all help each other?'

'You make me feel ashamed.'

'Good!' She laughed, and so did Connie.

On her way downstairs, Kathleen recalled what Connie had said. 'I'm not ill . . . as such.' It intrigued her. What did she mean? Still, there were other, more pressing matters to attend to now, and time was running short. 'Like it or not, I've promised to be there, and I will. Smiles and all.'

While Kathleen got ready with Maisie's enthusiastic help, Connie leaned over the bowl, retching and spewing, and feeling like death warmed over. 'There's no doubt about it now, my girl,' she said, splashing her face with cold water. 'You're carrying Christian Westerfield's bairn.' She hadn't been certain until now. 'It couldn't have worked out better if you'd planned it yourself,' she told her mirror image. 'But take your time. Be sure when you make your move. That drunken devil's as cunning as you ever were.' She leaned on the dresser, staring at her reflection. 'You might be past your bloom,' she muttered, 'but at last you've got your ticket to an easier life.' Patting her stomach, she grinned. 'This little bugger is the way to a fortune. Or my name's not Connie Blakeman!'

Going to the wardrobe, she put away the pretty lemon blouse and blue skirt she'd originally chosen to wear to church. Instead, she took out a grey dress and a sensible pair of shoes. 'Mustn't look like the sort of woman who would lead a man on,' she laughed.

Suddenly she was looking forward to attending the church, even if it did mean she had to stand at the back with the other servants. 'You won't be a servant for too long now, Connie, my girl,' she declared. 'Wait until after the wedding. A few days at the most, and then we'll see.'

———✦———

IN SPITE OF last-minute crises – Cook dropped a tray of meringues and the butler skidded across the floor on them; Melinda trod on her bouquet and the crushed gypsophila had to be replaced; Kathleen lost two hairpins and had to borrow from Maisie – the wedding went smoothly.

The church was ablaze with colour; flowers decorated the pews and lined the aisle, and a myriad blossoms made long, meandering trails down the centre columns. The bright autumn sunlight filtered in through the windows, and when the bride came in, all eyes turned to gaze on her.

Melinda looked very glamorous. In her long dress and wearing an exquisite pearl tiara, she looked almost regal. A gossamer veil of lace and silk flowed from her head to the ground behind her, moving gracefully as she walked, slowly and sedately, to the tall, handsome man waiting at the altar.

It was only a moment before all eyes turned to Kathleen. Dressed more simply, in a straight-cut primrose-coloured gown, she looked almost like a bride herself. Her long dark hair was swept up, leaving trails of tiny ringlets framing her face and neck. In her ears she wore small, pear-shaped drops of gold, and round her neck a single gold chain. Her feet were clad in silver slippers and her hands in gloves of the same, finer material. She carried her flowers low, moving with grace and confidence towards the altar – and the man whom she, too, loved with all her heart.

Maurice walked his daughter up the aisle, proud to do so but ashamed of the reason for it. At the altar, he turned to glance at Kathleen. Her beauty took his breath away. She smiled, and his heart tightened with love. Quickly he looked away. She must not see the longing in his eyes. He must be patient a while longer. Once Melinda and Murray were settled in Kent, his time would come.

Kathleen couldn't stop her gaze from rising to Murray's profile, strong and serious, his dark hair smoothed back, one small lock straying across his forehead. He looked so proud and fine, the way any man should look when he was making his vows. But Kathleen sensed his pain. When he made his vows, his tone was clipped and cold, not warm and soft like that of a man in love. There was no hint of nervousness, and no sign of pleasure either.

His back was stiff and straight, and he held his bride's hand as though it was a necessary duty.

Melinda didn't notice. Too wrapped up in herself, she smiled demurely, and when the service was over, she kissed him the same way.

Christian Westerfield made a handsome best man. He carried out his duty, and, to all those present, he seemed a good son and brother. Maurice had warned him unequivocally that if he did anything to disgrace the family or upset the united front they were presenting to the world, he would cease to be part of that family. And so he carried out his duty with dignity and presence. It was a small price to pay for a life of comfort.

After the formalities, the servants returned to Westerfield House, leaving the gentry to follow at their leisure. 'Can't say the groom looked very happy,' Cook remarked.

'I'm not surprised,' Maisie retorted. 'Who'd want to wed an uppity madam like her?'

'I reckon she's having a bairn,' the scullery maid said. At that everyone was silent, except Cook who instantly reprimanded her.

'That kind of talk will get you in trouble, my girl!' But her anger was mild. The girl was only saying out loud what she herself thought in private.

The reception went on into the evening, with music and dancing and a great deal of wine. Christian drank too much but he managed to remain sober enough to keep his advances to another man's wife reasonably discreet. The young wife was flattered, and her husband remained blissfully unaware of the flirtation, so no ugly scenes disturbed the proceedings.

Kathleen was danced off her feet by two persistent young men and then by Maurice, who was insanely jealous but managed not to show it. While they danced, Murray swept by with Melinda in his arms. Kathleen knew she should look away but couldn't, and his eyes met hers. The longing in them shook her to the core.

There was one forbidden moment of magic when she escaped out into the garden for a breath of fresh air. The relative quiet soothed her frayed nerves. Out here, under a star-decked sky, she could think more clearly. It was such a beautiful evening she decided to stroll to the cherry trees. She stood beneath them, her eyes raised to the sky. 'Help me forget him,' she whispered. The music gentled through the night air, touching her soul, freeing her mind.

Startled by a sound behind her, she swung round, and there he was.

He didn't speak, and neither did she. For a long, anxious moment, they gazed at each other, not sure what to do. Then, stepping forward, he took her in his arms and pressed her close. Looking down on her lovely face, he didn't have to say how much he adored her. There was no need for words. It was there, in his eyes, a love so profound it would last all her life.

They held each other close, and danced, hidden by the trees. When the music was over, he bent his head to hers and kissed her long and tenderly.

Another glance, one more kiss, and the heartfelt whisper, 'I love you, Kathleen. Always remember that.'

She watched him stride away. He turned only once, his gaze searching her out. A warm smile, a look of regret. Then he was gone, back to the celebrations. Back to the woman who was already wondering at his long absence.

Kathleen's stricken eyes followed him to the last. 'Goodbye, my love,' she murmured. Through the window she saw Melinda claim him. 'You belong to her, and the child. As for me,' she smiled through her tears, 'I will miss you for ever.'

***

'I HAVE TO find work,' Kathleen declared, restlessly pacing the kitchen, much to Cook's disapproval. 'But I don't know how, or what I'm capable of.' Right now, anything would do. Anything that would keep her busy and take her mind off Murray and his new bride. They had gone to Venice for their honeymoon.

Kathleen couldn't imagine a city with canals instead of roads. It sounded magical. Oh, if only—

'No good asking me,' Cook interrupted her thoughts, dumping kneaded dough on to the table and pushing her bunched fists into it. 'All I know is how to cook and bake, and anyway, what do you want to go working for when you have all you need right here?'

'I know, and I'm thankful for that. But it isn't enough. I need something to occupy my mind.'

'Talk to the master. He'll know best.'

'I've often thought I wouldn't mind learning about the world of merchandising.'

Cook was gently scornful. 'Oh no, miss, you wouldn't want to do that, handling money and suchlike. Best leave that sort of thing to the men.'

'I see,' said Kathleen with a grin, 'you don't think I'm capable, is that it?'

'Now, I never said that. I said it were best to leave such things to the men, and I meant it. Women are for getting wed and bearing children, not sitting at a desk poring over accounts and chasing after merchandise.' *Thump* went the dough as she threw it down again. 'Women ain't made for sailing the seven seas looking for treasure neither.'

'Maybe not.' Kathleen didn't entirely agree, but there was little point in arguing with Cook, who always had the last word.

'No maybe about it.' Eyeing Kathleen with concern, Cook asked tentatively, 'Is there any word from your brother, miss?'

'No.' Kathleen couldn't help but wonder what she might do if Adam did get in touch. Rightly or wrongly, she found it hard to forgive what he had done.

'I expect he's off on some adventure or other. He'll be back when he's found a fortune.' She pummelled the dough until the table shook. 'He'll be back before you know it,' she declared with conviction. 'You see if I'm not right.'

Kathleen smiled, but inside she was sad. 'I'm going out. If Mr Westerfield asks after me, would you tell him I've gone for a walk?'

'Course I will, miss.' Cook flopped the battered dough into a bowl, where it lay, limp and exhausted. 'A walk will do you good, if you don't mind me saying.' She draped a cloth over the bowl and then called out for the scullery maid, who pattered into the kitchen like a scared rabbit. 'Where the devil have you been?' Cook demanded.

Smiling to herself, Kathleen crept out. In the hallway, she collected a shawl and draped it loosely over her shoulders. She left the house and walked down the lane, towards Ilford High Street; past the White Horse public house, and the butcher's shop next door. Here she hurried her footsteps. The butcher's was a sight to turn her stomach, with its many pig corpses hanging outside, dripping blood on to the pavement and staring at her with big, dead eyes. Poor things, she thought, and hated herself for having enjoyed one of Cook's pork chops last night.

She bought a bobbin of cotton in the draper's, and two ounces of bull's-eyes in the grocer's two doors down. Kathleen had always been partial to bull's-eyes.

Sucking her sweets, she went on towards Valentine's Park, where she often sat and let the world go by.

She wandered over the crooked, rustic bridge and down to the stream. On the bank she sat and stretched out, not caring who might see her. In fact there was no one. She was alone, as she often was in this particular spot. 'Nobody can find me here,' she mused, closing her eyes to the autumn sunshine. 'This is my place. My very own private garden.' For the best part of two hours, she was undisturbed. Lying there, visited only by the birds and the bees, she could have stayed for ever. Eventually though, the daylight faded and evening began to creep in.

'Time to go,' she sighed. She brushed herself down and slowly retraced her steps back to Westerfield House, pausing at the bridge to mull over what she and Cook had talked about earlier. 'It's not a bad idea for me to learn a trade,' she said. 'I'll talk to Maurice this very evening, ask him if he can take me under his wing and show me the world of finance. After all, Adam's natural flair for figures only really came to light when he started working for Maurice.'

The idea wouldn't go away. 'Maybe I'll find I'm as good as he is. Why not?'

In the event, she had no chance to discuss it with Maurice that evening. As soon as she entered the house, he came hurrying towards her. 'Kathleen. Oh, thank goodness,' he exclaimed. 'Can you come to the study?'

'Are you all right?' she asked, thinking he looked ill.

'As soon as you can,' he said distractedly, and hurried away, back to his study.

Losing no time, Kathleen hung up her bonnet and shawl and followed him.

'Come in, my dear,' his voice called out when she tapped on the door.

Maurice was seated at his desk, his face grey with worry. On the opposite side of the desk, perched uneasily on the edge of her seat, was Connie Blakeman, her eyes wet with tears, and her face a picture of anxiety.

'Is anything wrong?' Kathleen asked, looking from one to the other. The question seemed foolish; it was painfully obvious that something was dreadfully wrong.

'Sit down, my dear.' He indicated a chair and then turned to Connie. 'Tell me again, please, in front of Miss Peterson.'

Connie played her part well. 'I'm not a liar,' she cried, appealing to Kathleen. 'Everything I've said is the truth.'

'I'm not calling you a liar,' Maurice assured her. 'I just want you to tell me again.'

Wiping her nose on her best linen hankie, Connie sniffed. 'You've been good to me, sir, and it grieves me to bring you such distressing news. But, as I stand before God, I'm telling you the truth. Some weeks back, your son took advantage of me, and now I find I'm carrying his bairn.' She glanced at Kathleen who was staring with shock. 'Miss Peterson knows how ill I was on the day of the wedding, sir. It was her who took me to my room.'

'Is this true, Kathleen?'

'Well, yes. But I didn't know she was . . . I mean . . .' Lost for words, she lowered her gaze. She was shaken by Connie's story.

What a terrible thing. And yet, she wasn't surprised that Christian was capable of something like this.

'Nobody knew,' said Connie. 'I wasn't even certain myself until very recently.'

Maurice rubbed a hand over his face. He could confidently lead a board meeting with a dozen or so men in fierce debate and still win the day; he could shake a good deal out of thin air, when the competition was baying at his heels; and there was no ocean he was afraid to cross. But here and now, confronted by a woman accusing his own son of violating her, he was utterly out of his depth.

'I'm truly sorry, sir,' Connie wailed convincingly, 'but it wasn't my fault. I swear on my mother's grave, I did nothing to encourage him.'

Kathleen felt the need to intervene. 'When did all this happen? Have you told Christian you believe you're expecting his child?'

Connie answered in a small voice, looking from one to the other and seeming exhausted by the ordeal. 'I haven't told anybody outside this room. I felt I owed it to the master to speak to him first.'

'And I'm very grateful for that,' he said. Turning to Kathleen, he asked solemnly, 'Could you please find Christian and bring him to me?'

Kathleen was on her feet in an instant. 'Of course,' she said.

When she returned with a puzzled and rather sullen Christian, Kathleen made to leave, but Maurice asked her to stay. Christian resented it but said nothing. As soon as he saw Connie seated there, looking forlorn, he was instantly on his guard. 'What's this all about?' he demanded of his father.

Maurice was blunt. He relayed Connie's claim, and then, in a voice that shook with anger, he asked, 'What have you to say for yourself?'

The row that followed was heard by everyone in the house. Christian vehemently denied the charge, while Connie accused him of creeping up on her that night when she was in the kitchen. 'He tore off my nightgown,' she cried. 'He was drunk out of his mind, and strong as a lion. I didn't stand a chance. I'm ruined.' Falling into Kathleen's arms, she sobbed her heart out. 'He's ruined me,' she said brokenly. 'What will I do now? No man will take my word against his son's.'

'Take her out!' Striding across the room, Maurice flung open the door, his face set like stone. Only when he looked at Connie's face did he soften. 'You're wrong, my dear,' he said. 'No other man has a son as wicked as mine.'

Kathleen took Connie to the drawing room, leaving her there while she went to the kitchen.

'You should have rung through,' Cook chided. 'But then, you never have, so why should you start now?' While Kathleen got a tray ready, Cook set the kettle to boil for tea.

Kathleen could hear Christian's voice, yelling abuse and denying everything. 'I'm sorry you have to hear all that,' she told Cook.

'So am I, miss.' She clicked her teeth. 'Dreadful business, if you don't mind me saying.'

Kathleen picked up the tray and carried it into the drawing room, where she and Connie waited, Kathleen anxiously walking back and forth, Connie noisily gulping her tea and silently congratulating herself.

Suddenly there was a lot of shouting, much closer now. Then a loud, rattling bang. 'Stay here,' Kathleen told Connie. She hurried out of the room and across to the study. The door was wide open, almost split from its hinges where Christian had flung it back in his rage.

Maurice was standing leaning on his desk, his hands spread in front of him. 'He's gone.' Looking up at Kathleen as she came into the room, he seemed like an old, old man. 'I never thought I would have to throw him out. My own son.' He sank into the chair and covered his face with his hands. 'Oh, Kathleen, Kathleen. What else could I do?' Into his mind came the image of his lovely wife, and how they had been a happy family once. Now, in his awful loneliness, only Kathleen gave him a reason for living.

She went to comfort him. 'Don't reproach yourself,' she said softly, putting her arm round his shoulders. 'You did what you felt was right.'

'He admitted it.' His voice was heavy with pain. 'She was telling the truth.'

'I'm sorry.'

'I couldn't turn him out penniless. He may be a weak, useless coward, but he's still my son. I've made him a generous allowance, but if he hasn't got work inside twelve months, he'll get no more. I've told him that. Now it's up to him.' He sighed. 'I'd better speak to her now.'

While Kathleen went to collect Connie, he took the brandy bottle and a glass from the cupboard, poured a small measure and quickly drank it down. He was not a drinking man, but now and then a small nip took away the heart's chill.

Connie listened while he told her what he had decided. 'In view of the fact that my son reluctantly admitted his part, and Kathleen witnessed how ill you were, I've decided not to submit you to a medical examination.'

'I should think not!' she spluttered. 'I want no man, medical or otherwise, putting his hands on me.'

'I shall make one, generous, single payment, to see you through until the child is born. After that, there will be an adequate allowance. However, I will not leave myself vulnerable to blackmail by any—'

'Never, sir!'

'And to that effect, you will be required to sign a document, drawn up by my solicitor.'

'Yes, sir.'

'As for the child, he or she will be my own flesh and blood but I shall be the one to decide whether or not I want to make contact. Do you understand?'

'Yes, sir.' Pity. She wanted him to be the loving, generous grandfather all his life, and maybe leave a hefty legacy when he was gone.

'At this point, I have no wish to see or hear of the child.' He glanced at Kathleen, who was visibly surprised by this. 'I've been disappointed enough in my own children.' He squared his shoulders and suddenly he was a man of authority again, tall and straight, his face expressionless. 'You must make no attempt to contact any member of this family, or let it be known to anyone who the father of your child is. Before I make a settlement on you and the child, I must have your agreement on that.'

Connie's quick mind calculated that, in the end, she might be better off doing it his way. 'How will I know the child and myself will always be cared for?'

'The document my solicitor will draw up will be legally binding on both of us. You and the child will be provided for all your lives as long as you keep to the terms I've outlined.'

'I'm very grateful, sir.'

His manner softened. 'So you agree to the terms?' She nodded. 'Then I suggest you leave this house as soon as arrangements can be made. Say nothing to the servants. They may guess, but if we all keep our silence, no one will ever know for certain.'

Kathleen was concerned that any woman should be left to bear and rear a child alone. 'Will you be all right?' she asked Connie as she prepared to leave the house two days later.

Connie was humbled by her kindness. 'After the way I've behaved towards you in the past, I'm surprised you don't want me kicked out and left on the streets.'

'I wouldn't want that for anyone.' Kathleen knew what it was like not to have a home and to search the streets for a roof. 'Take care of yourself,' she said as she waved her off, a small, pretty woman whose rage at the world was now tempered by the knowledge that soon enough she would be the sole person responsible for another human being, her own child, and because of the honourable generosity of her child's grandfather they would never want.

I N THE WEEKS that followed, Maurice learned to smile again, but he had lost some of his self-confidence, and he felt his age keenly. It seemed almost as if fate frowned on him, and he held back from declaring his love to Kathleen although his dream of marrying her remained undimmed.

Kathleen talked to him about learning the business of merchandising, and he was delighted. 'A woman in the business,' he laughed. 'It might raise a few eyebrows.' But he loved the idea, especially since it meant they would spend more time together. 'I have an important business meeting in Liverpool next week. Come with me, Kathleen.'

Thrilled, she accepted. This would be her first real introduction to the world of business.

But fate, yet again, intervened.

The morning before they were due to leave, Maurice came to her in the garden. Kathleen knew from the look on his face that something was wrong. 'What is it?' she asked nervously. 'Tell me.'

He took hold of her hand. 'It's Adam,' he said. 'I've just got news.'

From the kitchen window the servants saw him relay the news. 'God help us,' Cook sobbed, 'if it ain't one thing it's another.'

'Maybe he ain't drowned,' Maisie said hopefully. 'Maybe they've got it all wrong.'

The butler intervened. Shifting them from the window, he said quietly, 'They haven't got it wrong. The ship went down in treacherous seas, that's what the master told me before he went outside. "The ship was lost, and everyone with it. Including Adam Peterson. His name was on the passenger list." '

It was the worst week of Kathleen's life. Maurice set in train investigations, gleaning information from every possible source. Eight days after the initial news, official confirmation came through that the ship, bound for New York, had broken apart in a storm and sunk, taking every soul on board with her.

Unable to eat or sleep, Kathleen saw it as a punishment for her unforgiving anger towards her brother. In her mind's eye she saw his face, the way he used to laugh, the way he would look at her as a child when she'd done something wrong. At the service held in the local church, her grief was crippling.

One day ran into another, and when there was nothing to

distract her, the quiet was unbearable. She walked a lot, and kept to herself. She cried herself to sleep, and in her every waking moment she cursed herself for being so wrapped in herself and Murray's sudden appearance that she had not seen how deeply troubled Adam was. And so he had gone without a word of love, or forgiveness. She imagined his loneliness, and her own was tenfold.

Maurice's heart ached for her. He knew she needed time and space to come to terms with her loss on her own, without interference from him. But he cancelled all business trips and made sure he was never far from her, should she need him.

One warm October evening, she was strolling in the garden and caught sight of him at the drawing-room window, watching her. He smiled and waved to her. To his joy she beckoned to him to join her, and at last she spoke to him of her feelings, her sense of guilt. 'Adam knew I would never forgive him, that's why he went away. If it hadn't been for me, he would never have gone.'

'You know that's not true.'

'How can you say that?' She looked at him, and suddenly she realised what he meant. He knew. He had known all along.

'Your brother was always in love with Melinda,' he said softly. 'I knew that, and so did you.'

She gulped back the tears. 'But he left thinking I would hate him, and now he's never coming back.'

Gently, Maurice took hold of her hand. It was cold. Cradling it between his own, he fed back the warmth. 'I have no doubt your reaction to the knowledge that he had deceived you about Murray was something he did not relish having to face, but the truth is, Adam was driven from this house because of his love for Melinda. I don't believe he would have stayed even if you'd gone down on your knees and pleaded with him. You see, my dear, love is a powerful thing. I know.'

Something about the way he spoke made her ask, 'Are you lonely too?'

'Yes, I am.'

'Why have you never married again?' She shivered, and he put his arm round her and drew her close.

'You're cold, my dear. Do you want to go inside?'

'Not yet.' She felt warm in his arms, safe, protected from the outside world. 'You still haven't told me.' She moved in his arms. 'Why have you never married again?'

The moment seemed to go on for ever. He gazed down on that small upturned face and those lovely dark eyes, and his love for her was like a beacon inside him. 'Why do you think?' he murmured. All his need rose up in him, and it seemed so natural to lean forward and kiss her. When his mouth touched hers, it was as if his very soul took flight. He kissed her with all the love and tenderness of a man who would cherish and protect her always. 'Marry me, Kathleen.' Drawing away, he held her face between the palms of his hands. 'I won't ever let you down.'

She started to tell him, 'I'm not in love . . . with . . .'

'Don't say it,' he whispered. 'All that matters is that we're two very lonely people. We can stay that way, or we can make each other happy. Please, Kathleen. Will you say yes?'

'Yes,' she murmured. 'If you think I can make you happy.'

Overcome with emotion, he raised his head and looked to the sky, giving a silent prayer of thanks. When he looked at her again, he was smiling like a man at peace. 'You've made me happy since the first moment I saw you,' he said brokenly. 'And I've loved you . . . all my life.'

Kathleen didn't fully understand what he was saying. She saw the love in his eyes, and it warmed her. Murray was beyond her reach. Adam was gone for ever. She had no close friends and the loneliness stretched before her like a never-ending road. Maurice was all she had in the world, and he needed her. He loved her. She owed it to him, and to herself, to give back some of the happiness he had given her.

Strangely content, Kathleen nestled into his arms. She vowed to heal the wounds his own children had inflicted on him. She would be a good wife and, if there should be children, she would be a good mother.

At last, she had a worthwhile purpose.

PART FIVE

1892
THE
PRODIGALS

Chapter Sixteen

THE SCENE WAS one of domestic bliss.

On this balmy summer's evening, the windows were open wide to let in the cool night air and the chink of crystal heralded a celebration. 'Happy birthday, Kathleen, my love.' Raising his glass, Maurice drank a toast. 'To the woman who made me the happiest man on God's earth.'

Kathleen smiled. 'You're a very easy man to please.'

'No.' He shook his head. 'That's where you're wrong. Only you could have made my life complete.' He gazed on her with deepest love. 'Forty-two years old, and still the most beautiful woman I've ever seen.' The idea that his first wife might live on through Kathleen was long ago forgotten. Each of them was lovely. Each of them gentle and kind, but so very different.

'You flatter me,' she chided, a little embarrassed. 'Only this morning I found two grey hairs.' She laughed. 'I plucked them out so you wouldn't see them.'

He smiled. It was said that some women never realised their own special beauty. Kathleen was such a woman. He looked at her now. She had worn the years well. Her skin glowed with health, and her long dark hair shone as it did on the day he found her. The neck was firm, the dark eyes soft and wondrous, like those of a child. She carried her sadness deep down and never spoke of it. There shone from her face only a kind of contentment, and every day, every moment he was with her, he never forgot how fortunate a man he was.

For a moment Kathleen observed him across the table. Though only in his early sixties and working harder than ever, Maurice had grown old before her eyes. Still tall and handsome, still possessing a certain commanding presence, he had become slightly stooped at the shoulders, his hair was marbled with grey, and to her observant eyes his attractive face showed signs of stress. Though he never burdened her with his troubles, Kathleen knew he was saddened by the absence of his children and weary of the demands of his work.

'Are you tired?' she asked, hoping he might say no.

'No. You?'

'I'm too excited for sleep.'

He walked the length of the table and taking her by the hand led her to the fireplace, where he sat on the couch. Kathleen sat by his feet, as she often did. 'It's been a lovely day, Maurice.' She fingered the pearls round her neck. 'Such a beautiful present. Thank you.'

'Kathleen.'

She looked up.

'If I ask you something,' leaning over, he kissed the top of her head, 'will you be honest with me?'

'I always am.' But then he had never asked her the kind of questions where she might feel the need to deceive him.

There was a moment while he wondered if he should broach a subject so close to both their hearts. But tonight for some reason he couldn't fathom he needed to know if he had failed her in any way.

Inexplicably, Kathleen suddenly felt afraid. 'What's wrong, Maurice?'

'Nothing's wrong,' he assured her. 'I was just thinking.'

'About us?'

'Do you ever regret not having children?' There. It was said.

Stunned by his question, and wondering what had brought it on, Kathleen gazed into the empty fire grate. She didn't answer right away because she didn't want to make him feel guilty. Yes, she would have loved children, but they weren't to be. It was a bitter disappointment.

'I'm sorry.' Mortified, he drew her close. 'I should never have asked you.'

She looked up then. 'You have every right to ask me,' she told him. 'But why now? We've been married for over twenty years and you've never asked it before.'

'I had to know,' he answered simply. 'Don't ask me why, but I feel the need to know if I've failed you.'

Her smile was convincing. 'You haven't,' she lied. This was the first time she had ever deliberately deceived him. It gave her no pleasure. 'What about you? Do you regret we never had children?'

'Children can be a blessing,' he admitted. 'They can also be heartache.' He shook his head. 'All I've ever wanted is to make you happy.'

'And you have,' she said. Her assurance was all he needed.

They were quiet for a time, he leaning forward with his arms round her neck and his head close to hers; and she with her long legs stretched out over the rug, her hands enclosed in his, and a feeling of contentment filling her soul.

'I wanted it all to be so perfect for you.' There was a sense of urgency in his voice.

'What is it, Maurice?' Scrambling up, she sat beside him. 'You sound so strange, as if it's all going to end tomorrow. Something's worrying you. Is it work? Is it because you lost the shipment you so desperately wanted?'

'No. I did want that cargo of silk, but it wasn't the first and it won't be the last. I've come to accept I can't win all the time, and lately I've been thinking of taking a year off.' He chucked her under the chin. 'Maybe we'll sail round the world, what do you say to that?'

'I say if you haven't got your work, you'll be lost.'

'Ah, but there isn't the excitement like there used to be. Or the opportunities. In the old days I could buy a shipload of tobacco in the morning and sell it on in the afternoon for twice

287

what I paid. You know that. You saw it for yourself – before you decided it wasn't the kind of work you wanted and took yourself off to do voluntary work at the hospital.'

Kathleen recognised his evasive tactics. 'Is it Christian?' she persisted. 'Have you heard from him? Is he in trouble? Is that what's worrying you?' Strange how when she thought of Christian, she always assumed he was either in trouble or causing trouble.

'I haven't heard from Christian since the day I threw him out. If I never hear from him again, it won't lose me any sleep.'

'What about Melinda? You miss her, don't you?'

He bowed his head. Then, as if winning a fight within himself, he sat up, straightened his shoulders and answered with conviction, 'If she chooses to move to the other side of the world, there is nothing I can do about it.'

'It's my fault she went away. If I hadn't said yes when you asked me to marry you, she would still be here.' Their wedding had been a very quiet affair. Neither of his children attended the service. Rumours reached them that Christian was sinking deeper and deeper into a seedy world of crime and as for Melinda, she persuaded Murray to accept a post overseas, in Australia, as far away as she could take her husband and son.

Kathleen suspected that Murray had needed little persuasion. On the day Maurice told them that he and Kathleen were to be married, she had seen the pain on Murray's face. And she felt in her heart she would never see him again.

'I offered Murray a good position in the business, but he turned it down,' Maurice recalled. 'I know she was behind that, and I know it was her who stopped me from seeing my grandson.'

'It's him you really miss, isn't it? Not so much Melinda but David, your grandson.'

Torn between love and fear, he didn't know how to answer. 'I'm not sure if he should be anywhere near me.'

'You're too hard on yourself.'

Maurice didn't think so. 'What if he turns out to be like

Christian? What if he has the same selfish tendencies as his mother? I don't know where I went wrong but for both my children to turn out the way they did, it must have been my fault.' There was anger in his voice. 'I sometimes wonder if David even knows he's got a grandfather. Perhaps his mother has told him I'm a monster to be avoided at all costs, or that I'm dead. David was only a baby when they sailed away. He'll be almost twenty-four now, and he probably doesn't even know I exist.'

Kathleen was shocked. All these years he had never once spoken so openly about his grandson, or so bitterly. 'You never told me how strongly you feel about this. Write to your grandson,' she urged him. 'Tell him how much you want to see him.'

'And have her come between us? I'd rather he never knew me than got caught between the two of us. I don't want to be the one who causes him to choose between his grandfather and his mother. And she would make him choose, make no mistake about that.'

'He's your grandson, Maurice. He has a right to know. Why don't you find out exactly where they are? You know they settled in Melbourne. With your contacts it shouldn't be too hard to find them.' Briefly she wondered about that other grandchild, Connie's son – or was it a daughter? It troubled her, not knowing how mother and child had fared, or even if they were alive. As far as she knew, Maurice had made no attempt to find out, although presumably his solicitor, who was responsible for ensuring the allowance was paid, could have told him. Maurice never mentioned the subject, and Kathleen did not feel it was her place to probe.

Maurice seemed to be considering her suggestion, and she was glad. He was such a good man, he deserved to have the love of one grandchild at least, and maybe, just maybe, that young man might be the means of bringing the family back together again.

She smiled to herself. That young man – Murray's son. Was

289

he like his father? Did he have the same wayward fair hair and warm green eyes? Did he smile in a way that touched your heart? Was he quick to laugh, and did he have a mischievous twinkle in his eyes?

'I'm tired, my dear.' Maurice's voice shattered her thoughts. 'You don't have to come up if you don't want to.' He stood up. 'It's been a long day, and I'm not as young as I used to be.' In that moment he looked years older than his age. 'Shall I ask Cook to send you in a hot drink?'

'No, thank you. I'll just sit here awhile.'

'Goodnight then, my dear.' He held out his arms and she went to him. They kissed, a gentle, loving kiss. 'You've given me so much,' he murmured, 'and I've given you so little.' He cradled her face in his hands. 'Sometimes I fear I stole you from life. So young. So innocent. I wouldn't blame you if you resented me for it.'

Kathleen couldn't understand his melancholy mood. 'I could never resent you,' she said fiercely. 'You and I have given each other contentment and love. We made each other happy, and we've been good companions over the years. It was what we both wanted. Please, Maurice, don't regret what we've had together.'

'I don't think you'll ever know how much I love you,' he whispered. He kissed her again and left the room.

It was one o'clock in the morning when she climbed the stairs to bed. These days, Maurice slept in his own room, but she always went in to kiss him goodnight before she crossed the landing to her own room.

She went in now, tiptoeing across the room so as not to wake him. 'Goodnight,' she whispered. 'Sleep tight.' He stirred, glanced up, and smiled. 'And you're wrong,' she said. 'I *do* know how much you love me.'

'God bless you, Kathleen,' he murmured.

It was when she went to close the door behind her that Kathleen sensed something different. She stared across the room to where he lay, and suddenly, like the gossamer wings of an angel in flight, there came the softest, most beautiful sigh. It was unnerving, making every hair on her neck stand on end.

Instinctively, she hurried back to him. 'Maurice?' She looked into his face, and she knew instantly. 'Oh, no! Dear God, *no!*' Falling on the bed, she took him in her arms, rocking him back and forth, her cries filling the house.

Maurice had gone. And she was all alone.

<hr />

THE HEAVENS OPENED and it poured with rain on the day they buried Maurice Westerfield.

The news of his departure from this world had spread far and wide. People from all walks of life came to pay their last respects. 'Maurice Westerfield was a pillar of our community,' the vicar told his congregation. 'He was a respected businessman and a kind soul who cared for his friends and servants with equal compassion.'

His gaze fell on Kathleen who was seated in the family pew, head bowed and veil down to hide her red, raw eyes. 'Our thoughts and love go out to his widow and family,' the vicar concluded. He closed his prayer book and led the procession behind the coffin as it was carried on the shoulders of four strong men to its last resting place.

Kathleen came next, then Maurice's son and daughter. His grandson walked sedately with his father, two men out of the same pod. David was the same build as his father, with the same long, easy stride; the same green eyes and wayward hair. Kathleen had not noticed. She had been aware of very little since Maurice was taken from her.

As they walked in silence, huddled under their umbrellas, the sound of the rain seemed to echo their grief.

When the prayer was said, and the earth sprinkled, they made their way back. Kathleen climbed into her carriage alone, while Christian accompanied his sister and her family. 'She's beautiful,'

David remarked. Like his father, he had not been able to take his eyes off Kathleen.

They followed her now, the carriages moving slowly, respectfully. 'Why was I not told about her?' David asked his mother. 'Why did I never get to meet my grandfather?'

'This is not the time.' The years in Australia had done nothing to dim Melinda's jealousy and resentment of Kathleen. In fact her bitterness had grown in proportion to her disillusion with her empty marriage to Murray, until now she hated her with a passion so strong she could taste it.

'You never told me I had a grandfather. Why, Mother? Why was I not told?'

Murray intervened. 'Not now, David,' he said in a firm voice, his eyes flickering a warning. 'Like your mother said, this is not the time.'

At the house, everyone gathered round Kathleen, offering their condolences, comforting her with their fond memories of Maurice.

At a distance, Christian and his sister stood in a corner, talking in whispers and occasionally glancing in Kathleen's direction. When she looked up and caught their gaze, she smiled at them sadly, thinking that at least in their common grief they could be united. But her smile was not returned. Nor did they seem too grief-stricken. In fact, at one point Melinda let out a peal of laughter, drawing astonished looks from everyone there and a sharp, private rebuke from her husband.

When the formalities were over, Murray brought his son to meet her. 'This is David,' he said proudly. He stood back while his son stepped forward.

'He's so like you,' Kathleen said, and her heart was broken all over again.

Holding out his hand, David said warmly, 'It isn't the best way for us to meet, but I'm very glad to know you.'

'Thank you,' she said. 'And I'm very glad to know you.'

While she and David talked, about Australia, about the grandfather he had never known, Murray could not take his eyes off her. Seeing her now was like a knife through his heart. He devoured her beauty, her presence, her every word like a man starved for too long.

After a time, the guests began to leave, forming a little queue to wish Kathleen and the family the best for the future.

All this time, the servants had been weaving in and out, doing their duty and hiding their sadness. Now, however, they returned to their own private places, quietly shedding their tears for a man they had loved and respected, and wondering what would happen to them, and to the mistress.

'That Christian,' said Maisie unhappily, 'he told his sister that the mistress wouldn't get a penny. "If she thinks she's getting his fortune, she can think again." That's what he said.'

'You're not to carry gossip, my girl!' Cook warned. 'You heard nothing, do you hear? You heard nothing!'

Maisie went off in a huff, but when she'd gone, Cook told the butler, 'I've never known that girl to tell a lie. If she's right, and I'm certain she is, the mistress had better watch out for them two grabbing buggers!'

The butler was inclined to agree. 'There's bad feelings, running deep,' he muttered. 'If I know them two from old, they'll show their hand sooner or later.'

———✦———

THEY SHOWED THEIR hand the very next evening, when the solicitor came to read the will. After outlining some minor bequests, he came to the bulk of the estate and the Westerfield fortune: 'Three thousand guineas to my son Christian; the same amount to my daughter Melinda. My grandson David is to have my collection of silver sailing ships, and the sum of one thousand guineas, to be invested until he reaches the age of thirty. To his father, Murray, with my thanks and gratitude, I leave my coveted chess set.'

The solicitor looked up, his stern gaze travelling over the faces of those present. 'Now, to the bulk of the estate,' he said.

'As directed by the will of Maurice Westerfield, it goes in its remaining entirety to his widow Kathleen.'

'No!' Melinda was instantly on her feet and accusing Kathleen. 'Cunning bitch! You did this! You got him to turn against his own family. It's our money! Mine and my brother's.'

Incensed by her outburst, Murray leaped up and grabbed her by the shoulders. 'Get a hold of yourself,' he muttered, desperate to retain some kind of dignity. 'You don't know what you're saying.'

'She knows what she's saying right enough, and so do I.' Christian launched himself at Murray, sending him stumbling to the ground. 'I've seen you making eyes at that bitch. Is it *her* you want, or are you after getting your paws on my father's money?'

As Murray tried to get up, Christian knocked him down again with a vicious kick to the stomach. 'Want to fight, do you? Come on then!' He was about to land another kick but this time Murray was too quick for him. Grabbing his ankle, he tossed Christian aside.

'There'll be no fighting here.' Murray picked him up and held him by the scruff of the neck. 'Do you understand?'

Kathleen stepped forward, her eyes hard and unforgiving as she told Christian, 'You're a disgrace to your father's memory. All his life you caused him sorrow, and now that he's dead you tarnish his memory. Get out. And don't ever come back.'

He clenched his fists and tried to move towards her, but Murray still held him fast. 'You heard what she said,' he growled.

'Oh, I heard what she said right enough,' Christian sneered. 'I'll go, and gladly. I can't stand the sight of her. But you haven't heard the last of me.' Glaring at Kathleen, he told her in a trembling voice, 'None of this is yours.' Opening wide his arms, he embraced the house and land, a wicked smile creasing his face. 'Be on your guard, *Mrs Westerfield*.' He spoke her name as though it was a curse. 'I *will* be back, and when I am, *you'll* be the one thrown out of the house, for good.'

Melinda moved towards him. 'Go away, Christian,' she said. 'You shame us both.'

Shocked, he glanced up. He saw the look in her eyes and, without another word, took his leave.

Kathleen was grateful for her intervention, and for Murray's. 'Thank you,' she said to them both. 'I'm sorry it had to come to this.'

'No,' Melinda was kindness itself, 'it's us who should be sorry.' Turning her blue eyes on Murray, she said, 'Please, take me back to the hotel.'

'You know you don't have to stay in a hotel,' Kathleen said. 'I've told you, you're more than welcome to stay here with me.' It would be nice to have company. She might even get to tell David more about his grandfather.

Melinda graciously refused. They quickly left, with Murray giving a backward glance as he climbed into the carriage.

'Goodbye Murray,' Kathleen whispered. 'It seems we're destined to be always parting.'

The following morning David asked his parents to take him into London and show him the sights. 'I've never been there,' he reminded them, 'and you've told me so much about it.'

Murray was delighted, but Melinda begged off. 'I had a mind to do some shopping here in Ilford before we go back,' she said. 'I need a new hat, and my blue jacket is way past its best. You go ahead. I'll see you both when you get back.'

'If you're sure.' Murray had grown used to her impulsive whims and fancies.

'Of course I'm sure,' she said, kissing them in turn. 'You know I always like to shop on my own.'

The two men left, Murray's arm draped over his son's broad shoulders. 'Right, son, where would you like to go first?'

'The docks,' came the immediate reply. 'I want to see where you and Grandfather started out.'

Once the men were out of the way, Melinda took a carriage to the far side of Ilford. After giving the driver an address, she settled back to renew her acquaintance with all the sights and sounds of the town; past the old post office, down Barley Lane; along Oakfield Road where the authorities had earmarked a site for Ilford's first fire station, then out to the edge of town where the driver manoeuvred his carriage down a narrow street. Flanked either side by rows of terraced houses, the street was loud with playing children. Mothers watched from a distance, babes at their feet, and tattered shawls round their shoulders.

Bringing his carriage to a halt, the driver jumped down to open the door for his well-dressed passenger. 'Are you sure this is the right address?' he asked. 'It doesn't seem the sort of place a lady like yourself should be visiting.'

Ignoring his comment, she gave him a steely glare. 'Wait here,' she instructed, going at a smart pace towards number twelve.

'Get orf, yer buggers!' The driver ran at a number of ragged children who were stroking his horse. 'I don't want him catching no bleedin' fleas from the likes o' you lot.'

Inside the house, Melinda held a handkerchief over her nose. 'How can you live in a place like this?'

'Don't you come here with your high and bloody mighty ways,' he warned. 'I'm living here because I've got nowhere else to live.' He swaggered across the room. 'But don't worry, soon I'll be living in splendour. I'll have servants and a carriage and all the booze and women I want.'

'You're drunk.' Disgusted, she wafted the smell away. 'I thought we agreed there'd be no more drinking until it's settled.'

'I've only had one, to settle my nerves, that's all.'

'Make it the last, until all this is over.'

'Trust me.'

'I've got no choice. I can't be seen to be involved. Murray would never stand for it. Neither would David, come to that.'

'I'll need money. If I have to consort with solicitors and suchlike, I'll need to look the part.'

Digging into her bag, Melinda took out a fat wad of notes. 'This should be enough to begin with.' She flung the money on the table. 'You'll have all you need, but keep your mouth shut and stay sober.'

'She's really got under your skin, hasn't she?' Sneering, Christian grabbed up the money. 'Is it just because she married Father and cheated us out of our inheritance, or have you got it in for her because Murray looks at her the way he's never looked at you?'

Her face went white, and for a moment he thought she might hurl herself at him. Instead, she came a step closer, her eyes boring into his.

'*Ruin her!*' Her voice was quiet, shivering with emotion. 'I don't care how you do it, or how many years it takes.' She paused. 'I want her left with nothing but the clothes she stands up in.'

Chapter Seventeen

'THEY'RE HERE!' red-faced and anxious, Maisie came rushing into the kitchen. 'I've shown them into the drawing room.'

'How many?' Like everyone else, the butler thought it was a sorry business but there was nothing he could do about it.

'Four of 'em.' Maisie counted on her fingers. 'There was the awful Christian, a lady friend of his, and two men in dark suits and bowler hats.'

Cook gasped. 'They'll be the bailiffs, may God forgive 'em!' The impact of what was about to take place sent the strength from her legs. 'I'll have to sit down,' she said, dropping into the rocking chair. 'I can't believe it's come to this. It's been four years since the master died, and she's not had a minute's peace in all that time.'

The butler stood with his hands behind his back, staring out of the window at the two parked carriages. 'I wonder what's going on in there,' he mused.

'You know very well what's going on,' Cook exclaimed. 'The same thing that's been going on these past four years. Right from the start, Christian Westerfield was determined to get his claws on this place, and every penny the master left. Anybody who's followed the court cases and read the newspaper articles knows that.'

Maisie peered through the window. 'Who are all those folk gathering outside?' she cried. 'What do they want?'

'News travels fast round these parts,' Cook said with satis-faction. 'The local shopkeepers and tradesmen want to send her on her way with their good will, that's what they want. They all know what a disgrace it is. That good lady in there is besieged by them that aren't fit to wipe her boots. And them folk outside are waiting to show their displeasure.'

They didn't have to wait long.

'She's coming!' Maisie had been peering through the door and now she slammed it shut and ran to stand beside Cook. 'She's got 'er bags packed and everything, and she did it all by herself.'

'Course she did.' Cook's ample bosom rose with pride. 'She were never one to be waited on hand and foot, weren't Miss Kathleen. Sometimes I think she's more one of us than one o' them.'

'Aye, and it's them who's turned on her, damn their souls to hell and back.' The butler was not one for strong words but at this particular moment he felt like a fighting man.

When the door opened they all stood to attention. 'Sit down, please.' Leaving her bags outside, Kathleen came in and closed the door. 'Is there a cup of tea going begging?' she asked, and Cook had one in front of her in no time at all.

'Bless you, ma'am,' she said, wiping the tears from her eyes. 'Whatever will yer do?'

'I'll find work, and I'll do very well, I'm sure. There's no need for you to worry either. I've fought hard for you to keep your positions here. The solicitors and I have come to an agreement. Your jobs are safe.'

'How can we ever thank yer?'

'No need for thanks.' Kathleen was just grateful that she had been able to insist on that small clause.

Before she departed, the butler told her how sad they were to see her go in such a spiteful manner. 'The place won't be the same without you here.'

'Thank you,' said Kathleen simply. 'I shall miss you all.'

When she emerged from the house carrying a large tapestry

bag in one hand and a small portmanteau in the other, a great cheer went up. 'You don't deserve to be thrown out of your own house and home!' they yelled. 'Shame on them that did it to yer.'

As she went down the drive, head high and heart full, they called after her, 'God bless yer!' Cries of encouragement and anger followed her to the gates. Here she turned, her stricken eyes going over the house and the grounds, the home where she and Maurice had spent so many happy years together. In the autumn she had planted narcissus and daffodil in the flower urns outside the front door. Now, in the warmth of spring, the shoots could be clearly seen from where she stood.

'Goodbye, Maurice.' She raised her eyes and found herself looking straight into the triumphant face of Christian Westerfield. 'Badness never prospers,' she whispered.

With that, she went on her way. Out of the past and into the future, with only a few personal belongings. And the clothes she stood up in.

When she was lost from sight, her enemies began to disperse. The woman went off to roam the house. One of the men hurried to the carriage, anxious to escape the baying crowd. The second man remained behind, huddled in a deep and furtive conversation with Christian Westerfield.

'You're to follow her wherever she goes,' Christian instructed him, just as he himself had been instructed, by Melinda. 'You're to spoil every chance she has of work or lodgings. You'll hound her, day and night, until she has no friends, nor reason for living.'

'By! Yer asking me to ruin 'er!'

'Does that bother you? Because if it does, I'll get somebody else.'

'No, it don't bother me. As long as yer make it worth me while.'

Christian thrust a roll of banknotes into his sweaty palm. 'That's more money than you could earn in a year. If I'm satisfied with your work, you'll get more.'

The man grinned wickedly. 'Oh, you'll be satisfied, I can promise yer that, guv. She'll come up against all kinds of obstacles. When she thinks she's sailing before the wind, I'll set up a storm to send her down, and when she seems to be striding too far ahead, I'll put the skids under her. Everywhere she turns, there'll be bad luck and misfortune. There'll be no let-up.' Feeling bold, he nudged Christian, sniggering into his face. 'I reckon that should do the trick, don't you, guv?'

'Oh, yes,' Christian murmured. 'I think that should do it.'

Mutually satisfied, they parted company.

Christian lingered on the front step, watching as the people began to drift away. 'This is a good day's work,' he told his woman when she came to him. 'It makes a man feel good to know he's done something worthwhile.' Melinda would have been proud of him, he thought. It was one favour in return for another. She would not press for her share of the inheritance if he did as she asked. Ruining the lovely Kathleen seemed to be all she wanted.

Chapter Eighteen

Rosie Maitland sat back in her chair, the old lady's diary open on the desk before her. Her eyes were sore from reading in the gaslight but, like last night and every other night she'd been on night duty in the hospital, she felt compelled to finish the chronicles of the old lady who seemed destined to end her days here in a charity ward.

'Nurse Maitland!' Matron's soldierly voice startled her. 'Reading again?' She would have peered at the diary, but Rosie was too quick. Snatching it up, she rammed it into her apron pocket.

'Sorry, Matron,' she gasped. 'I was just about to do the rounds. Everything's quiet so far. Nothing to report.'

'Good.'

'Matron?'

'Yes, what is it?'

'She won't suffer, will she?' Rosie glanced down the ward. 'The old lady, I mean.'

'According to Dr Naylor, she'll probably just sink quietly away. Her injuries are slowly mending but she seems to have lost the will to live.' She marched briskly towards the door. 'Get on, nurse,' she whispered harshly. 'Get on.'

Rosie's first call was to Kathleen who was sleeping soundly. 'I don't understand,' she whispered. 'Maurice Westerfield was a rich and powerful man who adored the ground you walked on.' She observed the sleeping face; not young any more, but still a proud and lovely face. 'What happened to you? If you had all that, and the love of a good man, how in God's name could you have come to this?'

She finished her rounds and went back to her desk. Here she sat, watching Kathleen from a distance, and wishing she had known her when she was younger. 'What a life you've lived,' she murmured. 'What a tragic, exciting life. So many relationships of one kind or another, and yet here you are, all alone at the end.' It was difficult for her to accept. 'What happened?' she muttered. 'What happened to you, Kathleen Peterson?'

'Talking to yourself, are you?' The hours had passed and now the new shift was starting. 'That's a real bad habit, Rosie Maitland. Some people might think you were going out of your mind.'

'Maybe I am.' She prepared to leave. 'Miss Leatherhead wet the bed twice,' she reported.

The other nurse wrinkled her nose. 'From the smell wafting down the ward now, I'd say she's done a bit more than that.'

'She must have seen you coming,' Rosie laughed. 'It serves you right for confiscating her knitting yesterday.'

'She could have hurt herself with those needles, you know that.'

'Tell her, not me.' Swinging away, Rosie chuckled, 'I'm off to my bed.'

Normally the walk home took her only ten minutes at a brisk pace, but tonight she loitered, thinking about Kathleen. 'I can't understand it,' she kept saying. 'Where are they now? All the people she knew. Why have they deserted her?'

As usual when she got home, he was waiting. As usual, he wanted to row. Afterwards, he wanted to make up and use her in the same old way. 'No!' She was done with all that. 'Not tonight,' she told him, 'I'm too tired.' Sick and tired of *him*, that was the truth.

'Sod you, then!' Grabbing his clothes, he stormed out of the room.

'Good shuts to you.' Rosie settled down to sleep.

But she couldn't sleep. 'I have to find out what happened,'

she decided. 'Maybe there's something I can do to help Kathleen. There must be somebody, somewhere, who still cares what happens to her.'

With that in mind, she took up the diary and began leafing through it. As she did so, she made notes. Names. Places. Anything and everything that might help her unravel the mystery. The hospital owed her some holiday and the ward wasn't too busy at the moment. It might end up being a complete waste of time, but she couldn't let Kathleen just fade away in hospital without doing something to try and track down a relative or friend.

<hr />

ROSIE HAD NEVER been to Blackpool before. Fascinated by the wide promenade and glittering sea, she leaned over the balustrade. It was a beautiful spring day. The sun was on her face and the wind in her hair. Here, in this place, the hospital seemed a million miles away. So did her husband, and what a blessed relief that was. He thought she was staying with her sister in Cleethorpes. She'd told him Dora had been taken suddenly ill and she had to go to her. He'd been so taken aback by her spirited insistence, he'd hardly argued. It made her wonder why she hadn't done it before. In fact, it made her wonder why she shouldn't do it again, for good. Serve the bugger right if she just up and walked out on him.

She watched the many children playing on the sands. 'This is where Kathleen came as a girl,' she mused. 'This is where Markham brought her and Adam, and now here am I, trying to piece her life together.'

Turning round, she looked up and down the front. All the buildings looked the same: three storeys, bow windows with pretty curtains, and a narrow flight of steps leading up to each front door.

She consulted her notebook. 'If my instincts are right, Mabel's place should be around here.' She walked the length of the promenade and back again. In Kathleen's notes there was no address. Only a description, and a mention of the windmill.

Deciding to ask for help, she went into a quaint little teashop that straddled a busy corner. It had two entrances, frilled nets at the windows and clean white tablecloths. 'Tea please,' she told the elderly waitress. 'And a buttered scone.'

When the refreshment was delivered, Rosie asked, 'I don't suppose you know of a man by the name of Mr Mason, do you? He has a small hotel round these parts. There's a wife who used to be cook at a big house, and a young woman by the name of Nancy.'

'I'm not sure,' the woman answered. 'There was a family at number fourteen, used to take in guests. I've a feeling they were called Mason but I can't be certain. It don't really matter anyway, being as he died, oh, years since. His wife went soon after.'

This was a blow to Rosie. She hadn't anticipated that Mabel and John Mason might not be alive any more. She should have thought of it, though; they weren't young when they took on the hotel, and that was more than fifty years ago.

'And their names were Mason?'

The waitress scratched her chin. 'I think so, yes. And now I come to think of it, there *was* another woman, but I don't know as how she's young. More like in her sixties now, I'd say. Funny little thing an' all. Kept herself to herself after the other two passed on. Might have passed on as well, for all I know, or gone from the area altogether.' She shrugged her shoulders. 'Folk come and go,' she said casually. 'Can't keep track of 'em.'

'In her sixties, you say?' It sounded about right. Nancy must have been what? Eight, nine years older than Kathleen?

Rosie finished her tea and made her way to number fourteen. The house looked very much as she might have expected, but more downtrodden. The curtains were grimy and the door panels painted with dust. The whole place looked ready for demolition. 'Doesn't look like there's anybody living here,' she muttered, but knocked on the door anyway.

No answer.

She knocked again.

Not a sound.

Rosie put her mouth to the letterbox. 'Hello!' she called, coughing when the dust flew down her throat. 'I'm looking for Nancy. Is anybody home?'

Silence.

'Empty,' she muttered.

Turning away, she thought she heard a noise. She opened the letterbox again and called out, 'The lady in the teashop on the corner said Nancy might live here. My name's Rosie. I'm Kathleen's friend. She's in hospital.'

Nothing.

'I must be imagining things.' She shivered. 'Ghosts maybe.'

Returning to the teashop, she left her name and address. 'If you hear anything at all that might help me find her, I'd be grateful.'

Her next stop was Lytham St Anne's. She wanted to see where Markham had lived.

Waiting for the tram, she consulted her notes. 'Westerfield House sold last year, to a mystery buyer. Christian Westerfield killed in a bar fight, and Connie Blakeman nowhere to be found.' Frowning, she closed the book and replaced it in her purse. 'Not much for my troubles, is it?'

'Pardon me, dear.' An old woman cupped her ear and grinned toothlessly at her. 'Are you talking to me?'

Feeling embarrassed, Rosie shook her head. 'Just thinking out loud,' she said lamely. Three days left before she returned to work. After that there'd be no time for searching out Kathleen's friends.

There was still one avenue she hadn't explored. 'I have to find Murray.' Her fighting spirit returned. 'There must be a way.' Suddenly, a light flickered in her mind. 'Of course!' It was staring her in the face and she hadn't seen it. 'You stupid thing, Rosie! Why didn't you think of that before?'

'Beg yer pardon, dearie?'

'Sorry.' She wouldn't be at all surprised if the woman thought she'd escaped from an asylum. When the old dear gave her a funny look and shuffled away, Rosie had to bite her lips to stop from giggling.

NANCY STAYED HIDDEN in the staircase cupboard for a long time after Rosie had gone. 'That were Rosie,' she told herself, 'Kathleen's friend.'

She came out of the cupboard like a mouse, bent low and nervous. 'I should 'ave gone to the door. Cook said I were never to be afraid.' A smile lit her eyes. 'Cook liked Kathleen.'

Coming to the door, she peered out of the letterbox, recoiling when a man glanced her way. 'Rosie.' She liked the sound of that name. 'She said Kathleen were in 'ospital.' She began pacing the floor. 'Kathleen. Kathleen . . . so pretty.'

<hr/>

THE TRAM ARRIVED and Rosie got on. 'A tuppenny ticket, please,' she said, handing over the coins.

The conductor waited for the others to board the tram. 'Hurry along there, please,' he shouted impatiently. 'Hurry along.'

As Rosie turned to accept her ticket, she saw a ragged woman running down the road, a small, wizened little thing, with flyaway hair and a pixie face, and she knew her at once from Kathleen's diary. 'Nancy!' Her voice sailed out of the window and across the road. Nancy came to a halt. Staring this way and that, she couldn't tell where the voice had come from.

Rosie leapt off the tram and, dodging the traffic, ran towards her. 'Nancy!' she called. 'Stay there!'

Nancy stayed and Rosie fell into her arms, laughing and crying all at the same time. 'If you only knew,' she said, the tears running down her face. 'Oh, Nancy, if you only knew!'

They sat in the café for an age, going back over the years and reminiscing. Rosie told her all about Kathleen and the diaries, and Nancy told her about Cook and Mr Mason, and how they'd gone to heaven and left her behind.

Chapter Nineteen

ROSIE LEANED OVER the bed. 'Listen to me, Kathleen.' Her voice shook with excitement. 'There's someone here to see you.'

Kathleen opened her eyes. 'Hello, Rosie.' Her face lifted in a smile, but oh, she was so tired. 'Where've you been?'

Holding out her hand, she felt the warmth of other fingers, strong fingers, not like Rosie's at all. 'I missed you,' she murmured, her dark eyes half closed.

'Did you, my lovely?' The voice shook Kathleen to her very roots. 'I missed you too. More than you'll ever know.'

In a heartbeat, Kathleen was transported back over the years to when she was young and beautiful. In her tired old mind she saw herself standing with him in the garden of Maurice's house. That was the night they had said goodbye, when she told him she would miss him for ever. And she had. Every minute, every day and night since.

'No, it can't be,' she whispered. Her heart was beating so fast she feared it might leap out of her chest.

'Look at me, Kathleen.'

Slowly, she opened her eyes, desperately trying to focus on the face before her. It was a moment before she saw it, the same strong face and warm, green eyes, the wayward fair hair that fell over his forehead, and the voice, so soft, so loving. 'It's me, Kathleen. I've been searching everywhere for you.'

With a little cry, she covered her face, the chin dimpling with the effort of keeping back the tears. But the tears came anyway, spilling through her fingers and blinding her.

'Look at me, Kathleen. Please.'

It was a moment before she dared peep through her fingers. At first she couldn't speak, but then her eyes shone and her arms opened, and she knew she wasn't dreaming. 'Oh, Murray! Is it really you?'

Taking her in his arms, he whispered, 'It's been a lifetime, hasn't it?'

She clung to him and he held her tight, as though his very life depended on it. 'I'm taking you home, sweetheart,' he said, and her heart soared.

<hr>

T WO MONTHS LATER, her will to live restored and her body responding in kind, Kathleen went home.

In the carriage Murray sat beside her, holding her hand and thinking how their lives had turned full circle. He looked on this woman who had been his one and only love, and he could still see the girl. Though older and marked by the years, Kathleen was still Kathleen, with striking dark eyes and long hair, now grey and dressed into a long thick plait down her back. The smile was still the same. Kathleen touched his heart with a magic that no other woman had ever been able to do.

Kathleen, too, took stock of her companion. He was older, but straight and proud, and still possessing his fine handsome looks. His hair might be grey and his stride not so brisk, but she saw only the young man who had swept her off her feet all those years ago.

'Close your eyes,' he told her as they came down Ilford High Street.

Laughing like a girl, Kathleen did as she was told.

When the carriage came to a halt, he carried her out and, standing with her in his arms, said softly, 'You can look now, sweetheart. This is your new home, yours and mine.'

She opened her eyes and when she saw where he had brought her, she was filled with astonishment and delight, for she was looking up at Westerfield House, and wondering if she was dreaming after all.

Inside the house they waited for her: Rosie, Nancy, and Murray's strapping son David.

'Oh!' Kathleen walked in on uncertain footsteps, with Murray at her side. 'Oh, look!' she cried, and the tears started again. She shook her head and cried and laughed, and when Nancy ran forward, calling out her name and telling her, 'Bleedin' hell, miss, you ain't changed a bit!' everyone laughed and clapped. Then they were hugging and kissing, and Murray stood back, letting them take her for a while. But she was his, and he would never let her go again.

Kathleen couldn't take it all in. She turned once to glance at her man, and he smiled encouragingly. 'You're home, sweetheart,' he said. 'Now all you have to do is get strong and well.'

Rosie had already explained how she brought it all about. 'I found Nancy in the same guesthouse where she'd lived with Cook and Mr Mason all those years,' she told Kathleen. 'I had lost all hope of contacting Murray, but then I began thinking about the mysterious man who'd bought this house. After that, it wasn't too hard to find him.'

'Melinda never really settled in Australia,' Murray told her simply. He saw no reason to burden her with the details of his wretched marriage. 'After Maurice died, she was never the same. She seemed somehow consumed by devils. I don't know how else to put it. I couldn't reach her at all. Then when Christian was killed, she took her own life. I brought David back to England two years ago. We set up a merchandising company and now David is taking over the running of it.'

That evening, Murray made a speech. 'I want to give thanks for Kathleen's promising recovery,' he told them, 'and for Rosie Maitland who brought us all together again.' Here he paused, dipped into his pocket and brought out a small box which he gave to Kathleen. 'This is for you,' he said. When she opened it to find a sparkling engagement ring, he murmured, 'I think it's time we got married. What do you say, sweetheart?'

'I say yes.' She gave her answer wholeheartedly, and a rousing cheer went up.

'To Kathleen and Murray!' David announced, and everyone

raised their glasses. He turned and discreetly put his arm round Rosie. 'To us,' he whispered.

Kathleen saw the special way they looked at each other. It was too soon yet, she thought, but in her heart she knew that Rosie and David would find a way.

The celebrations were interrupted when the doors opened and in strolled a mangy, grey-whiskered old dog. Kathleen knew him instantly. 'Oh, look! It's Mr Potts!' Holding out her arms, she waited for him to come to her.

Just then a shadow fell across the doorway. Curious, she glanced up and for a moment she thought her mind was playing tricks on her. The hair was grey, and the figure seemed a little shorter than she remembered, but . . . No. It wasn't possible.

But then he grinned, and there was no doubt. 'Hello, sis,' he said, and the years rolled away.

She wasn't aware of the others watching; they'd all known he would be here. Adam had not been on the ill-fated ship bound for America. He was on the passenger list because he'd bought a ticket, but before the ship sailed he was suddenly and unexpectedly offered a job in India, which he promptly accepted. There he had made a new life, believing that Kathleen would never again want to see him. He had never married. Murray had managed to trace him, and when he learned of Kathleen's fate, he had vowed to be with her.

Now, as they held each other, no words could describe the joy in their hearts. 'We're together again, sis,' he murmured in her ear. 'Doesn't it seem like only yesterday?'

Through her tears, Kathleen answered. 'Someone up there's been good to us,' she said.

She looked round the room, at Rosie and David, Nancy and the little dog at her feet. Beside her stood the only man she had ever truly loved, and here before her was the brother she had prayed for every night since he'd gone.

It's been a long and difficult road, she thought, but, for all that, I would not have travelled any other.

As she gazed on her loved ones, Kathleen knew they would be together, for a long, long time.